THE THRONE OF DARKNESS:
RISE OF WAR

SAM FERGUSON

authorHOUSE®

AuthorHouse™
1663 Liberty Drive
Bloomington, IN 47403
www.authorhouse.com
Phone: 1 (800) 839-8640

Published by AuthorHouse 07/06/2018

ISBN: 978-1-5462-4901-6 (sc)
ISBN: 978-1-5462-4900-9 (e)

Library of Congress Control Number: 2018908065

Print information available on the last page.

This book is printed on acid-free paper.

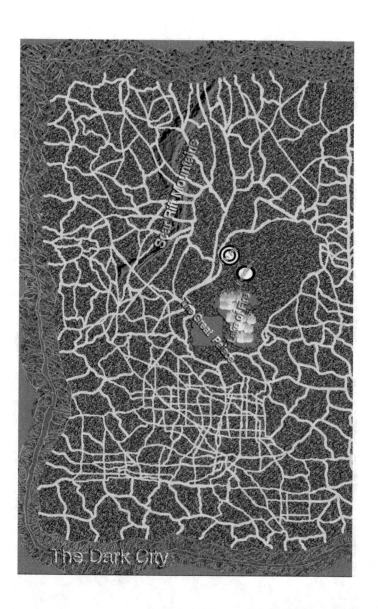

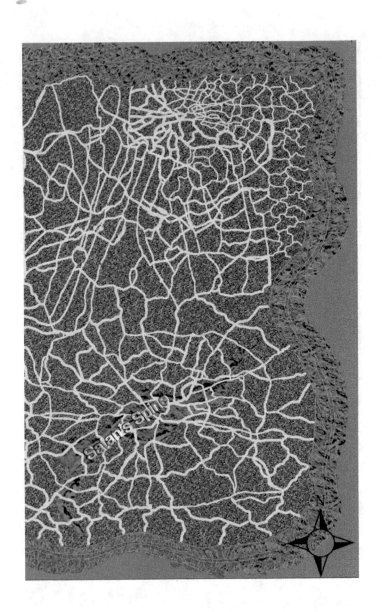

This book is dedicated to my best friend Nicholas, thank you for your dedication and support. And to my Father, who taught me how to dream.

PROLOGUE

Taken from the personal journal of Tobin Masters, Observer to the Throne of Darkness.

On the nature of betrayal, every Demon from the lowest Slave master, to the aspiring Satan, learns that nothing is to be trusted. In my short time in this world, as the Observer (Slave) to the Throne of Darkness, I have seen terrible acts of degradation and violence committed in the streets of the Dark City itself. These acts, no matter who commits them, seem to draw little or no attention from the passerby. I actually witnessed the maiming of a small Demonic boy by his own Father, and listened to the elder Demons, hearty laughter as he held up his sons' severed hand in the air like some grotesque trophy for all to behold. And even as I took a step from the curb, the natural human instinct to help the screaming child in my mind, the boy pulled a bone dagger from beneath his filth blood stained tunic, and slashed viscously across his Fathers' stomach. My mind refused to accept what I was seeing as I stood frozen in horror with one foot in the street, as the boys' Mother wrapped her arms around her one handed son and hugged him close, a look of happy affection on her face. All the while her mate lay in the gutter, his steaming entrails being trodden upon by his fellow demons, as they continued on their way as if all was right in the world.

Of course in Hell it was. One would think that with examples such as this, as a demon rose through the ranks of power they would grow paranoid, seeing plots to kill them everywhere. This would most assuredly be the case with the Demon Lord, who for whatever mad reason seeks to ascend to the Throne of Darkness to become the Ruling Satan. But I am told that even though the Throne has betrayed all that have come before them, every Satan that approaches it, believes that he, or she will be the One that finally tames the all powerful Artifact.

However, in the end, it is they who are taught a final lesson in betrayal. The Throne is the most powerful entity in all of Hell, and like Arthurs' great sword Excalibur, it cannot be defeated. And like most blades it is double edged. Eventually, just when they least expect it, when they have let down their guard, believing that they have indeed brought the Throne to heel, it cuts back. And that is when they learn that death is the best teacher of all.

Tobin screamed out into the silence of the huge, shadowy chamber that held the Throne of Darkness. On the black marble walls around him torches burned, throwing shadows about like macabre dancers, with his screams as the music.

"Please…" the dark haired man begged, as tears of blood seeped from his eyes. "No." He moaned as his burning eyes were forced open by some unseen force, so that he looked upon the True Power of Hell. The Throne of Darkness. The Throne was carved from the blackest stone, with reliefs of humans and demons writhing in either ecstasy or agony (at this very moment all bets were on agony) etched into its surfaces. As Tobin was forced to watch, the Throne began to glow with its' own dark light, causing the etchings to appear to suddenly come to life and move of their own accord.

"Please." Tobin sobbed as a fresh wave of agony tore through his eyes.

"**Observe. Bear witness**." The words echoed in his head, and Tobin felt his knees grow weak with the horror of it. It was the first time since he had come to this world, that the Throne had spoken directly to him. It was an experience that he did not want to have again.

"Oh God, no." The human wanted to scream, but his voice came out a quivering whisper as the creature that currently called itself Satan crashed through the large ebony doors that led into the cavernous Throne Room. Without wanting to Tobin turned to look at the Grand Demon. He knew, though how he could not say how, that once over a hundred and ten years ago, this creature had ruled over a small Kingdom on the west shore of the continent called Malice.

The Kingdom had once been filled with bright orange skinned creatures calling themselves Skarren. Shortly after ascending to the Throne of Darkness this thing, which had once been the King of the Skarren, had ordered the elite soldiers of the Dark City, the Royal Guardsmen, to raze his former Kingdom to the ground. Not a single Demon Lord or lowly human slave had survived.

Tobin gasped in fresh horror as his mind was filled with images of this slaughter. He wanted to vomit as he saw the streets of the Skarren Kingdom run red with blood. Of course by this time any resemblance that Satan had to his former race had completely faded, his skin, which had been a bright orange had shed in great patches to be replaced by shiny, midnight black scales. Horns had grown out of his forehead, reaching thirteen inches in length and at least five inches around. These horns were called the "Crown of Satan."

Great black and blood red bat-like wings had burst from his back, and talons as sharp as razors decorated each hand. The Demon grew to an impressive eight foot tall and his muscles had grown and hardened. To complete this transformation, the creature's eyes had become a blazing fiery red, which glowed with the promise of torture and pain whenever they fell upon potential victims. All in all, Satan was an impressive creature.

But tonight, Tobin saw that the monster had begun its final lesson with the Throne. Satan staggered as if drunk, his right claw clutching a ragged, bleeding wound that literally sprayed crimson like a fountain around his thick fingers. Tobin could see that the blood had spilled down the creature's sculpted chest, past his naked stomach to stain the loin cloth that barley covered the creature's maleness "I will not allow you!" The Ruling Satan screamed at the Throne, as he stumbled past the human without even a glance. "I own you, Hell is mine forever!"

If Satan had hoped for some response from the Throne, he was to be disappointed. Tobin could hear voices now, coming from the hallway where Satan had come from. Even as he turned toward the door four Demons entered the room. Three of the new creatures were Satan's own sons, beings called Throne-Kissed due to their lineage as offspring of a Ruling Satan, with thick black and green scales and small leathery wings. These three were being led by Satan's current concubine, a female Demoness named Severa.

Severa was a striking creature with soft red fur and glowing blue eyes. She wore a blood stained spider silk nightgown, and in her hand she clutched a bone dagger she obviously wished to use to cut out her lover's heart. At the sight of their prey the twisted family of Demons screamed out in triumph. They came at him as one, dragging claws and dagger across exposed scales, drawing fresh blood. Tobin watched as Satan struggled against them, raking his talons across one of his son's eyes blinding him. Even as the young Demon Lord screamed out in agony his Father turned to snap the neck of his brother, dropping him to the floor, dead.

But in the end nothing the Ruling Satan did mattered. The Throne of Darkness had spoken. It had passed its judgment and the sentence was death. The Human watched as the wife's deadly blade, slick with fresh blood, buried itself to the hilt into the thick flesh of Satan's neck.

Gagging the once Great Ruler of Hell pushed away from the two remaining combatants and stumbled up the steep steps to the raised dais where the Throne sat glowing. He fell to his knees in front of it, his clawed hand pulled the knife from his neck, spraying the Throne with blood. Slowly he drew back as if he intended to strike the Throne before toppling over.

Tobin watched as a bubbled made of blood foamed from the creature's mouth before it finally shuddered and died. Whooping in joy the two uninjured attackers rushed up the steps, intent on claiming their prize, as seven gems (each representing the Seven Deadly Sins) on the Throne began glowing with the power of Hell. At the top of the steps each victor, Mother and Son reached out trembling hands to grab one of the gems.

Suddenly, black lightning leapt from the Throne, engulfing the would be usurpers, burning them away until not even ash remained. Tobin felt the unseen force that forced his eyes to remain open disappear and he sagged to the floor. Alone in the Great Throne room except for the body of the fallen Satan and the low moaning son that had been blinded, Tobin began sobbing. His stomach roiled at the smell of blood and burnt meat. Even though he had control of his eyelids again, he could not stop looking up at the glowing stones upon the Throne. Their terrible beauty was hypnotizing and as he watched he heard the Throne speak again. Its terrible voice filling his mind like a backed up sewer.

"**A new era has begun.**" It whispered. "**You will be my Observer, watch and record the greatness that is me.**" With his eyes still seeping blood Tobin crawled up the steps, across the cooling body of Satan and pressed his lips against the cold base of the Throne.

"I hear and obey." He sobbed as his body shuddered with the horror of it all.

CHAPTER 1

Take from the personal journal of Tobin Masters, Observer to the Throne of Darkness.

When I was on Earth (It seems like a life time ago), I remember reading about certain cultures that celebrated death rather than mourning it. At the time I dismissed such thoughts as being repulsive and inherently unnatural. However, even if I had embraced such beliefs, I am certain that nothing could have prepared me for the Dark City's' reaction to the news that the Ruling Satan had been killed.

By any standard what went on that night(and many nights after) could only be described as rioting. No. Even this does not do those nights and days justice. Imagine if you can, a world gone completely mad. Where arson, rape, assault, and all manner of violence are not only acted out by the people celebrating, but are actively encouraged by the very people they are being perpetrated against. Indeed, I witnessed several demons thrown to the ground and beaten bloody, all the while they laughed and begged for more.

If this was not bad enough, I observed as several of the police force of the Dark City (called the Dark Guard) beat a young Demon Lord to death because he was sitting on a curb and not participating in the gang rape of a human woman behind him.

From time to time during this first night of insanity, one or more Demon(s) would look up and see me watching from my balcony at the Great Palace. At first they would point up at me as they drew closer to get a better look, but then one by one they would kneel, bowing their heads in my direction. This would only last a few moments before they were on their feet once again searching for other potential victims.

For that is what they had believed I was, a victim for them to torment. That was until they came close enough to see what I really was. Oh, I have no doubt that that it was not to me that they bowed. Oh, no. They bowed to their damnable Throne, for I bear that things mark upon me like a branded cow.

But I must admit that watching these beings of hideous power kneel below me has sent a thrill of excitement through me. God help me, part of me may have even liked it.

Six days ago. December 15ᵗʰ 2013.

"Hey buddy," Tobin could hear the voice echoing from some great distant place, intruding into his safe place. He didn't want to hear what the man on the other side of the darkness had to say. No. Here in this warm blanketing dark he was safe. Here there was no Throne of Darkness. No Demons walking through the streets with their tunics made from human skin. In the dark he could hide from their roaming eyes as they walked by, sizing him up the way a farmer would prize cattle at a county fair. He would not answer the distant voice. Instead, like a child hiding from the boogie man, he would crawl further into the dark and hope that he would never be found.

"C'mon buddy," the voice was followed by a strong shake that Tobin could not ignore. He should have known, there was no escaping the boogie man. The Beast had him. Gasping he sat up eyes wildly searching for the nightmare creatures that would tear him limb from bloody limb.

"You okay Mac?" Tobin turned toward the voice with a slight cringe. The voice belonged to an older man who was leaning over him. But he knew enough by now not to be tricked. Oh no. This was an illusion and just when he felt that he was truly safe everything would change. First the watery blue eyes would go, slowly changing to reptilian irises that would begin to glow red in the night.

Next, horns would split through the skin on his forehead, growing large and black. The old weathered skin of the face would slough away, dropping in sickly wet sheets on to the ground, or (worse) onto Tobin himself. Underneath this dead human skin there would be scales of the color of blackest night.

Finally those oh so perfect white teeth (so perfect in fact they had to have been ordered in the mail) would fall out, dropping one by one into Tobin's lap like tiny enameled tombstones, pushed out by thick curved fangs that would tear through his lips like a hot knife through cold butter.

Once transformed, the fake human would gurgle laughter and frothy black blood at him while he cowered and grieved the lost pocket of dark peace from which he had been torn. But the face stayed decidedly human and as the minutes passed and no horrific transformation ripped through the man, Tobin could feel himself calming down.

Slowly his mind began to orient itself and he came to realize that he was looking at a very anxious looking Cab Driver in New York City.

However it was the man who came up behind the cabbie that brought Tobin completely out of his stupor. This man was wearing a long heavy burgundy coat that was embroidered with gold thread. He wore a matching hat that was dusted with slowly melting snow flakes. It was the uniform of Doormen throughout New York City's most prestigious high rise apartment buildings. The uniform may have been standard, but the face was personal and as welcome as a hot drink on a freezing cold winter night (which it was, judging by the snow that was falling on the two men).

"Is there a problem?" The Doorman asked the cabbie in a voice that said that he would tolerate no disruptive drunks in front of his building. Slowly he leaned over the cabbie to peer into the back of the car. "Oh, Mr. Masters!" The Doorman (his name is Robert Tobin suddenly remembered) changed his demeanor quickly, as if the King of France had just arrived at his doorstep.

Tobin knew that this was something that the job called for, and yet it always made him feel like he was the most important man in the entire City. "Is everything okay, sir?" Robert's face changed into an almost mirror image of the Cabbie's.

"That's what I've been trying to figure out."

The cabbies angry Bronx accent was like beautiful music to Tobin's ears. He struggled a moment more between true memory and dream, trying to remember how he had come to be inside the back the cab. And then it all came back to him. He had left New York last week to go to an auction in London, England. He had heard that two seventeenth century cookbooks, written by a French Royal Chef, would be auctioned off. Had he gotten them?

Of course he did. They were in the old leather satchel that Robert was lifting out of the cab's back seat. In fact Tobin remembered that he had been able to broker a private deal with the Auction House which had only taken a few days and he had been able to return home a few days early. He had come to surprise his lover Richard.

Just thinking of Richard cleared away the last remnants of the terrible nightmare. He assured both men that he was fine, just a little tired. Slowly he pushed his way out into the cold winter air of the city. He laughed and waived Robert off when asked if he needed help with his bags. So happy to be home, he gave both men a five hundred dollar bill and wished them a good night. He left them standing there in the snow each looking at their tip with childlike shock.

Tobin pushed through the glass spinning door and found himself in the warm lobby of the building that he had called home for the last ten years. The lobby was sparsely decorated with a long black leather couch for visitors to sit while they waited for the people they had come to see to collect them, if they were not on the list. Said list being held by a security guard who sat behind a small security desk and kept unwanted people from running willy-nilly through the hallways.

The night guard was a big burly black man by the name of Jonas. Jonas looked up from his security monitors only long enough to register that Tobin was indeed allowed to enter the property and then back down again. It occurred to Tobin, as he waited for the elevator to arrive that he had never, in the ten years of living here spoken a single word to Jonas. He knew nothing about the man and in a way that seemed very sad.

For just a moment Tobin thought about going back out to where the desk sat and saying hello to the man, just to see what would happen, but then at that moment the elevator bell dinged and the doors slid open. Feeling a rush of excitement, the security guard forgotten, Tobin went into the car. He slipped his key into a special lock in the panel and turned it, knowing that it would take him all the way to the top of the eighty story building, where he lived in a Penthouse Suite with Richard.

Tobin had inherited the Penthouse from his father, as well as a considerable fortune and his love for antique books. Out of his older brother Thomas and younger sister Karen, it was Tobin who would always sit with his father for hours on end researching this or that ancient tome. By the time he was ten years old it had become a passion and he started doing his own research. By fourteen he was going on trips all around the world with his father.

Perhaps that was why, when both of their parents had died in a terrible plane crash ten years ago most of what they had went to Tobin. His brother and sister had been well taken care of in their own rights, but it was Tobin who had received over seventy five million dollars, with his father's New York Penthouse, and book collecting/selling business.

Thomas had taken his money and moved to Texas, had gotten married, and now had two little girls of his own. Tobin heard from him at least twice a month and he and Richard went to see him three times a year. Karen had taken a nice apartment in Manhattan and stopped by every couple of days. All in all both of his siblings seemed to be content with what they had been given, or at the very least they never complained.

After receiving the business Tobin began traveling the world and living a life that most people could only dream of. But still there was always something missing. Something that he could never put his finger on. And then one day, he flew into the Leonardo Da Vinci International Airport in Rome He was there to meet with a book dealer who said that he had a fifteenth century Bible. If the book was legitimate it would complete a set of Holy works that his father had started collecting over twenty years ago. Once complete the set could probably sell for close to a quarter of million dollars. Of course Tobin would probably never sell the books, given their connection to his father.

All of this had been going through his mind as he moved through the private gate and customs area reserved for VIPs and very (very) rich people.

"And how long will you be staying, Mr. Masters?" The young Customs agent asked in Italian. He was a man that Tobin had known very well.

"Only a couple of days, Vincent." Tobin smiled, his own Italian spoken with a slightly off accent, but otherwise it was almost flawless. Vincent waved him away as he brought out the official papers that would allow him to import/export "Specialty Books" from all around the world. Tobin smiled as he slid the papers back into their special carrying case. This was a game the two of them had been playing for years.

"I know that you are authorized to bring and take items out of the country." Vincent smiled and winked at him and Tobin knew exactly what the Customs Officer had in mind. This was another, much more private game that the two played. A game that always seemed to end with them in bed together.

"My new number." Vincent slid a small piece of paper across the counter to him. Tobin took it without looking and slid it into his jacket pocket. Yes, he was pretty sure that this was going to be a very good trip indeed. As he moved on from Customs Tobin could only think of two things; the book that would complete his father's collection, and the nights that he would surely spend in Vincent's apartment.

"Please, help me." The words spoken so softly in English pulled Tobin from his happy thoughts. It was his first instinct to ignore the plea and move on. After all, Vatican City may be considered by some to be the Holiest city in the world (except maybe for Jerusalem), but that did not mean that the City was without its' dangers. Indeed the streets of Vatican City could be just as dangerous as the back alleys of New York, if one was not careful. However, it was the utter despair in that voice that caused Tobin to stop and look for its' source.

He found a young man sitting just outside the airport doors leaning against the wall, his legs spread out before him. As he watched the young man repeated his plea to several people as they passed by. He never held out his hand for money or asked for anything other than 'help' from each person. Every person he spoke to moved away from him as if he smelled offensive and found something else to occupy their attention so they would not have to face this pathetic looking man.

Curious, despite his better judgment, Tobin walked

towards the man. At his approach he lifted his head to look Tobin in the eye, and he felt his heart ache for this stranger. The young man was dirty with short, greasy, unwashed brown hair. His face was smudged with grime that showed clean tracks down his cheeks from crying. To accent this, the mans' deep chocolate colored eyes were red and swollen as they filled up with fresh tears.

"Can you please help me?" The man whispered when Tobin stopped in front of him. "Please." He dropped his face down into his hands and began to sob so hard his whole body shook with the force of his sorrow. At that moment Tobin found himself just as embarrassed as those he had seen walk by earlier. He wanted nothing more than to turn his head, perhaps check his watch and simply drift away. Away from this terrible scene that he had placed himself in.

Perhaps that is exactly what he would have done if the police man had not shown up at that moment. The uniformed man seemed to materialize out of nowhere. One moment Tobin was alone with the young man on the ground, the next the Police man was dragging the pleader roughly from the ground.

"I told you to get out of here!" The officer screamed into the mans' face, speaking in heavily accented English. For his part the man looked terrified as he tried feebly to pull himself away from the other man's iron grip.

"Please, I have to stay," the young man begged. "I have to find somebody to help me." He tried again to pull away, only to have the officer spin him around and drag his arm up behind his back. At that the man's plea for help turned into a yelp of pain.

"I told you what would happen to you, if I caught you

out here again." The police man snarled into the young man's ear and jerked on the man's arm again. This time the man practically screamed in pain. Tobin had seen enough.

"Hey…hey!" he grabbed the officer's shoulder when he was ignored. The man turned his rage filled eyes to Tobin. "He's with me." He spoke quickly in Italian. "You can let him go, I'll take him." For a moment Tobin was sure that the police officer was going to ignore him and continue his assault, but after looking at Tobin up and down a couple of times he released the man who crumbled back to the ground.

"You will take him with you?" The officer asked suspiciously, taking in Tobin's expensive luggage and Italian suite.

"Yes," Tobin knelt down and gently pulled the other man to his feet. "I'll take him." And with that he led the man away from the Airport and into one of the many cabs waiting at the curb.

"Thank you." The man leaned his head against Tobin's shoulder and began to cry again.

"It's okay." He put his arm around the poor man as they drove toward the Hotel where Tobin had made reservations.

The man's name was Richard Murry and he had come to Rome two weeks ago on vacation. He had come to the Vatican City from Ohio, in the hopes of finding salvation and perhaps a little meaning in his life. He thought that maybe here he would be touched by something truly Divine. And that Divinity would lead him onto the right path in his life. His first two days in the city led Richard to believe that he was going to find what he was looking for. He felt that God himself was walking with him through the ancient streets of this Holy City.

There was something in the very air that seemed to call to his soul. He wandered the streets looking at the architecture and feeling the vibrancy of the people that lived and visited there. He had even stood in line for six hours for a chance to kneel and kiss the foot of the Holy statue of Saint Peter.

He thought that everything was on track. That nothing in the world could stop him from finding the peace that he was so desperately searching for. But then one day after going to the hotel pool and returning to his room, he found that someone had broken in. The thieves had taken everything. His money, almost all of his clothes, and his wallet and passport were all gone.

He had spent all of his savings on this trip and there was no one back in America that he could call for help. When he approached the American Embassy to ask for help, he was told to fill out some paper work and they would verify his identity. After that it would only be a matter of a couple of days before they could get him on a plane back to the States.

This had been three weeks ago. Richard could get no more information out of the Embassy. It was as if they were deliberately stalling him. Keeping him from getting out of the Vatican City. Finally he had given up on getting their help and went out into the streets to find a way to get home. By this time he had run out of money. He was kicked out of the hotel where he had been staying and found himself living on the streets. It was in the shadows of these streets that Richard found the darker, crueler side of the Holy City.

People ignored his pleas for help. Some had even spit on him, cursing him for being in their 'Great City'. Once he had been given a slice of flaky bread by a young woman who had taken pity on him as he sat on a street corner. But even this small kindness had been overshadowed when a man came out of the shadows and sucker punched him in the side of the head. Dazed he could not even struggle as the man ripped the precious bread from his numb fingers, and ran off into the night.

Finally a week ago Richard decided that his only hope would be to camp out at the airport and beg for someone, anyone, to help him. Once there, he had a little more success at getting food and the occasional cup of coffee, but that was as far as most people were willing to go. He had to hide several times from the officer that Tobin had saved him from. Each time the police man had caught him, he was roughed up a bit more. Finally he had simply given up all hope. He figured that eventually someone would report finding his body where he had either died of starvation or finally had been beaten to death by a so called officer of the law.

By the time Tobin had found him Richard had gone a full three days without food. He was ready to die. He had been lied to. This was not a Holy City. There was no Salvation to be found here. He had come here to find Heaven and found Hell instead. Tobin learned all of this on the short drive to the Hotel and his heart went out to Richard. He shuddered to think of all the poor man had gone through and what he might still be going through if Tobin had given into the impulse to abandon him as everyone else had.

Once they were in Tobin's room at the hotel, he sent Richard to the shower (the man did smell rather offensive) and placed a few orders with the hotel staff. By the time

Richard came out there were several carts of hot food waiting for him. While he ate Tobin got on the phone and spoke to a few contacts that he had in the Embassy here in the Vatican, and he was told that they would have all the necessary paperwork completed in a few days.

It took exactly three days for Richard's new I.D. and Passport to be delivered to the suite that he still shared with Tobin. Of course the suite wasn't the only thing that the two men now shared. It had only taken one day for Tobin to understand what had been missing in his life all of those years. It was this man, this stranger who had found him out of need and desperation and in those three days Richard and Tobin had fallen in love with each other.

That had been seven years ago, and they were still together today. Now here he was, riding an elevator up to see the love of his life. Tobin couldn't wait to see Richard again. He had only been out of the Country for five days, and yet every hour almost felt like a lifetime. Of course he wasn't due home for another two days, but Tobin could not resist the opportunity to surprise Richard.

In his mind he imagined how the night would go. First they would make love. Afterward Tobin would lie in Richard's strong arms and they would talk. Tobin would tell Richard about his horrible nightmare in the Cab on his way home. Richard, for his part would listen very intently to everything he said and then he would pull him closer and say all the right things, as he had every other time that Tobin had been plagued by these demonic nightmares. The same nightmares that he had been having since he was a little boy.

After that, Tobin would finally feel safe, and protected, and he drifted off to sleep in Richard's arms. That would be the perfect night. Tobin looked up into the mirrored surface of the elevator doors and found himself grinning from ear to ear. Just a few more floors. In the next instant Tobin felt a chill run through his body, and the hair on his neck stood up on end, as he realized that he was not alone in the reflection.

Standing next to him in the reflection of the elevator was a young girl of maybe eight or nine, with long strawberry blond hair. Her face was pale as if she needed to be out in the sun more often, and her pale blue eyes looked out at him full of sadness. She wore what could only be described as a tan tunic and leggings that made on think of a medieval peasant toiling away in the fields under a Lords' great castle.

Tobin didn't waste any time looking at his side for the girl. He knew that she would not be there. No, the only place that he would find her was in the mirror on the doors. Most people would found this to be unnerving, perhaps even terrifying, but not Tobin. After all he had been seeing this little girl for almost six years now.

It had started shortly after he had almost died (technically his heart did stop twice so maybe he had died after all) in Los Angeles five years ago. At the thought Tobin fought the impulse to run his fingers across his chest where scars marred his skin. That had been a truly terrible time. A time that had brought a lot of emotional turmoil for both Richard and himself. It was a time that Tobin had thought that maybe he had loved someone else, and that love almost ended his life.

However, one apparent side effect of this near death experience had been this little girl. Tobin had no idea who she was or why this ghost, for that is what she had to be, was haunting him, but here she was again. She always appeared in reflective surfaces and watching him with sad eyes, or sometimes trying to pass on some message that he never understood.

But this time the little phantom seemed to be begging with him, pleading for some understanding that he couldn't grasp. This new attitude was more the most disturbing display that she had put on. Whatever she wanted to tell him, it must have been truly heartbreaking, because she began to cry as she seemed to beat against her side of the mirror.

"I don't understand." Tobin whispered, his voice shaking in frustration and not a little fear. He would not tell Richard about seeing this girl again. He would not understand, not that he himself did. However, he did know without any doubt that this ghost, or whatever it was, was not a figment of his imagination. She was as real as Tobin himself. He couldn't explain how he knew this, he just did.

When Tobin tried to explain this to Richard, he had earned himself a house visit from a "Doctor," who was of course a Psychiatrist. After that Tobin kept the fact that he continued to see the girl to himself. It's better to keep the crazy to yourself sometimes.

"I just can't hear you." Tobin sighed. At this the girl pressed her hand against the reflection, her palm facing him. It was as if she wanted for him to reach out to her. He hesitated before finally lifting his hand. What would happen when they touched? Would there be some grand reaction between them even though they were separated by the dimensions of life and death?

Whatever might have happened was lost in the moment

just before his hand would have touched the mirror the elevator "dinged" to let him know that he had arrived on his floor and the doors split open taking the phantom with them. Slightly shaken by this latest encounter he stepped out of the car into home.

Tobin stood on a landing with a small oak table with a key bowel sitting on it Sighing again, some of the happiness now drained from him he set down his travelers' bag and dropped his keys into the bowl. He looked around the familiar Penthouse and felt a small twinge of pride at his home.

In front of him a short set of steps led down into the sunken living room, with its all black leather couch and easy chairs. Sitting in front of the furniture was an obsidian coffee table, hand carved from a solid piece of rock and then topped with glass. Two of the walls had been painted black. One sported a large eighty inch plasma TV that could be hidden behind a sliding wall plate. The second wall was dominated by a large marble fireplace and was one of Tobin's favorite things in the whole Penthouse. On either side of the fireplace were two doors, one leading into the Master Bedroom, and the other a guest room.

A third wall, directly across from him was made of glass and showed off a spectacular view of the New York City skyline. Tobin couldn't count the nights that he and Richard had sat out on that balcony just looking at the city lights. In the corner, to right, where the glass wall met the interior wall was a large nine foot white frosted Christmas tree. Tobin smiled as the lights blinked in its branches reflecting off the shiny glass globes hanging all through it. Underneath this tree was a small box hidden amongst the other gifts. In this box was the ring Tobin had bought and would give to Ricard Christmas day, when he asked if he would marry him.

Off to left Tobin knew that there was an open kitchen with the finest appliances money could buy. This was his home. This is where he was most happy. He thought about these things as he stepped down into his living room. Slowly he became aware of a few things.

First there was a fire burning in the fireplace. This seemed a little out of place, since Richard never seemed to care for a fire unless Tobin was home. There were rose scented candles lit all throughout the room, and sitting on the coffee table was an opened bottle of wine with two half-filled glasses. Tobin shook his head and smiled to himself. Tomorrow he would have to have a word with his assistant Amy. When he had called to tell her that he would be home early, he had specifically told her not to tell Richard. Well, obviously she had ignored him and called ahead so that Richard could surprise him instead of the other way around. Tobin inhaled the heady scent of roses and romance that hung in the air.

At that moment Richard walked out of the Master Bedroom and Tobin was delighted to see that he was completely naked. This night just kept getting better and better. "Hello, Lover." Tobin's voice was husky and filled with desire the phantom suddenly forgotten.

"Tobin?" Richard stopped dead in his tracks and all the blood seemed to drain from his entire body. "Wha….?" He started to say when another voice interrupted him. A decidedly feminine voice that came from the bedroom door that Richard had just left. The bedroom that he shared with Tobin.

"Richard," that voice was filled with sexual desire and heat. The sound of it, the familiarity of it made Tobin's stomach turn. "Are you coming back with the wine?" For several moments they stood like there looking at each other, Tobin feeling as if he were going to throw up, Richard, eyes wide and mouth moving but no sound coming out.

"Come on," the voice called from the bedroom again. "The bed's getting cold." Finally exasperated with the lack of response, the voice presented itself in person. "What the hell….." She started before seeing Tobin. Before him stood a woman of stunning beauty, her naked body catching the glow from the fire and the candles that had been lit for her perfectly. Oh yes, she was a beauty all right, there was no way Tobin could deny that.

"Hello, Karen." Tobin greeted his sister in a soft voice and marveled at how calm he sounded. "Nice of you to visit."

Tobin stood out on the balcony looking out across the light of the city. At one time (could it have only been an hour ago?) he had loved this view. But now everything had changed. Everything had lost its shine, its color. Nothing would ever be the same again. At some point it had begun to snow again, but Tobin didn't care. He found himself playing the ugly scene over and over in his head. Richard still standing there his mouth still working like a fish gulping for air after it has been taken out of its tank. Karen running up on him, not even trying to hide the smug look of satisfaction on her face as she tried to tell him that "it wasn't what it looked like."

As if. Tobin hadn't even looked at her. He only had eyes for the man that he had loved. The man that, not just broken his heart, but had torn it from his chest and thrown it into the fireplace to watch it burn.

"Tobin?" Karen had grabbed his arm and he was forced to look at her. To see her standing there next to him naked, sweat drying on her body. Sweat from fucking Richard. Sweat from destroying his life In that moment Tobin knew a rage like none other in his life. He didn't even remember moving his hand. One moment his sister was standing there talking, the next she was on the ground her eyes full of shock as she lifted her hand to her already reddening cheek.

This finally broke Richard out of his shock. Gasping he moved to kneel down next to Karen and looked closely at her face. In that moment, looking down at the two of them naked on the floor in front of him, he was sure that he was going to kill them. It would be so simple. Just turn around, walk around the large grey stone island and into the beautiful kitchen where he and Richard had cooked so many meals together. He could reach out and draw one of the large chef knives from the wooden block on the counter next to the silver stone. Then he would simply walk right back out to them. Neither one them would expect what was coming.

He wondered which of them he would kill first, but then he was pretty sure he knew. He could feel the knife as it slid right between Karens' firm tanned breasts. He could imagine the "thunk" the blade would make as it scrapped against the bone of her breast plate. Oh, how he would love to slash her pretty face up until no one would ever recognize her again.

19

All of this went through his mind in a matter of seconds and it took all of his force of will to stop his feet as he started to turn toward the kitchen. Instead he pushed himself forward, past the two cringing naked people on the floor, and through the sliding glass doors that led out to the balcony. This is where he had stood for the last ten minutes? A half an hour? He wasn't sure. He had not, would not cry. No, there were no tears left in him. Only an empty feeling that seemed to consume his entire being.

From behind him he heard the sliding door open slowly on its track. "Tobin?" Richard's voice came to him over the freezing wind. "Please come back in." There was a sadness in that voice that reminded him of that first day they had met. But unlike that day nothing touched Tobin's dead heart. Slowly he turned to the man that he thought was his everything. Richard had gotten dressed and now he stood just outside on the balcony the curtains billowing out in the wind.

Several feet behind Karen stood, also dressed. Her face had a small bruise from where Tobin had slapped her and she seemed none too eager to get any closer to her brother, good.

"Go away, Richard." Tobin spoke in a toneless voice and began to turn back to the city, but Richard was not ready to give up yet.

"Tobin, we'll go," he pleaded. "Just come back in, please." Tobin stopped and turned back toward the other man. He didn't want to know, but something inside of him pushed him to ask.

"How long?"

"What?" Richard blinked a couple of times in confusion.

He had expected many different reactions but this small soft question had not been one of them.

"How long?" Tobin repeated as he took a step forward. Behind him Karen must have seen something dangerous in her brothers' face for she took a step backward, even though Richard stood between the two of them. Of course Richard didn't sense or see anything in his confusion.

"How long?" Richard repeated stupidly. "What….?" This was as far as he got when Tobin's hand darted out and caught him by the throat and began to squeeze. Tobins' voice was as cold as the winter night as he chocked the other man. Gagging Richard slid down to his knees not even trying to fight, his face turning blood red as Tobin continued to choke him.

"Tell me you son of bitch, or I will kill you." Tobin let go and Richard gasped in air, his hand automatically going up to his throat. "Tell me." Tobin hated the sudden plaintive sound that filled his voice.

Richard's eyes slowly slid away from him and he was sure that he was not going to answer, but then; "Six years." Tobin felt all the air rush out of his lungs as if he had been punched in his stomach. All the rage and anger finally fled him leaving him with an overwhelming crush of despair.

Six years. He had been living a lie for six years. How could he have been so stupid? Had any of it been real? He asked himself but then immediately answered. No. Of course not. They had started sleeping together exactly one year after Richard had come to live him. How could he have been so stupid?

Slowly he backed away until he felt the railing of the balcony press up against his back. He wanted to scream into the night. He wanted to wake up from this terrible nightmare that had taken over his life. In that moment he even longed to return to the tortured creatures of his nightmares. Anything would be better than the reality of his life. But he knew that there was no waking up from this. Nothing would ever be the same again.

At that moment Tobin knew what he was going to do. Knew what he *had* to do. As he looked up from the floor to where Richard was struggling to get back to his feet he saw that he was no longer standing alone. Next to him in the reflection of the sliding glass door was his little ghost. Tobin could see that she had been crying and finally at least some understanding came to him.

"This is what you were trying to tell me, wasn't it little one?" He felt tears finally spill down his face as the little girl nodded her head. Richard looked from Tobin to the empty spot next to him and back again.

Tobin?" There was a new kind of fear in his voice now. He knew that Tobin was not speaking to him and he felt the hair on the backs of his arms stand up. But Tobin did not hear him, could not really even see him anymore. Oh, he knew that Richard was there, it was just that he no longer mattered. Only one thing mattered now.

"It's okay," Tobin told the girl trapped in the reflection. "I know what to do now." The ghost seemed to be wracked by sobs as she began slamming her fists against the window as she had in the reflection of the mirror doors in the elevator. She shook her head back and forth denying what he was telling her. But his mind was made up; there was no going back now.

"Tobin...?" Richard started to call to him again and at

that moment the glass door next to him exploded outward. Gasping he jumped to the side taking his eyes off Tobin for just a second. It was in that second that Tobin made his final choice. Bending his knees he pushed himself up and over the railing at his back.

Richard seemed to turn back to him in slow motion his hand reaching out as if he had the power to pull Tobin back with the force of his mind. His face was a mask of horror as he screamed Tobin's name. And then Tobin was gone over the ledge, the cold winter wind tearing all sound from his ears. In peace Tobin Masters closed his eyes and waited to die.

CHAPTER 2

Take from the personal journal of Tobin Masters, Observer to the Throne of Darkness.

In Earths' history there have been what humans have called World wars. These wars, while involving whole countries and thousands of lives cannot compare to the realities of a True World War. Every war that has ever been fought on human soil is a type of controlled chaos. Now imagine, if you can, a war that engulfs not just a few of the largest nations of the world, but instead spreads through every country, every city, every town on the planet. Such is the chaos of the War of Ascension. While there may be only seven Chosen, before the last arrow falls to the ground, before the victor Ascends to the a Throne of Darkness, every last Kingdom (save one) will have burned. Will have fought for and either had won or lost its survival. Some Kingdoms will have been purged of all life, while others will have grown through the call of war. But one thing has always remained the same throughout the untold centuries that the War of Ascension has been fought, whether a lone Demonic baby suckling still at his Mothers' breast, or a full-fledged Demon Lord or Lady leading their army into battle, every being will be affected in the months and years to come.

Tobin had not died the cold night that he threw himself from his balcony. No, death would have surely been more welcome compared to the nightmare that he found himself in. As he fell he passed through one of the strange dimensional gates that led to the world of Hell. Humans (according to the Throne of Darkness) stumbled through these gates all the time. These people came blindly through the gates only to find that they had left the sane world behind and now were in a place of living nightmares. People went missing by the thousands on Earth and while many were probably buried in the foundation of homes or sunk to the bottom of hundreds of swamps, many more had come to Hell.

Surprisingly some of these gates were very well known to humans. Forbidden places like the Bermuda Triangle or the deep dark rain forests of South America, where people went missing all the time. But these were not the only gates, they were the stationary ones. Other gates moved and opened randomly all over the world. It was one of these random gates that had opened and swallowed all the inhabitants of the lost Colony of Roanoke Island.

It was through one of these gates that Tobin passed while he fell. He had his eyes closed at the moment that he passed through, but he immediately felt a change in the air around him. One moment the icy air was rushing past him and the next everything was calm. And not only calm but warm and humid.

Feeling his heart hammering in his chest Tobin opened his eyes and found he was staring up into what appeared to be the eye of some great black and red hurricane. In the center of this eye Tobin found that he could see the building that he had just jumped from and for one wild moment he thought that he had hit the street with such force that he must have smashed through the black top and now lay in the sewers beneath the city.

He waited for the pain to begin, but when nothing happened, he began to understand that something else was happening. Above him the scene had begun to waiver like a reflection in a pool of water that had been disturbed. Slowly the eye began to close as clouds of black and red began stretching across it like the tentacles of some great prehistoric creature.

Slowly, foot by foot Earth disappeared and at that moment Tobin did not understand that it would probably be the last time he would see his home again. Of course even if he had understood this what could he have done?

Soon nothing remained of the portal and Tobin found himself looking at an alien sky of black clouds that roiled and lit up with red lightning. Slowly he pulled himself to his feet and began looking around trying to get his bearing. He was standing in a large ring of pillars carved from black marble. Slowly, on shaking legs he went up to one of these pillars and stared at it wonderingly. It was fluted in the style of ancient Roman Temples, with veins red running through it.

Slowly his heart still racing in his chest he reached out to brush his fingers along its cool surface. Yes, it was there. It was real. A soft wind suddenly blew across his face carrying on it the stench of sulfur and he had to force back a gag at the stench of burning meat. It was at that moment that he looked out beyond the rings and he felt his heart stop.

"Oh my God." Tobin breathed into the foul air. He was

standing on a hill overlooking what appeared to be some vast city, but unlike any city he had ever seen before. The first thing that drew his attention was that the city stretched out as far he could see in all directions, even climbing up the steep sides of a nearby mountain range. He felt like the city went on forever covering every inch of this strange world.

Not far (he guessed) from the hill where Tobin found himself, stood a great fortress, so huge that its walls threw a large section of the city in shadow. Tobin could see fires flickering in the shadowy streets, but of the people who might be living among them he could see nothing. Next to this fortress Tobin found himself drawn to a huge patch of rolling fire. This burning pit surged and roiled reminding Tobin of the motions of waves as they crashed against the many beaches he had been to. And then it hit him. He was not looking at some great burning pit, but a lake. A lake of fire.

Tobin was not a religious man in his heart, but he had read the Bible. He knew what he was looking at. The Great Lake of Fire that the preachers told of in their Sunday morning sermons. And with this knowledge Tobin knew where he was. His breath began coming out in short labored gasps.

Hell.

He was in Hell. That Infernal place that he had dreamed about for so long. In that moment he could feel the familiarity of this place, as if he was just returning after being gone on some long trip. He could feel the land calling out to him, welcoming back and he chocked a horrified sob.

At that moment some creature exploded from the flames of the lake. Tobin watched in horrified fascination as the thing spread great wings of fire and began flying towards the walls of the fortress. The creature banked up, gliding easily through the air, leaving a trail of dark smoke behind it like a missile fired from a jet airplane. Without warning the thing let out a shriek that echoed through the stormy night air and caused goose bumps to pop all over his body.

Tobin watched the creatures' flight with a mixture of awe and fear. Surly this was one of the demons that he had read about in that Good Book that he should have spent more time reading. Maybe this was Lucifer Himself come to collect the man who had lived in sin before finally committing the ultimate sin and killing himself.

As if this thought called to it, the creature changed direction, at the last minute pulling itself close to the surface of the burning lake and shot up in his direction. Tobin felt his legs grow weak and he fell against the pillar for support as the thing screeched again. He knew that he should turn and run, but his legs would not obey him. He could only watch as the thing came closer and closer.

At the last possible moment, just when Tobin was sure that the burning creature was going to slam into him, the thing pulled its' wings back, stopping a mere five feet in front of where he stood trembling in his terror. Tobin had no idea how tall the thing was, at least seven foot. He could now see that the thing was not exactly on fire as he first thought. Instead the creature's skin seemed to be made up of thousands of tiny dancing flames, covering thick blackened bones that made up the creature's body.

The beast's skull was that of some large Demonic Goat, with curved horns that dripped thick viscous looking black fluid. There were no eyes in the empty sockets of the skull, but Tobin could feel the thing looking at him none the less.

All of this he took in after only a few seconds, but it was the creature's flaming skin that held his gaze the longest. Inside each individual flame Tobin could see the writhing forms of people. Most of these were human men, women, and (oh dear god help him) children, though here and there he could see forms that were decidedly not human as well.

These tiny people howled in agony as they beat against their fiery prisons and if this weren't enough, some of them seemed to be aware of him standing there, as they reached out to him in supplication. Tobin felt tears of horror spill down his face as he understood that this is what was going to become of him. To be trapped inside the living fiery skin of this creature. To be tortured for eternity.

"Tobin." The demon spoke his name through a lipless mouth like an old lover calling him back to bed. The things' breath washed over him, smelling of a mixture of burned flesh and boiling blood. Tobin dropped to his knees as his legs finally gave out, vomiting acidic bile on the ground in front of the creatures' (there were people in its toes) feet. But none of this mattered. Only one thought dominated Tobin's mind.

It knew him.

Faced with this final horror Tobin felt the world begin to spin all around him. Somewhere, off in the distance he could hear someone screaming. It was the sound of a person who had been pushed to the very brink of insanity. The scream carried with it a message of agony that rivaled those pitiful souls trapped the creature's body.

Indeed it was these very souls that had to be the source of the scream and his heart went out to them once again. But then, just as the world began going black, Tobin realized that his head was thrown back and that terrible scream was coming from deep within him. That he was the tormented soul at the end of that wail of despair. And then he fell forward, landing in his own vomit and slipped into unconsciousness.

Tobin thought about all this as he stood on the balcony that led into his rooms in the Great Palace of Hell. Down below in the streets, the Dark City celebrated, the gutters running red with the blood of the revelers. So much had changed for him since that night that he had arrived in this twisted world. Could it have only been a nine days ago? Though in truth it felt like a life time ago.

Those first couple of days he was sure that he was going to die from just the sheer terror of the place. But he had survived, with what he hoped was most of his sanity intact, though his long ordeal was only just beginning. The Throne had told him, its' voice like a bloated slug in his mind, that he had been chosen to be the Observer. A recorder of events to come in the name of the Throne of Darkness.

He would watch and write down the significant events in the coming War of Ascension. A War of Ascension occurred at the end of a Ruling Satan's life. When this happened seven gems upon the Throne (simply called Stones) were filled with all the power of Hell. These Stones were then given to seven Demon Lords/Ladies called Stone Bearers. The goal of each Stone Bearer was to collect all seven Stones and bring them back to the Throne of Darkness. To this end the Stone Bearers would gather armies and go after each other (and anyone else who got in their way) killing one another until only one remained.

If this was not bad enough, there were no rules in a War of Ascension. Just because the Throne chose the original seven demons that would compete did not mean that those seven were set in stone (as it were). No, any demon in the world of Hell could be a Stone Bearer if he or she could find and kill one of the Chosen. In this way the War could shift in the blink of an eye and nobody (except the Throne and its' Observer) would know. The Throne told him that he was the first human to ever be chosen for this great honor. It was an honor that he could have (and would have) done without.

"Why me?" Tobin had asked in a plaintive voice. But on this subject the Throne remained silent. It had made its choice and that was that. There was nothing Tobin or anyone could do about it. This was a lesson that Tobin put to the test the day after the Ruling Satan had died. He had woken up in a Suite of rooms that was three times larger than his penthouse back on Earth.

Having no memory of how he got there he stumbled out of the large bed and stumbled into the next room. This room was large and decorated with furniture made of stained bone and gold. Three of the cold black walls were decorated with scenes of great battles that Tobin assumed to be from past Wars of Ascension. The forth wall had a huge fireplace that Tobin could have easily walked into and he briefly wondered if there was wood in Hell. Then quickly decided that he didn't really want to know what they used for kindling in the fireplace.

Dominating the center of the room was a large desk that appeared to be made from the skull of some large beast.

Slowly Tobin approached this desk, half expecting it to suddenly come to life and swallow him whole. Sitting on the surface of the desk were only three items. A large unmarked book, a black feather that he figured must be a quill and a small pot that contained red ink. At least he hoped it was ink, but was pretty sure was blood.

Behind the desk sat a large bone chair that was gilded in gold. It was almost Throne like in its stature. Slowly Tobin slid into this chair and was surprised to find that it was comfortable, almost as if it had been made to fit him perfectly.

After a moment he turned his attention to the book. It was large and thick and the cover of it was rough almost as if it were made from poorly tanned hide or...... Tobin snatched his hand away from the book.

Skin.

The book was bound together with skin. Whether Human or demon he did not know. Slowly, feeling as if at any moment he might throw up, Tobin pinched the corner of the cover and peeled the book open. Inside, the first page was blank. As was the second and the tenth and then he understood. This was to be his book. This is where he was expected to record the War of Ascension.

Tobin leaned backing his chair and sighed. So this was to be his punishment, to be the secretary to the Throne of Darkness. He felt a giggle building up in his chest and he knew that if he let it out, it would sound more than a little hysterical. He imagined sitting down at this desk every day after clocking in with a demonic Overlord. His desk would be decorated with small collectable toys like the ones found in happy meals. He could even set a silver framed picture of Richard on the corner.

Richard. The thought of his ex-lover ended all thoughts of merriment, hysterical or otherwise. It was Richards's fault that he was here. Richard's and Karen's. Oh how would like to make them pay for what they did to him.

"Master?" The single word spoken softly into the room caused Tobin to jump as if it had been shouted directly into his ear. He jumped up and spun around to face whatever horror the. Throne had sent to torment him this time. He thought that he was ready for anything, but he was wrong.

Standing just inside the room, next to what appeared to be a secret door in the wall was a human man. Oh, but what a human he was. The man looked like he was about twenty two yours old and stood almost six feet tall, with light green eyes and medium length red hair. His naked chest was hairless and well muscled and Tobin wondered for just a moment if he worked out. Below the waist the man wore only a loin pouch that showed off just how much of a man he really was.

At first Tobin had been surprised to see so many humans in Hell. But then the Throne had explained that while the gates only accounted for some of the Humans present. The ones that had been brought to Hell had bred creating an instant class of slaves to be raised. The Throne also explained that once a human was brought to Hell, depending on their age they stopped aging. If you were born in hell, you only aged to prime age, eighteen to twenty three or four, and then stopped aging. After all what good were slaves if they grew old and died?

Of course this limited immortality did nothing to stop one from truly dying. A Demon Lord could easily snap the neck of a disrespectful slave and he would expire as easily as someone on Earth. If a human was maimed he or she could not grow limbs back. They would just spend the rest of their long life crippled. If they were allowed to live on as defective toys.

Tobin was so stunned that for several moments he just stood their admiring the young man. It was only when he spoke again in that soft husky voice of his that he was able to come back to himself.

"Master?"

Tobin turned his head to look behind him to see who the man was talking to. Finding himself to be the only person in the room besides the man who spoke, he came to the conclusion that he must be speaking to him.

"What?" He asked in confusion.

"If you are ready my Lord, I will present the rest of your slaves to you." The man bowed low keeping his eyes to the floor.

"Slaves?" Tobin shook his head trying to understand what was being said to him. "What are you talking about?"

"I am called Stone, my Lord," the man spoke, his face still pointed toward the floor. "I am First Slave among those who have been chosen to serve here; it is my right to serve all of your primary needs." Tobin had no doubt what the Throne would have considered "primary needs". So this man had been sent as a kind of pacifier, a bribe. Well no thank you Mr. Throne of Darkness.

"I don't want slaves." Tobin told the man, the very thought of owning another human being was abhorrent to him. Stone flinched as if Tobin had yelled at him and he could see his already pale skin turn almost sheet white.

"If My Lord is dissatisfied with his slaves it is his right

to have them replaced." The man spoke in a soft trembling voice. "If he wishes it, I shall execute the others and then end my life so that others may be sent."

"Wait, what!?!" Tobin couldn't believe what he had just heard. Did this man just offer to murder several people and then commit suicide? This was insane! Without thinking he stalked across the room and the young man fell to his knees in terror.

"Oh for Christ's sake get up." Tobin was flustered by the turn of events.

"My life is forfeit, if my Lord finds me unworthy to serve him." The man spoke from the floor and Tobin wanted to grab him by the shoulders and shake him until he understood that he didn't want slaves. Of course he didn't want anybody to die because of him either.

"Stand up Stone," Tobin sighed in resignation. "It's okay I don't want you to kill yourself."

For the first time the other human looked up at Tobin's face and he saw hope and joy in the man's eyes. "You will let me serve?" It was as if Tobin had offered a small child a trip to their favorite amusement park. It sickened him, but all he said was.

"Yes."

"My Lord is very kind and wise." Steven gushed as he grabbed Tobin's hand and kissed his fingers in adulation. It took everything he had not to snatch his hand away from the groveling man, but he restrained himself knowing that if he did, it would not bode well for Stones' continued life.

After that Steven had taken him out to view the other slaves that had been selected to serve Tobin. All in all there were fifteen human men and woman that were to serve him in all aspects of his life. From cooking and cleaning to making sure that the water in the large stone basin that served as his bathtub was always hot.

Shortly after dismissing all (except Stone of course) of the groveling slaves Tobin found himself sitting at a large obsidian table that served as his dining room table, with a platter of steaming meat and strange radish looking vegetables called blood pods in front of him. These had been presented to him by his female cook who had called herself Nitta.

Tobin was not all together comfortable with Nitta, or her cooking. This stemming from the conversation that they had before she made him his dinner. The petite young woman had come to him while he sat in his study staring at the still empty book, his mind mercifully blank for once.

She bowed to him and asked if he would like to eat soon. After only a moments thought Tobin realized that he was indeed hungry, very hungry. But that was when everything went south. Upon telling his cook that he was indeed ready to eat, he was asked what kind of meat he would prefer. At this Tobin was at a loss, what kind of meat did they serve in Hell? Did they also kidnap cows and raise them in Demonic pastures? He didn't know.

Nitta told him in a no nonsense voice that she could cook a variety of meats including human. Before Tobin could say anything else, she went on to explain that if he preferred very tender meat she could acquire a baby from one of the many nursery/pantries throughout the Palace and cook it for him. They were especially good when basted in mother's milk.

In a horrified panic Tobin had told her in no uncertain

terms that he did not want her to cook a baby for him, no matter how delicious her spicing of the flesh would be. Instead he settled for a large rat like creature called a Tog. That had been several hours ago and now Tobin wondered if he had made the right choice in requesting meat. Perhaps he would have been better served with a new, all vegetarian diet.

"Is there a problem My Lord?" Stone asked as he poured what Tobin assumed to be wine into a fine red crystal goblet at his side. Tobin thought about telling him to take the meat away, perhaps he could share it with his fellow slaves, but then again would such and act sign Nitta's death warrant? This place was just too damned complicated.

"No," Tobin lied in an unsteady voice. "Everything is perfect." Slowly he picked up the knife and fork (both made from hardened bone) and began slicing through a large chunk of meat. Tobin had to admit that the smell of the cooked meat and the spices that Nitta had used made his mouth water and his stomach growled in anticipation.

As he moved the cut meat to the small metal plate in front of him Tobin suddenly realized something. He was holding a knife. A tool that could possibly end his torment here and now, but would Stone try and stop him? He thought that he probably would.

"Stone?" Tobin turned to where the slave stood off to his side, always waiting to be served.

"Yes Master?" The man's eyes instantly dropped to the floor. "How may I serve you?"

"I would like to eat in privacy now." Without a word the red haired man bowed and slipped out the door that Tobin figured led into the kitchens. He couldn't believe it. He was alone and had the chance to end it all right now.

Gripping the knife by its off yellow handle Tobin turned the blade toward himself and closed his eyes. Silently he counted in his mind, trying to keep his breathing under control.

One….Two…Three! Tobin shoved the knife into his throat and nothing happened! He felt the blade enter the skin and muscle of his throat, but there was no pain, no blood. Panicking he opened his eyes and thrust the blade deeper into his neck. Still nothing.

After several attempts, changing tactic, stabbing himself in the eye (no pain but unpleasant to say the least), and trying to slit both of his wrists, he had finally given up. He should have known that the Throne was not going to make it that easy on him. He was not allowed to die. Resigned, Tobin turned to the food and began to eat. Despite the fact the meat was as tender as any steak he had ever eaten and spiced perfectly as well, Tobin could not enjoy the meal.

He never thought that he would be so depressed about not being able to commit suicide, but here he was. After dinner he decided to take his first real bath in Hell. The basin was filled with steaming water that was tinged red. This would have made him uncomfortable had he not found out earlier that all the water in Hell had that reddish color to it. Almost as if it were permanently tainted with blood.

Tobin had allowed Stone to help him undress and thought about how under any other circumstance the situation would have probably aroused him. But he was afraid that those days had passed. Sinking into the hot water Tobin sighed and waved Steven off as the man come forward with sponges that he intended to use to wash his Master. Instead the human slave watched as Tobin washed himself and then soaked in the cooling water. Finally a thought came to him.

"Stone?" At the mention of his name the slave perked up. "What do I look like?"

"You are the Observer Master." The man seemed confused by the question. "You are magnificent."

"No, that's not what I meant," Tobin said in exasperation. "Do I look different?" As soon as he asked the question he knew that it had been a foolish one. What did Stone know of how he looked before coming to Hell? So he cut the other man off before he could speak.

"Wait, what about a mirror?" He asked.

"Mirror?" Steven rolled the unfamiliar word around in his mouth and looked at Tobin in confusion.

"Uh…um…a shiny piece of metal or something polished so I can see myself."

"Oh!" Steven looked relieved. "My Lord wishes to see a looking glass." And with that he left the room to presumably retrieve a looking glass. He was back in only a few moments with a small piece of polished metal. He held it up before Tobin and he gasped in horror at his reflection. Everything looked the same, except his eyes. Gone were the ever changing hazel color they had been. Now his eyes were like two black tar pits set in his face, showing no white, no other color. It was the mark of the Throne. Just as Stone was a slave to Tobin, so Tobin was truly slave to the Throne. There was no denying it.

In that moment the dam finally broke and Tobin began to silently cry. "Yes my Lord." Stone's green eyes gleamed with fanatical joy. "It is a great honor that you have been given." Tobin could say nothing in his despair and only continued to cry.

That had been seven days ago. Things had gotten only slightly easier for Tobin during those intervening days. He had found ways to get around having Stone offer to serve him every moment of every waking hour. The man had even offered to serve as a sex slave should Tobin desire it. He had turned him down as gently as possible, but he could tell that the slave felt that he had somehow failed. This was very aggravating. There had been times when Tobin had wanted to scream at all of those who served him, to ask them what their problems were. Why did they accept their servitude so willingly, while he fought against it with every fiber of his being?

But of course he knew the answer to that. They had all been born into slavery. To them there was nothing wrong with a Lord demanding a human child to be cooked for his afternoon meal. Or to order a First slave into his or her bed. There was absolutely nothing he could say or do that would change anything for them. As a matter fact they had looked at him in horrified awe the only time he had tried to explain to them what Earth was like.

They had wanted to know who ruled the humans and Fireal, a young man of about fourteen who acted as a kind of squire for Tobin had actually began to tremble when Tobin told him that all humans were free to do as they wished on Earth. After that none of the slaves wanted to hear any more about this place they had dubbed as Chaos World. They had even tried to explain to Tobin about how lucky he was to have been brought to Hell. No, he did not speak to them again about his home.

"Master?" Stone called to him from the open door that led back into his bed chamber and Tobin sighed heavily to himself. He turned and the red head bowed to him as he always did.

"What is it, Steven?"

"If it would please the Master it is time." Stone's voice trembled with excitement.

The Banquet. It was time to go down to the Great Hall and prepare for the arrival of the sseven Stone Bearers. Time for them to formally declare that they were ready to ascend to the Throne of Darkness. Tonight Tobin would come face to face with the worst that Hell had to offer. If he thought that the horrors that he had endured so far were bad, things were about to get one hundred times worse.

One of these creatures might become the next Ruling Satan. They had been chosen, hand-picked so to speak, by the Throne of Darkness and tonight Tobin was to be their Host.

God Help him.

CHAPTER 3

Taken from the personal journal of Tobin Masters, Observer to the Throne of Darkness.

The War of Ascension serves more than one purpose in what passes for the natural order Hell (if Hell could be said to have any real order). The obvious of course is the placing of a Ruling Satan upon the Throne. Though in my very short time here in Hell I have come to wonder why there must be a Ruling Satan at all, given the fact that the Throne itself remains the most powerful thing in Hell. My best guess is that without a mortal being sitting upon it, fighting for it, there would be less chaos in the world, and the Throne thrives on pure chaos. The other purpose of the War is the simple culling of the weak. Like lions that separate the weakest animals from a herd, so the War of Ascension weeds out the weak demon Lords and Ladies and devours them. Indeed, whole Kingdoms will have been scoured clean of all life in ways that would have made Hitler himself cringe in horror. So the motto of the War has always been "only the strong will survive." But what happens when one of the weak are at the very heart of the conflict? What happens when the weak are given the hope that they can one day rise to the level of the truly powerful? The answer is as obvious as it is simple.

Chaos.

The Great Hall which had been used to host the Banquets since the first War of Ascension was a round domed room that had exactly eight doors leading into it. Seven of these doors led into special chambers set aside from the rest of the Great Palace that were set up for the Stone Bearers. These demons were kept apart until it was time for the Banquet to begin for obvious reasons. It would not do for the now enemies to kill each other before the true War had begun.

The eighth door led back into the Great Palace itself and it was through this door that Tobin had arrived to find an army of twenty or thirty human slaves rushing about making sure that all was in place to honor the seven Chosen. It was his duty, as Observer to make certain that all was ready when the time came. Of course he had no idea what needed to be done, though he had no doubt that the Throne would alert him to any discrepancies that might arise.

The center of the room was dominated by a large table made of (of course) bone that had been stained black by foul magic and pigments. Around this table seven chairs (also made of bone) had been evenly placed. This was to be certain that none of the Stone Bearers would feel as if one or another was being honored more.

An eight chair had been placed at the head of the table. The bones that made up this chair were gilded with gold and had gems decorating the eye sockets of the large Demon skulls that had been mounted on it. Two of these horrid skulls made up the armrests. This was to be Tobin's seat.

A statement to the Stone Bearers that he spoke with the Throne's authority. Tobin looked at this throne like chair for several moments and felt fear rising up inside of him again. He couldn't, wouldn't do this. He would run out of this Hall and go back to where his rooms were. What would the Throne do to him for refusing? Kill him? Oh how he longed for that final death.

He turned and found that he suddenly could not move. He stood frozen like a statue for several minutes his muscles refusing to obey him before finally giving in. He would not fight this. He would stay.

As soon as he formed the thought he stumbled slightly and several of the slaves stopped to look at him. Tobin smoothed the thick black spider silk robes that he wore and turned to glare at these looky-loos. Under his withering stare they started as if he had lashed out at them and hurried to continue their work.

"Now you are getting the hang of it, Observer." The Throne chuckled in his mind.

"Fuck you." Tobin growled as he moved on with his inspection of the room. Torches on the walls provided the light, causing shadows to dance in the darkest corners of the Great Hall. Banners had been hung on the walls, one next to each door. Each of these banners was crafted of the finest spider silk (when had he started thinking about craftsmanship) and bore the symbol of the demon Lord in that room. Tobin thought about each of them as he walked by.

First there was an Egyptian Ankh that seemed to be made of bones and skulls on a field of crimson. This was the mark of the Vampire Lord Set. It had come as quite a shock to Tobin, who had heard the name Set before. Indeed he was the Egyptian god of chaos and evil. He then learned that many of the Ancient Gods of Darkness were actually demons in the world of Hell. Several of these creatures fostered their own blood lines in the "mortal" realm. Set had the head of a black jackal with blazing red eyes and long fangs. From the neck down he had the muscular body of a pale human male. He ruled a great Kingdom of shifting black sand on the continent of Malice.

Next came the green scaled claw crushing a burning globe that could have very easily been Earth. This was the symbol of the Demon Lord known as Deceiver. This Demon appeared in Tobin's mind looking like a seven foot tall anthropomorphic crocodile with black and red scales and blazing orange eyes. His right arm had pieces of metal armor that seemed to grow right out of his scales, ending in a wicked looking gauntlet that completely covered his large hand. To Tobin the arm and gauntlet looked like some bio-mechanical armor from some science fiction movie. Deceiver's jungle Kingdom was on the continent of Wrath.

After Deceiver, came the Purple and black flag of a demon Lord known as Severikhan. This demon resembled a seven foot tall humanoid dragon, with dark royal purple scales. Unlike the other Chosen Severikhan did not rule over an empire of his own. Instead he was a priest of Lust in the great church of Sins. His symbol was two demons engaged in sex embroidered in gold.

Next up was the broken goblet that represented Lord Thanatutus. A fat slug of a demon, with pale grey skin and rolls of disgusting sweat covered fat, which literally hung off his body like under baked dough. He was kind of like a

Mafia Don, overseeing a vast network of slavers, drug lords, and soldiers from his compound in the City of Darkness.

This had been another piece of information that actually interested Tobin. What in the world of Hell could be considered a criminal act? What could be so depraved that even Demons would condemn it? Apparently Thanatatutus dealt in a powerful drug made from rendering Demons down to their basic essence. This essence was then snorted or added to human blood and drank.

This drug entered the blood stream of the user infusing them with some of the power of the Demon used to make it. It fed their ego making them feel as if they were truly invincible. Most users simply enjoyed the rush of extra power and the high that came with it. While others rushed off to do battle with their enemies, only to find out that while they are indeed slightly stronger, they were still very mortal. Those who could not control these impulses usually died.

If this were not enough, it was rumored that Thanatutus was involved with the breeding of half breeds. Creatures resulting in a human demon union. Half breeds were not uncommon amongst those Demon Lords perverse enough to use their humans as sex slaves, but Thanatutus was said to make deals amongst the Demon Lords and ladies throughout Hell for their semen or eggs.

Once in his possession he would turn these materials over to his alchemists who would begin working their magic, trying to create the most powerful hybrid warriors and assassins. It was his hope that one day he would be able to turn his bastard army loose on all those that called him enemy. Now that he had been Chosen, perhaps his time had finally come.

After Thanatutus came the first female Demon to be chosen. Her name was Legacy and she ruled over a Forest Kingdom on the shattered continent of Armageddon. It was said that she stood at least ten foot tall with the head of a feral wolf and her body was covered with light grey fur. It was from her wolf like people that ancient legends of werewolves on Earth had come from.

Apparently some of Legacy's people had some how made it to Europe in the fifteen hundreds and terrorized as many countries as they could before finally being hunted down and killed. Legacy's symbol was of a great wolfs' skull on a field of white

After Legacy came the Lady Darkstar, the only one of the Chosen to fit the classic description of a demon. Her symbol was that of a great bloody sword with batwings coming from the hilt. She stood six feet tall, with shiny black scales covering her well muscled body. Small red horns grew from her forehead, looking like a miniature crown. She was the daughter of one of the past Ruling Satan, making her Throne-Kissed. After her father's death at the hands of one of his own elite guards, she had been banished by his successor. Left with nothing, Darkstar went out into the world and simply took what she wanted. She traveled to the continent of Blasphemy, chose a Kingdom at random and single handedly slaughtered the ruling family, and took over.

Finally there was the Nameless One, whose banner held no sign or symbol and yet as Tobin stopped to stare at the empty field of black he swore that it shifted and roiled like a chaotic storm. The Nameless One was said to be so hideous that to look upon her uncovered form would drive both human and Demon insane. This being always appeared in ever shifting rags that covered her from head to toe. Not much was known about the Nameless One, other than the fact that she ruled a Kingdom of madness on the continent of Sheol.

All of this information flooded his mind, coming from the Throne, and Tobin knew that tonight the first lines would go into that hideous skin bound book that sat on his desk. Tonight he would truly begin his work as the Observer to the Throne of Darkness. Somewhere off in the distance a gong sounded and Tobin's heart froze in his chest. It was time. Even now those hideous creatures were moving from their private rooms towards the Great Hall. Panicked Tobin looked around the room and realized he was alone. Alone, getting ready to face seven horrors and there was nothing he could do.

At that moment the first of those terrifying doors began to open. Even though he felt that he was going to pass out in any moment, Tobin forced himself to look at the creatures that began entering the Great Hall. First came Deceiver, his reptilian eyes searching the room for hidden dangers even though he, like the other Chosen, had been assured that this room was considered neutral ground. Of course one did not rise to the level of Demon Lord by trusting other people's assurances. Finally those powerful eyes came to rest on the human that stood near the head of the table.

Tobin shuddered as the image of the Lord of Deceit standing over the ravaged body of some poor human slave filled his mind. He could see the man's intestines thick and covered with blood and some jelly like fluid running from the ruined stomach up into Deceiver's mouth as the Demon chewed on them like a long strand of obscene spaghetti.

Tobin felt his stomach turn and his heart suddenly leaped against his rib cage like an animal trying to tear itself free from its' prison. He fought the temptation to turn away from the opening doors. After all wasn't it possible that if he refused to acknowledge the horrors that were about to present themselves that they would simply go away? This thought was so comforting that he began to turn to stare a blank wall. Once again he felt his legs lock and knew that the Throne would not even allow this small mercy. There was no escaping the Boogie Man. After all the vilest of creatures no longer lived in the shadows of fear. Instead they slithered like some disease infested rat in the corridors of his own mind.

Feeling bile rising in the back of his throat, Tobin gave into the Throne's will again and was released once more. One by one the doors opened and the Chosen began filing in. Thankfully, no other images came to Tobin's mind.

"Where is the Observer slave?" Thanatatutus demanded. Tobin turned toward the fat creature and the demon gave a start of surprise.

"You will be seated in no particular order." Tobin spoke without meaning to. "Any seat is open to whomever would take it, save this one." Tobin pointed at the large chair at the head of the table.

"And who shall be sitting there?" Set asked, his deep voice deep and dark. There was power in that voice and Tobin could feel it wash over him like waves pounding against a beach.

"I will."

"That is unacceptable!" Thanatutus roared. "No human will sit above his station in my presence." His flabby grey flesh quivering like it had a mind of its own. As the demon came closer Tobin became aware of two things. First, he smelled of rotting meat, and the second was that the movement of his skin had not been an illusion. Even as he watched it bulged and crawled in places all on its own and Tobin knew (through the Throne) that Thanatutus was carrying a Groach nest deep inside of his guts.

Groaches were a kind of demonic cockroach about three inches long with a black and crimson exoskeleton and eight legs. They infected beings in many ways. One was through sleep. If a victim slept to close to an infected person a Groach queen could crawl out of any opening in her host's body and lay eggs in the victims mouth, or nasal passage. One could also be infected by tainted blood or food. The disgusting little creatures could even be passed on through sex.

These sightless parasites burrowed deep into the soft flesh of the stomach and intestines where they nested, effectively turning their host into a walking hive. If the Groaches were not discovered in time, they would multiply and spread throughout the body and begin to cause the victims muscles to putrefy (hence the smell of rotten meat). If the Groach infestation was not halted the host would find themselves dependent on the parasites for movement as the insidious things took the place of the muscles they destroyed.

The only way to be rid of a Groach infestation was to dig through the body in attempt to locate the Groach queen. However, this was not a simple thing and many demons died during the procedure. Hence the fact that there were several thousand Groach nests in the Dark City alone. It was possible for one infected demon or human to infect a whole neighborhood.

As Tobin's mind filled with these details a groach drone forced its' was out of Thanatutus's nose. The blind parasite crawled around just below his right eye buzzing like an Earth cicada. This went on for several moments before the thing then scuttled down into Thanatutus's open mouth. The human watched this with disgust and quite suddenly all of his fear of these monsters evaporated. Let them do as they will, but this thing in front of him, this diseased slug did not deserve his fear. He was obviously weak and beyond pathetic. How could the Throne have chosen such a thing for the War of Ascension?

"You are an imposter," Thanatutus voice was slightly garbled as the Groach crawled down his throat and through his voice box. "You will pay for your trickery human." The demon spat the last word as if it was a curse.

Tobin had had enough. "How dare you!?" He snarled and his voice echoed through the Hall like thunder. "Who are you to presume to know the workings of the Eternal Throne of Darkness!?!" He raged and he would have sworn that the shadows of the room seemed to darken with his anger. "How dare you even approach me, you worm!"

With each word Tobin could feel his fury grow. He felt more powerful than any of the creatures in this room. He knew that he had only to reach out and twist to break this puny Demon's neck like a dry twig. Then it would take no effort at all to tear his head from his shoulders. Tobin imagined what that would look like, a fountain of blood and bugs splattering across the floor.

As he raged, Thanatutus stumbled back from away from him until he found himself up against the big table, his eyes wild with fear. "Forgive me, Lord." He whined in a high nasally voice. "I beg thee forgive me."

"There will be no forgiveness, though you will not die this day." Tobin turned to where the remaining five Stone Bearers stood watching the exchange with dark amusement. "To your seat, worm." Without looking Tobin pointed at the chair farthest away from where he would be sitting. After Thanatutus fell shaking into his appointed seat, the other Demon Lords chose seats for themselves.

It was only after Tobin sat down in his Throne like chair at the head of the table did he realize what had just happened. He had just threatened a Demon Lord of Hell. Placing his very life at risk. After all could he have really counted on the Throne to protect him? The same Throne that betrayed every one that had ever approached it? However, as the human searched his mind he found something even more disturbing. Earlier when he had spoken, it was the Throne using him the way a ventriloquist would use a dummy.

But not this time. He had not fell the Throne's influence at all during the whole exchange, which meant that it had been his tirade alone.

Deep in the back of his mind Tobin heard the Throne's dark laughter, and it spoke once again. "Oh yes, my Observer," it whispered to him. "You are definitely getting the hang of it now."

CHAPTER 4

Taken from the personal journal of Tobin Masters, Observer to the Throne of Darkness.

While it is true that the War of Ascension serves the purpose of clearing away the weak from the surface of Hell, I think that it is really a game for the Throne. A giant chess board to be manipulated at its dark whim. However, every good chess player knows that your most powerful pieces are always your pawns. No matter how many other pieces you still have on your board, it is the pawn that can be anything that it desires. The pawn can cause havoc in an enemy line if it can survive long enough to reach deep into enemy territory. So it is with the War of Ascension. So many beings of Supreme Power that call themselves Kings and Queens simply ignore the weak looking pawn until it has reached within striking distance. Only then do they realize their mistake, when it is too late and they lay bleeding out in the ruins of their once great Kingdoms. It is then that they realize what the pawn really is. The truly perfect assassin. I am curious to see what the pawns of the War of Ascension will become.

Tobin set his personal journal aside and looked at the large book where he had started writing about the War of Ascension. Only fifteen pages had been filled but already it felt like a thousand. So much happened two nights ago that he had to stop writing, his hand trembling with the remembered horror of it all. But he could not stay away from the Great Book for much longer. He could feel it in the back of his mind like an itch that he could only relieve once he began to write again. He had to record the rest of the banquet and after that he would be summoned to the Throne once again. There he would be given the seven Stones so that he could travel all over the world to deliver them to their Bearers.

He was putting all of this off but now he knew that he must push forward. Slowly he pulled the large book over to him and jumped as the cover suddenly flipped open on its own. All the hair on the back of his neck stood up on end as the pages slowly turned, stopping on the last page on which he had written. The book wanted to be written, wanted to be completed. Tobin put the tip of his quill in the jar filled with blood (he was sure that was what it was now) and placed it against the page. In that moment the present faded away and he was back in the past two nights ago. His mind filled with every minute detail as he recorded it all.

The Stone Bearers had all taken their seats and turned their expectant gazes towards the human now sitting at the head of the table. For an awkward moment Tobin wasn't sure what to do and he felt himself break out in a sweat as the Demon Lords and Ladies continued to stare at him. Just when he was sure he was going to get up and flee from the room, the Throne spoke through him once again.

"You have all been chosen to compete for the right to become the next Ruling Satan." The Throne's dark voice echoed through the Great Hall. "In the next couple of days each of you will be visited by this human, my Observer." At this last statement all eyes turned to Thanatutus who tried to slump further down into his chair.

"He will carry with him a Stone for each of you. You all know that to earn the right to ascend to the glorious title of Satan you must bring all seven Stones back to the Throne Room. Only one of you may achieve this." The Throne/Tobin waited as the Stone Bearers murmured amongst themselves as they looked around the table at their competition, already scheming on how they would take from them their prize.

All that is except for Lord Set, who instead of looking at the others, had locked his blood red eyes on Tobin. Inside of his mind the Throne chuckled in delight. "No Lord Set." The Throne (through Tobin) spoke directly to the Lord of Vampires. Instantly all attention was focused on the two of them. "You may not attack my Observer and take from him any extra Stones he may have" At that all heads turned toward Set who bared his fangs in what might have been a smile, but looked more like a snarl and shrugged his shoulders as if to say "Oh well, can't blame me for trying."

"Any who would lay a hand upon my Observer will find themselves utterly destroyed and his or her Stone shall be passed on to another. Is this understood?" One by one the Stone Bearers nodded their understanding. Satisfied the Throne spoke one last time before giving Tobin his body and voice back to him. "Good, then let us feast and honor each other one last time before the War of Ascension begins."

With those words Tobin's hands came together twice clapping in quick snaps. The sound summoned the slaves that would be serving the banquet. Instantly the doors to the Great Hall flew wide open and a group of six human males came forth bearing a large ten foot tray between them. They made their way to the table quickly and slid their burden onto it before the waiting demons (and Tobin). The smoky scent of cooked meat filled the room and he stared at the tray in sickened horror. The main course lay before him and he felt his stomach turn and he fought not to vomit. Lying on the large tray were the remains of the last Ruling Satan.

His body had been skinned of tough scales and the flesh underneath had been spiced and perhaps even marinated for cooking. Without waiting for any kind of signal all seven of the Stone Bearers reached forward as one and began tearing gobbets of tender juicy meat from the body and stuffed them into their mouths. They smacked their lips as if they were eating at some Gourmet restaurant and were tasting the best food there was to offer.

How much more could his mind take? Tobin wondered. There had to be a limit that he would (hopefully) soon reach and then he would break. Go blissfully insane, perhaps even catatonic. Struggling with this hope Tobin looked up and Set caught his attention. He could see that the Vampire Lord had none of the foul meat in his hands. Instead he held a large wooden barrel up to his muzzled face, gulping its contents as they poured out faster than he could swallow. The thick liquid slid from the corners of his fanged muzzle to drip on his pale human like skin. Here it ran like red rivers down his body. Blood. Of course it was the Ruling Satan's blood. Set was a Vampire so what else would he feed on? They must have drained the blood before cooking the body and now everyone (except Tobin) could take a piece of the last victor into themselves.

"Will you not eat with us Chosen One of the Throne?" The Lady Legacy growled at him from her position at the table, her voice a guttural bark. The mere thought of reaching out to touch the ravaged body was enough to sap all the strength from his limbs. Tobin swooned back into his chair, darkness crowding at the edges of his vision. Seeing this reaction the Lady Darkstar laughed merrily. The sound of her laughter was a thing of beauty, like the sounds of crystals rubbing against each other on a warm spring night. Tobin focused on this sound and the darkness retreated a little. Perhaps in any other setting this creature could have been considered beautiful, a fallen angel of sorts.

Even as these thoughts filled his feverish mind Darkstar reach across the table with one black scaled hand. Tobin watched (unable to tear his gaze away) as she ran her thick talons across the soft meat of the stomach, hovering there for a moment before moving further down. Suddenly her hand darted and ripped a perfectly roasted testicle free with a sick tearing sound. Her eyes never leaving Tobin, she popped the testicle into her mouth and squeezed it between her sharp teeth. With a slight popping sound the meat broke open spraying juice all over her chin.

Tobin couldn't hold back any longer and he let the darkness over take him as the others laughed at him.

Tobin blinked and found himself back at his desk. The open book in front of him several more pages had been filled. For a moment he gasped trying to catch his breath. It was as if he had been there once again. Like he had traveled back to the past to relive the horrors of that night. And when he looked down at all that he had written he saw that he had captured every detail in perfect clarity. This is what it meant to be the Observer Tobin understood now. He would travel in his mind to places and times throughout the world and hewould watch and record events as they happened. He would miss nothing. He would live every nightmare moment of the war of Ascension no matter how long it took to crown a victor. Tobin had only been in Hell for eleven days and the War could easily go on for decades, maybe even centuries.

"Master?" Steven's voice broke into his despair.

"What is it?" Tobin asked without looking back at the slave.

"A Royal Guardsman awaits you." Trying to control his trembling Tobin pushed himself up from the desk and in front of him the book slammed shut. After he returned from his journey passing out the Stones all across the world he would record everything that he saw. He thought about taking the book with him, but something inside told him that he would not need it.

Slowly he walked out into the front room of his suite and found the creature that would be taking him to the Stone Bearers. The thing had not changed since the first night he had seen it fly out of the lake of fire. It was shortly after he had awakened after passing out that night that he discovered that these creatures, and there were thousands of them, served the Throne as Royal Guardsman. Each of these things was terribly different, but for each difference they all shared one horrible trait. That burning skin of fire with souls trapped within the flames.

Tobin recognized this one immediately. It was certainly the one that had greeted him on the hill overlooking the Great Palace. "Hail Observer, it is time to deliver unto the Stone Bearers their trophy." The Royal Guardsman bowed slightly in front of the human and offered him a sack which looked empty to Tobin.

Taking it the human felt the sides and discovered that it was indeed empty. "I suppose we have to go to the Throne itself to get the Stones." Tobin stated and was rather happy to note that his voice did not tremble as his body did. For a moment the creature turned its' horned skull like head to the side as if it were listening to a faraway sound and Tobin felt sure that the Throne was talking to its servant.

"The pouch is made with powerful magic, Observer." It suddenly spoke as it turned toward the door that would lead them out into the hall of the Great Palace. "You have all that you need, it is time we go." And with that they were off. Tobin moved quickly trying to keep up with the larger creature. As they passed slaves and Demons in the hallway they each dropped to their knees until they passed and Tobin could not figure if they trembled in fear of him, or the Guardsman. Perhaps both.

In just a few moments Tobin found himself standing out in a large open courtyard. He looked up at the perpetual storm that covered the sky and found himself longing for the sun as he had never before in his life. He missed its' warmth and light. But Hell had no sun, just the storm, lightening and darkening in a perverse imitation of night and day.

Pushing these meaningless wishes from his thoughts, Tobin turned to his large companion. "Thanatutus will be first?" He hated the thought of seeing the disgusting Demon Lord again and wanted to get it over with quickly.

"No Observer, the first to receive their Stone will be the Lord Deceiver."

"Okay," Tobin looked around for anything that might resemble a personal airplane. "How are we going to get to Wrath, walk?"

"Have more faith in your Master. All things are possible through the Throne." The Guardsman turned and before Tobin could react he found himself pulled into its long arms. Expecting to feel the burn of its flaming body Tobin clamped down on a scream, but instead of burning the human felt a tingle begin to spread through him as if his entire body was falling asleep. He opened his eyes to find himself staring at the miniature souls as they continued to scream for help. He could even feel their little fists beating against him and he shuddered as he realized that they were the cause of the tingling across his body.

Without a word, with Tobin cradled against its' chest like an infant, the Guardsman leapt into the air and flew out over the Dark City. Though Tobin could not see, he could smell several fires as they ravaged different parts of the city as the party was beginning to wind down. Slowly the Guardsman banked to the right and Tobin found that he could see part of the city. He found himself looking at it in a new light. The Dark City had a terrible beauty that could draw someone to it like a poisoned flower just to get one whiff of its' fragrance. And there you were, knowing that you were going to die if you did this, knowing in your very soul that this is true as you put your nose to that blossom anyway.

No. Tobin shook his head as if he could shake these thoughts loose. He would not allow this place to take root in his soul. He refused to see beauty in this decadent place. And most of all he would not give in to the Throne of Darkness. Just as he thought this, the creature carrying him suddenly dropped into a dive and Tobin had just enough time to scream before they plunged into the Lake of Fire and he was truly engulfed in flames, his body bursting in agony unlike anything he had ever felt before.

The pain seemed to last for an eternity before Tobin suddenly found himself on his hands and knees gasping for air. Slowly he became aware of his surroundings and came to realize that he was no longer on the continent of the Dark City. With a great effort he pushed himself up on legs that felt like they were made of rubber. The first thing he noticed was that he and the Royal Guardsman were standing next to a small (twenty foot) lake of fire. He became aware that instead of the buildings that dominated the Dark City they were surrounded by jungle. But a jungle like nothing Tobin had ever seen before in his life.

First there were the trees. Large, towering things with sickly mottled grey trunks that had what appeared to be black veins running through them. The branches of these trees were thick and decorated with human hands. Yes, human hands instead of leaves, whose fingers wiggled when the wind blew through them. If that were not enough, then there were the sounds. All around him the sounds of the hellish jungle filled the air. The clicking of fingernails as they rubbed together in the wind. Animals moved around in the thick red and orange underbrush and though Tobin could not see them, he could hear their growls and grunts as they moved passed. All in all, this place seemed to be even more dangerous than the streets of the Dark City.

"Come Observer," the Guard spoke causing Tobin to jump. "Lord Deceiver awaits his prize." And with that the Demon stalked into the jungle. Tobin knew that he had to move or he would be left alone and he had no illusions about how long he would survive here without the protection of the Guardsman. After all, the Throne said that any demon that touched him would die; it never said that nothing could eat him out in the wilderness. Moving as quickly as he could, the human went after his escort.

The air in the jungle was thick and humid and only after a few moments Tobin found himself sweating in his black robes. Several times he had to stop just to catch his breath and he wondered if he might not have to worry about being eaten alive after all, first he just might die of a heart attack.

"Help me." The soft voice came from behind a large black bush off to his left. Upon hearing it Tobin froze and instantly he was back in the past seven years, standing on the sidewalk outside the airport in The Vatican City. "Help me Tobin." Richard's voice was ragged from screaming.

"Richard!" Without thinking Tobin moved from the path that he and the Guard had been following and into the brush. Instantly the leaves of several of the black bushes slashed him like miniature razors and by the time he reached the small clearing beyond them he was bleeding from his hands and face. Once in the clearing Tobin froze. Before him Richard hung in what appeared to be a huge gossamer spider web. The man writhed in agony as small black shapes moved across his naked body. Tobin could see that Richard's once perfect, tan skin was now covered in hundreds of swollen, bloody bite marks from the insidious spiders. His eyes were puffy and red rimmed as he begged Tobin to free him from his torment.

Tobin stepped forward and a large flame covered hand slammed onto his shoulder and pulled him back. "No, Observer." The Royal Guardsman held him in place. "You will go no farther."

"Let me go!" Tobin yelled at the Demon and struggled against its' powerful grip. "I will not leave him here. I don't give a damn what the Throne says, I will not leave him!" Still struggling Tobin felt himself lifted off the ground and into the air.

"Stop this idiocy." The demon growled into Tobin's face. "Stop and look, see not with your frail human eyes but through the eyes of your Master." Tobin's head was turned forcibly away from his captor to look at poor Richard once again. For just a moment everything looked as it had before, Richard pleading with his words and eyes to be rescued but then the trapped man began to waiver, like a reflection in a disturbed pond.

In only a few seconds the man that had been trapped in the web was gone, in his place Tobin found himself looking at a large black spider, its carapace dotted with crimson markings, as it had been spattered with blood. At first these markings appeared to be random but after looking at them for a moment Tobin could see that they were there by design, that they formed a red skull on its abdomen.

"Help me Tobin, please." Richard's voice slid from

between the terrible things mandibles. "Please Tobin, don't leave me here." This creature was using his memories of Richard to try and lure him into its' web. Much like the Venus flytrap used sweet smelling liquids to draw prey to their deaths. If Tobin had not been stopped by the Guardsman, Tobin would have stumbled blindly into the demonic spider's trap.

"Okay," A subdued Tobin turned to look at the Demon still holding him in the air. "I see it, put me down." Without a word Tobin was set back down on his feet, much in the same was a human child set their action figure down. Standing there Tobin stared at the creature in the middle of the web for several moments. This thing had tricked him but Tobin was angrier with himself. How could he have been so weak? After all wasn't Richard the reason that he was trapped in Hell in the first place. And here Tobin was rushing off to rescue him.

Again.

Was that all Tobin was to be, a victim over and over? "Help me, Tobin." The thing tried again, not knowing that its' illusion had failed. Once again Tobin felt rage bubbling up inside of him but this time there came with it a sense of power with it. A pressure that pushed against his skin from the inside, begging to be released. In awe Tobin lifted his right hand and found it engulfed in black flames.

"Tobin?" The spider asked plaintively, perhaps sensing the change in Tobin from prey to predator.

"No!" Tobin screamed and threw his hand toward the spider in its web. Instantly the creature burst into black flame. Tobin watched as it squealed in true agony and tried to climb up and out of sight. But Tobin was having none of it. He willed the flames to fly from his hand and again in a long continues jet, which he moved with the demonic spider until finally it dropped to the ground, smoking and lifeless. In an instant the power was gone, leaving Tobin gasping for air.

"Feel better?" The Guardsman asked as Tobin turned and stalked by it.

"Immensely."

Deceiver's castle jutted out of the jungle like the discarded tooth of some great prehistoric beast. It appeared out of place surrounded by trees and untouched by the savage jungle. Tobin stood in the large courtyard in front of the ugly structure. Sitting in front of him in a large throne made of bones on a raised dais, was the Lord of Deceit himself. Tobin felt no fear as he had two days before. Not now that he was beginning to understand some of the powers that he was able to wield. For a moment he wondered idly if it were possible to burn the scales right off the Demon sitting upon his petty throne.

In his mind he saw the scales charring and peeling back from the boiling juices just below the muscles. The pink flesh underneath the scales would liquefy next and pour from the bones like hot wax to pool at the base of the bone throne. Finally, the bones would blacken and snap under the immense heat before crumbling into ash. Would Deceiver scream in pain or would he die silently, cursing a power greater than himself? How easy would it be to find out? Just reach out and caress that dark anger that seemed to be festering within his soul. Find that piece of him that had surely already accepted the Throne of Darkness as its Lord and Master.

"I see the way that you look at me Observer. Does the Throne fill your mind with visions of my glorious victory to come?" This was the first time that Tobin had heard the demon's voice and the sound was deep and resonating.

Suddenly he found himself something quite different from his earlier fantasy of killing Deceiver. Perhaps the Throne would allow him to take the would be Lord of Hell back to the Palace. He could keep him as a personal slave. He could just imagine what it would be like to hold complete and total power over a creature such as this. He could dominate the Demon Lord in all things, even the bed.....

No! Tobin pushed the thoughts away. What was wrong with him? He searched his mind for anything that would tell him that the Throne was influencing him, putting these horrible thoughts in his head. But he found no trace of that malignant thing. This was more troubling than anything he had experienced so far. If the Throne was not manipulating him, then the thought had been his own. The desire to kill and to subjugate his own.

"Have you been struck with some ailment Observer?" Deceiver's voice washed over him again and he felt a shiver run through his body. Never in a million years would he admit to anyone that the shiver had not been one of fear, but one of desire. Behind him he heard the Royal Guardsman chuckle and Tobin had the distinct feeling that the creature could read his mind.

"I am fine Lord Deceiver." Tobin was pleasantly surprised to find that his voice did not quiver when he spoke. "I have brought you the first Stone." With the flourish of fanfare he slid his hand into the flat pouch and pulled forth a small ornately carved box that contained the Stone of Power.

"You have honored me this day, Observer." Deceiver stood revealing to Tobin that even though he looked like a crocodile he had all the male parts of a human. "As you can see my people even now prepare for the Great War." Indeed Tobin noticed the lizard men of Deceiver's kingdom running to and fro carrying weapons and armor. There were even some warriors riding large snake like creatures bearing Deceiver's symbol. These were the Demon Lord's elite army and one day soon they would explode out of their jungle kingdom to lay low any who would stand before them.

Trying very hard to keep his eyes above Deceiver's waist as he walked up the stairs of the dais Tobin spoke in a loud clear voice. "To you Lord Deceiver, I give a Stone of Power. Accept it now and declare yourself a Stone Bearer."

With reverence and a little awe Deceiver took the box from Tobin's hand. "I declare before the Throne of Darkness that I accept the title of Stone Bearer."

"May you prove worthy of that title, show no quarter to your enemies and remember that only one can ascend." Tobin spoke the words but he knew that it was the Throne providing them. All around them the reptilian warriors stopped what they were doing and dropped to their knees, bowing their heads to the ground in front of them.

"All hail the mighty Deceiver, Bearer of the Stone and the next Ruling Satan." Their hissing voices filled the air in a chant. "All hail the Chosen Chronicler of the Great War of Ascension. All hail the Throne of Darkness." Tobin turned to look at these creatures who were preparing to slaughter their neighbors in the name of putting their Lord upon the Throne. They honored not only the Throne of Darkness and their Lord. No, they honored a lowly human chosen to be the slave of the most powerful thing in all of Hell. But at that moment his connection to the Throne didn't matter to him at all.

Sometime later Tobin stood next to another blazing pool of fire, in yet another place, another continent. This time he found himself standing in what could have been considered a traditional castle from Earth's medieval Europe. Tobin had visited such castles in Great Briton, but he had never seen anything quite like this one. The castle was literally built into the very side of a mountain, giving it the appearance of a natural feature. Of course for all that Tobin knew it was, and for once the Throne remained silent.

Tobin and the Guard stood on a ledge overlooking a great walled city. From this height it was impossible to tell many details but Tobin thought that the city was building in the same style of the Dark City. Of course this city would have not even have even been considered a neighborhood in the Capital City, it being so small. In the center of the city Tobin could see a large coliseum and he had no doubt that bloody battles of survival were fought behind those walls for the entertainment of the castles' Mistress. Turning back towards the castle Tobin dismissed these thoughts as irrelevant. He was still floating on the heady mixture of killing the spider and the honor of Deceiver's men. At the same time all of these new thoughts confused him. He could almost feel himself changing. Part of him wanting to give in completely to the Throne. After all what was he getting for fighting? Nothing. But if he gave in, what then was the limit of his potential. If he gave in, then demons would truly tremble before his might. Wouldn't they?

The other half of his mind tried desperately to hold on to his humanity. He feared the end of the War more than he feared the Throne itself. After all was said and done would he still be Tobin Masters, or would he simply be the Observer to the Throne of Darkness? And then there was the little thing of not knowing what happened to all of the Observers that came before him. From all that he could tell, they simply ceased to exist.

Tobin blinked and found that while he had been thinking about these things he and the Guard had moved down the path and now stood in front of a large portcullis that lead into the castle. "Damn the Throne!" Tobin cursed under his breath. He hated the feeling of being moved about like a marionette under someone else's control.

"Who dares approach the Castle Darkstar?" A croaking voice demanded from behind the portcullis. Tobin saw that the voice belonged to a squat demon with six eyes and four arms. The things' skin was a dusky red while its' long stringy hair was black and tied back into a greasy pony tail. It held two long spears in its hands. These creatures were the actual natives of this kingdom, though they looked nothing like their Queen. This was to be expected considering the fact that the Lady Darkstar had come one night and simply took the kingdom from the ruling Demon Lord. It was said that blood had flowed down the side of the mountain to flood the streets of the city below, when Darkstar had slaughtered all those who lived in the castle.

"I am Tobin Masters, Observer to the Throne of

Darkness." Tobin announced himself and waited for the gate to be lifted.

"To the Throne with you." The little creature spat surprising Tobin. "Do you think me stupid? I can see you plain as night human." At this Tobin could feel his anger rising again and he could feel that delicious power filling him.

He stepped closer to the portcullis. "You will open this gate now you little piece of Groach shit, or I will tear it down and rip your filthy heart from your chest and shove it up your ass."

"I would like to see you try." The pitiful thing crouched down into what may have been a fighting stance but more resembled someone preparing to take a shit out in the wilderness. Snarling like an animal Tobin grabbed the gate and pulled with all of his might. To his surprise he heard the sound of screeching metal as the thick gate bent toward him. He knew that he could do exactly what he had threatened and he began pulling harder, looking forward to making this creature suffer.

"Hold, Chosen One of the Throne of Darkness." A new voice called out. Tobin looked from his intended victim to see another demon hurrying across the courtyard. This demon was larger than the residents of this miserable kingdom, standing at least seven foot tall with short grey fur covering his body. His head was that of a skeletal bat with glowing red eyes. Tobin knew that this was Darkstars' lover and second in command. His name was Chantric.

"I beg that you forgive this ignorance My Lord. Chantric dropped to one knee in front of Tobin on the other side of the portcullis. "We had not expected you so soon."

"Regardless Chantric, our welcome should have been better." Tobin's was cold. He took great satisfaction that the Demon flinched at the mention of his name. "Now open this thron damned gate before I decide to take your Lady's Stone to another, more worthy Bearer." It was an empty threat. Tobin had no authority to choose a Stone Bearer but it did have the desired effect. Chantric practically fell over the little guard getting to the lever that opened the gate. Tobin ducked under the gate before it was fully opened and he and the Royal Guardsman stalked toward the castle proper. The gate guard stood very still as Tobin passed his eyes, wide and staring at the bent bars of his precious gate.

As they were lead through the dark corridors of the castle Tobin noticed the same kind of frenzied activities that he had seen while visiting Deceiver's Kingdom. Finally they were shone into a large War Room where the Lady Darkstar awaited them. When they entered she was bent over a table where a large map of the world had been drawn. Next to her was yet another type of Demon. This creature stood nine foot, with stone thick grey skin and large wings. The thing had a short muzzle and orange eyes. It was a gargoyle right out of legend.

This route will take you to your first conquest the quickest My Lady." The gargoyle was saying as Tobin approached. Tobin could see that he was tracing a path that would take her across the lower half of Blasphemy and across one of the Blood Seas toward the continent of Malice, which suggested that she was going against Lord Set first. Suddenly she became aware of the new comers and she quickly covered the map with several pieces of parchment before turning to face them.

"Fear not Lady, I am simply an Observer, neutral in all things." Tobin couldn't help but smile to himself. Such paranoid things, these Demons.

"Very well Chosen one," Darkstar's eyes dropped to the floor. "You have brought me my Stone." Tobin could hear the plaintive almost begging sound in her voice and his smile deepened. He had her, just as he had had Deceiver, even though she did not honor him as the reptiles had, he knew that she would drop to her knees and beg if he wanted her to do so.

"Of course." Tobin pulled another small box from the enchanted pouch. "To you Lady Darkstar I present a Stone of Power, accept it now and declare yourself a Stone Bearer."

"I take this Stone and call myself Stone Bearer." The demoness announced as she snatched the box away from Tobin's hand. Without a second glance Darkstar retreated to the far corner of the room and opened the box. Tobin and his escort left her standing there the glow of the Stone illuminating her eyes. She seemed mesmerized by the object and Tobin wondered if she would still be standing there when one of the other Stone Bearers came to collect her Stone. In the end it really didn't matter to him, he had four more Stones to deliver. Of course he took a few moments to stop on his way out and kill the gate guard, just as he promised he would.

A short time later Tobin stood on a huge sand dune and looked around the kingdom where Set ruled. He now understood why it was called the Kingdom of Black Sands. The place seemed to be devoid of any features except blowing black sand and a few large pyramids that dotted the land like strange tombstones marking the graves of mysterious giants. Then there was the sound. It filled the air, enveloping the Guardsman and Tobin like a thick, uncomfortable blanket. It was the sound of moaning and Tobin swore that it rose out of the sand itself. If this was not enough every step that the human took was struggle, as if the sand was trying to pull him under.

After a long arduous walk the two were met at the entrance of the first pyramid by Lord Set and a group of black robed figures. Tobin noticed that these figures were actually demons from all over the world. There were even some humans amongst them. These were Set's people, both living and undead. They were graduates from his Necromancy Academy, and vampires. It was an interesting fact that while vampires existed, many of the legends surrounding them were false. Vampirism was not a curse to be passed on to unwilling victims. Instead one had to be born to at least one vampiric parent. Then depending on which gene was most dominant, the child would be either born a vampire or a normal example of the living parent.

Then there were the rare times when two vampires produced offspring. These children were called True Vampires and were the most powerful of their kind. As for the Necromancers, they were Set's elite magical force. Training from the time they arrived at the Academy until they either mastered the art of Death Magic, or provided an example by dying themselves. Set's minions searched the world over for any who showed the spark needed to learn Necromancy. Trying through bribery and sometimes outright force to recruit them into service to the Lord of

Death, all those who completed their training, whether brought by force or own free became fanatical followers of Lord Set.

"Greetings, Lord Set." Tobin stepped up to the jackal headed demon. "To you I give a Stone of Power, accept it now and declare yourself a Stone Bearer." Set bowed low and slipped the box from Tobin's hand.

"I declare myself a Stone Bearer and say that I will be the next Ruling Satan." Set announced. Tobin expected to hear a cheer or maybe a battle cry from those present but the only sound was the soft moaning.

"Behold, Observer!" The Demon Lord lifted his voice. "Bear witness to that which no living eye has seen except for those in my service. See the army of The Dead." With these words the sound of the moaning deepened in pitch causing Tobin's ear drums to vibrate in his head. Slowly he turned to see the sands of the black desert begin to shift as huge shapes began rising from underneath several large dunes. At first Tobin did not understand what he was looking at. He was expecting some great skeletal beast or perhaps a flock of undead bats. But as the shapes rose further out of the sand he realized that he was looking at ships.

They were not the modern war ships of Earth, of course. Instead they were old sailing ships. However, Tobin knew that these ships did not travel the wind swept seas. Indeed as he watched the ships broke free from the sands that had imprisoned them and began floating up into the dark sky. As they rose the Observer found that the information concerning these ships filled his mind. They were called Dread Ships. Powered by the souls of the dead and mastered by Necromancers, their hulls were made from the bones of those who failed to survive their necromantic training. The sails were made of skin (of course), sewn together and kept alive through the darkest magic. They were manned by Necromancers, vampires, and other undead. From where he stood Tobin could see humanoid skeletons moving across the decks of the Dread Ships, preparing them for war. It was the most impressive show of power Tobin had seen thus far.

The next stop landed the two unlikely companions in a wooded clearing on the continent of Armageddon. At first Tobin thought that they were going to have to go off into the trees once again to locate the next Stone Bearer. Not a prospect that he relished. Then he got a good look at their surroundings. They stood in a large grove of crimson red trees but they were not alone. Standing in a large circle were eighteen demonic wolves. These wolves stood on two legs with black fur covering their bodies. Each creature had paint marking its muzzle or chest and Tobin was reminded of pictures of Native Americans that he had seen. Tobin was sure that he was seeing the actual truth behind the legends of werewolves from Earth.

Hail Chosen of the Throne!" Tobin found the Lady Legacy striding toward him with a large spear clutched in her clawed hand. In that moment Tobin was sure that he was about to be attacked as she raised the spear above her head but instead of throwing it at him, the she-wolf drove it into the ground at Tobin's feet. At this the gathered wolves howled their approval into the darkening sky. Tobin was sure that there was something significant in the gesture, but he couldn't figure out what it could be, and the Throne chose that moment to remain silent.

Tobin felt weary all of a sudden. He just wanted to be done with all of this. He found that he longed for his chambers in the Great Palace. "Hail Lady Legacy. I give thee a Stone of Power, accept it and declare thyself a Stone bearer." Tobin lifted the next box out of his pouch.

"I declare it so." Legacy spoke without much fanfare and the wolves pounded their spears against their shields and howled again. From all around them throughout the forest more howls lifted into the air. Hundreds, perhaps even thousands of voices joined in the call. Listening to them Tobin felt the hairs on the back of his neck stand up on end. For just a moment he knew what the rabbit must feel like, hearing that sound out in the night.

The terror of being prey with nowhere to hide. And with that Legacy and her followers were gone, disappearing with the speed and silence of ghosts. Tobin turned to the Guard and waited to be taken to the next location but the Demon stood looking at him. Finally Tobin had to ask.

"What?"

"The spear." The Guardsman pointed to the weapon still sticking in the ground. "It is a gift to you, the Lady Legacy would be insulted if we left it behind." Sighing Tobin turned and pulled the spear out of the ground and found it to be remarkably heavy.

"There, can we go now?"

Next they appeared in what seemed to be some great cathedral with seven giant statues of humanoid dragon like creatures. Each dragon stature was carved from a different gem, representing their connection to the seven deadly sins, ruby for Wrath, emerald for Envy, amethyst for Lust, obsidian for Greed, diamond for Pride, zircon for Sloth, and sapphire for Gluttony.

It was said that in some great war in the past a great seven headed demon dragon known as Von Helix rose up to slaughter the army of the Angelus. It was believed that this beast was unstoppable until the Arch Angel Michael confronted it in single combat. The two were said to have fought none stop for seven days and seven nights, neither being able to gain the upper hand, laying waste to the lands around them.

Then on the dawn of the eight day, Michael struck a terrible blow to one of Van Helixes' heads, severing it. From the first two drops of blood to hit the ground grew two creatures, humanoid dragons. And as each head was severed two more demon dragons, one male, one female were born. These new creatures fled off into the wilderness, and later came together to form the Church of Sin.

This church started out small, but soon gained power and prestige and today it was recognized as the most powerful origination in all of Hell. So much history filled Tobin's' mind that he felt dizzy and he knew that he could have filled volumes of books with all that he had learned. But there was no time for history lessons. He had a Stoner to deliver.

"I declare the monk Severikhan to be an aberration." The red demon dragon declared in a booming voice. Here she paused as the large amphitheater burst into gasps, and hushed conversations. To be declared an aberration, a demon with true feelings, was almost assuredly a death sentence for the accused. IF it could be proven. However, this was Hell, and "proof" was always easy to come by, if one told the right lies.

"Bring forth the accused. The Master of Ceremonies, a green, called out. Tobin and the Royal Guardsman stood at the top of stairs leading down to a huge stage, watching the drama unfold before them. No one had noticed them yet, and Tobin was hoping to watch a little while longer before interrupting.

Down below three demon dragons of different colors, dressed in the armor of the churches elite warriors (the Knights of Satan) marched to where Severikhan was seated. Slowly the monk stood, and even from where he was standing, Tobin could have sworn that the demon was smiling.

"The accused." The Captain of the Knights announced as they reached the center of the stage. For the first time Tobin became aware of the raised dais in the middle of the room, where the leaders of the Church, seven Cardinals of Sin, sat on their marble thrones. And above them all one ornate throne where the true leader of the church sat watching everything.

Tobin looked at this leader, on odd creature that looked much like one of his race, but not of one single color. Instead his scaled were a patchwork of all the colors of the church. Representing them all. Below the Lord of Sin Tobin noticed that one of the seven thrones sat empty and realized that Severikhans' accuser was none other than the Cardinal of Wrath herself.

"My Lord of Sin." Severikhan spoke drawing Tobin's'

attention back to the lower part of the stage. The monk bowed low, his snout almost touching the floor.

"And how do you plead?" The red Cardinal demanded as the purple dragon straightened.

"Well….I suppose that I would plead innocence in these allegations brought against this most humble servant of the church." Severikhan spoke and there was no mistaking the jovial tone in his voice. The red glared as members of the gallery broke into quite laughter.

"I am prepared to deliver to the Ruling Council irrefutable proof…."

"Are you sure," Severikhan cut the Cardinal off in midsentence. "that doesn't have anything to do with the Red Lord that I killed last week, or maybe the contracts that he carried on him at the time?" Suddenly every eye was locked on the monk. He had them right where he wanted them, capturing his audience with only a few words.

"I have irrefutable proof….." The red started again, and again was cut off.

"I mean, exactly what was the Faction of Wrath going to do with seventy thousand mercenaries anyway?" Severikhan asked, his voice dripping with false innocence.

"You shut your filthy mouth!" The red Cardinal screamed, her eyes bulging in rage. "I will hear no more of your lies." She snarled as she drew from her back a wicked looking axe. At that moment the Royal Guardsman moved forward, making its way down toward the stage. Sighing, Tobin followed. Now he would never know how all of this would have ended.

Gasps and murmured conversations broke out as they passed the seated spectators. Even the six upon their thrones turned away from the drama unfolding in front of them to watch the intruders as they approached the center stage.

"If you speak again you filthy son of a human, I will cut your head from your shoulders." The Red snarled, completely unaware of the two who had arrived at her back. She raised her axe to show how serious she was, only to have the weapon snatched right out of her hands.

"None shall touch the Lord Severikhan at this time." The Guardsman commanded as he tossed the demon dragons' axe away. The red turned, her mouth hanging open in shock at being thwarted in her threats. At that moment the amphitheater exploded in noise. Voices being raised in anger, cries of astonishment. Never before had the Throne meddled in the affairs of the church. It was unheard of, and was not to be allowed. Now, several of the other factions were calling for Severikhans head, if for no other reason, than to teach the Throne its place in the order of the church.

"How dare you!" The Cardinal for Pride shouted. "The Throne oversteps itself. We will kill who wish and the Throne be damned!"

"The Throne is Master of all and as such knows no boundaries, and by decree of your Lord and Master, Lord Severikhan is to be remain unharmed."

"Lord?" The Red Cardinal howled at the Guardsman that stood less than five feet away from her. "He is no Lord, he is a petty murdering thief monk and I will end his life with my bare hands." With that the doomed Cardinal turned and took one step toward the openly smiling Severikhan. One step, that was all she got to take before the Guardsman struck.

Everyone in the amphitheater fell silent as the tip of the

Guardsman's black crystal sword exploded from the chest of the red slicing through her armor like a knife through hot butter. As soon as the blade penetrated flesh the blades' terrible magic began to work and as the whole congregation watched, the Red Cardinal began to shrivel. Flesh, scales, and muscles melting away as she was consumed by the Guardsman's weapon. In only a few seconds, the reds' empty armor clattered to the ground, and Tobin knew that if he looked hard enough, he would find a new flame, with a new soul on the Guardsman's body.

"Um....anybody else?" Tobin spoke into the now silent amphitheater. "NO? Well okay, Lord Severikhan I declare you the Lord of Lust do you accept?" Tobin held up the box with the Stone in it.

"I accept the honor of being a Stone Bearer in the War of Ascension." Severikhan lifted the box high above his head for all to see.

"I apologize for the inconvenience," he turned to the stunned Cardinals on their thrones, but I think we will have to hold my trial later. After all, I have a war to prepare for.

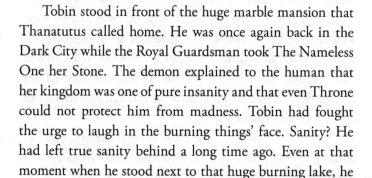

Tobin stood in front of the huge marble mansion that Thanatutus called home. He was once again back in the Dark City while the Royal Guardsman took The Nameless One her Stone. The demon explained to the human that her kingdom was one of pure insanity and that even Throne could not protect him from madness. Tobin had fought the urge to laugh in the burning things' face. Sanity? He had left true sanity behind a long time ago. Even at that moment when he stood next to that huge burning lake, he had known that true insanity would have been better than living with the knowledge that this was his reality now.

Damn Richard and his betrayal. If not for him Tobin would not be here right now. Oh, how he wanted to see his former lover suffer. Pushing this thought from his mind Tobin turned back to the task before him. This was where the worm Thanatutus lived and he had to face him alone. Tobin wanted nothing more than to leave the box he held in his hand on the step outside the large metal door. Maybe there was a mailbox? But Tobin knew this was not to be. There was ritual that needed to be followed.

Feeling even more tired Tobin lifted a large bronze knocker and pounded it against the door. After only a moment the door slowly swung open on rust hinges. Inside stood one of the most beautiful human men that Tobin had ever seen. He stood at least six foot tall, with long flowing blond hair, and deep green eyes that flashed at Tobin for just a second before the man bowed.

"My Master bids you welcome Observer, and asks that you allow me to serve you during your stay in his home." The man's voice was deep and husky. Tobin found himself wondering if he could take the slave back with him. Just imagine the nights with this one. But on the back of this another thought came to him. Maybe this was exactly what Thanatutus had wanted. This thought unnerved him. It showed that Thanatutus was more cunning than Tobin had first thought. Somehow the Demon Lord had figured out that he desired male companionship and had sent this oh-so perfect man to distract him.

But to what end? Did he hope to steal the other Stones while the Observer was otherwise occupied? If so, he was going to be disappointed. Perhaps Tobin was over thinking things. Maybe the man was meant to be a gift to try and repair the damage done the night of the Banquet. No, that was not it. Thanatatutus was a worm and a coward, but he was not one to try and make amends. No matter what his trap was Tobin was determined not to fall into it.

"Lead the way slave." Tobin snapped his voice cold and hard. Part of him (a small part), felt ashamed when the man in front of him flinched and bowed his head lower, but this passed very quickly. He would not allow Thanatutus to play him like a fool, no matter who else it hurt.

The human (funny how Tobin had begun thinking of himself separated from that word in his own mind) led him through hallways in silence. Tobin for his part did not really care if the man ever spoke again. After all wasn't he nothing more than just another version of the spider that had tried to kill him in the jungle? Bait. With this thought came anger again but this time there was no feeling of power behind it. It was just anger.

The halls were opulently decorated with many gold and gem encrusted items openly displayed as if they were nothing more than mere trinkets worth nothing at all. This was more Thanatutus's style, to show off his wealth in an attempt to prove his superiority. Instead, in Tobin's mind it only served to accent the Demon's weakness. None of the other Lords that he had visited this day had felt the need to show off who and what they were. They allowed their power to speak for itself. To his surprise Tobin found that he actually respected the other Stone Bearers, while Thanatutus fell even farther in his estimation.

"My Lord?" The slave interrupted his musings. Tobin

found that while he had been lost in thoughts (again) they had traveled through the mansion and come to a stop in front of a set of golden double doors. Each door had a likeness of Thanatutus carved into it so that the Demon Lord appeared to be looking down on anyone that stood in front of them. From beyond the barrier came the muffled sounds of many voices and what Tobin swore was music.

"The doors will only open to one who kneels to my Master's likeness." The slave explained when Tobin turned to look at him.

"Well then kneel quickly so I may get this over with and be on my way." Tobin snapped, his patience beginning to wear thin.

"My Lord gave specific instructions Chosen one, only you may be allowed to open the doors." The slave trembled in terror.

"Oh, I am sure he did." Tobin laughed out loud. "Now understand this," he lowered the tip of the spear toward the man. "You will kneel and open these doors, or I will walk away and the Throne can choose another to fight in the War."

"But Lord please..." Tobin cut him off by placing the sharp spear against his throat.

"Hear me," he hissed. "I will not bow to this worm, so do as I say or I swear by the Throne I will wear your guts like garland." His eyes bugging wide the human slowly slid to the floor and the doors swung open.

The scene in the room beyond was a miniature version of the chaos that had ruled the Dark City after the death of the ruling Satan. Demons cavorted throughout the room swaying to a band playing on a small stage in the corner, or drank themselves into a stupor. This did not surprise Tobin at all. While the other Stone Bearers were preparing themselves for war, each in their own way, Thanatutus threw a party. Did he believe himself untouchable? Perhaps he believed that he had all the time in the world to prepare himself. If that were the case Tobin knew it was pure folly. There was never time in the Great War. The Stones had been delivered; the War had technically already begun. Once the seven were chosen, time became liquid, in the blink an eye the balance of the War could and would change. Tobin had no idea that this was a lesson that he was about to learn first hand this very night.

The assassin watched her prey from the floor in front of the dais. She was dressed in dingy rags that barley covered her muscular body, just as every other human in the room was dressed. However, unlike the other slaves this woman was not sickly or frail. Her skin was soft where it wasn't criss-crossed with scares and firm. Her hair was long, dark, and clean. However none of the beings in this room, human or demon would be seeing these things. They could not see past the powerful spell that cloaked her true form. Instead they would only see an ugly girl with ratty hair and open postulating sores that leaked black puss.

Of course the young Demon Lord that had hired her to kill his father would have been very surprised to find out that she was human. But then of course she was not your typical human either. She was the only human to be raised by the Seekers, the greatest assassins in all of Hell. She had been trained in their traditions and magic for as long as she could remember. The very fact that she was human made her even more deadly. After all how many Demon Lords believed that such a lowly creature could kill them. The assassin enjoyed the look of confused horror that came into her victims eyes when they realized that they were about to die at her hand.

She was the servant of death and soon all in this room would meet her Master. She was not afraid, only excited. Soon the air would be filled with the screams of the damned and the floor would run red with their blood. These powerful beings would flee before her and drop dead at her feet. Those who believed themselves to be Gods would die at the end of her swords. There could be no better rush. To add to the excitement the Lord that had paid her the five hundred thousand souls stones (the common currency in Hell) to kill Thanatutus had also told her that anything she could carry out with her would be a bonus to her pay.

She had already spied many fat purses strapped to the belts of several Demon Lords. Even now as she watched a new human slave dressed in black robes approached her target. She watched as this man passed right by her and she was drawn to a small ornate box that he carried in one hand. Surly there was something of great value lay within that box. In any event she would know soon enough, for that box and everything else in this room now belonged to her. Laughing to herself, the assassin began moving toward the dais.

Tobin glared at Thanatutus as he climbed the raised dais where the Demon Lord sat. He had had one moment of pleasure when the doors had swung open and Thanatutus had leaned forward, eager to see the Observer kneeling on the ground. But his disappointment had shown clearly when he found Tobin still standing and his slave on his knees. Tobin's feeling of victory had only lasted a moment before he found himself pushing through the stinking sweating bodies of the partiers on his way across the room. Oh how he wanted to reach out and call forth those black flames and burn a path through these creatures but he found that he could not find that power any more. He was more than a little disappointed.

Now he climbed the steps at the end of the room and he was sure that he was going to have to burn these robes when he got back to the Great Palace.

"Thought I told you that the Observer was to have the honor of opening the doors." Thanatutus snarled at the slave accompanying Tobin.

"It was an honor I could do without." Tobin said dryly.

"How dare you." Thanatutus whined. "This is my house, you have come here to honor me and honor me you shall."

"Oh please." Tobin tossed the box into the Demon Lord's lap. "Here's your Stone, declare yourself a Stone Bearer." Tobin turned to leave. He wanted away from this disgusting creature as soon as possible.

"You can't leave yet Observer." Thanatutus's voice was touched by dark glee. Tobin turned to look directly into the others' eyes.

"I am the Observer to the Throne of Darkness worm, I come and go as I see fit." He spat on the floor at the demon's feet before heading back down the stairs.

"Be that as it may Chosen One, but I am afraid that the

doors have been sealed with powerful magic, they cannot be opened from this side until morning." At these words a chill moved down Tobin's spine. He looked up and found the doors had closed sometime after he had entered.

"Open them now!" Tobin hated the panicked sound of his own voice.

"Oh, I am truly sorry, My Lord," Thanatutus spat the last words as if they left a foul taste in his mouth. "But I gave strict instructions that after your arrival the doors were to remain sealed for twenty four hours. The demon smiled happily and Tobin could see Groaches climbing behind his teeth.

"There are no more Stones and you know the penalty for attacking me." Thanatutus's face took on a hurt look that was about as real as Karen's breast implants.

"I have no desire to attack you Observer," he held his hands out as if imploring Tobin to understand. "I only thought that since we had such a hard time the first time we met that we could take this time to become better acquainted. After all this party was put together in your honor." Shaking his head Tobin turned and continued down the stairs.

"Yes," Thanatutus called out from behind him. "You go out and enjoy yourself with the others and when you tire of their company you come back to me. After all we have twenty four hours to get to know one another". Tobin sped up as Thanatutus's laughter followed him across the room.

The human that had carried in the box brushed passed the assassin as he hurried back down the steps in his eagerness to be away from his Master. She paid him no attention at all. Just a few more steps and she would be up to where her Mark sat. Then the blood would flow.

"Stop!" A gruff voice commanded as she drew near the top of the stairs. The assassin's view of her target was suddenly blocked by a guard as he stepped out on front of her. Trying to look cowed the assassin looked up at the guards slime covered face.

"Where do you think you are going?" The guard was a large flabby creature covered in loose grey flesh that hung from its' body like partially melted wax. It had no arms, instead two long grey/green tentacles sprouted from its' massive shoulders.

"I am to entertain the Lord." The assassin dropped her face back to the floor as much to avoid the smell of the guards disgusting breath as to appear subservient.

"The Lord has his entertainment." The guard snarled at her. "Be gone whore." Sighing, the woman took a step back and drew in a deep breath. From deep within her she felt something stir. There was the spark of magic taught to her by her Seeker Masters and granted by the Throne of Darkness. She concentrated on this spark feeding it until it began to blaze like a wildfire in her body.

When she had gathered sufficient strength the assassin spoke the ancient incantation summoning her swords and armor. The guard yelped, a very undignified sound, as suddenly the human woman that had been standing in front of him changed. Gone was the soft fleshy woman that he could have killed so easily. In her place was a creature wearing what appeared to be black, living chitin armor which gleamed in the torch light like the carapace of some giant beetle. In her now clawed hands she held two red glowing rapiers that appeared to be made of crystal.

This was a creature from nightmares of Demons all across Hell. Every Demon had heard of the legends of the Seekers and their name was enough to make entire Kingdoms tremble in fear. Many of the inhabitants of Hell did not believe that these assassins actually existed, that they were stories created to instill fear. Those fools invariably screamed out the impossibility of their existence even as they died at the hands of the legend made flesh.

These thoughts and more shot through the guard's mind in an instant. He should have known in that instant that his life had come to end, but like so many before him he ignored the warning that rang in the back of his mind. This could not really be a Seeker, she was a human after all and he had killed his fair share of Throne Bound magic users. This was just another illusion. By the Throne the girl must be terrified. If she were truly one of the Seekers he would have been dead already. The illusion was a good one; he gave her that, but that is all it was.

"Assassin!" The Guard screamed drawing his tentacles back to snap the magic user like a whip. The assassin was in motion from the moment the guard had shouted his warning, sliding to the right dodging the almost certainly lethal blow that would have struck her in the face. Instead the tentacles struck an unfortunate Demon that had been walking up to speak to Lord Thanatutus, catching him in the chest, crushing his ribs and causing his heart to explode out of his back.

Before the shocked guard could react the assassin moved again, her swords whirling as she danced back to the left.

The guard felt a stinging across his stomach but ignored it as his eyes tracked his prey as she moved away from him. She would not escape a second time he vowed. Only he could not seem to make his tentacles obey his commands. Looking down in confusion he became aware that he was standing in a steadily growing pool of blood. Still not completely sure what was happening the guard took note of a large coil of green intestines that lay in the blood, like some thick segmented worm.

"Who lost their guts?" The guard asked himself as he followed the line of intestines up to the gaping hole in his own stomach.

"Oh." He said and fell forward, dead before his face smashed against the stone stairs. All around the room shouts of alarm rose into the air, followed by the sounds of blades being drawn from their sheaths. Behind her chitin face guard the assassin smiled. Nothing like a challenge to keep a girl happy.

"Assassin!' Tobin turned away from his futile attempts to open the doors at the sound of the panicked scream. "What now?" He thought to himself as the body of a guard toppled off the dais. He watched as two more guards rushed the dark armored figure at the top of the stairs. The first one to reach the assassin kept running right on past her as his now headless body tumbled into the crowd below. The second one put up a valiant fight but in a matter of moments he was separated from his legs and tentacles. Ignoring the wailing guard the assassin looked to Thanatutus who sat dumb founded upon his throne.

"Protect me!" The Demon Lord screamed and a human stepped out in front of him. Under normal circumstances Tobin would have found it laughable that anyone would send a human against the killing machine that stalked toward her target, but this was no normal human. He was Throne Bound.

Throne Bound were beings, both human and demon, who received the ability to cast magic through the Throne of Darkness. They were dangerous people who tapped into the very power of the Throne itself. Upon the dais the Seeker must have recognized her latest foe, for she paused to see what the Throne Bound would do. The human did not disappoint as his hands moved in intricate patterns and he spoke arcane words of power. Suddenly, a ball of fire leapt from the Throne Bound's out stretched hand. Tobin recognized the spell (and didn't question how) and braced himself for the fiery explosion that would envelope the assassin when it hit.

At the last moment the assassin jumped up and over the fireball, dodging the spell completely. Someone in the crowd below screamed and then the spell exploded frying several Demon Lords to a crisp. The seeker was already in motion dodging the Throne Bounds' second spell, which turned out to be a bolt of lightning that struck harmlessly against the far wall. With a flash of her hand the Seeker sent a small dagger at the Throne Bound, catching the surprised human directly between the eyes.

"You can't do this." Thanatutus wailed as the assassin moved towards him once again. "I'll pay you to let me live." He begged but one cannot bribe death once it has come, not even a Demon Lord. Tobin watched as the young slave that had met him at the door stepped in front of the assassin.

"Please Lady, spare my Master." Without a second glance the Seeker slashed her sword across the man and his upper body fell to the floor.

Tobin watched as Groaches poured out of the truncated corpses and he now understood what Thanatutus had planned for him. He was hoping to infect him with Groaches. Oh, how he wanted to be the one to deliver the killing blow, but up on the dais, the deed was already done. After that the assassin moved quickly through the room, killing anything that moved, and a few things that did not.

After being passed over for the third time as some pitiful demon fled by where he stood, Tobin came to realize that the assassin could not see him. So he watched the killer moving from corpse to corpse collecting pouches. The last item to be taken was the lacquered box containing the Stone of Power. As the assassin used her magic to open the doors that led back into the halls of Thanatutus's Palace Tobin followed her. He understood that this woman had no idea what she had just done. Had no clue what she carried with her at this moment. He also understood that even though nobody knew it, the first blow in the War of Ascension had been made. The dice had been rolled and chaos had won. For the first time in the history of Hell, a human was now in possession of one of the Stones of Power.

CHAPTER 5

Taken from the personal journal of Tobin Masters, Observer to the Throne of Darkness.

In any society that oppresses an entire class of people one must expect problems. Not from those who are oppressed, but from the very system of oppression itself. Do you only distinguish the lower caste by race? What about wealth? There are so many reasons why we as a people can declare others as lesser than we are. On Earth the biggest things are race, money and sexuality. In Hell these lines are blurry at best. To set only one group of restrictions on which to determine ones superiority would be to restraining. After all, what good is hate if you can only hate one thing or another about a relatively small group? To this end, it is the duty of every Demon to hate just about everyone around him (or her) for a variety of reasons. What you are hated for today, may not be the same tomorrow. However, the most universally hated people in Hell are of course the humans. How can one be expected to have respect for ones food, pet, or breeding cow? You may as well respect the ants you walk on every day. But, in their single minded hatred and oppression of the entire human race, the ruling Demon Class has overlooked humanities natural inclination to want to be free. They have also ignored the inevitable reaction to any type of mass oppression. Rebellion.

The man known as Father Michael sat staring at the object in front of him. Anyone seeing him sitting there would have seen an older man of about fifty, with watery blue eyes behind a pair of bent glasses. These glasses had been broken and repaired as best they could, considering that one could not simply go down to the local optometrist to get replacements. His full head of hair had turned white long ago. Before he came to Hell he had been drastically over weight perhaps waiting for the dreaded heart attack to take him off to Heaven. But, in his time fighting in this twisted world he had become lean and muscular.

Sometimes all of this still caught him off guard. He had been forty nine years old when he first arrived in Hell. That had been what, fifty three years ago now? He should be an old man now, sitting in a nursing home while living in the lucid past through Alzheimer's. Instead he found himself at one hundred and two in the best shape he had ever been in his life, fighting an entire world full of demons bent on enslaving any human they could find. He himself had been rescued from demonic slave masters by a small group of free humans. This group had been led by the Blade Master known as Forgotten Child. This of course was not the man's real name. Father Michael learned from these people that names, true names, had power in Hell. A Demon Lord that knew the true name of a human could cast terrible magic against them. The demon had to know the first and last names, so most free humans went by first or nicknames only.

Forgotten had taken from him any identification he carried on him when he had passed through the gate and burned them.

"No one," he explained "Not human nor demon must ever know your full name." Not even the "free humans" as one of them turned against their own kind from time to time. Forgotten's real name was Nick. Father Michael had learned that twenty years after that first meeting. The two had become friends and together they had began to wage a different kind of war against the demons. Father Michael had gone from Parish Priest in the Catholic Church to Guerrilla warrior in the span of six months. There had been a time when he couldn't even imagine running a single mile, but now he knew that he could run five without even breathing hard.

He had also become a fair combatant, learning the basics of the Bo staff, crossbow, and the composite long bow. But by far his favorite weapon was the War Axe. He was by no means a Blade Master; those were few and far between. But he fought in his fair share of battles over the years. His body bore the scars of many close calls. He did not know how he had survived so long when so many had fallen in their war against the Demonic Kingdoms. Perhaps it was just blind luck, or maybe God had not truly abandoned him after all.

That had been another type of battle all together. The fight to hold on to his faith in the Almighty God and believe that his coming to this cursed place had been part of His master plan. It had been a hard fight, but in the end his faith had won out, though there were times that he slipped and questioned it all. He had slowly risen up through the ranks to take control of the Rebellion. To be the leader of all the free humans in Hell. It still amazed him to know that thousands of people that were hidden throughout Hell depended on his strategies to help them win a war against almost impossible odds.

He had become a General, not actually fighting as much as he had when he first arrived. Each time he sent out orders to begin a raid or an attack on a high profile target his heart broke. He knew that he was sending men and women to their deaths and he felt that he should be with them; bleed with them, instead of pacing in some hidden cavern awaiting reports. But this is where he was needed. His head knew that, even if his heart did not.

There were resistance cells on every continent, including the Dark City itself. It was a known fact that during a War of Ascension the Dark City was sacked and burned. Each new Satan rebuilt the Capital upon the bones of the old city, leaving catacombs and ruins beneath the streets of the new Dark City. It was here, in these ruins that a small group of humans had hidden themselves. They knew that it was dangerous, but where in Hell could they be considered safe?

They knew they risked discovery every day from treasure hunting demons, but also add to that to the fact that the ruins often held lairs and nests for various demonic creatures and animals. But the humans braved these dangers and had lived under the current city for more than thirty years.

As a matter of fact at that exact moment Father Michael, leader of the Free Human Resistance, sat in rough round room under the City, less than ten miles away from the Great Palace itself. It was a place that the residence called the Pit. They called their home the Pit because they had found a great hole that lead down at least seven levels of ruins.

They had built bridges across this pit and lowered ladders so they could travel from level to level. The Pit was now the second largest free human settlement, with close to five hundred souls living in it. Only Haven, a hidden city on the continent of Malice had more people living in it. Sometimes when Father Michael lay down to sleep, he thought he could feel the Throne's malevolent presence in the dark with him. It was unnerving to say the very least.

Light from the fire pots in his room/office caused shadows to dance across the room but Father Michael hardly noticed. His attention was rapt on the object sitting on the desk in front of him. It was a small lacquered box and even as the priest looked at it, he swore that it covered itself in shadow, rejecting the fire light. Of course considering what was inside of it he thought it entirely possible. He shuddered just thinking about it.

What was he going to do? He asked himself for the hundredth time since this terrible thing had been brought to him. For just a moment he raised his eyes to look at the only other person in the room. She was a beautiful woman with long flowing black hair and soft hazel eyes. Her face was lightly rounded and perfectly positioned for beauty. Her skin was dark as if tanned though the Priest couldn't figure out how this was possible since there was no sun in Hell. She looked soft and innocent, but he knew better. She was one of the most dangerous people in the entire world.

Her name was Shard and she was human, at least in looks. However, she had been raised by a Demonic sect known as Seekers. She knew their ways, studied their magic, which made her demonic in nature. With her human appearance she could easily infiltrate any free human cell with little difficulty. They would be dead before any of them realized the threat. How many of his warriors had fallen to this beautiful woman's blades. Too many for him to count and now she sat across from him, watching his every move. He looked down at her petite hands expecting them to be stained red with blood.

The assassin had shown up two days before, sneaking past the sentries into the Pit. She had come right to the room where Father Michael had his sleeping mat which showed that the humans of the Pit had some very big security leaks that needed to be plugged. Father Michael had woke up to find the assassin standing over top of him and he knew that his luck had finally run out. He may die, but he was not going without a fight. Moving quicker than he could have when he was twenty years old the Priest rolled to his left, coming to his feet with his axe in his hands. Shard looked at him with amusement before lifting her hand in a dismissive gesture. Father Michael flew in the air like a child's doll, slamming into the wall. He gasped as wind was knocked from his lungs and the axe fell from his suddenly numb fingers.

"Silly, silly man." Shard whispered her voice soft and husky. "If I had wanted you dead, then you would be dead already."

"What...do...you...want." The older man asked her between gasps of air. Without a word she brought out the small box that now sat on his desk and held it out to him. "What is it?" He looked at it his eyes filled with suspicion. Again without speaking Shard lifted the hinged lid to reveal what lay within. Light danced from the interior of the box, moving in a hypnotic power. It was hard for the Priest to concentrate on what he was seeing. His mind was suddenly filled with a need to reach in and touch the source of that light. He knew that he only had to claim the object, call it his own and everything he ever dreamed of would be his. But then his mind focused and he saw the thing in the box for what it was. He had only heard of the Stones of Power through rumor and legend, but he knew in his heart that this was one of them.

"Dear God help us." The Priest whispered, his voice trembling. "Close it." He hated the plaintive sound of his voice, but he could not gather his thoughts while looking at the dark artifact. Laughing low in her throat Shard did as she was told and the room was plunged once again in darkness.

"So," the assassin set the box down between them and looked directly into the other human's eyes. "I believe we have much to talk about."

That had been two days ago and once again the box sat before the Priest. He had not told anyone else in the Pit about Shard's arrival, keeping her hidden in some of the lower storerooms. He had kept the secret, not out of greed or any other type of personal gain, but out of fear. What was he supposed to do with this thing? What *could* he do with something of this magnitude?

"Why did you bring this to us?" He asked the woman again. It felt he had asked her this question a hundred times the last two days. He could suddenly feel the weight of all those who had died under his command settle on his weary shoulders. He wanted to bow down under that weight, let it drag him to the floor, but he knew he could not allow that to happen. If he broke now there would be no one to take his place. This was his fate, like it or not.

"I have already told you." The woman sounded irritated. Perhaps sleeping on the cold stone floor among barrels of dried food had not been to her liking. Well, welcome to the Rebellion. The Priest thought snidely. He had been sleeping on the ground with only a thin mat between him and the stone for as long as he could remember. It would be good for this twisted human to know hardship.

But then he pushed those thoughts from his mind. They were not helping him decide what he was going to do. As for his question, the assassin had told him, at least ten times, how she had come to the Pit with her cursed object. Nine days ago she had been hired by a young Demon Lord named Belial to kill his father. The youngling had grown tired of waiting for his father to get himself killed so he could take over. Payment for this assassination did not matter Shard glossed over that part which hadn't really mattered to Michael any way. However the woman was told that anything that she could carry away from the mansion was hers.

No one could have guessed that Thanatutus had been chosen by the Throne of Darkness to be a Stone Bearer. Or that the night he was celebrating his great victory Shard would kill him and leave with the Stone of Power that had been just delivered. She had not known at the time what she had in her possession, but that changed all too soon. Belial discovered what his father had been celebrating and what had been taken from him. He wanted the box back, of course. Enraged he contacted the Seeker Council demanding Shard return his "property". Shard had been contacted by her Master and she explained the contract to him. It was decided by the Council that since the contract specifically covered any and all objects that could be carried out as part of the payment, it was up to her what to do with the box.

Of course by now she had already opened the damned thing and realized what she had. The assassin wanted nothing to do with the artifact. So in the end she agreed to return the Stone for the sum of two million Soul Stones. Belial agreed quickly enough and an exchange had been arranged. But Belial betrayed her, sending a great many of his father's half breed demons after her. She had barely survived the encounter. To make matters worse Belial's warriors talked and rumors of one of the Stones of Power being lost in the streets of the Dark City spread like fire from neighborhood to neighborhood. Now several hundred Noble Families had their warriors searching for her and the Stone she carried.

So after spending a couple of days playing hide and seek and almost dying on three separate occasions, she had decided to seek out the humans under the City. She had come to see what they could offer her in return for the Stone. She felt reasonably sure that they would honor any agreement that they came to. She had wandered two days before stumbling upon the Pit. It had just been blind luck that she overheard two of the perimeter guards talking about Father Michael, the leader of the free humans and the fact that he was here in the Pit. After that it had only taken the assassin an hour to find him.

That was it. Blind luck had brought to him one of the most powerful artifact in all of Hell. Could it really be as simple as that, or was there more to it? Was there a purpose here? Could this be the reason that god had allowed so many of His Faithful to this world? Was this father Michael's ultimate test? Sitting on his desk made of old stone was an object that could possibly destroy every living free human in the rebellion. But could it also save them? For two days he had dwelled on it, prayed on it. But no easy answer came to him. What he was considering was so far beyond anything that he had thought of before. It was most likely impossible, but the possibility alone was worth the chance, right? If they could pull it off they could change the very face of Hell itself.

If.

It was the biggest word he had ever heard. There was no way around it, he must make a decision. Sitting there looking into the assassin's eyes he finally made that decision and prayed to the Lord above that it was the right one. If not, then by his actions today he would surely be dooming every free human to a life of slavery and horror. Again the old Priest felt his heart break. Across from him Shard saw the change come over the man's eyes and smiled. Good, it was now time to negotiate.

Forgotten Child whirled away from the incoming blade while bringing up his blade to parry a second strike coming from the opposite direction. The two swords come together with the sound of metal against metal. Behind him the attacker he just dodged moved in for what he thought would now be an easy kill. He swung his axe up over his head intent on splitting the Blade Master in half. Forgotten waited until the very last second when the axe wielder was fully committed to his attack before suddenly sidestepping, releasing the pressure he had been using to hold the other's blade at bay.

The other man, not expecting this move stumbled forward to occupy the space where Forgotten had been. The man with the axe saw all of this, but could not stop his attack. The axe slammed into the other man's outstretched sword causing sparks to fly. The sword wielder, a woman, yelped as the shock waves sent up the hilt of her weapon numbed her fingers, causing her to drop the sword. For a moment the two attackers gawked at each other before throwing themselves apart as if they thought they would now have to fight one another.

The now weaponless woman stumbled back into Forgotten's spinning sweep kick. For a moment the woman caught a glimpse of the cracked and dirty ceiling of the room framed by her booted feet, before slamming hard on to her back. Forgotten Child heard the air rush out of her lungs and knew that he had a few minutes before she would recover enough to get back into the fight. He allowed his kicks' momentum to carry him around and without looking brought up his sword in a defensive posture. Once again the axe wielder found himself blocked when he was certain that the quarry had not known he was coming.

Screaming in frustration the man swung his axe in a wide arc which Forgotten dodged easily. This time as he slid around the attacker he drew the flat of his blade against the man's stomach. For a split second the man stood there dumbfounded, but then he remembered the rules and he fell to the ground "dead". At that moment another attacker launched himself from the shadows to Forgotten's right. The man's hands were a blur of motion as he threw a barrage of knives at the Blade Master.

Forgotten was already moving even as the man came from the shadows. Without a thought he dropped his sword knowing that it would be of little use to him now. The world began to slow around him showing the Blade Master intricate details that no one without Blade Master training could see. He saw each of the six throwing daggers heading for him in perfect clarity and he allowed his mind to calculate their trajectory, pinpointing in seconds where each one would strike. One each in the right and left shoulders, one in his throat, one in his gut, and one in his heart.

Allowing his Blade Master's instinct to take over, Forgotten's hands darted around his body catching each of the knives and sending five of them back at the man who had thrown them. He put the perfect spin on them causing the hilts to strike the man in both knee caps, and both shoulders. The last one that would have struck him in the heart was caught before it could hit its' target. However the damage had been done, and with a grunt of pain the knife thrower dropped to the floor. The sixth blade, the one that would have stuck in Forgotten's stomach went off in another direction, catching the swords woman in the forehead as she sat up. Without a sound she fell back to the stone floor with an uneremonious thud. Forgotten stood still for a moment waiting to see if there would be any more attacks, his face hidden by his long sweat dampened blond hair.

"Okay." He finally spoke into the now silent cavern. He turned to a large group of humans that had gathered to watch from the other side of the room. Around him his "enemies" stirred and began pulling themselves to their feet. "What mistakes did they make?" Disappointed he watched as one by one the students dropped their faces, looking away from his intense blue eyes. He had just about given up getting an answer from the group when a small voice rang out.

"They attacked independently, without regard to those who fought with them." Trying to keep his face from cracking into a pleased smile, Forgotten turned slightly to face the young girl that had spoken. She was by far the youngest member of this group at only nine years old. For just a moment he regarded her long reddish blond hair, blue eyes, and beautiful face still full of baby fat. Then, he turned away from her to pace in front of the class.

"Very good, you must always remember your allies on the field of battle." He looked at the students as he paced. "Without teamwork death is the only thing you will achieve." He turned and looked at the embarrassed combatants. "You are not competing with each other for the kill." One by one they bowed their heads knowing that they were guilty of thinking they had to be the one to take down the Blade Master.

"Being a Blade Master is more than knowing how to wield the weapons. You must learn to sharpen your greatest blade in your armory, your mind." Forgotten turned back to the class. He knew that any of them becoming a Blade Master was very slim. It was a gift that only three hundred men and women had in all of the resistance. Of course there were no demon Blade Masters, nor were there any in captivity.

These people had come to him in the hopes of making their way down that path and though probably only one of them would make it, they would leave knowing all they needed to know to survive the war with the demons. But if any more did show promise, he would send them to the

Academy in Haven. To tell the truth, there was only one student in the group that he hoped and dreaded would succeed. The nine year old girl who had answered his question. Cassandra.

"Excuse me Master." A new voice brought him out of his thoughts and he realized that he had been standing, silent for several moments. The class seemed to have taken his silence for anger at them for not answering his question. Good, let them worry for a few minutes longer. He turned to the new comer, a young man named Trevor who had lost his right arm to a Demon five years ago. Unable to continue his life as a warrior Trevor had become a runner for Father Michael. In many ways accepting this had been harder on the man than the training to become a fighter and Forgotten Child knew that Trevor longed to lift a weapon again. His heart went out to the young man.

"Welcome Trevor." Forgotten smiled warmly at his one time student. Trevor had shown much promise back then, and for a time Forgotten thought that he would be going to the Academy, but while he had been a very talented swordsman, he could not learn other bladed weapons. And so the young man had become just another warrior in the rank and file, going on to fight many battles before the loss of his hand.

Trevor bowed low to Forgotten. "Father Michael requests your presence in the War Hall." Forgotten felt his heart freeze in his chest. For the last couple of days he had been on edge. It was as if he could sense danger just around the corner, but couldn't quite see what it was. But maybe his unease came from something else. Could something have happened to his wife, Rachael?

She had gone on a mission four days ago to check into

some disturbing rumors that more and more Noble Houses were sending their warriors down into the ruins under the City. If this was true, then it was only a matter of time before one of these groups found the Pit. Rachael had volunteered to lead a small group to scout out the situation. There had been no word from her since then and now Father Michael was calling for him. Could he have been sensing her death? The thought was enough to paralyze the Blade Master.

Fighting to keep control of his emotions Forgotten turned back to his class. "Run through practice drills one through seven and then meditate for one hour." He told the students before looking back at Trevor. "Tell the Father that I will join him in a moment." Bowing his acknowledgment the runner turned and strode from the room. Trying to keep from running, Forgotten walked stiffly toward another part of the Training Room, where a small pool of water was used by the students. Slowly he cupped a handful of reddish water and splashed it on his face.

"Master?" A soft voice called to him as he ran his damp fingers through his hair.

"Yes, Cassandra?" Forgotten turned to look at the girl and felt his heart clinch again.

"I would like to accompany you to the War Hall." Forgotten's first impulse was to deny the request. He did not want her there if they had brought back Rachael's body. He couldn't bear the thought of Cassandra seeing the agony this would bring him. This was a selfish thought. Hadn't he just told her and the rest of the class that they had to learn to rely on one another? Sometimes an emotional battle could be even more devastating than a physical one. Without speaking he nodded his okay, before turning back to the pool.

Quickly he stripped off the spiders' exoskeleton that he wore as armor and splashed more cool water on his chest. He then applied a thick sweet smelling paste to his underarms and armor. The paste came from large demonic birds that the resistance bred. The birds, called Lures, used the paste to attract prey. The humans used it as soap and deodorant. Finally, with fear still in his heart he donned his armor, clasped his sword to his back and dipped his head deep into the pool of water to cool his feverish brain. Please, oh please don't let it be the worst, he begged a God that he was unsure even existed, what would he do if his plea went unanswered? He didn't know and for just a moment he thought about just not going. He could simply walk back to the class and continue their training session. By this action the fear of loss and death would be reversed. Of course these were the thoughts of a first year Novice and hardly befitting a Blade Master.

"Fear is my enemy." He whispered the Blade Master Creed to himself. "To fear is to allow the enemy to occupy the house inside my heart, this I cannot allow. I will kill my fear and thus kill my enemy." For the first time since the Creed had been created, Forgotten found that the words brought him no solace. One thought drowned out all others in his mind.

"Please, please don't let her be dead."

Cassandra walked briskly next to the man that everyone knew as Forgotten Child, her short legs moving quickly. She knew that he was worried, but would it have killed him to slow down just a little bit? She wanted to ask him this, but knew that she wouldn't. She would endure as she had been taught to do all her life. Suddenly, as if he had read her mind Forgotten Child slowed his pace and Cassandra found that she could now walk and still keep up with him. She blushed slightly knowing that in all likelihood he *had* read her mind and responded to her unspoken request. This was just one of the many powers of a true Blade Master.

"It's alright." Forgotten spoke in a soft voice confirming that he had indeed been in her mind. In shame she dropped her eyes. She had shown weakness to the man that she admired most in the entire world. He had taught her that weakness, all weakness, was an even greater enemy than fear. One did what one had to do, even if they thought they couldn't achieve their goal. Weakness killed the spirit, allowing a physical enemy to kill the body.

"Never fear weakness around those whom you trust Little Dagger." He turned to look down at her with a twinkle in his eye and Cassandra knew that he was up to mischief. "Unless you think of me as an enemy."

"Do not say it Father." He smiled down at her, obviously happy with her quick response, and turned to face the caverns that would lead them to the War Hall. Cassandra watched all the mischief leave her father's eyes.

"You worry that the Father has word on mother." She made it a statement not expecting an answer.

"Who is reading whose mind now?" He spoke without looking at her and she saw a ghost of a smile return to his face. "Maybe a little." A snort escaped Cassandra's mouth before she could stop herself.

"Okay, a lot." It was Cassandra's turn to regard her father as they continued on their way. He was a handsome man with blond hair that had been shaved around the sides leaving the top long, which was pulled back into a golden pony tail. His face was strong with a thin scar running down the left side and a crooked nose that had been broken several times. His eyes were sparkling blue and although they had always looked upon his daughter with gentleness, she knew that he was said to strike fear in the hearts of his enemies with just a glance. But there was sadness in those eyes, as if her father carried the weight of terrible memories with him always. Cassandra never knew what tore at her father's heart, but she thought it had something to do with his time in his other world. The world called Earth.

Forgotten had once been known by another name on this Earth and he used to regal her with stories of this world. First there was this big ball of light that filled the sky bringing warmth to the many people of this world. Cassandra could not even begin to imagine what purpose such a thing would serve, except to maybe blind ones' enemies. But then if this light covered the whole land, would you not be blinded yourself. It just seemed impractical. Forgotten had also described white clouds that drifted through the sky, moved by gentle warm winds.

Then there was something called grass, which grew everywhere it could take root, turning the ground into a carpet of vibrant, living green. He even told her of oceans and rivers and lakes that were blue, not blood red and people actually went into the water for fun. It was amazing to hear that not many were eaten in these waters. Nobody went into the waters here in hell, not even the Demon Lords. Nobody wanted to die.

Some of the other things that he told her she just couldn't

believe, they sounded just too fantastic. Like giant metal birds that flew free humans from kingdom to kingdom. Her father had grown up in a Free City called Los Angeles in the kingdom of California. He had grown up by himself learning what he called "The Streets". When he had come of age he joined the army of the Empire of the United States. He went into what he called the Special Forces where he killed many humans in the name of his Empire.

When he told her this Cassandra had asked why he killed humans? After all wasn't he now fighting for the humans? Forgotten had sighed and shifted his eyes away from his daughter as he explained that on Earth there were no demons, just many humans. These humans always seemed to be fighting amongst themselves for one reason or another. He also told her, with his head hung low, that he had done a great many things that he was ashamed of. Whenever he said something like this Forgotten Child would touch the small sword necklace that he wore around his neck as if it were some sort of magical talisman. He would not go into specifics, and Cassandra knew that whatever these things were that he had done, they hurt him deeply even today.

When she asked how he came to be in Hell, he told her that he had been on a special killing mission deep within some jungle kingdom. It was here during a great battle that a gate had opened up and swallowed him and his men. One minute they were fighting humans, the next they were fighting demons.

He had been fighting ever since. He was the only soldier to escape that terrible first night, leaving the bodies of seven slavers in his wake. He spent the next seventeen years wandering the lands killing demons and freeing humans when he could. It was during this time that he began to understand some of the special abilities he had.

It was also when he started gathering humans together and began training them to fight with him. He found that he was not alone, that others could be trained in the amazing powers he developed and his group began to get bigger. And the larger they got, the bolder they became in their attacks against the demons. They began targeting slavers, tracking them to where the gates would open. Here they could rescue humans just arriving and add to them to their ranks. It was during one of these raids that Forgotten killed a slaver that would have captured Father Michael.

Forgotten had tried to teach Father Michael the Blade Master ways, but the older man did not have the ability. However, he did show talent in recruiting and tactics, talents that seemed to come to him with ease. Father Michael was convinced that there had to be a way to open the gates back to Earth and send the free humans home. But then there was the question of time. Even if they could open the gates backwards, who knew where, let alone when they might arrive? Of course in the end did it really matter as long as they were free from Hell?

All around the world, humans pledged themselves to this dream, until the rebellion really began to form. It was during the building of the first free human city (Haven) that Forgotten first met the woman who would become his wife. Rachael had come to them, a freed slave from some Demon Lord in the Dark City. She joined Forgotten's training class and soon discovered that she had the spark that would allow her to become a Blade Master. It had been hard to admit that he was falling in love with the red headed woman.

There had only been one other person that had laid claim to his heart and through his actions he almost destroyed that person. Forgotten had vowed that he would never open his heart again, but in the end Rachael would not be denied.

Father Michael performed the marriage ceremony on the steps to the Academy where they had met. Being born in Hell Rachael had never seen anything like this and this added to Forgotten's joy at seeing her wonder at the words of promise he spoke for her alone. A short time later they came to the Pit. And then nine years ago Rachael had given him the best gift he had ever received in his life, their daughter Cassandra. It was Forgotten's dream to take his wife and daughter beyond the barriers to the world of his birth. Once there he could tell them his true name and give them the gift of his last name.

Walking next to her father Cassandra blinked, there was quite a bit of information in those thoughts that she had never been told. And yet, there were holes in what she had gleaned from her father's mind and she got the distinct feeling that most of the history that he gave his wife and daughter was made up to hide something more profound. Perhaps that was where he hid the sadness that she always sensed within him.

Never before had she been able to get so deeply into her father's mind and while she was sure that part of this was because he had lowered his shields to allow her more access, she knew that he had not intended for her to see through the lie of his past. This both terrified and thrilled her. Did this not mean that she was becoming a Blade Master? For as long as she could remember she dreamed of this, knowing that she had to achieve this to make her father proud.

Forgotten stopped suddenly just as they reached the center of one of the bridges that crossed the Pit. All around Cassandra could see other people coming and going using various bridges and rope ladders to gain access to the different levels of the Pit. A few people stopped as they passed by them to offer greetings to the Blade Master before they moved on. Forgotten only nodded his head in acknowledgment, never taking his eyes off his daughter.

"Yes, you have the gifts of a Blade Master, which is why you are already in my advanced class." He smiled down at her, his eyes filled with warmth she rarely saw in her father. "You will be the youngest adept to ever enter the Academy, of this I have no doubt, but know this Little Dagger, if you had never shown any inclination to ever pick up a blade, I would have been just as proud of you."

His words shocked her. Never pick up a blade? How could he even think of such a thing? Even if she had not known that she would one day become a Blade Master she knew that she would have to learn how to fight. Every man, woman, and child who lived as a free human had to fight. It was the price for not being a slave. It was the only way they could live. How could her father have thought that she wouldn't do what was expected of her.

Through her connection to the Blade Master's mind she felt a flash of pain and regret before he threw up his mental shields, blocking her out. For just a moment longer he looked down at her, his eyes searching her face. Cassandra felt her heart begin to race. Had he sensed that she now knew that he had been lying about parts of his past? That she had been on the verge of finally penetrating his best defenses and reading the truth? But then he turned away and she knew that she had not been discovered after all. Without another word he began walking away and Cassandra shook her head and followed behind.

Forgotten Child found himself slowing down as the doors to the War Hall came into sight. He was not ready to face what lay beyond those doors. How many demons had he faced over the many years? Surly there were thousands dead by his blade by now. In battle he never once hesitated. And yet, in this moment he fell back.

"Get a hold of yourself." He whispered to himself. If Rachael had fallen, he knew that she had not done so without drawing her blade. This was the best that any Master could hope for, dying with the blood of their enemies on their sword. This thought brought fresh pain to him, for if she was dead then she was beyond caring about the life they had had to live. No. This time he thought of his daughter. Cassandra deserved better than this. Was this to be her life's destiny, to grow up in a world of constant blood and pain? She deserved to know peace and happiness, a life without never ending fear and war. However much he longed to give her this world of peace, short of taking over Hell, he could see no way of achieving any of it.

Even moving slowly he soon found himself in front of the double doors. There was no avoiding the truth that the room beyond would give him. Taking a deep breath he pushed through the doors and into the War Hall. The War Hall was one of the largest rooms in the Pit with walls decorated with large maps of each of the six continents of Hell. A large marble table sat in the center of the room.

This was the table where a map would be placed where the leading warriors could view it by gathering around. How many times had Father Michael stood at the head of that table and outlined some plan of attack? Forgotten could not possibly count. He only knew that he stood here with other warriors in awe of the Priest's ingenuity and tactical prowess.

Today there were no maps littering the table. No gathering of able warriors to prepare for some daring raid. Today there were only two people standing in the wavering light of the fire pots. The first was Father Michael wearing his black Priest's outfit with white collar and familiar axe hanging from his belt. The priest stood almost six feet tall, with a crown of wispy white hair, and strong muscular body. The old Priest turned his warm watery blue eyes to the Blade Master and his daughter as they entered, but Forgotten barely noticed him. It was the other person in the room that commanded all of his attention.

The woman stood next to the priest wearing tight red studded hide armor and a long sword strapped to her back. Her face was perfectly shaped with green eyes that tilted slightly downward giving her the appearance of Asian ancestry. Her perfectly shaped mouth lifted in a smile as she ran a hand through her short fiery red hair. Her body, Forgotten knew, was lean and muscular with firm breasts and tight buttocks. He also knew from experience that her nails were as sharp as the sword on her back.

Rachael. She stood next a large map of the Dark City which she turned back to after a moment of acknowledgement to her husband. He could not read her mind since she was shielding herself against such intrusions, but there were a great many promises in that momentary glance and

Forgotten found that he could not wait until they were alone. His earlier concern made him feel like a fool, after all Rachael was a Blade Master. Of course this hardly meant that she was immortal. Blade Masters could and did die just like anything else in Hell. Hell may have stopped humans and demons from aging, but people died every day here.

They had lost at least a dozen Blade Masters in the years since the Academy was founded, but they had died bravely with blades in their hands. The sword was the preferred weapon of the Blade Master, though anything with a blade became a deadly weapon in the hands of a Master.

Forgotten had even heard a tale of a Blade Master that killed an entire tavern of demons with the equivalent of a butter knife. Of course there were stories and legends like this throughout all of Hell. Some of the stories were created by humans as a kind of propaganda machine to help build morale in their compatriots and fear in their enemies. Other tales, like the one about the tavern were completely true.

Rachael turned to face him again and he made sure that his mental shields were up. It would not do for her to read his mind and find out how worried he had been. She was a proud woman and would take his fear as an insult to her capabilities. Without a word Forgotten moved forward and all of a sudden she was in his arms, her lips against his. In that moment he was complete, it didn't matter that there was a war going on, didn't matter that they all could die any day, Rachael was here and he was complete. Slowly they parted and stood looking into one another's eyes. At that moment no one else in the whole world mattered.

"I am sorry to interrupt your reunion children." Father Michaels' soft sobering voice called them back to the room.

"But there are things that we must discuss." Feeling his face fill with rushing blood Forgotten turned toward the smiling Priest.

"Cassandra." Rachael called happily to her daughter. Behind them the girl made no indication that she had heard. Instead Cassandra stared at the map of Wrath which hung on the far wall.

"Little Dagger?" Forgotten touched her shoulder and was surprised to find that he could not read the little girls' mind. Her shields were more powerful than he had ever experienced. He had no doubt that no matter how hard he tried, she could keep him out with little or no effort. At his touch Cassandra jumped as if he startled her, and turned her wide eyes up to her father.

"You are trembling, what it is it?" He asked suddenly concerned. For a moment his daughter did not answer. Instead she looked from the map to her mother and then back to her father.

"It's...nothing." She shook her head as if to clear it. "Hello, mother." She spoke the words and even managed a smile, but Forgotten was struck with how formal she sounded. He thought about how children on Earth would burst out in laughter and joy at seeing their mothers return after only a couple of hours, let alone days. But here it was dangerous to get to close to anyone, even your parents. After all, just because they were here today did not mean that they would not be dead tomorrow. Death was the only constant companion to the children of Hell.

"Listen, I am sorry but there are matters most urgent that we must discuss with Forgotten." Father Michael's voice cut into his thoughts again. Slowly Forgotten Child turned and looked into the now very grim faces of his wife and friend.

"Very well." He said after a moment. "Cassandra, go back to the class and begin working on drill number fifteen." It was a more advanced drill than any of the others were currently working on, but she had already mastered one through fourteen. With a curt nod in his direction Cassandra walked silently out of the room. He did not watch her go, instead he was looking at Father Michael, who seemed to visibly relax as Cassandra left the Hall. It was almost as if his old friend was afraid to be in the same room as his daughter, but that was ridiculous. What could the leader of the free humans have to fear from the daughter of his best friend?

"There's trouble." His wife spoke as soon as the doors closed behind her daughter. She turned back to the map in front of her. "The rumors are true, the demons have begun pushing into the under city. We came across a small patrol not seven miles away from the Pit last night."

"That close?" Rachael nodded her head. "But what are they looking for? Surely not us." Forgotten's mind reeled at the implications. They may have to start evacuating immediately.

"Have there been any raids that I don't know about?" The second the accusatory words left his mouth Forgotten wanted to snatch them back, but it was too late.

Father Michael's eyes flashed in anger. "Of course not!" he snapped. Forgotten winced at the wounded sound of the Priest's voice. "I have always included you in the decisions I make." He may have continued his tirade had the Blade Master not threw up his hands in a sign of surrender.

"Forgive me old friend, I spoke without consideration."

Slowly Father nodded his acceptance of the apology and though he didn't say anything more he could still see that the Priest was still angry.

"If these patrols continue to move deeper, they could stumble upon the Pit any day."

Rachael steered the conversation back to the subject at hand. Are we prepared for this?"

"You are quite right my dear," Father Michael turned to look at her. "Why don't you go and begin getting the word out. We must be ready to move at a moments' notice." Forgotten turned to go with his wife, but the Priest was not done with him yet.

"Forgotten, could you please stay a moment longer?" He asked as if unsure his friend would comply with the request.

"Of course Father." Forgotten quickly kissed his wife and watched her walk out the door. He had the distinct feeling that Michael had wanted both his wife and daughter out of the room so that they could talk about something even more dire than possible discovery. The sense of dread he had felt building the last two days seemed almost overwhelming. Slowly he turned back to the table to find his old friend sagging forward, his hands flat on the table. It was as if the entire weight of the world had suddenly come crashing down on his shoulders. Even as he watched, a shudder ran through the old man's body.

Instantly Forgotten was at his friend's side. "What is it?" He asked worried that the old man might be suffering some sort of heart attack. "Tell me that you're not still troubled by what I said earlier."

Father Michael turned to look at the Blade Master and even though he was smiling sheepishly Forgotten could see tears in the old man's eyes. "No my son, that has already passed from my heart."

"Then what is it, what troubles you so?"

"Oh dear God, forgive me." The Priest whispered as if to himself.

"Please Michael, tell me." Forgotten had never seen the old Priest like this. It was almost terrifying.

"I know what the demons are looking for." The old man spoke, dropping his eyes back to the table.

"What?" Forgotten looked at the other man completely confused. "How could you possibly know?"

"I've had it for the better part of two days now." The Priest's voice was filled with misery.

"Had what?" Forgotten had had enough of all this beating around the bush. "Tell me plain, what are you talking about?"

"You can come in now."

Forgotten looked up as the map of Wrath suddenly moved and someone slipped into the room from the secret passage behind it. He had known of the doorway hidden behind that map, that led back to a secret library. What he had not known was that someone had been standing back there listening. He then remembered the way his daughter had stared at the map before Father Michael had ushered her out of the room. She had felt the presence of the person when he had not. Forgotten didn't know whether he should be delighted or terrified.

Then he saw who had been hiding behind the map and he decided to be terrified. He of course recognized the person. They had fought on several occasions over the years. It was too late to evacuate the Pit, death had already come.

CHAPTER 6

Taken from the personal journal of Tobin Masters, Observer to the Throne of Darkness.

It is an old Earth saying that history is written by those who are victorious. While this may be true, one must consider that it is impossible to wipe the slate of history clean and rewrite it. Inevitably something from what came before always survives. Whether it be an ancient rune covered stone buried in the earth, or a collection of writings from someone who experienced the events, these clues always surface. Once they do they could be more dangerous than any weapon of mass destruction. For in the history of any world (even Hell) knowledge, when wielded properly can lay waste to whole armies before they even take the battlefield. What happens when one discovers that their whole lives have been a lie, rewritten by their oppressors? Beware those who would manipulate history for their own gain. Truth is a sword wielded by the oppressed and it bites deep, unraveling the tapestry of lies that you have spent so much time creating. And as the sword cuts the threads away more and more of the truth is revealed. And truth is the ultimate weapon.

Tobin sat at his desk in his study, the book for the War of Ascension open in front of him. His mind seemed numb as he slowly came back to himself. He had been writing about the human Blade Master named Forgotten Child and even though the man's story had appeared in his mind he had not actually seen any of the events as they had begun to unfold. He was not sure why the Throne was holding him back, but he knew that he was not yet done with the humans. Even now he felt events moving forward and knew that his rest would not be long. Soon enough he would be compelled to write once again.

He set his blood stained quill down and flexed his black gloved hands, trying to work the stiffness from his fingers. Tobin found that his mind kept wandering back to the tragic hero named Forgotten Child. He could feel for this man, trapped in a world he didn't want to be in. Lost in a war that he could not possibly hope to win and even now, faced with his own death Tobin knew that he would not go down without a fight. If he was going to die, then he was going to die with his blade in his hand.

It was funny how Tobin found himself thinking about those he wrote about. For a moment he wondered what would become of Forgotten and the Stone of Power that Shard had brought to him. He wanted Forgotten to survive, perhaps even needed him to. Forgotten and his people represented hope. A hope that maybe one day he himself could also be free from the leash the Throne of Darkness had placed upon him. What if he wrote the ending he wanted into the book of history? Would it change the outcome in reality? Did he, as Observer have that much power?

The thought was tantalizing. Trying to keep his hand

from trembling he dipped the quill back into the ink well and took a deep breath as he allowed himself to become one with the Throne once more. His hand once again began to move across the page and he read the events as they began to unfold. The Priest, Father Michael standing beside the Blade Master, both staring at the assassin as she presented herself to them. Tobin could imagine the look of betrayal that had to be on Forgotten's face. He could almost feel the man's confusion and knew that his hesitation would mean his death.

Shard moved deeper into the room, death dressed in black leather breeches and shirt, her soft boots making no sound on the stone floor. In front of her Forgotten woke up and drew his sword faster than any eye could see and Tobin knew that he had counted the human out before his time. The Blade Master was ready to face the assassin. The Observer let all sense of himself go and immersed himself in the story in front of him. The battle for the Blade Master's life had begun.

Forgotten leapt forward, his sword slashing out in front of him. He ignored Father Michael's cry of surprise. The Priest had been tricked or worse had betrayed them. Did the old man not realize what he had done by allowing this monster to walk the halls of the Pit? For just a moment his mind flashed back to the last time he had faced the assassin in the streets of a small free human village. The huts now burned and all those who had lived there lay dead. They had battled with the bloody bodies of mothers and their children lying in the dirt around them. He would not allow her to do the same thing here. His blade passed through empty air slicing the map of Wrath in half. Shard was behind him, ducking the blade and rolling past him.

"Forgotten wait!" Father Michael yelled as the Blade Master spun around leading with his sword again, trying to cut Shard in half. Once again the assassin dodged, back flipping up onto the War Table. Had Forgotten been a normal fighter he would have found himself spinning away from his quarry by his own momentum. But he was not a normal fighter and he stopped exactly where he needed to, directly facing the enemy.

"Hello Forgotten," Shard smiled down at the Blade Master. "Long time no see." The man refused to be baited and simply moved into to attack again. Shard spun around snapping her foot out. The kick connected with the side of Forgotten's head causing bright stars of pain to bloom in front of his eyes. Not waiting for the Blade Master to recover the assassin jumped up into the air coming down in between the man's outstretched arms. Shocked by this move Forgotten found him face to face with the woman his arms around her in a strange embrace, clasping his now useless sword in both hands.

"Hi." Shard's hot breath caressed his check just before she brought both of her elbows down in the inside the bends of his arms. Forgotten gasped as pain shot through the nerves in his hands causing him to reflexively drop his sword.

Following through with her sudden advantage the assassin pushed against the man's chest with the palm of her hand sliding back, kicking the sword across the room as she moved away from him.

"Stop it!" Father Michael bellowed, but Forgotten wasn't sure if he was talking to Shard or him. The Blade Master backed away rubbing his tingling hands together. If she thought he was defenseless without his sword she was going to be in for a big surprise. Slowly he bent his knees slightly slipping into a fighting stance. A small smile crossed Shard's face and her eyes lit with a light that under different circumstances might have been considered seductive. As it was, the look reminded Forgotten of a starving lion that had finally found prey.

Suddenly Shard exploded forward striking with a flurry of hands and feet. Forgotten had been expecting the attack and moved at the same time blocking each blow as they came, waiting for an opportunity to strike back. This moment came when the assassin tried to use of her fists to hit him in the chest. The Blade Master used his left arm to force the blow downward, pushing her off balance while he brought his right fist around in what was called a right hook. He smiled happily at the sound of crunching teeth when his fist connected with Shard's jaw, causing her to stagger.

He moved in, not wanting to lose the advantage, landing blows against her head and chest. Shard stumbled back under the relentless attack until the back of her legs stuck the table toppling her onto its' smooth surface. Sensing that this was the moment to end it all Forgotten whipped out a bone dagger from a hidden sheath at the small of his back. He aimed the blade at Shard's throat, determined to avenge all those that this human monster had killed.

The dagger stopped inches away from the woman, burying itself into the wooden haft of the axe that moved to block the weapon. Confused Forgotten looked up to see that it was Father Michael who had saved the assassin's life. Their eyes locked and Forgotten felt his heart break. He was going to have to kill the Priest, his oldest living friend. For just a moment his resolve faltered, but then the image of his daughter rose up in his mind. In his mind he saw Cassandra laying, her body broken and bleeding at the bottom of the Pit. He would not allow this to happen. Even if this once great man had to die.

Something must have crossed his face because the old Priest's face visibly paled and he took a step back. "Forgotten," Michael spoke his voice trembling as tears spilled down his face. "You don't understand."

"Your right." Forgotten backed away from Shard who stayed unmoving on the table. His voice was cold. He wanted to keep the other man occupied with talking so that he wouldn't notice his left hand sliding yet another bone dagger free from his back. With a flick of the wrist he would send the dagger flying with deadly accuracy into the Priest's heart.

"Forgotten, please." Michael tried again. Oh how the sound of that soft cultured voice tore at his soul, knowing that this was the last time he would ever hear it. "It's not what you think, she came…."

Forgotten threw his dagger, not giving the old man a chance to finish his sentence. The weapon flew like a homing missile targeting the man's heart. Father Michael flinched knowing that he had made a terrible mistake and that he would be paying for that mistake with his life. Time slowed and he wondered if he would finally find himself in the Kingdom of Heaven, or would he simply remain bound to this world. A ghost doomed to haunt Hell for all eternity. But this question would have to wait for another day, as the dagger hit an invisible barrier inches away from the Priest. For just a moment both Priest and Blade Master stared dumfounded as the dagger fell to the ground with a metallic clang. Neither of them could understand what had just happened.

"You should really watch where you toss your toys Blade Master." A deep voice that was tinged with a British accent spoke into the sudden silence. "Someone might get hurt." Forgotten's shoulder slumped in defeat as he recognized the voice.

"Uh.... is it okay if I get up now?" Shard asked sitting up on the table. Her lips were bleeding, and Forgotten could see that her face was covered in several bruises and her right eye was already turning black. He wanted to feel at least a little pride in all of this, but he could not. Actually for at least a couple of minutes he had forgotten that she was there. The assassin could have killed him at any time.

Not wanting to dwell too much on those thoughts he turned to face the newcomers in the room. They stood just outside the now exposed secret doorway, a man and a woman. The man stood tall at six foot five with long flowing black hair and Asian features, wearing a black spider silk Kimono. The woman at his side wore long crimson robes that accented her coal black hair and eyes. Her face was deceptively small and she was smirking at the Blade Master. Her delicate hand was still raised in the position she had used to cast the spell that had saved Father Michael's life. The man's name was Raven and his wife was Kara. Both of them were Throne Bound magic users.

Forgotten knew that he could never hope to defeat all

four of them, especially with the addition of magic, but he would not kneel down in defeat. "Can I at least die with my sword in my hand?" He asked, determined to honor the Blade Master Creed which he had founded. Shard hopped off the table and began scanning around the room as if she had misplaced something. After a moment she knelt down and began fishing under the table. Forgotten considered striking out at her again, but then rejected the idea. The Throne Bound traitors would have surely prepared more protection spells by now. Such was the nature of the magic given by their damned master, the Throne of Darkness.

The Blade Master had always hated Throne Bound, knowing in his heart that they served the Throne before anyone else. He had especially disliked these two who had come to them six years ago from Sets' dark Kingdom. They had come seeking asylum from the humans in the Pit. Forgotten had argued vehemently against allowing this. There was no way that they could be trusted, especially since the man was the half -blood son of Set himself, a vampire. But Father Michael had allowed them to stay and now they all worked together to betray the Pit. He wished that he had fought harder to keep them out. Of course it really didn't matter any more. Now he was going to die and his wife and daughter would soon be following him.

Shard came out from under the table holding Forgotten's sword. For moment she looked at the blade as if she were admiring it before turning and walking towards him.

"What are you doing?" Father Michael demanded, but Forgotten knew what was about to happen. Shard was going to kill him with his own blade. Showing none of the sorrow he felt he turned to face her as she approached. She stopped in front of him and looked directly into his eyes. Forgotten suddenly realized that hers' were a brilliant hazel. Standing there looking at her he thought he saw something familiar there, as if they had stared into each other's eyes before. He tried to look beyond those beautiful eyes and read the mind beyond, but could not.

"This blade is well crafted," Shard whispered her voice soft and husky. "It has seen much bloodshed in the years you have wielded it." Unexpectedly she flipped the sword up into the air. Reflexively Forgotten's hand shot out catching the hilt of the blade in mid-air. Confused he looked from the sword back to the woman in front of him. For a moment he thought he saw something new move through her eyes, something softer and, well….. human. Then it was gone as she turned back, giving him the perfect opportunity to strike her down. But in that moment he could not bring himself to act.

"Okay," Forgotten looked around the room. "What's going on here?" The two Throne Bound stood quietly by the secret doorway, while Father Michael slumped down into a chair, his whole body trembling violently.

"If you are done trying to kill everybody, I'll explain." Father Michael spoke in a halting voice.

"Explain quickly old man."

"First, you will put away your sword." Forgotten hesitated for a moment, his eyes flicking over to Shard who now leaned against one of the maps looking bored. Finally he slid his sword into his sheath.

"Good, now we must go back to the library." Father stood up on legs that felt like they were made of jelly. "There are things that you must see."

In a single line the five people made their way down the short dark corridor that led to the hidden library. Forgotten had balked at allowing any of them to be at his back so with a shake of his head Father Michael led the group, while the Blade Master brought up the rear. Beyond the hallway they came into a medium sized room about twenty by twenty feet long and wide. Four small fire pots threw shadows around the shelves of books that were hidden in this room. The only furniture in the room was a large desk made from bone in the center of the room, and the chair sitting behind it. The books had been collected over the years and kept here out of the way where those who didn't need to know couldn't accidently read them. They were mostly spell books and other foul things that they had taken from raids on Noble Houses. Sitting on the desk were three volumes that Forgotten remembered well.

Three years ago there had been a raid on a Demon Lord's estate on Wrath specifically to get these books. The battle had lasted three days and about two hundred humans had died but Forgotten had never been told by Father Michael why these books had been worth so many deaths. All he knew is that they had been smuggled across two continents before being brought to the Dark City. After that they were brought to this room and for all anyone knew, simply left to gather dust.

"Why are we here?" Forgotten asked. He thought that this room was a very good place to hide a body, but he kept that observation to himself.

"I know that I have a lot of explaining to do," Father Michael's voice sounded weary, as if he hadn't slept in a long time. "I know that I should have come to you days ago, but

I just didn't know what to do." The old Priest looked at the Blade Master through blood shot eyes. He almost felt sorry for the man, but could not bring himself to let down his guard. After all the man had brought a killer into the very heart of their home.

"You're not explaining anything." Forgotten snapped. Michael sighed and turned toward the desk.

"Before I explain everything, there is something that you have to see." He pointed to a small box that had appeared as if by magic on the surface of the desk. "Go ahead, open it."

Preparing himself for a trick, Forgotten walked up to the desk and lifted the top of the box. The gem inside sat in what looked like black velvet. It flared to life as soon as the firelight hit it, glowing a soft sickly green. He watched in fascination as the facets of the gem shifted colors, fading and brightening at random. Not really knowing what he was doing Forgotten's hand reached for the gem, he only knew that he had to touch the gem.

"No!" Father Michael reached for his friend, but it was too late. Forgotten Child jerked his head back as if he had been physically struck. His body went rigid and his eyes opened wide. He was no longer seeing the library or its' occupants. Instead he saw himself leading a great army of demonic and human soldiers, the gem hanging from a necklace made of bones around his neck. He led this army in a swath of destruction across Demon Kingdoms leaving nothing but burning ruin in his wake.

Suddenly, the scene changed and he found himself sitting in a great chamber upon the Throne of Darkness. Before him two Demon Lords knelt on trembling knees awaiting judgment from their God. Indeed, for that is what he was now; a Dark God to be worshiped and feared by all. At one time he may have been just a mortal man named Forgotten Child, but no longer. He was now Satan, tamer of the Throne of Darkness, ruler over all of Hell.

The vision faded and Forgotten Child gasped as he jerked his hand away from the vile thing in the box. His mind reeled and the room began to spin. He slowly became aware that Father Michael was at his side, holding him up.

"….can you hear me?" Michael was speaking, but he only heard half what was being said.

"What the fuck is that thing?" He gasped, but deep inside he already knew. But he listened as his old friend explained how the Stone had come to him and why then he protected Shard from him. But Forgotten was not ready to let things go.

"What were you thinking?" He asked, pushing the old man away from him. "They will not stop until they find that thing and when they do, they will kill every person in the Pit."

"Do not judge me until you here the rest." Anger was finally seeping into Michael's voice. He had had enough of Forgotten's accusatory tone.

Forgotten laughed harshly, a sound like breaking glass. "Oh, there's more?" Without answering him Father Michael turned toward Raven who had retreated to the shadows with his wife. It was a good place for them as far as the Blade Master was concerned. Now he glided forward, moving with an unnatural grace.

"Greetings Blade Master." Raven spoke, his English accent making him sound worldly and sophisticated. Raven was the vampiric son of Set, the product of a human woman and a True Vampire. Kara, the fully human woman that claimed Raven as her husband was a beautiful woman. She had been a slave in Set's Kingdom, kept for breeding and food. Raven broke her out of her personal Hell and the two had fled together to the Pit. At least that is the story that the two had given the humans. Forgotten didn't believe it for one second. Raven was a vampire, the son of a Demon Lord. To believe that he could love and show compassion implied that he had humanity.

"The tale I will be telling you comes from these volumes here." Raven pointed to the books on the desk. "We have spent a great deal of time translating the passages within them." He turned and smiled lovingly at his wife who remained in the shadows. Forgotten shuddered. The man had fangs.

"The tale is a long one and I would ask that you reserve any questions you may have until I have finished." Raven spoke as if he were preparing to lecture at a college. The vampire waited politely to see if Forgotten would object. After a few moments of silence he smiled (fangs) again.

"I will be telling you the history of a world that once was called Elysium."

The History of Elysium.
(Abridged)

No one knows for sure how or when the world of Elysium came into being. Perhaps it had always existed, but even the elders were unsure. What was known was that there had been seven continents separated by pure blue oceans.

Throughout the world there was peace and prosperity for all. There were two types of people living in the world. First there were the humans. Beautiful people with fair skin and golden hair. Then there were their Great Protectors the Angelus. These beings looked human, except for their white feathery wings which they used to glide through the air. Both races served the Master of this world, a kind and benevolent being known as Yahweh.

The people of Elysium knew powerful magic and used their art to explore the various dimensions around them. And through this exploration they discovered a world connected to their own; this world was called Earth. To their surprise the explorers found humans like themselves, though they were troubled by the lack of Angelus on this sister world. Magical gates were created, linking the two worlds and the people of Elysium began teaching their Earth cousins magic.

Yahweh looked upon all of this, but said nothing, allowing his people to visit Earth as they saw fit. At this time Yahweh had two sons. The oldest was an Angelus with long black hair and eyes of darkest night. His name was Lucifer. His second son was a human with long flowing brown hair and eyes the color of honey and was called Jesus.

Together the brothers couldn't be more different. Lucifer with his fiery temper and passion. Always trying to out- do his younger sibling to prove to their father that he was more worthy of his love. For his part, Jesus was content to allow his brother the spot light. He only wanted to live a life of simplicity and quiet. Their pursuits in magic were also different. Jesus studied the arts of healing and magic for the joy that the knowledge brought to him and others. He took this knowledge and used it to help those around him.

Lucifer however worked aggressively to conquer magic. Desiring to make its power his slave. He experimented with spells, twisting them from their original purposes, turning them dangerous and deadly. It was during this time that Lucifer began making his own search of the many dimensions beyond Elysium and Earth. When he returned after visiting some unknown world he was changed. He was calmer and showed gentleness in all of his actions. He claimed to have discovered a great teacher out in the multi-layered universe and that his teacher had shown him a great many mysteries. What nobody had known was that Lucifer himself had been tainted by darkness unlike anything Elysium had even known. He began teaching those humans and Angelus that would learn from him, spreading his corruption. His influence even stretched between worlds, infecting the humans of Earth.

The war erupted without warning taking from Elysium the peace it had always known. The battle for the world was pitched, but surprise had been on Lucifer's side. By this time dark magic had twisted his form, covering his body in black scales and giving him large red and black bat like wings. Great horns split through his forehead and his once beautiful eyes now glowed crimson red. It was not only their leader that had changed. All of his followers found themselves changing into horrific forms. They called themselves Demons.

For Yahweh, the war was going badly. He had little chance of winning so he did what he thought best. Using the most powerful of magic, he ripped the seventh continent, the only one not tainted by Lucifer's foul power, from Elysium and hid it another dimension. He would call this world Heaven.

Jesus seeing that Lucifer's influence would destroy the world of Earth as well, declined to go with his father. Instead he travelled to Earth once again. There he taught as many who would listen his message of hope and peace. He healed the people and even used his powers to raise the dead. He told of a time when his father's Kingdom would come to Earth, bringing about a great change in their world. He fought his brother's encroachment, removing from people the taint of Lucifer's magic.

But even with all of his might, Jesus was only one person and he could not stem the tide of his brother's relentless work. So by performing a powerful ritual Jesus sacrificed his life to close the permanent gates between Earth and Elysium. Elysium became Lucifer's dark and twisted prison, a tortured place called Hell.

Trapped, Lucifer changed his name to Satan and had a great city built over the entirety of one continent. He built a palace and a throne upon which he could sit and rule. However, Lucifer had taught his followers the nature of betrayal and after a time another Demon Lord rose up against his Master and killed him. But in the end it was Lucifer who got the last laugh. In the moment of his death he cast a spell that bound his soul to the throne from which he ruled. Thus creating the living Artifact and tying himself to any who would claim the title of Satan.

Forgotten stared at raven in stunned silence. His mind reeled with all that he had been told over the last two hours. His first inclination was to reject the information. How could any of it be true? He wanted to disbelieve, but deep in his heart he felt the truth of it. Humans and angels had once ruled the world of Hell.

"But what does any of this have to do with the Stone?" He asked in a subdued voice.

"Don't you see?" Father Michael was desperate to make Forgotten understand. "We have an opportunity here." Forgotten started to shake his head, and then it hit him like a brick. They had a Stone of Power. It was possible, for the first time in the history of Hell to put a human being on the Throne of Darkness. If a human was in control of the Throne then maybe he or she could open the gates leading back to Earth. They could all go home. But at what price?

Forgotten turned to look at his friend, his eyes wide with fear. "You're mad."

CHAPTER 7

Taken from the personal journal of Tobin Masters, Observer to the Throne of Darkness.

Deceit is not only practiced by demons. Humans are by their very nature liars as well. History is filled with those who rose to power on lies and subterfuge. So why would those humans trapped in Hell be any different. Some will lie to move up in status amongst their fellow slaves, while others would lie to simply impress those around them. Whether for status or protection, a lie is the first strand of a web that must eventually be spun. You see what starts out as one lie must be followed by more, until one finds themselves trapped in a net of his or her own creation. It took me coming to Hell to understand this, and learn one more valuable lesson on the nature of lies. No matter what we lie about, or who else we may lie to, it is the lies that we tell ourselves that haunt us the most.

Forgotten Child sat next to a small pool of red water and looked off into the dark ruins of the under city that used to be the capital of Hell. He was no longer inside the Pit, but instead he was about one hundred yards away from the human stronghold. This was his place, where he came to decompress and let his mind wander. A secret place where he could let down his guard without fearing that his wife or daughter might see things within his mind that he kept buried.

After his "meeting" with Father Michael he had been so confused and full of fear. There was, even now, sitting in the place he had called home for so long two of the most dangerous things in the entire world. The first and probably most dangerous was the Stone of Power. This would almost surely spell doom for the Pit. Then there was the assassin who had brought them the Stone. Forgotten viewed her as a rabid dog bidding its time before turning on those around it. It was only a matter of time.

But in the end the biggest threat could very well come from the humans themselves. After Father Michael had revealed his "plan" Forgotten had looked at him and told him that he was mad, but his mind was already calculating the odds. Could they truly succeed? Could they really force the Throne to open the gates backwards to Earth? If so then would any sacrifice be too much? Confused he left the library and took his wife to their private rooms and confided all to her. He told her everything, the histories, Shard and the Stone. They speculated on the insanity of the Priest's plan to put one of their own on the Throne. They had talked well into the night finally drifting off to sleep in each other's arms.

Sometime later Forgotten woke up alone to find that Rachael had slipped out. This was not particularly upsetting; she was often on nighttime guard duty. After all, considering all that he had told her he had not expected her sleep very well. He slid into the next room to watch

Cassandra sleeping for a few moments. She rolled over and whimpered in her sleep and Forgotten felt his heart break at the sound.

"No," Cassandra mumbled. "Don't go up there." Forgotten had no idea what nightmares plagued his daughter but he would do anything to give her peaceful dream. Even go with father Michael's plan. Unable to watch his daughter sleep any longer he had slipped out of their cave like home and came to this place.

Now he looked at his reflection in the water next to him. After telling Rachael about his meeting, he had dreaded sleep. He knew that he would dread the return of the horrifying vision he had upon touching the stone. Instead, after drifting off, he dreamed of his past. Not the story that he told everyone else when they asked about his life, the story that he made up so that his wife and daughter would not be ashamed of him. No, he dreamed of his real life, and had he been given the chance he would have preferred the vision. He felt the weight of his guilt and shame pull him down as he looked deep into his past.

The man who was to become Forgotten Child was born on October thirty-first, nineteen seventy six in the city of Los Angeles. Even though both of his parents were living in the same house, he grew up without them. It was the streets that taught him all that he needed to know about life. At the age of twelve he started getting into drinking and drugs. It started with a joint here and there, and maybe a beer or two. But by the age of fourteen he was not just cooking and selling Meth, he was also using. He spent at least two years in Juvie for drug possession and assault. He murdered his first man at the ripe age of twenty. His life was spiraling out control and he didn't seem to care. He had a woman, money, drugs, and booze, what else did he need?

Just after his twenty third birthday he was busted trying to sell Meth to an undercover cop. He was given two years in the California State Prison. Once on the inside, he had been given "The Speech". This was the time to change his life, to get the skills he would need to return to the world as a productive member of Society. The same line of bullshit they gave in Juvie. The only things that would make his life better was a hit of meth, and woman. Both of which would be waiting for him the minute he stepped out the gate. He knew better than to listen to all the shit they tried to feed him.

The true meaning of life was getting as much as you could. The only person that truly mattered was you. How many times during his younger years had he been taught that lesson? How many times had he been used, and then tossed aside? After all, everyone wanted something from him. Drugs, money, sex, a place to stay, nobody cared about him, but him. He met people in prison, and came to see that nothing had really changed. He had money so he gathered followers who came to him with hands held out wanting a cup of coffee or maybe a cigarette. He in turn got a soft job and was generally left alone by the Guards. Then, after four months, he met the man that would change his life forever.

He had been out on the yard shooting basketball when one of the users that hung around him stopped and pointed. He turned to see a heavy set man with dark brown hair pushing a cart across the yard. The man was wearing an obviously expensive suit though Forgotten didn't recognize him as one of the regular staff at the prison.

"Who's that?" he asked.

"Some rich fag from the streets." One of the leeches answered him. "He comes in every couple of months to pass books out to the lames." The others on the court laughed as they watched a group of nerdy looking inmates came up to the man. He greeted each one with a handshake and a smile before turning to his cart, selecting a book and passing it out to each individual who came to him.

Back in the Great Palace Tobin tried desperately to stop writing. His mind was beginning to be pulled back into Forgotten Child's past, but he struggled against it. He knew what he was going to see. He railed against it, fought with every fiber of his being, and yet he found himself standing in Forgotten's memory, looking across that prison yard at himself as he passed out books to the inmates. His breathing came in short gasps as he turned to the basketball court. This was why the Throne stopped him from seeing Forgotten Child before. Tobin knew him. His real name was Nicholas Miller. He knew what was coming and he didn't want to relive this sad part of his life. But the Throne cared little for what Tobin wanted and he was forced to continue to watch and write.

"Any of you need a book to read?" The man (Tobin) asked at the basketball court.

"Get lost you fucking fag!" Somebody behind Nick shouted and the court exploded into laughter. The man never stopped smiling, but Nick saw a look of sadness cross his face as he turned to leave.

"I'll take a book." Nick was shocked to hear himself suddenly say. Instantly the court fell silent around him. For a moment the man studied Nick with intense hazel eyes, as if he was waiting for him to spring some nasty comment on him. After a moment he must have decided that Nick was serious and he turned to his cart.

"I think I have just the book for you." The man spoke as he rummaged through the drawers on his cart. "Here you go." He turned and put a large paperback book into his hand. "Please take good care of the book, I usually pick them back up so that others can read them."

"No problem." Nick turned back to the people on the court, his eyes challenging anyone to say something. No one did. Later that night, after they had been locked down in their cells Nick finally looked at the book that the strange man had given to him. It was by a famous author and was about a group of witches living in the city of New Orleans. It turned out to be the best book that Nick had ever read. He spent every moment of his free time reading and when he got to the end he found that the man had written his name on the back cover, Tobin L. Masters.

It took Tobin three months to get back to the Prison, but when he did Nick was one of the first people to greet the other man. He was excited to see him and wanted to know if Tobin had the other two books that completed the series. Not only did he have the books. But he was so pleased by the man's excitement, that he let Nick keep the first book. After that day Tobin would visit Nick on a more regular basis. They were two different people from completely different worlds, one from the hard streets and the other from the penthouses above those streets, but none of that mattered. When they sat together, whether on the yard, or in the visiting room, it was if they had known each other all their lives.

Though Tobin could not admit it to himself back then, he had fallen in love with Nick during those times they spent behind the prison walls, but there was no way they could be together. Not only was Nick not gay, but there was Richard to consider. Now the fantasies of what could have been flooded his mind like a wave being pushed by Richard's betrayal. How many nights had he lain in his L.A. hotel room feeling guilty after spending the day talking to Nick? How much of his fate would have been changed had he given into his feelings back then and pursued Nick? The pain of what could have been mingled with the ache of betrayal in his heart.

Ultimately Tobin knew that none of this mattered, nothing would have ever happened between Nick and him. It wasn't that they couldn't be together; it was more due to the fact that Nicholas couldn't bring himself to love anyone. It was a dream that could never come true, but this did not stop Tobin from being there for the man through his entire incarceration. He had even been there the day he was finally released. He had still been dreaming then. It was a dream that almost cost him his life.

Tobin was an enigma to Nick. He came to prison of his own free will, simply to pass out books to the inmates. When Nick had asked him what he got out of it, Tobin had shrugged and told him that he didn't want anything. The same was true of their friendship. Tobin wanted nothing from him, except his happiness. Nick found that he could talk to Tobin about anything and not be judged. He knew that there was something between them that could have gone much farther than just friendship, but there was no way that Nick could reconcile these confused feelings.

But even this did not stop Tobin from being there for him. As a matter of fact, it was Tobin who sat in his Limo, waiting for him the day he was released. Nick had been sure that his so called friends would have been there had he told them he was getting out, but he was equally sure they would have had their hands held out to him to collect as much from him as they could. Instead of heading back to the old neighborhood, Tobin took him into the city of Los Angeles, and so it came to be, not long after being released from prison Nicholas Miller found himself standing in a Penthouse suite high in the sky.

It was a huge suite, with a large open front room with a fire place (in Los Angeles?) and a balcony. The room was furnished with black leather couch, four matching chairs, and a round crystal coffee table. Off to the left of this front room was a huge kitchen that gleamed with stainless steel appliances. Three doors led of from the main room. The first lead into the Master Bedroom, while the other two were for guest rooms. There was even a private elevator.

"Man, what I wouldn't give to live like this." Nick exclaimed after Tobin had given him the grand tour. He had meant it as a joke, but Tobin turned to him and smiled happily.

"You can."

"What do you mean?" Nick's defenses went on high alert.

"This isn't my place," Tobin turned to look directly at Nick. "It's all yours, if you want it." So that was the way it was going to be. Nick knew that all the talk about not really wanting anything from him was a set up. This was where Tobin tried to draw him in. Using this fancy apartment as bait he would then try to talk him into his bed. Something must have shown on his face because Tobin's smile vanished.

"You're upset."

"You bet I am." Nick snapped and Tobin looked around the room as if looking for whatever had changed the mood in the Penthouse so quickly. Nick wished that he had a mirror to hold up.

"I thought that you said that you liked the place." Tobin's voice sounded like a hurt child.

"I did." Nick looked around the room in contempt. "What do you expect me to do for your generosity?" The last word was dripping with venom. Tobin's face went blank and then Nick could see hurt behind his eyes.

"If you thought I would try and blackmail you into sleeping with me, then you don't really know me at all, do you?" Nick could hear the pain in the other man's voice and suddenly realized that Tobin's offer of the Penthouse, like everything else in their strange, confusing friendship had been sincere, with no strings attached.

"Tobin…." Nick tried to apologize, but the other man was having none of it.

"Your key is sitting on the kitchen counter, along with a letter from a friend of mine willing to give you a good job." Tobin cut him off. "You are right about one thing, this is not a free ride. I expect you to put the past behind you, no more drugs and go to work. That's the only two things that I ask of you." With that Tobin turned and walked out of the Penthouse, leaving Nick to feel guilty for not trusting his friend.

Later that night he found a bottle of champagne in the fully stocked refrigerator. Around the bottles' neck was a card with the words "Welcome Home" written in Tobin's fine cursive. Nick felt renewed sorrow for jumping to conclusions and hurting Tobin. He wanted to take it back, but he had no idea where in L.A. Tobin was staying. If he even was still in L.A. Leaving the champagne unopened he went to lie down in his new fancy bedroom.

The next day he called the man whose phone number Tobin had left, and began working that afternoon. The job was (of course) at an antique book dealer that Tobin did regular business with. At first Nick wasn't sure that he was going to work out. He knew nothing about antique books. But, soon enough he found that he really enjoyed the work. Every day was something new, from helping the owner Mark Baxter to translate texts that were hundreds of years old, to researching the origins of a recently purchased book. Mark was a good man who seemed to genuinely like Nick and he was a patient teacher who enjoyed sharing his knowledge.

Tobin called two weeks after Nick's release and it was if the ugly scene that had taken place the last time they had been together had never happened. He was glad to hear that things were going so well and that Nick was enjoying his new job. They talked about the possibility that after a few years under Mark's tutelage, Tobin would help him open his own shop. Nick brought up the still unopened bottle of champagne and they agreed that they would open it on Nick's birthday and drink it together.

October thirty first came quickly and Nick found that he was looking forward to Tobin's arrival. The night before they had stayed on the phone until two in the morning about the meeting that Tobin had to attend before coming to Nick's apartment, and what they would do to celebrate that night.

"You okay?" Mark Baxter asked him for the third time that day. "You don't seem to be all here." Nick couldn't explain it. It wasn't like he and Tobin didn't talk on the phone at least three times a week, but it wasn't the same as being with him. He tried to make Mark understand, but he couldn't find the right words. Finally Mark slapped him on the back and laughed.

"Get out of here kid, you are going to drive me batty." Nick didn't need to be told twice and he rushed out the door and headed home. When he made it to his street from the bus stop, he felt his pulse suddenly race. There, sitting next to the ally way that led to the penthouses' private entrance, was a sleek black limo. Leaning against the limo was the driver that Tobin used every time he was in L.A. His name was Carl.

"Hey Carl." Nick walked up and shook the diver's hand. "He upstairs already." Nick could hear the happy anticipation in his voice and could barley stop himself from running past the man. Carl lifted up his head and looked directly into Nick's eyes for a full minute before answering.

"No Sir, I am afraid not." Nick felt as if someone had punched him in the stomach. All the joy that had filled him only seconds before fled, leaving a pit of cold dread to replace it. Why was Carl here, but not Tobin? And then the thought came. He tried to keep it down, but it rose to the surface of his mind like some prehistoric monster. There had been some sort of accident; Tobin had been hurt, or worse. Nick felt his legs go weak and he was afraid that he was going to fall.

"Where is he?" He asked, his voice sounding small and strangled. Carl stood up straight concern filling his usually impassive face.

"Mr. Miller, are you okay?"

"Tobin. Has he been hurt?" Carl looked confused for a moment and then it dawned on him what Nick was asking him.

"No Sir," he actually reached out and grabbed Nick's shoulder, which was a good thing, because Nick was sure he would have fallen at that moment. "Mr. Masters wanted me to supervise the delivery of your gift, and to let you know that he regrets that he will be running late this evening." Nick felt the pressure in his chest ease and his legs became stable again. Suddenly Nick felt angry with himself. What in the hell was wrong with him? Swooning at the thought that Tobin had been in accident like some flighty housewife. He felt ashamed at himself and he took his anger out on Carl

"He could have called to tell me that." He snapped. If Carl noticed Nick's sudden change in attitude, he didn't show it.

"Yes Sir, he could have." Carl stepped back and picked up an envelope from the hood of the limo and handed it to Nick. "He could not however, give you this over the phone." His task complete the driver donned his chauffeurs' hat, slid into the driver's seat of the limo and drove away. Nick watched the car drive away and felt bad about his outburst. He would have to remember to apologize to the man the next time he saw him. He then turned his attention to the envelope in his hand. Inside he found a set of keys and a remote starter for a nineteen sixty nine Chevy Corvette. The car was midnight black with white highlights. It looked like it had just rolled off the manufacturing line. Opening the door with trembling hands he looked inside and found the seats were made of burgundy leather that he thought may be Italian. There was also a complete sound system and a built in GPS that slid out of a hidden compartment in the dash board. Sitting on the driver's seat was a pair of driving gloves and a card. Feeling his eyes fill up with tears Nick opened the card and read the words Tobin had written inside.

My Dearest Nick,

I regret that I will not be there when you "open" your gift, but I have been delayed at my meeting. I hope that the car meets with your approval and that you will enjoy using it in the future. I am sorry that you will miss riding the bus, but I thought it passed time that you had your own vehicle. I will see you soon. Happy Birthday.

Tobin

All in all Nick was sure that the car had run anywhere from fifty to sixty thousand dollars. He didn't know how to react. Nobody had ever given him anything like this in his life. Trembling he slid into the front seat, inserted the key and turned it. Instantly the engine turned over purring to life. Nick sat there for twenty minutes listening to the rumble of the engine feeling the car vibrate around him. Finally he went upstairs to get ready.

Tobin arrived an hour later carrying Chinese take out and smiling from ear to ear. Nick found that tonight whatever there was between them, that unspoken feeling that he could not express, was much stronger tonight, and for the first time he let down his defenses. Tonight anything was possible, but not because of the things (the life) that Tobin had given him. But because he felt somewhere deep in his soul that there was a whole new world just beyond his reach, and the only way to explore the infinite possibilities that this world offered was to open himself up to Tobin.

After dinner they sat together on the couch sipping Champaign and talking. At one point Nick felt himself drawn to Tobin, pulled toward him as if he couldn't help himself. He leaned closer to him, not knowing what he intended to do, but knowing that it felt right. As if he and Tobin were at some great turning point and the rest of their lives depended on what happened at that moment.

But they would never know what might have been, because at that exact moment, just before their lips touched Tobin's phone rang. Both men jumped as if they had been burned and Tobin pulled back grabbing the cell phone out of his pocket. Nick wanted to tell him not to leave, to continue where they had been going, but found that he couldn't make himself speak.

"Hello?" Tobin's eyes slid over Nick's face and then quickly away again. "Hey, Richard." With those two words the moment was shattered, lost. After Tobin finished speaking to his lover back in New York, he moved away from Nick to sit on one of the large chairs across the room. The conversation lagged and soon enough Tobin stood to leave. He wished Nick a happy Birthday and slowly walked out the door. It never even crossed Nick's mind to offer him the guest room. That would have been too awkward.

The next day Tobin flew out to San Francisco. They said their good-byes, neither of them mentioning the night before and what might have happened. After watching Tobin's private jet take off, Nick went in to work. He tried to forget what had almost happened but his mind kept returning to that moment just before the phone rang. He felt that he had somehow lost something very important at that moment. Finally, as they were locking up for the night, Nick asked Mark about Richard even though he and Tobin had spoken about the man in the past, Nick knew next to nothing about him. The old man sighed and took a seat. For a moment he searched Nick's face and then told him the story of how Richard and Tobin had met.

"Is it me, or do you not like him very much?" Nick asked after Mark fell silent.

"Now don't get me wrong, Tobin is one of my best friends, but there is something kind of….oily about Richard, you know what I mean?" The old man suddenly looked sly. "Why all the questions about Tobin's boyfriend?"

Nick shrugged his shoulders and tried (unsuccessfully) to look nonchalant. "Just wondering."

"Just wondering my ass," Mark smiled. "You looking to break them up?" Nick suddenly felt defensive and more than a little ashamed of what he had almost done.

"Why would I want that?" He snapped. Now it was Mark's turn to shrug.

"I don't know, maybe you like him more than you are willing to admit." This hit way to close to home for comfort and Nick found himself speaking before he had a chance to think about what he was saying.

"What the fuck are you saying?" He was suddenly up on his feet. "Do I look like a fag to you?" Mark's smile vanished in an instant and his voice dropped low with his own anger.

"Now you listen real good. That's my friend, and yours too if you get your head out of your ass and think about it." He spoke slow and deliberately. "He's given you a whole new life and deserves more respect than that."

"Whatever." Nick snapped and stalked out of the back door slamming it behind him. That night Nick would make a choice that would alter his (and Tobin's) life forever. Instead of driving home, he took his brand new shiny car to his old neighborhood. There he found two of his old dope buddies, Matt and Tony. He also picked up an old crack head girlfriend named Kelly. He took them back to his Penthouse and they were suitably impressed with the life he had been given. They went out and scored some Meth and spent the night partying like they did in the old days.

The next day he woke up in the afternoon with Kelly lying naked next to him. He called Mark and told him that he was sick, and that he would be in the next day. After that he rolled out of bed, picked up his pipe and took a hit of Meth to start the day right.

Slowly, over the next couple of months the new life that Tobin had given him began to unravel. His work, when he bothered to show up at all was beginning to slip, and Mark was quick to notice the change. Several times the two men found themselves in shouting matches that had almost come to physical blows. He had to hide his money before returning to the Penthouse each night, since Kelly and Tony had pretty much moved in. Once, shortly after they had started hanging out again several hundred dollars had come up missing out of his wallet while he was in the shower.

Neither Kelly nor Tony would admit to taking it. Another time he had caught Kelly sifting through his clothes looking for money, though she claimed to be searching for a lighter. She begged him for money so that she could buy some crack, but he refused. He was a Meth Head, but he wasn't going to be around Crack. Ordinarily he would have thrown them out on their asses, but now he had something to prove, and so they stayed and he kept using.

Tobin came to visit a few times during this period, but Nick managed to keep everything from him. Hell, it was during these times that Tony and Kelly were their most compliant. After all, if Tobin found out what was going on, he would kick them all out in to the streets. They wanted to live the High Life just as much as Nick did. They had even taken to calling Tobin the "Meal Ticket". How many times had he laid next to Kelly in the dark of his room laughing at the stupid fag who had honestly believed there could be something between them? To many to count. But there were times deep in the heart of the night, when it was pitch black outside, as if someone had poured ink over the whole world; Nick would wake up with a feeling of crushing guilt. He would lay there and think about all that Tobin had been to him and the memory was often too much to bear. He would get up long enough to get some Meth which he now used to hide from these painful thoughts.

Then one day, four months after his Birthday the inevitable happened. Everything finally came apart. Had Nick known how everything would end he would have done things differently. He would not have taken that drive back to his old neighborhood, would never had brought his past back into his present. But he could not see the future and even though he didn't know it that final morning, his fate was already set and nothing would ever be the same again.

It began with Mark firing him. He told Nick that he just couldn't continue to lie to Tobin for him and that his books were too valuable to have him around them anymore. He seemed genuinely sad about his decision, but this only served to make Nick angrier, he cussed the old man all the way out the door. Instead of driving home Nick cashed his severance check and simply drove around all morning his mind spinning. He didn't think things could get any worse, until he pulled into the gas station to fill up his tank and found Carl, the limo driver waiting at one of the pumps.

"Mr. Miller, what are you doing here?" The Chauffeur asked. Nick had been about to ask him the same thing, but his eyes were drawn to the tinted back windows of the limo. Was Tobin sitting back there right now on his phone talking to Mark Baxter? Of course Tobin might not be here at all. It wasn't as if he owned the company that he rented the limo from. Tobin usually called before coming to see Nick, which always gave him a chance to clean up everything before he got to L.A.

"I'm just heading home," Nick plastered a fake smile on his face. "You know, getting off work." Carl shrugged and slid a platinum credit card in a slot on the gas pump in front of him.

"Have you heard from Tobin lately?" Nick tried to sound casual as he began pumping his own gas. He figured that if Tobin had been in the back of the car he would have made his presence known by now.

"Yeah...uh......well, Mr. Masters flew in earlier this morning." Carl looked slightly uncomfortable. Nick felt his stomach drop. It was over. There would never be enough time to cover up everything before Tobin came from whatever meeting he had to the Penthouse. Everything was about to be taken away.

"Oh? When will his meeting be over?" Carl looked away from him and began to fidget.

"Look Mr. Miller, Mr. Masters said that he and you had been growing apart these last few months. I am not supposed to say anything, but Mr. Masters flew in specifically to see only you." Carl turned to look at him and a terrible thought struck Nick. The thought was so troubling that he thought he was going to double over and empty his stomach on Carl's gleaming black shoes.

"Where is he Carl?"

"I...we.... I dropped him off at your place about two hours ago." Nick felt like he had been kicked in the groin. Tobin was at the penthouse, with Tony and Kelly. Tobin, the man who only wanted to help would find himself faced with Nick's betrayal. There would be no excuse this time, no second chances.

"Are you okay Mr. Miller?" Carl reached out and

touched Nick's shoulder and he felt an overwhelming sense of déjà' vu. For just a moment it was his birthday, he and Carl were standing outside the Penthouse. This was a chance to change everything. He wouldn't let Tobin answer his phone. He wouldn't go back home. He would make everything right.

"Mr. Miller?" Carl's concerned voice shattered the illusion and Nick blinked at him as if waking up from a long sleep.

"What..? Oh yeah, I'm fine." Nick smiled and knew he suddenly looked like a maniac. "Hey Carl, any way you can cover this for me?" Carl shrugged and slid his card into the pump.

"Thanks." Nick jumped into his car and went home.

"Tobin!" Nick called out as soon as the elevator doors slid open into the Penthouse. Instantly he was overwhelmed by the thick cloying scent of Crack Cocaine in the living room. Choking he stumbled over to the sliding glass doors and opened them to allow fresh air into the room.

"Kelly, you stupid bitch, where are you?" He yelled, noticing that a small mirror that hung on the wall was shattered. Nick stomped over and threw open the door that led into the Master Bedroom. Inside he found Kelly naked in his bed with Tony. Both them were sitting wide eyed against the headboard passing a glass pipe between them.

"Hey dude, wanna hit?" Tony smiled up at him. Fury rose up inside of Nick and for a moment he forgot all about Tobin. He knew on some level he should be upset that they had been having sex in the bed he slept in, but only one thing was on his mind at the moment.

"Where did you get the money?" He asked. They had

to have stolen something from him. His eyes darted around the room making sure his sound system and entertainment center were still in their respected places. They were.

"I come up." Tony laughed stupidly as he sucked on the end of the pipe while holding hiss lit lighter to the other end.

"Bullshit!" Nick snapped. "The only way either of you can get anything around here is by leaching off of me." That is when he saw it. The wallet was made of soft leather, stained black and looked well worn. It sat on the corner of the bed like a black satin on the white silk sheets. Nick reached out with numb fingers and picked it up, turning the wallet over in his hands. Tony and Kelly ignored him now that he was no longer shouting at them.

Of course Nick recognized the wallet. He had seen it dozens of times over the last year and still his mind tried to reject what he already knew to be true. Slowly he opened it up. There, staring up at him was a picture of Tobin with a dark haired man sporting a goatee. This had to be Richard. The second picture in the small plastic cover was of Tobin and Nick, taken the night of Nick's birthday. There was no money in the large pocket, and all the credit card slips were empty.

"Where did you get this?" Nick's voice was barely above a whisper. Ice had formed deep in the pit of his stomach. "Where the fuck did you get it!" Nick screamed when the two people on the bed ignored him. His hand shot forward and grabbed Kelly by her greasy hair and pulled her off the bed. She screamed at the sudden attack and Tony rose as if he was going to get up.

"Hey, just chill dude...." Nick punched him square in the nose. The other man squealed in agony and blood exploded across his face.

"Where is he?" Nick demanded his voice called and hard.

"Who?" Kelly sobbed and tried to dis-entangle her hair from Nicks' iron grip. He shook her hard enough to make her neck pop.

"Don't fuck with me Kelly." There was a dangerous edge creeping into Nick's voice. Kelly must have heard it because she stopped struggling and fell deathly still.

"You mean Meal Ticket?"

Meal Ticket.

That was what he had relegated his best friend in the whole world to. He looked at the woman that he held before him, with her pale ashy skin, sagging breasts and dark rings under her green eyes. This is what he had given up everything for? He was disgusted by her, but not as much as he was with himself.

"His name is Tobin." His voice had fallen completely calm as if they were talking about what they would be watching on t.v. later that night. "Now where is he, Kelly?"

"We left him in the kitchen." The words chilled Nick to his very soul. He had not seen anyone when he went through the front room, and surely Tobin would have said something had he been there. Right?

(We left him…)

Nick felt all the anger drain out of him to be replaced by a panic that tried to sap his strength away from him. Numbly he let go of Kelly who crumbled to the floor sobbing. He turned away from her and ran back out into the front room. He stared at the open kitchen with the its' large island counter in the center and wondered if Kelly (we left him in the kitchen) had been lying to him. Maybe they just robbed him and threw him out of the Penthouse. Maybe Tobin was even now sitting in the police station filling out a report. The Police would come and they would be arrested, but Nick didn't care. Tobin would be safe, that was all that mattered. That was when he saw the shoe. It was sitting on the floor near the edge of the bottom of the marble island.

"Tobin?" Nick felt tears slide out of his eyes as he ran across the room. He gasped when he made it behind the couch and saw that the carpet was stained with blood. "Oh...oh God." He sobbed as he followed a path of crimson that led into the kitchen. Nick followed to where Tobin had crawled trying to escape his attackers. Tobin sat with his back against the kitchen island where his strength had finally given out and he succumbed to his injuries.

Wordlessly Nick screamed and lunged toward Tobin. He slipped in a pool of blood and had to crawl the last few feet to him, covering himself in the other man's blood. "Tobin?" Nick chocked on a sob as he wrapped his arms around the fallen man, laying the back of his head against his chest. He held him tightly as if he could will him alive with the strength of his embrace. He kissed the back of Tobin's head smearing his face with sticky blood.

"You're going to be okay." He whispered over and over again as he rocked Tobin back and forth sobbing.

"Nick?" The voice was so soft that Nick thought for sure that he had imagined it, but then Tobin's hazel eyes fluttered open and he tried to focus on Nick's face. "Why are you crying?" Nick half sobbed, half cried as he used one hand to pull out his cell phone from his shirt pocket. With blood slicked fingers he dialed 911.

Thirteen hours later Nick sat in a cell wearing the

familiar tan jumpsuit of an inmate awaiting arraignment in the Los Angeles County jail. After calling 911 Nick had wrapped both of his arms back around Tobin and whispered softly into his ear. He promised him that he would never let him go again, and that he would gladly give his life right now if he would just be okay. He promised him the world, if he would just stay.

When the Paramedics arrived they had to force him to let go of Tobin so they could take him to the hospital. The police arrived before Tobin was loaded into the ambulance. Nick begged to be allowed to go with him, but one look at him, covered in blood and the drug paraphernalia strewn about the Penthouse and Nick found himself in hand cuffs, right beside Tony and Kelly. The next few hours were spent with one detective after another questioning him about what had happened.

No, he was not a crack head.

Yes, he did use Meth regularly.

No, he did not hurt Tobin, would never hurt Tobin.

On and on it went until he finally was told that he was going to be charged with drug possession, drug paraphernalia, and attempted murder. He asked several times about Tobin, but the only thing the Detectives would tell him was that if Mr. Masters died, he would be charged with murder.

What had he done? What was he going to do if Tobin died? He thought at that moment he would die himself from the ache in his heart. Tobin had to survive. Even if he never wanted to see him again (and who would blame him?) Nick wanted more than anything for Tobin to live.

"Mr. Miller." Nick jumped at the sound of the voice in

front of his cell. Standing at the gate was a finely dressed man with a brief case dangling from one hand. "My name is Nathan Stone." The man introduced himself as Nick walked over to the gate. The man appeared to be about sixty years old with round rimmed glasses and silver hair. He smelled of Old Spice cologne.

"Who are you?" Nick asked his voice full of suspicion.

"I am your Attorney."

"I told the Cops that I didn't want an Attorney." He said as he turned away from the gate. "Besides, you don't look like a Public Pretender." Nick used the derogatory nickname inmates used to describe the free lawyers that defended indigent felons.

"I am not a Public Defender, I am Mr. Masters' personal Attorney and I have been retained to represent you." Instantly Nick was back at the gate.

"Tobin, is he okay?" That was all that mattered.

"No, he most certainly is not." Stone spoke as if he were addressing a child. "Mr. Masters was stabbed seven times with a butchers' knife and had to receive two blood transfusions and eighty five stitches. Nick felt sick as he sagged against the bars.

"Mr. Masters will recover however." The Lawyer continued. "During a short time that he was conscious he was able to give a brief statement to the Police as well as call me from the hospital."

"You said that you had been retained to represent me, by whom?" Nick asked, but in his heart he already knew the answer.

"Initially I came to L.A. to make sure that Mr. Masters would face no charges due to the fact that his name is on the lease for the Penthouse where you lived. But then Mr. Masters found out through the Detectives that you were being charged with his attack and he sent me to represent you." Even though Nick had suspected it, to hear it out loud caused his heart to leap in his chest.

"Tobin actually sent you to be my Lawyer?" "Let's get something understood Mr. Miller." Nathan Stone's face turned hard. "I am only here because Tobin begged me to come. I do not want to represent you. As a matter of fact, I would like nothing better than to talk to the Prosecutor about burying you. However I will do my best because Tobin asked me to, do you understand me?" Nick slowly nodded.

"Good, now I have already talked to the Prosecutor and due to Tobin's statement to the Police, the charge of attempted murder against you has been dropped. In the next hour I will be going before an Arraignment Judge on your behalf, Tobin has authorized me to pay any bail set."

Three hours later Nick walked out of the holding area into the main room of the Police Department. Mr. Stone had delivered some clothes from his closet, since what he had been wearing when he was arrested had been taken for evidence. He found out while getting dressed that both Kelly and Tony had been held without bond. It turned out that Kelly was the one that actually stabbed Tobin and Tony was the one that took the money to find crack. All of Tobin's credit cards had been found in his pants pocket.

Out in front of the Police Department Nick found Nathan Stone and Carl waiting for him. "Mr. Masters wants you driven directly to the hospital." Stone said his voice flat and emotionless. Carl for his part refused to even look at him as he opened the back door for Nick. At the hospital Nick paused outside of Tobin's room, his trembling hand inches away from the door handle. He could turn away right now, walk back outside and never look back. But, even as he thought about it, he knew that he could never really do it. He had an obligation that he would never be able to escape. He had to see Tobin and if he would allow him, he had to try to make up to him all the wrong he had done.

"You happy now?" The voice hissed out of the shadows right next to him, causing him to jump. He turned and found himself staring directly into Mark Baxter's rage filled face. "You come to finish him off then you son of a bitch?"

"Mark….look, I am so…." Nick began, but was cut off by the older man.

"Don't you dare say you are sorry." He spat. Several nurses turned toward them and Nick had the distinct feeling that they knew that he had been responsible for what had happened to the man laying in the room beyond the door in front of him.

"His heart stopped twice, did they tell you that? He died and they had to electrocute him." "I don't know what you want from me, I was not the one that stabbed Tobin." Even to Nick the words sounded like a lie.

"Oh yes you did." Mark's eyes filled up with tears and Nick had to look away from the man's pain. "You cut him up just by taking everything he ever gave you, and shitting on him for it." The old man turned and walked away, his shoulders shaking as he sobbed.

Nick watched him go and had to admit to himself, that the old man was right. With his heart feeling like a stone in his chest he turned the door knob, and stepped inside. The room was the stark sterile white of all hospital rooms with a single bed, a night stand and an old beat up chair. Tobin lay in the bed his chest wrapped in thick white bandages. His skin was ashen grey as if all of his color had bled out on the kitchen floor.

Tobin's hazel eyes were dull, with rings so dark around them that Nick thought he had two black eyes. His once vibrant brown hair had lost its' shine and looked brittle and old. His lips were dry and cracked. Overall, he looked like a corpse propped up in a hospital bed. The only thing that told Nick that he was still alive was the steady beeping of the heart monitor connected to the bed and the fact that Tobin's eyes turned slowly toward him.

Sitting in the old chair next to the bed was the man from the first picture that he had seen in Tobin's wallet. He sat up as close to Tobin as the bed would allow him, his hand resting on the injured man's arm. Richard turned to him with a look of pure hate.

"I don't want him here." He said to Tobin though his eyes never left Nick.

"I….need to…talk…" Tobin's voice was soft and filled with pain, is if speaking hurt him. Richard turned to look at him. "Please." Finally Richard nodded his head and stood up.

"I love you." He whispered as he bent down to kiss Tobin gently on the cheek. Nick turned away from these words and display of affection. Not because they offended him, but because of the sudden flare of pain that threatened to burst his heart. Richard left the room without another word, leaving the two of them alone.

"Sit….please." Tobin whispered. Nick came closer to

him, searching his eyes for the anger he knew must be there. What he found was so much worse than anything he had expected to see. Love and disappointment. Nick fell into the chair and for one insane moment he thought about reaching up under the railing and touching Tobin's arm as Richard had done.

Instead he said "I am so sorry."

"It's...okay....just....mistake." Tobin smiled and his lip began to bleed a little. Looking at him Nick felt the urge to scream, because he knew that if he started he would never be able to stop. For a moment he was sitting on his kitchen floor again, with Tobin's bloody body pressed against him. And then Tobin brought him back to the present. "Nathan ...will ....help ...you."

"Why?" Nick finally broke and tears spilled down his cheeks. "Why are you still helping me?" For a moment Tobin watched him cry before sliding his hand under the railing and took Nick's hand. The touch was leathery adding to the illusion that Tobin was a corpse.

"Because....I...lo..." Tobin began but Nick couldn't bear to hear the words. He stood up, pulling away.

"I can't do this." He gasped. "I am sorry, I have to go." A look of infinite sadness crossed Tobin's face and Nick almost ran for the door. He knew that if he didn't get out of there soon he was going to go crazy.

"Wait." Tobin spoke just as Nick was getting ready to open the door. Slowly, as if he were a puppet on a string Nick turned back to the man in the bed. Tobin held a small box in his outstretched hand. His arm trembled as if the box weighed a hundred pounds and Nick knew that it was an effort for him to hold it out to him.

"Take...this." Nick wanted to argue with him. Gifts? Now? Really? This was the last thing that Nick wanted, or needed, but to argue meant staying in the room even longer. He crossed the room grabbed the box and fled the room as fast as he could. Out in the hallway he ran, not heading in any particular direction, just putting space between him and the room where Tobin lay. Finally he could go no farther and he stopped by a dark hallway to lean against the wall and catch his breath. He stood there several moments, wiping his eyes before he realized that he was not alone. He looked down the shadowy hall and found to people, one man and one woman standing just a little way away from him.

The couple was standing close to one another and Nick got the impression that he had interrupted something. At that moment an overhead light tried to flicker to life, sending light dancing all around the hall, before going dark once again. But in that brief flash of light Nick recognized Richard. For an instant he felt an intense dislike for the man who had been able to touch Tobin. But what was he doing here with this woman?

They turned and walked toward him, the woman leading the way and when she got close Nick finally got a good look at her. She was five foot six, or seven, with long golden brown hair, and sharp hazel eyes that reminded him of Tobin. Her skin was perfectly tanned and she had a small beauty mark next to her supple mouth. Her lips were full and sensual, with lipstick the color of cotton candy covering them. The lipstick was smeared.

"So you are the one that almost got my brother killed." She stopped directly in front of Nick and he found that he took an instant dislike to the woman. She didn't seem particularly upset that her brother was in the hospital. As a matter of fact, Nick got the impression that she was checking him out, as if they were at a night club and she was looking to pick him up.

"Let's go Karen." Richard stepped in between them. "I want to be away from this filth." He grabbed the woman by the arm and began dragging her away. Karen did not fight him, but she did turn and give Nick a little wink just before they disappeared around the corner. Nick was glad to see them both go.

He finally made it back to his Penthouse at eleven thirty that night. He had left the hospital through one of the side doors, not wanting to run into Carl again. He wanted to be alone. So he had walked randomly through the city until well after sun set. And then after he felt he could walk no more, he had come home. Outside the building he stopped and ran his fingers across the hood of the Corvette before breaking the yellow "Crime Scene" tape that blocked the entrance to the elevator and went upstairs.

The front room still smelled of crack, but underneath that smell Nick could catch the sickening scent of dried blood. Slowly he walked over to the kitchen and looked down at the pool of crusty brown blood that had dried on the floor. A little over twenty four hours ago Tobin had lain in this spot awaiting death. A death that Nick would have been personally responsible for. And for whatever reason Tobin was not angry with him. Instead he wanted to profess love for him.

These thoughts were too much for him and Nick dropped to the floor, his hands sliding into the cold crusty blood. "I'm sorry." He sobbed over and over as fresh tears fell from his face. Suddenly the tile floor in front of him gave away, and Nick found himself being pulled, not into a dry puddle of blood, but a glowing frothing pool of crimson that seemed to have no bottom. He struggled, pulling back, only to slip on the fresh blood pouring from the fountain in front of him.

Nick Miller fell face first into the pool of blood, his whole body swallowed into the pit. A second later he surfaced, his hands scrabbling across the edges of the kitchen floor, looking for some sort of purchase. He screamed as he felt himself being dragged back under by some invisible force, and he knew that he was not going to win the battle to stay above the roiling blood. He disappeared once again, surfaced and was pulled down for the last time.

The pool of blood continued to boil and froth for several moments after Nick disappeared and slowly the pool calmed down and the glow faded. In moments the crime scene had returned to its original state and Nicholas Miller had left the world of Earth for good. Now Forgotten Child sat and dwelled on his past, reliving some of the most painful memories of his life. As he thought of these things, his fingers absently caressed the leather thong he wore around his neck. At the end of this leather strap was a gold medallion with a sword carved into its surface. This had been Tobin's final gift to him that day in the hospital room.

The day when he chose to run rather than accept another man's love. He wore the talisman to remind him of the mistakes of the past. He wore it as a promise to those who loved and trusted him, a promise that he would never fail them. He wore it for Tobin Masters.

There was not a single day in the last seventy years

that he had not thought about Tobin and all the mistakes he made. He would give anything to be able to go back to those days and change the choices that he made, but there were no more second chances for him. His fate had been in stone and there was no way he could change it. He fervently hoped that somewhere out there, beyond this world Tobin was safe and happy.

"Father!" Cassandra's mental voice slammed into him with the force of a physical blow. He reeled from the panic and fear that flowed from his daughter to flood his mind. "Father, where are you?" Forgotten wanted to reach out to her and ask what was wrong, but her panic was beginning to overpower his sense of self. If he did not do something soon, he would be locked in her terror, unable to act. So, he did the only thing he could do, he slammed his shields closed, cutting Cassandra off.

The guilt he felt was immediate and crushing, but he would have been no good to either of them if he had allowed himself to be swallowed by her emotional title wave. Free of the mental connection Forgotten became aware of echoing sounds coming from the tunnel that led back to the Pit. They were the unmistakable sounds of a battle raging.

CHAPTER 8

Taken from the personal journal of Tobin Master, Observer to the Throne of Darkness.

Throughout human culture there is a varied belief in what we call Fate. The idea that our futures are already determined for us from the minute we are born and that we are nothing more than mere pawns in some cosmic game of chess. Many who hear of this belief balk against it, unnerved by the lack of control that it implies. Before coming to Hell the idea seemed ridiculous to me, but now I am not so sure. As I recorded Forgotten Childs' memories I began seeing a disturbing pattern emerge. Was it possible that from the moment I decided to rescue Richard I had sealed not only my own fate, but that of Forgottens' as well? If there is no such a thing as chance, then the next step was easy to predict. By bringing the Stone to the Pit, Shard changed the Fate of all those who lived there. By that one action she took away their ability to control the direction in which way their lives would go. Their futures were taken out of their hands. Their Fate was sealed.

The attack had come without warning to the sentries whose job it was to warn the Pit of any nearby Demonic activity. These guards who, in spite of being told to be on alert, had been enjoying what appeared to be just another uneventful night. Then suddenly half of them were on the ground, killed by a silent spell cast by a Throne Bound Demon. The remaining guards froze in stupefied horror, not quite believing that their fellow humans had been snuffed out with no more effort than one would expend on blowing out the flame on a candle.

And then the demons began pouring into the cavern all around them. The sight of the enemy was enough to galvanize the guards into action. They had been able to ring the warning bell exactly three times before the demonic hoard was upon them. They all died within moments, overrun by sheer numbers and cut to bloody ribbons. Moments later the demons broke through into the Core of the Pit and began slaughtering the disorganized defenders.

Soon the sounds of metal against metal rang out through the central cavern, mingling with screams (both human and demonic) to create symphony worthy of the damned. Not a single level of the Pit was spared battle and those who were trapped in the lower levels fought as red and black blood rained down on them from above. Every once in a while a screeching form would plummet past the various bridges on its' way to death at the bottom of the central cavern.

The Pit was already dead and its' defenders knew it.

Forgotten Child entered the chaos on a rope bridge two levels below where he and his family lived. In a single glance he understood what the rest of the defenders had already discovered. After tonight there would no longer be a Pit. The place that so many had called home was lost forever. The only thing they could do was fight for their individual survival and hope that they could make it to a new place and start over.

A scream in front of him drew his attention and he watched as one of the defenders, a woman who had been standing on the other end of the bridge, dropped. Forgotten watched in horror as the woman's skin blackened and split open, oozing blood and a thick clear jelly like fluid. Within moments the poor woman was dead and her murderer turned its attention to Forgotten Child.

The demon that the Blade Master found himself facing was six foot tall, its muscular body covered in a hard midnight black exoskeleton that served as armor. The thing's eyes glowed red, and a large scorpion like tail danced behind the creatures' back as if it had a mind of its own. It was the poison from this tail that had killed the woman on the bridge in front of the demon.

Forgotten searched his memory as he prepared for battle, trying to remember details about this particular breed of demon. He didn't know what they were called, as a matter of fact, if there was a name for this sub-race of demon, then nobody knew it. What was known was the fact that they were the Elite Soldiers of a minor Demon Lord known as Belial. Belial was known to be the bastard son of a Demon Lord who lived in the City of Darkness, named Thanatutus. Though forgotten had never actually seen Belial himself, he was described as a large humanoid cat like creature, with large tusks protruding from his mouth, much like a Saber-Tooth tiger.

By all accounts, Thanatutus was a fat slob that lived in decadence that was beyond most demons. The Demon Lord would rather throw extravagant parties than fight. There were no Soul Stones to be had in fighting. This was not true with Belial. He was a ruthless killer, not hesitating to shed blood, and in some instances seemed to revel in violence, just for the sake of violence itself. Belial was here for one thing and one thing only. Somehow he had tracked Shard and her damned Stone to the Pit and now Free Humans would pay the price.

Forgotten had only a moment to think of these things before the demon was upon him, leaping over the still melting body of the woman it had just killed, to swing at the human with a large broad sword it clutched in its hands. Forgotten stood perfectly still, waiting until the last possible second, and then with blinding speed he drew his sword, blocking the creatures attack. The movement had been so unexpected to the demon, that it stumbled back away from the human that it thought was going to be an easy kill.

The Blade Master anticipated this move and pressed forward quickly, causing his enemy to stumble over the body lying on the bridge. The demon screeched as it tumbled onto its' back. Instantly Forgotten was upon it, his sword swinging in a whirlwind of death. Within seconds the creature found both of its' hands and tail cut from its body. Forgotten watched as the thing mewled in agony and tried feebly to crawl away from its tormentor. Forgotten watched the creature for a moment, knowing that what he was doing was cruel, but he wanted the creature to suffer as the woman had suffered. He walked slowly behind the demon until finally his strength gave way and it dropped to the bridge.

The Blade Master had no time to collect his thoughts before three more attackers appeared in front of him. He set himself with his Blade at the ready.

"I will die with my blade in my hand." He whispered to himself as he prepared for battle. At that moment two figures floated up from under the bridge. One was a twisted demon with four rail thin arms and mottled grey skin. The other was a human (Forgotten had to do double take) woman wearing a long flowing red robe. The human's hair floated around her head like she was submerged in water and she turned and twisted as she and the demon flung deadly spells at one another. Forgotten recognized Kara just as she deflected a blue lightning bolt that was cast at her with a casual, almost contemptuous flick of her hand.

Slowly the two continued floating up, raining death and destruction all around them, until they were out of sight. With the distraction gone, the combatants turned once more to each other. At that moment somewhere above them a bridge exploded. Forgotten instinctively jumped back as chunks of rock and burning pieces of wood began falling all around him. In front of him one of the demons moved forward thinking that Forgotten was retreating in fear. It was a mistake that it would not live to regret. A huge boulder smashed through him and the bridge severing the ropes that held the bridge in place. Without warning Forgotten found himself tumbling forward out into open space.

Calling upon all his training the man twisted his upper body up and back, his hand snagging one of the boards that had made up the rope bridge. Swinging wildly Forgotten slammed hard into the cavern wall. Instantly his left side went numb and he almost lost his hold. Gasping in pain he blinked his right eye as blood from a cut on his forehead ran through it. Slowly, he began pulling himself up the shattered bridge gritting his teeth against the tingling pain in his left arm.

Ten feet away from the top of the ledge, the unthinkable happened. Forgotten had stopped for just a moment to catch his breath when another human fell from above him. She missed him by only five feet, and although she passed by him so quickly that no normal human would have been able to see anything except a blur; Forgotten Child was no mere human. He had no trouble seeing the strawberry blond hair swirling in the air, or the haunting look of terror in her blue eyes as she passed out of his reach.

"NOOOO!" He screamed and reached out with his hurt arm, knowing that he was too late. All he could do is hang there and watch as his daughter tumbled away from him like a rag doll. Suddenly, in a blur of motion someone dove out over the center of the Pit, catching Cassandra in mid-air, and forcing them both to land on a solid wooden bridge fifteen feet below him. The unknown savior hit the bridge and rolled, ending with Cassandra lying on the bridge a few feet in front of them.

Forgotten felt his heart start to beat again and tears burned his eyes when he saw his daughter stir and then sit up. He didn't know who the brave human was who had saved Cassandra, but Forgotten swore that if they survived the attack, he would owe them a debt that could never be repaid. At that moment the savior turned and looked up at him, and he found himself staring down at Shard. The Blade Master could not believe his eyes as the assassin smiled at him. How could he reconcile the fact that the person that saved his daughter was a monster that he had sworn to kill?

Shard's smile deepened as if she could read his thoughts and for just a moment their eyes locked. Forgotten noticed for the first time that her eyes were a deep clear hazel and once again he felt something familiar pull at him. What was it about her eyes that called to him. She suddenly reminded him of someone, but whom?

The moment was shattered as he forced himself to look away from the assassin and began once again climbing. He did not have time for guessing games. Not if he wanted to get out of the Pit alive.

Shard watched as the Blade Master began climbing away from where she and the little girl now stood. Shrugging she turned her back on the girl and began to walk away. Why had she done it? Jumping out to catch the little girl as she fell past? She didn't know. It had been an impulsive action, made without any real thought and this bothered her. She had never been one to be impulsive and to suddenly start in the middle of this fight could very well mean her death.

She turned and looked into the girl's blue/green eyes and couldn't understand it. The child meant absolutely nothing to her and her father even less. And yet, when she had heard the Blade Master's scream of despair and had seen the girl falling, she hadn't thought twice about jumping out and saving her. She should kill the girl right now, find the Priest and get her Stone back and get out of here.

It was at that moment that she noticed a small group of demons gathering at the end of the bridge. A quick glance the other way revealed that they were surrounded.

"Well girl," Shard growled. "You may yet wish I had let you fall, that death may have been far better." Shard knew that if the girl was not killed outright, she would be taken to the Slave Pits. She would spend the rest of her life in the service of Belial or some other Demon Lord. Perhaps she would get lucky and end up with a more lenient Master. Either way, the girl's fate didn't matter. At least that's what Shard told herself.

"Try not to get in my way, or I am liable to kill you myself." She snapped.

"I'll fight with you," the girl drew a short sword from a hidden sheath on her back. "If you'll have me." This last was said almost a whisper, as if she expected Shard to deny her outright. And she might have at that, but then an idea formed in Shard's mind. The girl would surely die within moments of stepping up to one of the demons, but there was a look of fire in the girl's eyes. She was ready to fight. Oh yes, this little girl had her father in her for sure. Yet, this child was no Blade Master. However, she would make an excellent distraction to those who would be coming at Shard's back. True she would die quickly, but the assassin only needed a few seconds.

"Which group do you want?" Shard asked. She hoped that the girl would choose the group that gathered at their backs. Shard had seen a robed figure with the three warriors and that meant a Throne Bound magic user. Without a word the girl moved past Shard heading toward the group that held the Throne Bound. Smiling to herself the assassin called forth her armor and weapons from their magical hiding place and began dealing death to her enemies.

"I will die with my blade in my hand." Cassandra whispered as she moved away from the woman who had saved her life. In front of her four demons were beginning to make their way out onto the bridge. She felt sick to her stomach as her body began to tremble in fear. This was the first time she faced an enemy in true combat. She had, of course been trained to use a sword since the day she took her first steps, and her technique had only improved as she had gotten older. But then one only had to look at her parents to understand, after all they were the two most powerful Blade Masters in all of Hell, how could she not get better?

Cassandra had hoped to one day take her Test of Blades and get into the Blade Master Academy in the Free City of Haven, but it would seem that fate had other things in mind for her. She would probably die here today, but she wanted to die in way that would make her father proud of her.

She couldn't believe that only a short while ago she had been sleeping in the safety of the ruined building that had been her home since she had been born. Her dreams had been particularly haunting and vivid tonight. So real in fact that they were etched into her mind as if they were true memories.

She dreamed of her father before he came to Hell. There had been a man with him, a man that she had been dreaming about since she had been five or six. A man named Tobin. She knew that her father had a connection to Tobin, but when she saw them together in this new dream she knew that he was very important to her father. She also knew that Tobin loved her father. There had been pain and blood in the beginning of this dream. She watched in horror as some woman with ash colored skin drove a knife deep into Tobin's chest time and again, leaving him on the floor of some strange room in a towering palace. She listened as her father sat next to him and watched his agony as Tobin forgave him for some betrayal. She followed her father back to the dark tower where Tobin had almost died. There she watched him being pulled into Hell through a portal of blood.

Tobin had been devastated by her father's disappearance not knowing what to believe. By this time there was another man at his side now, whispering into his ear that her father had abandoned him. Cassandra did not like this other man. She railed against his lies screaming at Tobin to not listen to him. He needed to get up and go find her father. But he could not hear her. Slowly she moved with Tobin through the next five years of his life as he moved on. It didn't take Cassandra long to figure out that while Tobin could not hear her he could, at certain times see her. During those times she tried so hard to make him understand where her father went, but she just couldn't get through to him.

And then came that horrible moment as he traveled in the strange metal box up to the grand tower that he lived in. She tried desperately to stop him from going up, knowing somehow the pain that was about to rain down upon him. But she could not stop what had already been set into motion. She stood a secret witness to his lover's betrayal and wished with all of her broken heart that she could take away Tobin's pain.

She stood on the balcony of his tower home and wept as he turned to look at her. His soft sad smile making his face strangely beautiful. "It's okay." He spoke to her. "I know what to do now." Cassandra broke down into sobs shaking her head back and forth. She knew what he meant to do and there was no way to stop him. She wailed and slammed her fists against the invisible wall that kept her getting close to these dream phantoms, and then Tobin vanished over the rail out of sight. Cassandra's heart stopped.

"Nooo!" She screamed and the barrier in front of her shattered. Without thinking she rushed to the railing and looked over the edge, but Tobin was gone. Rage like none she had ever felt in her young life filled her as she turned to the man standing behind her. He stood looking at her in terror.

"I'll kill you!" She howled and rushed him, only to tumble out of her bed onto the cold hard floor. She sat up gasping for air slightly disoriented. Slowly she became aware of her surroundings and heard the sounds of battle coming from the small window in the wall. Suddenly alert she ran to the window and looked out into the Pit. What she saw caused terror to rise up in her heart. Everywhere she looked demons and humans were locked in combat. The corridors of her home ran red and black with blood. Over the sounds of metal on metal she could hear the wailing of mothers and children as they rushed through the fighting looking for escape.

Suddenly a shadow moved up in front of her and a claw darted in through the window and clamped around her throat. Cassandra tried to scream as she was lifted off the floor, but all she could manage was a choking gasp as she struggled to breath. She struggled, but there was nothing she could do. And then just as black spots began appearing at the edge of vision, the arm holding her up stiffened and the clawed hand spasmed open. Cassandra fell back to the floor sucking great gulps of air into her oxygen starved lungs.

Slowly she pulled herself back up to the window and once again looked out into the chaos. The demon that had been choking her lay on the broken road below her window, an arrow sticking out of the back of his neck. Dazed she looked across the way and found a young human girl with a bow and quiver looking back at her. Cassandra couldn't remember the woman's name, but she knew that she would never forget her face, the face of her savior.

"Oh no." Cassandra sobbed, her throat raw as a large blood slick blade exploded through the woman's back and out of her chest. Blood poured from her mouth as she worked her lips as if she were trying to say something and then she was gone, just another human body laying broken in the streets of the Pitt.

"Father!" Cassandra cried out with her heart and mind. "Father where are you?" And for a moment she felt him, knew that he had heard her and then the connection between them was slammed closed. She reeled as if she had been slapped. Had her father just died, in that single moment that she called to him? Did her call distract him long enough for some hell spawned creature to run its' blade through him? No, she refused to believe that. She had to get herself together, she had to get to her evacuation cave. With these thoughts filling her mind she quickly moved to slip on her clothes and strapped on her sword belt. She didn't intend to stop and fight unless she had to. Just before going out through the door to her room she turned once more to the window and thought of the woman who had saved her life. Her eyes welled up with tears, she had given her life for Cassandra and all she could do was stand and watch her die.

Without thinking she took a step away from the door back toward the window not really knowing why, but that one step probably saved her life. The door exploded in a storm of shards and a huge battle axe dug into the floor, in the exact spot where she had been standing only seconds before. Cassandra yelped and fell back into the room. A large demon pushed through the ruined door and turned toward her. It had to be about seven foot tall, with the head of some great cat. Two huge yellowing tusks jutted from its upper lip and it was covered in dirty fur that seemed to be falling out in clumps, leaving bright pink bald spots all over its body.

Slowly the demon turned its orange glowing eyes toward her. It snarled and the smell of rotting meat rolled through the room. With the only door to the room blocked Cassandra turned and ran for the window. Behind her she heard the demon roar but then she was at the window, her foot pushing her up onto the window-sill and then she was out into the air hurtling above the street the street. She landed on the roof of the building where the woman with the bow had died, her forward momentum dropping her roughly on the black stone. Breathing hard she smiled to herself and allowed a feeling of triumph to fill her, she made it, she had escaped. Or so she thought.

Behind her the wall around her bedroom window exploded and the cat like demon came flying directly at her, its axe above its head. Cassandra screamed and scrambled forward, her feet slipping on the smooth stone underneath her. The demon landed five feet behind her and the roof underneath it shattered dropping it into the room below. Cassandra felt the whole building shift as cracks shot through the stone in all directions.

Gasping in terror Cassandra pushed herself forward, trying to stay ahead of the cracks as chunks of the building began to crumble and smash into the street below. At the last moment, just as the roof completely folded in upon itself Cassandra launched herself once again through the air only to find that the only building in front of her was made of old wood, and was at least four stories shorter than the one she just left.

She had just enough time to raise her arms up to shield her face before she smashed through the rotting wood roof. She crashed through three more floors before finally stooping flat on her back in someone's dining room, crushing an old rickety table underneath her. Coughing, her body aching all over Cassandra slowly sat up.

"Die!" A shadow rushed at her and she was forced to roll painfully to her left or get her head smashed in by a heavy black cooking cauldron.

"I'm human!" She yelled as the old man struggled to lift the cauldron up for another swing. He paused and squinted at her and the looked up at the hole in his ceiling.

"So you are." He huffed and dropped the cauldron back to the floor with a heavy "clang". "Why you coming in through the ceiling?" He demanded.

"Well it wasn't my first choice." Cassandra snapped as she stretched her back and the old man cackled.

"You the Blade Masters' daughter?" The old man asked as he watched her.

"Yes, sir."

"Oh-Ho Sir?" The old man cackled again and Cassandra decided she did not like the sound at all. "I like that."

"Are you the only one here sir?" For just a moment a shadow of sadness crossed the old man's face.

"Tink went down to the market just before the bastards attacked." Cassandra had no idea if 'Tink was his wife or daughter, either way chances were she was dead, but that was not something she was going to say out loud.

"Sir, come with me, we have got to get out here." The man nodded wordless and lifted up the cauldron again.

"Uh...sir, I am sorry, but with all due respect, there is no way you are going to carry that all the way to the evacuation site." The old man turned to look at her as if she had suddenly grown a second head.

"Well of course not." He cackled again as he dragged the cauldron over to a fire place and hung it up on a hook set in the wall. "Tink would kill me if I left things like this." He turned his sad eyes to the mess on the floor beneath the hole in the ceiling.

"Sir....we don't have time." Sadly he nodded and turned back to her. "Good, put your hand on my shoulder, and if I go to fast just let me know."

"Child I was moving through the trenches killing Krauts a hundred years before you were born, lead on." Cassandra had no idea what he was talking about, but she didn't take the time to press the issue, instead she led them out of the building into the chaos of the undercity streets.

The going was slow as they darted from shadow to shadow trying desperately to avoid drawing the attention of any demons. Surprisingly they made it all the way to the central shaft without incident. But that is where their good luck ended. Cassandra was leading them across a stone bridge when two floating Throne Bound rose on the left side of the bridge. The two magic users were flinging deadly spells at each other with blinding speed, but the spells were bouncing around them shattering walkways and walls of the city. Cassandra ducked just as a bolt of dark energy whizzed inches from the top of her head. Behind her the old man muttered a curse under his breath.

"Back!" Cassandra turned and pushed the old man in front of her. "We have to get back!" But at that moment a huge bolt of red lightning struck the center of the bridge behind them. The explosion was deafening and Cassandra stumbled forward as she felt the bridge lurch under their feet. She knew that the bridge was coming apart and there was no way they would both make it back to solid ground. Knowing what she had to do she shoved the old man as hard as she could and was rewarded by the sight of him falling across the threshold of the broken bridge onto the walkway at the end.

The old man scrabbled around and he reached out for her in a desperate and futile attempt to catch her. For just a moment Cassandra hung there in the air and she had an odd sense of Deja' vu, only the old man was her, and she was Tobin. Then she was falling backwards towards her death.

But instead of dying, Shard had saved her life and now she faced her first real battle. Cassandra felt her heart drop as she noticed the robed figure behind the first three armored demons. The magic user would be her biggest threat. She had to get to it as quickly as possible. The lead demon, another cat-like monstrosity looked down at her and laughed, a coughing sound that grated on Cassandra's ears.

"Look at the human whelpling." At first Cassandra thought that the thing had spoken out loud, but she quickly realized that what she heard came not from the demon's lips, but from its mind. "This is going to be easy." The creature thought and Cassandra suddenly knew everything it planned to do. It swung its' axe in an arc that would cut her head off if she didn't move. But she had no intentions of dying that easily.

Without thinking about it, her body was moving, reacting to the attack even before it had begun. Up into the air she went, twisting and turning away from the killing strike. While the axe swung below her, she lashed out with her sword catching the demon in the crook of its axe arm. The creature roared in pain and surprise as its axe and arm continued on without the rest of its body out over the edge of the bridge. Black blood sprayed Cassandra's shoes as she landed back on the bridge. In front of her the lead demon continued to wail until she darted forward and buried half the length of her short sword into its' throat. The demon's eyes went wide as it dropped to its knees and slumped over dead.

Cassandra had no time to contemplate her victory, as two more demons rushed at her both attacking at the same time. Again she knew what they were planning before they executed their moves and her body moved without conscious thought. This time she jumped up, her feet catching the rope guides on either side of the bridge, her body leaning forward until she was vertical with the wooden planks of the bridge below her. In front of her the demons were already committed to their attacks. One swung high, hoping to cut her head off, the other swung low in the hopes of cutting her feet out from underneath her.

The low swing continued on with nothing to stop its' momentum, until it struck the second demon just above the knee, severing the leg. At the same time as it was losing its leg its swing passed above Cassandra's prone body, and she lifted her sword up and deflected the blade up and away from her. The first demon gasped and tried to back away, but it was too late. Its friend's axe cut its head cleanly off at the shoulders.

The second demon screamed in pain and terror as it spun off balance on its remaining leg and toppled over the guide rope into open air. Blood stained Cassandra from head to toe, but she didn't care. In that moment of clarity she understood what it truly meant to be a Blade Master. It was not enough to die with a blade in your hand. Her death would be meaningless if she had been too afraid to fight. Never before had she believed in the Blade Master chant against fear. It didn't matter if she died, she had to send as many of the enemy into the abyss of death as she could. That is what it meant to be a Blade Master, a warrior, a protector of free humans everywhere.

The sounds of chanting brought her back to herself and she found that she had forgotten about the Throne Bound. It was a mistake that would most likely cost her life. Suddenly the magic user held its' hand up and it began to crackle with red electricity. Acting on pure instinct Cassandra rolled her body backwards, her legs still suspended between the ropes. The movement saved her life, but she hadn't moved fast enough.

She gasped in pain as the red lightning bolt grazed her left side, burning her clothes and skin. Her body seized as the electricity coursed through her. Bonelessly she tumbled to the bridge. Gritting her teeth in agony she pulled herself up to her feet and swayed as the Throne Bound began chanting again. Cassandra was aware that she had lost her sword somewhere, but it really didn't matter, she knew that she didn't have the energy to mount any defense against the magic the demon was about to throw at her.

In front of her a ball of black fire blazed into life in the demon's hand. Slowly the fiend looked from the fire to her and stretched its' lips back in a parody of a smile.

"Die!" It hissed and threw the fireball directly at the human girl. Knowing there was nothing she could do Cassandra closed her eyes and held up her arms before her in a defensive posture. It was a purely reflexive gesture, borne out of fear.

The fireball exploded, engulfing her in black flame. She waited for the agony of being burned alive to come, and when it didn't she slowly opened her eyes. Black fire swirled around her and even though it danced across her skin she only felt a slight tingling sensation. Suddenly her hands began to glow with a pearly light.

Cassandra watched in horror as the glow began creeping up her arms. Everywhere the light touched the black fire it turned golden. She gasped as pain shot through her shoulder blades and two ghostly feathered wings unfolded from her back. Without warning she felt her feet leave the bridge and she rose out of the golden flames, like a phoenix rising from ashes.

In front of her the Throne Bound stared up at her glowing form in horror and it began to cast another spell, its' voice trembling in terror. Cassandra gestured with her right hand, and a bolt of golden energy slammed into the creatures chest killing it instantly. Slowly Cassandra rotated in the air until she was facing Shard where she stood with the bodies of several demons at her feet. Suddenly the little girl gasped as pain welled up inside of her. It was if she was burning from the inside out. She tilted her head back and screamed as her body exploded in golden light.

Throughout the Pit demons found themselves in agony as the sudden light burned their skin, or melted their eyes. One by one they fell before human defenders, or simply burst into flames. On the rope bridge in the middle of the Pit Cassandra found herself on her knees, head bowed gasping for breath. Her sweat covered body trembled as she slowly pulled herself to her feet and looked up at Shard. A new look crossed the assassins face, it was only there for a second and then it was gone. But it was a look that Cassandra recognized all the same.

It was fear.

Forgotten Child ducked a swing from a large sword and drove his blade up and through the chin of the demon in front of him. The thing gurgled and twitched as the light of life left its eyes as it died, but the Blade Master didn't have time to celebrate his victory as three more creatures rushed him from the shadows. He ached from several short gashed that criss crossed its body and he could feel blood running down his back. He had killed at least two dozen demons but they kept coming, in a seemingly never ending wave.

Forgotten knew that he could not keep this up forever, even a Blade Master had his limits. He ducked under the first new demon's swing, blocked the second one's axe and gasped in pain as the third one scored a glancing blow on his left shoulder. Fresh blood mixed with old and Forgotten knew that if he didn't do something soon, he was going to die.

With effort he slowed his breathing and opened his mind, concentrating on the demons standing in front of him. Instantly he was in their thoughts, his mind processing each of their planned moves like a computer, separating the more dangerous from the feints. The first demon moved in, his sword slashing at his left, but this was a false move, meant to make him dodge to the right, into the third demon's axe which was already in motion.

Instead of moving to the right Forgotten stepped up and left catching the surprised demon with the sword with an elbow across its furred snout. Grunting in surprise the demon tried to step back to get a better swing on the human, but Forgotten was already moving, rolling off to the right and lifting up into the air to deliver a spinning kick to the third demon with the axe. He heard a satisfying crunch as the things' jaw broke under his heel, but he realized in that moment that he had made a fatal mistake. He forgot about the second demon, the one that had not attacked. He felt it move up behind him, and knew that he did not have time to get out of the way, but he started to throw himself forwards in the hope of lessoning the blow.

Behind him the demon's roar of triumph was suddenly cut short, and its' head bounced across the floor past where Forgotten fell. Stunned he turned to look at the headless body as it wobbled, fell to its' knees and slumped to the stone floor. And there stood Father Michael, his large battle axe in his hand. Wasting no time, the human Priest uttered a war cry and fell on one of the remaining demons, driving it back before his mighty blows. In that moment he looked every bit the Holy Warrior, dealing out God's judgment to his enemies. Forgotten pushed himself up and engaged the final demon and within moments both creatures lay dead at the human's feet.

"Good to see you." Forgotten smiled at his old friend.

"It's good to be seen." Father Michael smiled back. "We've got to go, the evacuation is complete." Forgotten knew the plan, after all, he was the one who designed it. In case the Pit was ever attacked the defenders would fight, even a losing battle, giving the non-combatants, the elderly, women and children a chance to make it to secret caverns hidden on every level.

These caverns were stocked with everything from trail rations, to extra weapons. Each cavern was separated from all the others, just in case one was discovered by the enemy and attacked, the others would not be compromised. Each cavern had a scout, an Escape Master, men and women trained in different levels and paths that ran through the ruins under the Dark City. It was their job to get their refugees from the Pit to the safety of other human settlements, either under the city, or even on other continents. These Escape Masters lived in their assigned caves so that they were always ready to receive refugees. Ultimately it was the goal to get as many survivors to the Free City of Haven.

After word was out that the evacuation was complete, the remaining defenders would begin retreating to their own caverns. They would, of course kill any enemy they came across, but they would also burn any bridges they crossed to keep anyone from following them. Determined to get to their evacuation site, the two humans turned toward the opening of the cavern, just as six demons walked in.

Sighing the Blade Master moved to stand next to his oldest friend, and knew that one, if not both of them were going to die. There was just to many for the two of them to face.

"Go." He told the old Priest. "I'll hold them off for as long as I can."

"I'm not going to leave you." Father Michael protested.

"I'm not asking you, I'm telling you, go!" Forgotten snapped. "Find my wife and daughter and get them out of here." Michael looked as if he were going to argue before nodding his head in resignation.

"God be with you my friend." He touched the blade Master's shoulder before turning away, and stopping instantly.

"What?" Forgotten asked, but he already knew.

"There's more behind us." The old man confirmed. "Looks like it's a fight to the end after all." The Priest positioned himself at Forgotten's back, his axe at the ready. Standing together the two humans prepared to die fighting.

Somewhere off in the distance a howling rose and Forgotten felt a shiver run through him. The sound echoed through the tunnels, as if it came from many different directions at the same time. Then he noticed something else, the cavern behind the demons in front of him started to brighten, as if someone were slowly turning up the flame on an old lantern.

For a moment Forgotten thought that his eyes were playing tricks on him, but then the demons began to react to the light as it grew brighter. The two in the back spun around snarling in anger and pain as steam rose off their backs. The Blade Master blinked as the light suddenly exploded into a beam of pure white light, and the demons began howling in agony.

Forgotten watched in fascinated horror as the creatures threw themselves against each other, and the rock walls, trying desperately to get away from the light. It was as if they were covered in invisible flames, as their fur and skin curled and blackened. Several of them clawed at their faces as their eyes burst. The light only lasted a few seconds, and then it was gone, leaving ghostly after images in the human's eyes, but in those seconds every demon in the tunnel had died, horribly.

"What in Gods' Holy name was that?" Father Michael's voice shook. Forgotten could only shrug as they walked passed the still smoking bodies. They passed many more bodies, both human and demon on their way to the evacuation cavern. All the human remains showed signs of violent deaths at the end of blades, or infernal magic, as did quite a few demons. But by far, more of the invaders seemed to have been burned to death by the mysterious light. It was all that Forgotten could do to keep from gagging at the smell of charred meat and fur that hung in the tunnels like a thick fog. He was happy when they finally arrived in the larger hidden cave, and they found that the air was smell free.

The cavern was large and filled with about fifty or sixty men, women and children, preparing themselves for their journey through the underground. Forgotten felt saddened by the fact that even though so many had survived the attack on the Pit, many more would die on their way to Haven. How many people had died today because of the actions of the man beside him? How many more would die?

For just a moment the Blade Master felt the anger building inside of him. How could Farther Michael have allowed this to happen? For surely every dead body back in the caverns could be laid out at the old man's feet. How could he have allowed Shard and the cursed Stone she brought with her, to stay?

"Father Michael." A voice cut into his thoughts and Forgotten found this caverns Escape Master standing in front of them. A woman, with long brown hair and bluish green eyes. She was wearing tight fitting leathers and had a small sword strapped at her side. Her name was Stone. Or at least that is what the young woman called herself. Forgotten had fought next to her on several missions in the past and knew her to be quite capable and resilient.

"Blade Master." Stone bowed low in honor to him, before turning back to the old priest. "The others have gathered in my sleeping alcove, as you requested."

Father Michael smiled warmly at the woman as he took her hands into his. "Thank you so much Stone. How long can you delay your departure, there may be a few members of my group who may yet wish to go with you."

"Not long Father." The woman looked around at the restless people in the cave. "Will you be traveling with us?" Forgotten noticed a small sound of hope as it crept into the Escape Master's voice and he looked more closely at her. And there it was, that gleam in her eyes that gave her true feelings away. He wondered if Father Michael knew just how much the young woman cared about him. If he did, he surely didn't show it. He sighed and let go of her hands (much to her obvious disappointment).

"I honestly don't know child." Forgotten blinked, he didn't know? Of course he would be traveling with them, where else would he go? "If not, then may God be with you and I hope to see you in the streets of Haven someday soon." There was a resigned quality in the old man's voice that Forgotten didn't like.

"God Bless you, Father." Stone looked as if she was going to say more, but then she abruptly turned and went about preparing people for their journey. Without another word

Father Michael turned away from her and began walking toward the side cave. After just a moment Forgotten turned and followed him. The sleeping alcove was as large as a studio apartment, with rough walls, and a high rock ceiling. There about twenty men and women standing at the ready, with packs on their backs, and weapons in sheaths. One look at their grim faces and Forgotten knew that whatever was happening here, he was not going to like it.

Father!" That one shout shattered all doubts in an instant. He turned just in time to catch his daughter as she flung herself into his arms. Nothing could ever match the feeling of Cassandra's warm body pressed against him. He admitted to himself that he had been burying the feeling that she had died during the attack. Covering up the pain by trying to not to think about it, but she was here, alive and well. Having her in his arms made the world feel just a little more right.

But what about Racheal? Would he have to trade one death for another?

"No my love." A hand squeezed his shoulder and Forgotten fought down a tear as he felt his wife's aura fill him. For a moment there was nobody else in all the world, just his wife and daughter and Forgotten wished with all of his heart and soul that they could stay like this forever. But then he looked up and the moment was shattered as he found himself looking at Shard. Slowly he stood up and looked intently at the assassin, searching for whatever had called to him back in the caverns, but there was nothing.

"It doesn't mean that we are even, not by a long shot," Forgotten kept his voice neutral. "But thank you for what you did back there." Shard shrugged as if it didn't matter, and perhaps to the demon raised human it probably didn't.

"She fought like a Blade Master today, you should be proud." Shard spoke to Forgotten, but her gaze never left Cassandra standing at his side, before turning and walking away from them. Forgotten felt the little girl stiffen and sensed that something was bothering her, but before he could ask Father Michael's voice cut through the air.

"Listen up everyone, you all know that you have been chosen for a very difficult mission." He looked at each man and woman, finally stopping at Forgotten. "Any who wish to go may do so now, and know that I hold no judgment against you." Forgotten knew that even though he spoke so that everyone could hear, this message was for him and him alone.

Slowly the Blade Master moved up to the old man. "Michael, what are you planning." For a moment the Priest looked uncomfortable and Raven, the Throne Bound half vampire stepped up next to him. Forgotten could see that several blood stains covered the half damneds' robes and he walked with a slight limp, but it was what he carried with him that drew his full attention. It was the ornate box containing the Stone of Power.

"You still have that thing?" Forgotten hadn't meant to shout, but his anger burst forth like an explosion. "You have gone fucking insane, hasn't that thing done enough?" He ignored the gasps and angry mutterings that came from some of the others in the cave as he moved right up into the old man's face.

"We have an opportunity that no other human has ever had." The Priest kept his voice calm and refused to back away from the Blade Master.

"Was it worth having our home destroyed, this

'opportunity' of yours?" Forgotten screamed spittle flying into his friends face. "Why don't we go ask all those people who are laying dead back in the tunnels and see what they think."

The blow came out of nowhere, and Forgotten stumbled back in shock. A small trickle of blood formed at the corner of his mouth where Father Michael had punched him. Silence filled the cave as every eye watched the trembling old man as tears spilled down his worn face.

"Don't you think that I know that I am to blame for this?" He railed at the other man. "You can stand there and judge me all you want, but your judgement won't be near as bad as my own." All the fight seemed to drain out of the old man and he looked at the ground defeated. "Don't you see? We have to try or all of this would have been for nothing."

"What would you have me do?" Forgotten whispered, all his anger gone, replaced with a terrible emptiness.

"One of us, you or me, has to become a Stone Bearer, and then we must gather an army to fight in the War of Ascension." Forgotten flinched away from the thought of claiming the Stone, there was no way he would ever touch the vile thing again. Seeing his reaction the old man sighed.

"Very well my old friend, take your family and go with Stone, and may God be with you always." With that he turned and reached for the box, his shoulders already sagging under the weight of what he was about to do.

'It's not my problem.' Forgotten thought to himself as he started to turn away and then he froze. At his throat Tobin's sword medallion shifted against his skin and a feeling rose up inside his chest. It was the same feeling he had the night he and Tobin almost kissed. The feeling that the rest of his life depended on the path he chose at this moment, a crossroads in time. He could follow his gut reaction, and leave, or he could turn back and except the dark road to the War of Ascension.

Those were the two paths laid out before him. Back with Tobin he had followed his knee jerk reactions instead of giving into his true feelings and that choice had led to Tobin laying in a pool of blood, and ultimately brought him to Hell. Could this be another time when if he went running blindly away from his fear that others would pay the price. No! He could not allow that to happen. Behind him Father Michael began to speak.

"I Father Michael accept....."

"Stop!" Forgotten spun back around and the old man jumped back as if he expected Forgotten to attack him. Gently he pushed the old man out of the way, and turned to face Raven. "I am Forgotten Child and I accept the title of stone Bearer." Forgotten felt a tremor run through his body and he suddenly wished that he could take a bath to wash away the feeling of filth that suddenly filled him. But, he knew that no amount of water would have made him feel clean.

"I am so sorry." The Priest sobbed next to him. "Please.... Please forgive me." Forgotten lifted the box out of Raven's hands and turned his back on the other man and walked away.

Cassandra missed the argument between her father and his ultimate acceptance of the Stone of Power. If she had perhaps she would have been afraid for him, but the moment he stepped away from her, someone else in the cave caught her attention. He was a lone figure wearing a long black cloak with the hood pulled up to hide his face. Slowly Cassandra moved toward the mysterious man, her heart beating like a caged bird within her chest.

"Hello little one." The stranger spoke when she got close enough and Cassandra felt her legs grow weak. Could it be? Was it possible?

"Tobin?" Her voice was a shaky whisper, but she knew that he heard her. And then it truly hit her, he heard her! Gasping she threw herself against the man and wrapped her arms around him in a crushing hug. Everything was going to be alright. Tobin was here. And then a thought came to her. Her father needed to know, needed to see Tobin so he could let go of his pain and guilt.

"No little one." Tobin caught her as she turned to cry out. "He would not be able to see me."

"But...." she turned back to him and the words froze in her throat. His eyes. His beautiful, soft kind hazel eyes were gone, replaced by two black voids. What did it mean? What had happened to him?

"I have been marked by the Throne of Darkness." Tobin's voice was filled with such sadness that she felt tears well up in her eyes again. "I can't even save myself, let alone your father." Then just like that he was gone and Cassandra found herself standing alone. Slowly she turned to watch as her father lifted a box out of a man's hands and then she looked at the place where Tobin had been standing.

"Don't worry Tobin, you both will save each other." She whispered to the empty air.

CHAPTER 9

Taken from the personal Journal of Tobin Masters, Observer to the Throne of Darkness.

If one looks beyond the basic needs of food and good health, we find that our most complex needs are almost always emotional in nature. And of all the emotions love has always been one of the most powerful. We need to love and to be loved in return. This need is so overpowering that we sometimes blind ourselves to our own reality. We create a world where those we love are perfect. We simply refuse to see their faults and even overlook the fact that they may not love us as much as we love them. Since coming to Hell I have asked myself why I was chosen to become the Observer to the Throne of Darkness. Why a human after the demons of its own world had always served before? I believe it has something to do with the human ability to feel. Since my arrival I have felt a confusing flow emotions. Fear, anger, hate, the pain of betrayal, even the sadness of love lost and rediscovered. It is for these things that the Throne called me from my suicidal leap. Through me the Throne can, for the first time, experience true emotion, as I bear to it the depths of my soul. In return for this the Throne has shown me a different need. Before I believed love to be stronger than anything, but the throne has showed me differently. This new need, this all powerful, horrifying need is in all of us. It sleeps in the depths of our hearts, like some great prehistoric monster, waiting for some darkness to come along and awaken it. Once awake, it grows like a cancer within us, until it consumes every fiber of our being. It is a hungry need that must be sated. It is a need that can easily make humans into monsters that rival the demons of Hell. What could this need be, you ask? Nothing could be so terrible, you say? It is the simple human need for revenge.

"What do you want?" Tobin demanded of the ebony Throne resting on its' raised dais, The human felt disgust and anger rise up within him as he looked upon it. Even after being its' servant for the last six months had not changed these feeling every time he was summoned before it.

"I can taste your hate Observer, like sweet honey." Tobin shuddered at the voice inside of his mind. Even after all this time it felt as if some huge maggot was squirming through his brain when the Throne spoke directly to him.

"What do you want?" Tobin repeated and was happy to hear that his voice remained steady, despite the trembling of his whole body.

"You still fight me." The Throne almost sounded like a petulant child whose parents had denied them a piece of candy. "I have honored you above all in Hell, have given you power beyond your mortal dreams, and yet you refuse to use it." Tobin remembered the rush of power he felt when he had killed the spider on Wrath when he had been delivering the Stones to the Chosen. The feel of the black fire licking along his hand, tingling pleasantly. He had felt that he could have done anything, he was a God with the power to give and take life. He had taken life that day, snuffing it out as easily as one would blow out a candle.

Oh yes, he remembered the thrill of watching the spider burn and then the death of the guard at Darkstar's gate. Both creatures had died in agony, and at the time he had relished their death throws, drinking in their suffering like it was fine wine. But after he had returned to the Great Palace the images refused to leave his mind. They haunted him for months every time he closed his eyes and their screams echoed in his nightmares.

He knew what the Throne really wanted from him. It wanted him to open up and let it inside his soul again. The very thought of it sickened him. The Throne fed of his emotions like a leech fed off the blood from an unsuspecting host. Except when the Throne had finished its feeding, another part of Tobin's soul would have turned cold. Evil. The ultimate goal was to taint Tobin, corrupt him until he lost his humanity. That was what the Throne was asking him to do. To open himself and willingly allow it access to his inner soul. To invite it in.

This could never be allowed to happen again. He would fight it until his dying (may it come soon) breath. In his mind the Throne chuckled darkly.

"I know you would my Observer, but I offer you a bargain instead."

"There is nothing you could offer me." Tobin stated, but he wished that he felt as confident as he sounded. "I will never use your power to kill again."

"Oh, but I shall prove you wrong on both accounts." The Throne declared with confidence. "You will kill again and then you will take my offer."

"Never!" Tobin screamed. At that moment a large demon stepped out from behind the Throne. Tobin stared at the new comer in shock, he had thought that he was alone in the Throne room. The new demon was almost six feet tall, with a black skull like head. Its eyes glowed a malevolent orange as they fixed themselves on the human. Without speaking it began walking down the steps toward him, taking its' time as if it didn't have a care on the world.

"Who are you?" Tobin demanded, just barley keeping his voice from quivering. He had a very bad feeling about what was about to happen. The creature ignored him and for once the Throne remained quite. The demon stopped in front of the human and looked down at him. Suddenly, without warning the thing lashed out, backhanding Tobin across his face.

Gasping Tobin stumbled back, barley keeping his legs under him. "What....?" He began, but was cut off by a second blow. This one, a closed fisted punch that sent Tobin flying through the air. He smashed into one of the fluted columns that held up the ceiling, knocking the wind out of him.

"You are weak. The demon spat at him. "You are no true Observer." The creature moved up, and wrapped its' clawed hands around Tobin's throat and began to squeeze. Gagging, the human tried to struggle, but it was no use, the demon was much stronger than him.

"You do not have to be weak." The Throne whispered to him. "All you have to do is accept the power which I offer you." Tobin would have laughed if he could. This was the Throne's big plan? If so, then it had sorely miscalculated. If it thought that Tobin would kill this creature to save his own life it was wrong. He wanted to be free of the Throne, and it had unwittingly given him his way out. Black spots began to appear in front of his eyes, and he knew it wouldn't be long.

"The Throne has promised me your position human." If he could have, Tobin would have told it that it could have it, no problems there. Soon he would be dead. Dead and free.

"The Throne also promised me a special human slave." The demon laughed. "I will take this human and kill him piece by piece over the next hundred years."

"Forgotten Child." The Throne whispered again and Tobin realized that this was the human that it had promised the demon. If Tobin didn't fight back, if he died now, the Throne would give Forgotten to this demon to be tortured for centuries to come.

Part of him still wanted to give up, let himself die, but then images of Forgotten (Nick) sitting next to that pool of water six months ago, remembering their time together rose up in his mind. Deep in the core of his being he felt a cold ball of power building. He imagined Forgotten dying because Tobin was too weak to do what he must to survive.

It wasn't fair. How much would he have to sacrifice for this man? But he knew the answer before he even thought of the question. He would sacrifice everything for him. Even his soul.

"I will rape him over and over." The demon hissed, unaware that its time had already come to an end. This thing would never lay eyes on Forgotten Child, let alone harm him in any way. "I will… what?" The demon howled and snatched its' hand away from Tobin's throat with a pained screech. Smoke rose lazily from its' burned flesh, as black flames began dancing along Tobin's entire body.

"You will not touch him." Tobin told the demon, his voice filed by dark power as it filled him, and the black fire began spreading out from him. Snarling, the demon swung its fist, only to have it to be stopped short by Tobin's gloved hand. Instantly the fiends' clawed hand began to burn, causing it to howl in agony.

Tobin waited a few moments before letting go, and the demon fell to its' knees in front of him, cradling its' charred hand to its chest. It watched as Tobin began to rise, his feet leaving the floor.

"Kneel before your superior, dog!" Tobin's voice boomed with dark authority. He hovered twenty feet above the floor, in the center of a dragon made of swirling black flames.

"But the Throne promised." The demon wailed as if the Thrones' promises truly meant anything.

"Promised?" Tobin laughed. "Fool, the Throne only promises betrayal and death. Today it has betrayed you, and I bring you death." At that moment, the fire dragon surrounding Tobin reached out and covered the kneeling demon with one of its large claws. The creature didn't even have time to scream as it was reduced to ashes.

Tobin watched in a mixture of horror and fascination as the creature's soul slid into the black fire around him. Gasping he felt the soul merge with his own, causing the dragon surrounding to flare with even more power. Moments later the fire began to recede and he slowly drifted back to the ground. Slowly he moved back to the bottom of the dais and glared hatefully up at the Throne.

"Now what?" He demanded, his voice cold and hard.

"Listen, and I will offer that which you most desire." So, Tobin listened to what the Throne had to offer him, and when it was done speaking, he willingly offered up another piece of his soul for the Throne to feed upon.

Richard Murry sat in a large leather overstuffed chair in the bedroom that he had once shared with Tobin and cried. It had been two weeks since that terrible night when Tobin had walked in on him and Karen. The night that Tobin had thrown himself from the balcony, rather than face the betrayal Richard had committed against him.

That night replayed in his mind every time he closed his eyes. Tobin stepping off the elevator to find Richard standing there in the candle light, naked, with sweat cooling on his skin from just having sex with Karen. The look of happiness on Tobin's face when he thought that Richard had been waiting to surprise him, then the crushing realization and pain when Karen called out from the bedroom.

That look of pure lost sorrow had hit Richard like a brick in the gut. He would have given anything at that moment to take that look off of Tobin's face. To stop what he knew was about to happen. But of course nothing could stop it. Karen had walked out of the bedroom (Tobin's bedroom) as naked as Richard. There had been no way to hide the awful truth of their affair.

Richard had just stood there, holding the two crystal flutes half filled with champagne, the crushing guilt and horror robbing him of the ability to do anything but stare. Karen rushed passed him, babbling that nothing had happened between them, and that everything was going to be okay. Her brother looked as if he had never seen her before. Then without warning Tobin had back handed her across the face.

The slap broke the spell Richard had been under and he dropped the flutes to rush over to the fallen woman. That had been another mistake. He knew that now. He looked up from trying to comfort his lover to find Tobin looking down at them. There had been a look of such pure hatred on Tobin's face, that Richard hardly recognized the other man. A part of him honestly believed that he was about to die in that moment. That Tobin would fall on the both of them and tear them apart with his bare hands. But instead Tobin had stalked past them and out into the cold air on the balcony, leaving them alone.

They dressed in silence, Richard unable to look at Karen as she slid on her panties and short skirt. Confused thoughts jumped around in his head like a mad pinball. What had they done? What would happen now that they had been exposed? Tobin would surely throw him out. The thought caused his heart to go cold in his chest. He didn't want to lose Tobin. How had things gotten so far out of control? How had it come to this?

Seven years ago Tobin had rescued him in the Vatican City. Back then he had been Richard's Knight in Shining Armor, never questioning whether he should help the stranger on the street. At first he slept with Tobin out of a feeling of obligation, but then Tobin and he kept in touch after they returned to the states. It hadn't taken Tobin long to ask Richard to move in with him.

To his surprise Richard found himself genuinely attracted to Tobin. There was just something about the man that drew others to him like a moth to a flame. He couldn't count the nights he had sat up and watched Tobin sleep, marveling at his feelings for the man. Richard had never been in a same sex relationship before, and he couldn't understand how he could sometimes physically ache to hold another man in his arms.

But, after only a year things began to change. Tobin began going to Los Angeles more often. It was true that he owned two auction houses and a few Antique Book stores in the city, but there was also a man that he went to see. Tobin never hid the fact that he went to visit his "friend" while he was in prison, and the two of them exchanged letters and phone calls. At first this did not bother Richard, after all the man was locked up, what could he possibly do with Tobin? Plus, it was just in Tobin's genetic make-up to help someone in need.

However, Tobin continued to go and see this Nick Miller even after he was released from prison. He even discovered that Tobin had provided his "friend" with an extravagant apartment to live in. Free of charge. At least once every two months Tobin would fly out to Los Angeles on the pretense of attending meetings, but Richard knew the truth, he was really going to see the other man in his life.

Many nights Richard lay in the bed that he shared with Tobin, images of this mystery man holding Tobin in his arms, eating away at him like worms in his guts. And then there came the Halloween when Tobin had flown off to L.A. to celebrate Nick's birthday. Richard had been upset, lost, trying to figure out what he was going to do. He knew that he was losing the man he loved. He called Karen over so that he could talk to her about her brother. He never meant for anything to happen. One moment he was pouring his heart out to the woman, and the next they were locked in an embrace, kissing.

Richard felt a fire rise up in him, and all thought fled before this flame. He lifted Karen up and carried her into the bedroom, and made love to her in Tobin's bed. Afterward guilt filled him, and while Karen was in the shower, Richard called Tobin's cell phone. They talked for a few moments and Richard got the impression that Tobin was nervous. He wondered if he had interrupted him in his own affair. After they hung up he told Karen that they could never be together again. That he had made a mistake. They were back in bed three weeks later, when Tobin took a short trip to Russia to attend another book auction.

Karen had been sleeping next to him one night when the house phone rang. Tobin was in Los Angeles, again.

"Hello?" Richard looked at the clock trying to figure out the time. Four o'clock in the morning. Who in the hell would be calling at four in the morning.

"Richard?" The unfamiliar voice was thick, like whoever it was had been crying.

"Who is this?" Richard demanded. Next to him Karen groaned and rolled away from him.

"It's Mark." The man answered. "Mark Baxter." Baxter, Baxter. The name bounced around in his head until he remembered that this was one of Tobin's friends in the book trading business.

"Do you have any idea what time it is?"

"I'm sorry, it's....it's." The man chocked back a sob. "It's Tobin." Those two words drove all sleep and anger from Richard as he sat up straight in bed.

"Wh....what's happened." Fear tried to rob him of his voice.

"He's been stabbed." Mark's voice wavered as if he were

about to break down again. "You better get here, he's in surgery, and the Doctor's aren't sure if he is going to make it."

Richard had felt himself go numb as he mumbled a reply and hung the phone up. Within a few hours he and Karen were at the airport, waiting to fly west. Karen managed to whine the whole time, saying that if her brother was going to die, he would do so whether they went or not. It had taken every ounce of his control to keep from wrapping his hands around her throat and choke the life out of her. He didn't want to hear anything about Tobin dying.

Once at the hospital Richard refused to leave Tobin's bed side. He sat with him, holding his hand and trying to make deals with God to keep Tobin alive. He watched each rise and fall of the other man's chest fearing that each breath would be his last. It was then that Richard decided that he would do the right thing. He would tell Karen that it was over between them. He loved Tobin and he would not lose him.

She would threaten to tell her brother, but let her. Maybe he would confess to Tobin himself, and beg for his forgiveness. Just after twelve noon Tobin's eyes fluttered open and focused on Richard. In that moment he saw his future in those blood shot hazel eyes. Nothing would stand between them, Richard would fight for his life with Tobin.

At that moment the door opened and a man slid into the room. Richard looked up at the new comer and instantly felt his anger rise. Here was Nick, the man that Tobin had been seeing in L.A. Richard had seen pictures of him, but had never met the man face to face. He looked at Nicks long blond hair that looked like it had not been washed in days, his face was drawn and dark rings circled his blue green eyes. His clothes were wrinkled and unwashed.

This man was unworthy of Tobin. Not even fit to be in the same room. It was his fault Tobin lay in the hospital bed. Richard hated him. He didn't want to leave him alone in the room, but Tobin had begged, and so he slowly stood up, his eyes never leaving Nick's face. Slowly he turned and kissed Tobin's cheek. A look of pain flickered across the other man's eyes and Richard was glad. Good, let him see who Tobin belonged with.

Out in the hallway Richard ran into Karen as she returned from the hospital cafeteria, holding a cup of coffee. Without speaking he grabbed her arm and dragged her deeper into the hospital.

Ow!" She complained. "Stop. You're hurting me." He ignored her, only stopping when they came to a dark hallway where they could talk privately.

"What's with you?" Karen snatched her arm back when he let go, spilling most of her coffee. "We're done." Richard told her, his voice cold and hard. Karen blinked and then laughed huskily.

"Is that what you think?" She moved up to him and rubbed her body against him, and despite his convictions he felt his body respond to her. "You can't leave me." She whispered and slid her tongue up the side of his neck. Gasping, feeling betrayed by his body, he grabbed her roughly by the shoulders and pushed her against the wall.

"Oh yeah, baby." Karen purred and slid her hand down to cup his crotch. "You know how much I like it when you get rough." Richard growled in angry frustration and then he was on her, his mouth covering hers in a crushing kiss. He tried to fight it, but he couldn't win. There was no going back, no matter how much he loved Tobin. He loved Karen as well.

He may well have taken her right then and there in the hospital, with her brother in his bed weak and almost dead had Nick not stumbled upon them in their dark corner. Shame and anger warred with Richard as he pushed past the man in his rush to get away from Nick's accusing glare. What right did this prick have to judge him?

Richard had stayed at the hospital during the days that followed, holding Tobin's hand and whispering words of love to him. He spent his nights in the bed he and Karen shared in a nearby hotel. At first he expected to come in to Tobin's room to see Nick standing over him, telling him all that he had seen that first day, but as the days passed he began to feel that the other man had gone. He was thrilled when the police came to ask Tobin if he had seen Nick. Apparently the man had missed his court date and was now considered to be a fugitive.

Nick Miller never tried to contact Tobin again, which suited Richard just fine. Tobin on the other hand was devastated by Nick's betrayal. At first he sent out private investigators out to find him, swearing that something must have happened. But Richard sat with him and explained that this guy was nothing more than a drug addict, that he had used Tobin for his money and charity. That Tobin had never really meant anything to him.

Soon after returning to New York, Tobin sold his Auction Houses in Los Angeles, and refused to go back to the city again. This was agreeable to Richard, especially when Tobin was able to begin traveling again, it was mostly out of the country, giving Richard days, sometimes even weeks alone with Karen. The situation was perfect, he had Tobin's love, and Karen's body.

It was during this time that Richard began to worry just a little bit about Tobin's mental health. He started talking about seeing a little girl in various reflections around the penthouse, or on one of his many trips. He claimed that she was trying to communicate to him, like some ghost from beyond. He could not understand what she was trying to tell him. At first Richard thought that Tobin was just playing with him, but then one afternoon, he walked into the bedroom to find Tobin talking tensely to the mirror on the wall.

This incident completely freaked Richard out, and he forced Tobin to see a shrink. Shortly afterwards, Tobin claimed that he no longer saw the girl, though there were times that Richard would catch him looking at a mirror or reflective window with intense concentration, and the hair on the back his neck would stand on end.

Now all that came before that night when he and Karen had been caught seemed a distant dream. After dressing they went out to face Tobin on the balcony. Richard tried to make Tobin understand what he did, even though at that moment he didn't understand it himself. All he knew was that he would have given anything to be able to go back in time and start all over again.

"It's okay." Tobin spoke, and Richard's heart leaped in his chest. He was going to be forgiven; he was going to be given a second chance to make everything right. "I know what to do." Tobin continued to speak, and Richard realized that he was not even looking at him. Instead he was looking at his own reflection in the sliding glass door. He felt a shiver run through his body that had nothing to do with the freezing winter night air. He opened his mouth to say something, anything, and Tobin threw himself over the railing behind him.

For just a moment Richard stared in horror at the empty balcony in front of him. His mind refused to accept what had just happened. Beside him the glass door shattered and Richard knew that he was going mad as he watched the ghostly image of a young girl run to the spot where Tobin had stood only a few seconds before. The girl had long strawberry blond hair and was wearing some sort of leather shirt and pants. This was the girl that Tobin had claimed to see all those years ago. Suddenly the girl spun around and Richard flinched at the look of rage and hate in her bluish green eyes.

"I'll kill you!" She screamed and charged at him. He braced for impact when at the last moment the girl faded away like the phantasm she was. Shaking himself, Richard turned and pushed passed Karen and grabbed the phone. As he sobbed at the 911 operator, horrifying images rose up in his mind. He saw Tobin lying flat on his back in the middle of the street, his body curiously flattened. Bones had shattered, their splintered ends tearing through muscle and skin. Blood radiated out from the point of impact and if one would look down from the scene from above, he or she would be reminded of the old snowflakes they used to cut out of paper in grade school. The snowflake was red, but the pattern was still there.

It was at this final horrifying image that Richard began screaming and did not stop until paramedics showed up and sedated him. He woke up two days later in the hospital. The doctors told him that he had gone into shock and had spent a day and a half in a catatonic state. They were concerned about his mental state and suggested that he spend some time with their staff psychiatrist. They spoke in soft soothing tones, as if they were afraid that the very sound of their voices might shatter him.

In truth he kind of felt that way. As if he were a fragile piece of glass sitting on the edge of the counter, waiting for some force to push him over the edge to shatter on the hard floor. 'Kind of like the way Tobin must look' the thought rose up unbidden in his mind and he began to hyperventilate. He began to shake, and the doctors sedated him again. A little while later he woke up and found a young dark skinned man with short black hair and glasses sitting next to his bed. The man introduced himself as Dr. Malhood, and Richard found his deep African accent soothing.

Malhood was the psychiatrist and wanted to know if Richard was willing to talk to him. Sure. Why not? Nothing mattered anymore. There was only one truth in Richard's mind now. Tobin was dead. Nothing would ever be the same again. For just a moment he was back on the balcony again, watching Tobin going over the ledge, his hazel eyes locking with Richard's, cold, accusing.

Richard felt a scream rise up in his throat and bit it back. He knew that if he started again, he would never stop. After Malhood came the police. Richard had expected them, and answered their questions about that terrible night, getting through most of the questions without completely breaking down into hysterical sobs. He admitted the affair with Karen, unable to look the detectives in the eye. He finished with Tobin throwing himself off the balcony. For a few moments the detectives sat in silence after he finished his tale and looked at him.

Finally one of them, the one that had introduced himself as Lance Strickland, broke the awkward silence.

"Mr. Murry, are you sure that all of this happened the way you described?" Richard took a moment to look at the man. He had a hard face, with a small scar just under his right eye. He had a square jaw and a large over bite that caused him to lisp. His eyes were a dark green and seemed to bore into Richard's very soul. Richard did not like the man.

"Yes detective it all happened just as I said." The Detectives shared a look and Richard got the impression that there was something that they were holding back from him. Surely they weren't thinking that he had pushed Tobin off the balcony. Surely but then he realized that was what they had to be thinking. Of course it was. Richard felt his heart begin to race. These men thought he had murdered Tobin.

"You think I killed him." It wasn't a question.

"That's enough for today, Mr. Murry." The other Detective, a black man named Alexander, with kindly brown eyes and a bald head stood up. "We will be back in a couple of days and talk to you again."

"No, tell me now, do you think I killed him?" Richard pulled himself upright in his bed and glared at Strickland where the man with his accusing eyes still sat.

"Listen, the rest can wait." Alexander seemed to be talking to his partner, urging him to get up. "The doctors say...."

"Fuck the Doctors." Richard spat and realized that it felt good to be angry at someone other than himself. "You look like you have something to get off your chest Detective Strickland." He baited the big man, but it was Alexander who once again spoke.

"Well, you see Mr. Murry....we kind of have this.... situation."

"What are you talking about?" Richard was growing impatient. "Just fucking spit it out."

Finally Strickland couldn't contain himself any longer. He leaned forward, putting his face directly into Richard's. "You see there is a big problem with your little tale there buddy." The Detective's breath smelled of old cigarettes and stale coffee. "You see, we haven't been able to locate Mr. Master's body."

"What...?" Richard started to ask again, but Strickland cut him off, his voice rising in a shout.

"You say that your boyfriend, the very wealthy Tobin Masters threw himself off the balcony of his penthouse after discovering you banging his sister!" Strickland had hit his stride now, and he would not be denied his moment. Alexander moved away from them and slowly closed the door on several people who had stopped in the hallway at the sound of the shouting.

"The Doorman, Mr. Mattingly confirms that Mr. Masters arrived home at about nine thirty P.M. Mr. Masters was in good spirits when he entered the elevator that took him up to his Penthouse." Strickland emphasized the word *his*, as way of reminding Richard who had the money between the two of them.

"After that nobody has seen Mr. Masters. You claim that he committed suicide, but no body has been recovered. Explain that!" It was a challenge that Richard had no answer to.

"I don't understand, he jumped, I watched him." He began to cry. "I swear."

"Well, you swear, I guess we can just close this case now." Strickland sneered as he stood up, towering over Richard in his bed. "Maybe this will help jog your memory." The large Detective pulled out a digital recorder from his coat pocket and slid a beefy finger over the touch screen. Instantly a new voice filled the room.

"Nine one-one, what is your emergency?" The woman asked.

"He's...he's dead, oh my god he's dead!" Richard heard himself yelling.

"Sir, please calm down, tell me what happened." The operator was the picture of calm, her voice both soothing and controlling at the same time. "Who's dead?"

"Tobin...oh my God Tobin!"

"Sir, I need you to calm down, just tell me what happened." It was at this point that Richard began screaming hysterically, losing all composure. However, it wasn't his screams that had drawn the Detective's attention. Richard felt the blood drain from his face as he listened to himself screaming over and over.

"I killed him...oh God Tobin....I killed him."

The Detectives had not arrested Richard. Yet. This was not because they believed him innocent, oh no, they, Strickland in particular believed him to be guilty as hell. But, there was a spectacular lack of evidence that anything had happened to Tobin. The Detectives had yet to come up with a theory on how Karen and he could have killed Tobin so cleanly and then have gotten the body out of the building without being seen. Not to mention the lack of a body.

The Detectives visited him two days after getting out of the hospital, this time at the Penthouse. At this time they put forth the theory that Richard and Karen had bought off the Door Man and that all three of them would be arrested as soon as a body could be found. Richard had almost laughed at that. The thought that Mattingly would help Richard was hilarious. The Door Man refused to acknowledge his presence since returning to the building, allowing Richard to open the door for himself. Even the security guards had turned on him. The next day Robert Mattingly quit. After that Richard was left alone for a couple of days. Alone except for the ghosts that haunted his nights.

And then the Detectives had come back today, armed with new information. They had been to see Nathaniel Stone, Tobin's Lawyer. They had seen a copy of Tobin's Will and told Richard that he had left everything to Richard. Millions of dollars and property spread throughout the world. That, they said would be motive for murder. But that was not all they brought with them this time. They had interviewed Gwen, Tobin's aging secretary at the New York auction house. She had revealed, probably through tears and heart wrenching guilt that Karen had known that Tobin was coming home early that fateful night.

Apparently Tobin's sister had told her that she wanted to know when Tobin was coming home so that she could surprise him. Well, she had certainly done that. Karen had set up a last minute all nighter with Richard, ensuring that her brother would walk in on them. This final betrayal had threatened to break him for good. To know that Karen had used him to hurt Tobin in such a way was like a knife twisting in his gut. But even all this new information still didn't prove that he killed Tobin, only that Karen was a heartless bitch. Richard pointed this out to the Detectives as he stood up, effectively ending the interview.

"Why don't you just tell us where the body is?" Strickland

asked as they walked toward the elevator. The man was like a dog with a bone, gnawing and chewing until there was nothing left. "We'll tell the D.A. that you cooperated, see what deal we can get for you." The man smiled and Richard was reminded of a shark movie he watched on the Discovery Channel.

"I don't even know if Tobin is dead." Richard snapped. As each day passed and no body was found, Richard began to harbor the fantasy (hope) that Tobin was actually alive. That he had somehow faked his suicide and was making him suffer for his betrayal. But, would he let Richard go to jail for a murder that never happened? He hoped not.

"Oh, yeah?" Detective Alexander spoke while pretending to examine his perfectly manicured finger nails. "You seemed pretty sure the hospital." The man's voice was calm but he may as well have been shouting, as his words rang in Richard's head.

"I have had time think since then."

"Oh, I bet you have." Strickland turned to glare at him. "Time to come up with a better story, I'm sure."

Richard had had enough of the two Detectives. "Look, I have told you a thousand times, and I will tell you a thousand more if that what it takes to get through your thick skulls, Tobin threw himself from the balcony." He pointed to the glass door across the living room. "I did not conspire with Karen Masters to kill her brother. We did not push or throw him off the balcony! Furthermore, we did not shoot, stab, or poison him and put his body into the garbage disposal!" By this point Richard's face had turned beet red, and he was screaming.

"Now, if you two fucking idiots would stop trying to pin

something on me that never happened, and focus on doing your jobs, maybe you could go out and find my boyfriend!"

"Who the fuck you talkin' to like that?" Strickland stepped up to Richard. "You talkin' to me?" He grabbed Richard by the front of his shirt and physically slammed him into the closest wall so hard his teeth rattled. In a flash Alexander was at his partner's side, his hand on his arm.

"Let's go, Lance. Now." The other man's voice brought Strickland around and breathing heavily he let Richard go. "We are going to find a body, and when we do I am going to watch you fry, you little piece of shit." And then the doors to the elevator slid closed, cutting off anything else the Detective may have said. Screaming wordlessly, Richard snatched a vase off a small table and threw it at the elevator. It smashed against the golden doors, but did little to elevate Richard's frustrations.

That had been two hours ago. Now Richard sat in their room, Tobin's and his, remembering the past, reliving his mistakes. His eyes burned from all the tears he shed and his throat was raw from sobbing. Was it really possible that somewhere out there right now Tobin was alive? Hiding away from the pain that Richard had caused him?" If so, then couldn't there be a chance that he could make things right with him. That thought was the only thing that kept him sane.

He had learned many things this week. He saw his own weakness and accepted his blame in all of this. Most of all he learned (as corny as it sounded) that you really didn't know what you had until you lost it.

"Tobin." Richard whispered hoarsely. "I am so sorry, please come home." Slowly he closed his bloodshot eyes and rested his head on the back of the chair. Within minutes he drifted off to sleep.

Richard dreamed.

He found himself standing on the sidewalk just down the street from the building where he lived. The sky was a dark grey, bulging as if pregnant with precipitation. The air was cold and the wind that whipped down the deserted street cut through him like a knife made of ice. The street that had always been safe and happy, took on a sinister quality. The shadows that had always been there now seemed to be hungry mouths waiting for him to stumble into them.

The cars lined up along the curb were dirty derelicts, left behind like the remnants of some dead civilization. The trees that had been decorated with festive Christmas lights this morning were barren, like black skeletal hands reaching towards the dark sky.

Feeling his heart racing in his chest, Richard began walking back towards his building. "Hello?" He called out, his voice echoing along the glass and steel canyons of the city. Off in the distance something let out an inhuman scream, causing him to jump. His feet began to move a little faster, trying to reach the front door of his building and the safety that he always felt in the Penthouse. The safety he felt in Tobin's arms.

Tobin's name sounded like a bell inside of his head, and he suddenly knew that he had to get up to the penthouse, Tobin was there, waiting for him. "Tobin!" He yelled and took off running. In front of his building he skid to a stop, horrified by what he saw. The place he had called home for so long had changed along with the rest of the world. The building had once been a seventy story glass and concrete giant, beautiful, home.

Gone were the mirrored windows that used to reflect the sun, empty frames like the eyeless sockets of giant's skull. The front door where Tobin and Richard had so often passed through had been ripped from its hinges and lay on the ground. As he stared at the abomination, this defilation of his home, the air began to swirl with grey flakes, as if the wind had stirred up a pile of ash. It took him a moment to realize as the ash touched his skin and melted that he was looking at black snow.

Suddenly he heard a sound behind him, and his heart leaped up into his throat. Terrified Richard turned around to see someone kneeling in the street behind him.

"Hello?" He called out his voice trembling. The wind picked up, carrying to him the sound of someone weeping. Slowly Richard began moving toward the figure in the street. "H...hello?" He had trouble finding his voice. As he stepped off the curb and into the street itself, his foot slipped out from underneath him. The air rushed out of him as he crashed painfully onto his back.

He lay there a few moments looking up at the sky and the swirling flakes of black snow, before rolling to his side, and then back up to his feet. He winced in pain as he put pressure on his left foot. He must have twisted it when he fell. Looking down he searched for what he slipped on, and instantly wished he had not. The street seemed to be covered in blood.

Feeling his stomach twist he moved his eyes from the street to his body. His clothes and hands were covered in sticky reddish black blood. "Oh my God." He moaned and tried without success to wipe the blood off his hands, and managed to smear it over more of his clothes. In front of him the figure sobbed again, drawing his attention. Still smearing blood across his chest, Richard took another tentative step forward. Suddenly the snow parted and he got a good look at the man kneeling in the blood stained street.

"Tobin?" Richard whispered, recognizing the man's blue suit even though it was soaked through with blood.

"It's my blood on your hands, Richard." Tobin sobbed. "Why did you do this to me?" Richard lifted his hands and watched in horror as blood, thick and red began flowing from his palms.

"Oh...oh God no, Tobin I'm sorry." Richard dropped to his knees.

"Sorry? You're sorry?" Tobin laughed bitterly into the night. "You don't know sorry yet." "Please." Richard begged, holding out his blood stained hands. "Please forgive me."

"Forgive?" Tobin roared and the wind howled violently around them. Richard screamed when Tobin raised his face to look at him. Tobin's face was a rotting mass of maggots and putrid flesh. His lipless mouth showed bright white teeth that stood out against his blackened flesh, almost glowing in the night.

"Come here my love." The Tobin thing gurgled and grabbed Richard by the front of his shirt. "How about a kiss?" The creature pulled his head against it's face and Richard gagged as he felt its' cold black slug like tongue lick across his lips.

"Don't you want me anymore?" The thing sounded hurt and Richard struggled not to vomit.

"Tobin, please." Suddenly the thing that had been Tobin let go and Richard tumbled onto his back. He lay there gasping, tears running down his face. Tobin slowly rose up above Richard and looked down at him, his dead white eyes showing no emotion.

"You don't deserve to be forgiven." It snarled.

"Please." Richard sobbed. Tobin leaned over him and opened his mouth, vomiting a mass of worms and maggots onto his face. Richard's still bleeding hands slapped across his cheeks as the creatures squirmed into his eyes and burrowed into his skin. He writhed in agony as thousands of pincers began digging into his flesh all over his body, and he realized in horror that he was covered in maggots. Knowing that he was going to die he opened his mouth (allowing a tangle of maggots to crawl into to his throat) to Scream.

Richard threw himself out of the leather chair where he had fallen asleep. He landed on the floor, screaming his hands slapping at imaginary maggots. After a few moments he realized that he felt no pain, and that he was lying on the carpeted floor of his bedroom. He lay there for about a half an hour, his breath coming in ragged gasps, his heart beat slowly returning to normal.

As he lay there he became aware of the fact that he was drenched in cooling sweat, and his left ankle throbbed. Slowly he pulled himself to his feet and stumbled over to the edge of the king-sized bed. He sat there trying to shake the horror of the nightmare from his mind and body. Suddenly the phone on the table next to the bed rang and Richard screamed despite himself. With a trembling hand he leaned over and lifted the receiver terrified that he would hear Tobin's rot filled voice on the other end.

"Hello?'

"Jesus Christ, where the fuck have you been?' Karen's voice came from the receiver and Richard tensed. She was the last person he wanted to talk to.

"What do you want Karen?" He asked his voice dull and emotionless.

"I've been calling for the last two hours, where have you been?" She demanded again. Deep down inside of him Richard felt something snap. For far too long he had been answering to Karen Masters. He had been her pawn, the weapon she chose to use against her brother. It was time she answered to him.

"I talked to the police today you bitch!" Oh but didn't that feel good to finally get that out? Richard knew that he had a lot more to get out before this phone call was done.

"What?" Karen sounded shocked. "What did you just say to me?"

"They told me that you knew that Tobin was coming home early that night, did you?"

"Richard." Her voice had gone soft and husky. At one time that voice would have caused goose bumps to jump across his body and a chill to run up his spine. It was a voice that promised pleasure and so much more. All you had to do was surrender to it. Surrender to her. Now however, the sound of her voice reminded Richard of the maggots from his nightmare and he shuddered.

"I asked if you knew."

"Come on, Richard."

"I asked if you fucking knew your brother was coming home!" Richard roared into the phone cutting off what she was about to say.

"Yes." Karen sounded small and defeated on the other end of the phone.

Richard felt his eyes begin to fill up with tears again.

Hearing it from the Detectives had been one thing, but to have Karen admit it was almost too much for him to bear.

"Oh get over it Richard." Her voice went cold and hard and Richard realized that for the first time he was actually speaking to the real Karen Masters. The Karen that she kept hidden from the world. This was the voice of a woman who could easily take years to plan the pain she would inflict on her own brother, without a speck of remorse entering her icy heart. If she even had heart.

"Get over it?" He couldn't believe she had said it.

"Listen, everything is going in our favor. Tobin left everything to you in his Will." Excitement flowed into her voice. "If they don't find a body in seven years you can have Nathan declare him legally dead. Then we get everything."

We. Richard heard the word and recoiled from the phone as if she had reached through the receiver and slapped him.

"You knew about the Will?" He wanted to ask when she found out, but was afraid of the answer.

Karen laughed, the sound like nails being drug across a chalkboard in Richard's ear. "Of course I knew. Nathaniel tells me everything my brother does. So listen, he says that he will represent you and that you should stop talking to the cops." She sounded very pleased with herself. "See? I've taken care of everything."

Richard felt his stomach twist. She had taken care of everything. Of course she had. Most likely she had been fucking the Lawyer the whole time she had been doing him, maybe even before. Oh yes, she had been planning something for a very long time.

"Don't call me again." He said after a few moments of silence.

"You can't just cut me out of this Richard." She spoke with the conviction of a person who knew exactly what they were talking about. She believed that she had all the pieces laid out before her and that she was in control. While that may have been true three weeks ago, things had changed and it was time for her to see the light.

"Well, there is nothing to cut you out of Karen." Richard was surprised at how upbeat his voice suddenly sounded. "You see if I was interested in the money then things would be different, but I'm not. Sorry, you lose."

"What the hell are you talking about?" There was a slight edge of panic in her voice that Richard found he liked. A lot.

"After thinking about it for oh, thirty seconds, I have decided that I won't be declaring Tobin Dead. Ever."

"No!" Karen squealed, her carefully laid plans unravelling in front of her eyes. "Richard you have to, you don't understand."

"Oh you're right about that, I don't understand how you could do something so vile, but I do know that my part in all of this ends right now."

Wait!" She cried in desperation as he started to hang up. "I can still give you something that my brother never could."

"I don't think so."

"I'm pregnant." Karen blurted and Richard froze his mind reeling. How much more could he endure before he broke down for good? How much more could the world dump on him?

"Did you hear me Richard? I am pregnant with your baby."

Richard nodded his head dumbly as if she could see

him. "Yes, I heard you." This had to be another nightmare, more terrible than the last one. This was not the way things were supposed to be happening. Karen had to be lying. And then he suddenly understood, the baby was her backup plan. Her go to if all else failed. If she hadn't been able to get her brother to walk in on them, then she would have showed up pregnant and declared Richard the father.

"So you see, we'll need to get the money so that we can take care of our child." Again with the money. Richard just didn't understand it. He knew that Karen was wealthy, maybe not as wealthy as Tobin, but she certainly had enough money to keep her comfortable well past her senior years.

"I don't believe you." Richard said, though they both knew that he did.

"Well in about seven months you'll have no choice but to believe me, now about the Will...." Richard slammed the phone down in its cradle cutting her off. He didn't want to hear any more. He was done with Karen Masters.

The phone rang and he snatched it up in anger. "I told you not to fucking call me again!" he yelled.

"Hello Richard." Tobin's voice was soft with a hint of humor in it. Richard felt as if a cold bucket of water had been dumped over his head. He was suddenly afraid.

"Tobin? Oh thank God, where are you?"

"I have come home." Richard's eyes darted around the room finally stopping on the large mirror that hung on the wall above the bed. Standing behind him in the reflection was Tobin. He wore a long flowing black robe that was embroidered with gold and silver thread. Strange symbols had been stitched into the hem of the robe and as Richard watched they seemed to move and flow, constantly changing.

232

Around his neck Tobin wore a gold chain with a medallion hanging from it. On the medallion was a pentagram with a ram's skull in the center of the star. In his left ear was a gold hoop earring.

"Tobin." Richard gasped and turned around to find the room empty. Feeling goose bumps rising up on his arms he slowly turned back to the mirror, but Tobin was no longer there. And yet he could feel Tobin's presence in the air, like a suffocating blanket surrounding him.

"Tobin?" he called out again, feeling more than a little silly. There was no way that Tobin was there, and he did not believe in ghosts. Sighing he walked slowly across the room and into the master bathroom.

Tobin sat on the bench in front of the white Grand Piano that his father bought for him for a birthday in another life. He looked around the penthouse that he had called home his whole adult life, and marveled at how alien everything appeared now. He listened for a moment to the sound of the shower running in the other room and thought about Richard. He was in so much pain now that he was coming to understand his role in Karen's schemes, but was it enough? Was the little suffering that he felt now enough to cover the debt of rage that he felt toward him? It would be so easy to just let it all go. To return to his place in Hell and continue recording the War of Ascension.

After a moment of contemplation he lifted his black gloved hands up to the ivory keys of the piano and began playing a soft haunting melody. No, he decided, they had not paid nearly enough. If it had only been Karen that had betrayed him then maybe he could have simply killed her and moved on. But Richard had betrayed him as well.

Richard whom he had loved more than life itself. He had never done anything to deserve this. He had even allowed what could have been the true love of his life slip through his fingers all for the man who threw his love away.

To think that Tobin had carried the guilt of his feelings for Nick, while the whole time Richard was fucking his sister. This was almost too much to bear. He wanted to go into the bathroom right now and rip the man's penis from his body and shove it in his own mouth. But no, he would take his time with this. He had paid the price to come back to this world and he would savor every bit of his vengeance. They would pay for what they had done, and then they would pay some more.

How much would have turned out differently had Richard had not called the night of Nick's birthday? How much pain would have been avoided if he and Nick had been able to see that night through? Would Tobin be sitting here playing a song for Nicholas, allowing their love to fill him rather than hate? The possibilities were endless as were the ways to make them suffer. And suffer they would.

Tobin closed his eyes and swayed to sound of the music as he played. Even now Karen was moving across the city, coming here to meet her just reward. He could feel her panic and anger trying desperately to find some way to salvage her plans. Well, let her plan, Tobin had a few of his own. Soon all three of them would be together again and then Tobin would begin in earnest. Until then he had Richard all to himself. Without missing a note he reached out with his mind and found the other man in the shower. Slipping like a deadly snake into Richard's mind he listened to his thoughts until the time was just right, and then he struck again.

Richard allowed the hot water to run over his head, washing away the stale sweat that had cooled on his skin while talking to Karen. After the incident with the mirror, and his hallucination of Tobin he decided not to go back to sleep, though he felt exhausted. Instead he went into the bathroom, started the shower and stripped down. He hoped that the hot water would help sooth his feverish mind.

After only a few minutes he felt his tense muscles begin to loosen and he sighed happily. But this only lasted for a few seconds. Images of Tobin rose up in mind and he closed his eyes. He imagined that he could hear Tobin out in the front room playing the piano as he had done so many nights before as Richard had showered.

How many nights had they been together in this very shower, their hands and mouths exploring each other's bodies? Afterwards they would lay in bed, arms wrapped around each other whispering words of love in the darkness. Those had been the good moments, the moments of true happiness. It was during those times that thoughts of Karen had been furthest from his mind.

For just a moment Richard let his mind drift, imagining the feel of Tobin's hand sliding across his stomach, his hot breath against his neck. As he fantasized he felt himself become aroused and he slid his hand down toward his erection. Suddenly Richard's eyes snapped open as he realized that someone was with him. Startled he looked down to find two black gloves rubbing his stomach, just above his pubic hair.

Feeling the hair on the back of his neck stand up on end despite being wet, and he started to turn around. Instantly arms snaked around his body and squeezed him, cutting off his breath. And then the bottom of the bathtub disappeared. Richard had just enough time to scream once before sinking beneath the surface of a bottomless pool of sewage. Gagging he resurfaced, feces clinging to his face and hair.

"Help me!" He screamed as he struggled to cling to the side of the tub, but no one heard him and black gloved hands grabbed him by the back of his hair and pulled him back under. Suddenly Richard exploded from the tub, landing on the cold marble floor of the bathroom. Coughing and gasping he crawled over to the toilet just in time to vomit his lunch into the bowl. He dry heaved several minutes before being able to pull himself to his feet, using the sink to hold himself up.

"What's happening to me?" He sobbed to his reflection in the mirror on the wall. Without warning Tobin appeared behind him. Richard squealed as his head was shoved violently forward shattering the mirror. Grunting he stumbled back his hand going up to a small gash in his forehead. Sobbing in terror he spun around to find that he was alone. He was going completely mad, that was it. He struggled through the door and into the bedroom, heading for the phone.

"Richard!" Tobin's shout caused him to scream in terror. He whirled around, blood running down his face in rivulets. Richard's breath came out in short gasps as he watched various pictures on the walls come to life. Slowly Tobin turned to glare out at him from behind dozens of glass frames.

"You can't get away you son of a bitch." Tobin hissed at him with twelve mouths. And just when Richard thought that it couldn't get any worse he watched in horror as each of the pictures began pushing past their frames, and into the real world. Richard ran for the bedroom door with only one thought in his terror filled mind. He had to get out of the Penthouse. Now! Never mind the fact that he was naked and that it was ten below zero outside. The only thing that mattered was that he had to escape.

Karen walked through the lobby of the building where her brother used to live, ignoring the hard stares of the afternoon security guards. They didn't like her, but they were just the hired help, so they could just go and fuck themselves. She had more pressing things on her mind. She had worked hard to destroy her brother's happiness and she wasn't about to allow his faggot boyfriend to take any of her reward away from her.

She slipped her key into the plate on the wall and twisted it hard to the right. She was this close to getting everything. When she set Tobin up to find her and Richard together she had only wanted to show him that she had taken what he thought was his, the way he had taken their parents money away from her. But then he had gone and threw himself off the balcony. She couldn't have asked for anything better. With Tobin dead Richard would inherit everything, and through him Karen would have it all.

But then Richard had started to act all funny, and then

the phone call this afternoon. Who did he think he was? Did he think that she was going to let him get away from her? No, he was hers, to do with as she pleased, until she was done with him that was. She would bring him back to heel and everything would be alright. She might even keep the baby growing in her belly instead of going to her abortion appointment tomorrow. She didn't like the idea, but if the kid was the only way to make Richard cooperate, then so be it.

"Richard?" She called out as soon as she stepped off the elevator, her breath steaming in the frigid air of the penthouse. Jesus, it was colder in here than it was outside. Shivering Karen walked into the front room to see frost covering all the furniture. What the fuck?

"Richard?" She called again. Somewhere in the back of the Penthouse someone screamed, an agonized scream of terror and she stopped. Suddenly the main bedroom door smashed open and a naked Richard fell half in half out of the room. Karen watched as the man crawled across the floor, sobbing.

"Please Tobin!" The man on the floor screamed back at the empty doorway. Karen could see blood running down the side of his head. "Please forgive me."

"Richard!" Karen grabbed the naked man by the shoulders and he screamed again. "Richard, get ahold of yourself." She shook him and some of the wild fear left the man's eyes.

"Karen?" He whispered her name. There was a look in his eyes that she didn't like, a look that boarded on insanity. Blood flowed from a cut on his forehead, and there were pieces of mirrored glass in his hair. "Oh my God." He wrapped his arms around her legs and began to sob again.

"What's wrong with you?" She snapped trying to pull free of his grip.

"He's here." Richard looked all around the room, eyes wide.

"Who's here, what are you talking about?"

"Tobin." That single name, whispered with such fear sent a fresh chill through her body.

"That's impossible, we both saw him jump." She said, even as her eyes searched the freezing Penthouse. "There was no way he could survive such a fall." She tried to push him away from her again. The man was weak and he disgusted her. If it hadn't been for her brother she would have never gave him a second look. But he had been Tobin's lover and she had long ago decided that she would take whatever she could from her brother.

"He didn't survive." Richard crawled up her body smearing blood on her tan coat. "He's dead and now he's come back for me." Karen rolled her eyes and looked up at the ceiling trying to contain her anger. How much would she have to endure before getting what she deserved? There were no bounds to the hatred she had always felt for her brother. All their lives Tobin had been the 'special' one to their family. Their father had always doted on him like he had been an only child. Even their Grandfather treated him better than any of the other Grandchildren.

How it galled her to think that her father hadn't even listened to her when she came home from school and told him that she wanted to get into books the same way that he had. No, that honor had been given to little Tobin. He had ignored her and Brandon, his two oldest children, to groom his 'perfect' son He had even ignored them in death, leaving her and Brandon small trust funds of fifteen million dollars, while Tobin got everything else. Everything!

Well, he had nothing now. She had taken his precious love away from him, and then he had killed himself. Oh, how thrilled she had been that night when he saw her standing there naked next to his lover. The look of twisted pain his eyes had been like sweet nectar on her tongue. And the scene out on the balcony, when Richard had been forced to admit that they had been together for six of the seven years that he had been living with Tobin.

Karen had watched Tobin's tears freeze on his face. How she had wanted to taste those tears. She wondered if they would taste salty just as any other tear, or would they have an exotic flavor due to the pain that he was suffering. And then Tobin threw himself from the balcony. In the instant that his body vanished over the balcony railing she was already making plans on how to get the money to where it belonged. With her. She spent the rest of the night trying to play the horrified sister, when all she had wanted to do was laugh and jump up and down.

After fucking Nathan Stone's brains out she found out that Tobin had changed his will after being stabbed in Los Angeles. Instead of leaving the money to his brother and sister he instead left it all to his weak lover. At first this had pissed her off, but then a new plan began forming in her mind. After all, by that time Richard already belonged to her, she had stolen him fair and square. As long as she kept Richard under her control, then she would control the money.

She had not expected the man to have a mental break down. She needed to put an end to this idea that Tobin was haunting him immediately.

"Richard." She grabbed the man's face and forced him to look at her. "Can you hear me?"

"Yes." He shivered.

"Good, now you listen to me, Tobin is dead." She squeezed his face when he tried to look away from her. "In a couple of days they will find his body, you'll see." She spoke slowly, her eyes never leaving his.

"But...." He started, but she cut him off.

"There are no ghosts, Tobin is gone and nothing can bring him back." Richard searched her eyes before finally nodding his head. "Good, now let's get you cleaned up." She turned him back toward the bedroom. That was when she lost all control of him. Richard screamed and fell bonelessly to the floor, sobbing incoherently. Karen couldn't believe what she was seeing. Standing in the doorway to the bedroom was her brother.

For one shocked moment Karen felt her heart stop. This was not possible, it had to be trick. And then it occurred to her that perhaps it had been she and Richard who had been set up. Could Tobin have found out about the affair and then set into motion an elaborate scheme to fake his own death. To make her think that she had finally won, only to snatch victory away from her at the last second? No, she would not allow this to happen, not when she was so close.

"Hello Karen." Tobin's voice was soft and pleasant as if he were asking her out to see a movie, but behind it there was a hint of anger and something else.

"Yeah, whatever you son of a bitch." She spat. "Nice contacts." The black eyes were a nice touch, no wonder Richard was a basket case. All alone in the penthouse, eaten up with guilt, her brother playing ghost to mind fuck him.

Perhaps he had been hoping that Richard would snap and kill himself. Not a bad plan, really. She kind of wished she would have thought of it.

"Oh, you like these?" Tobin slid out of the bedroom like a coiled snake, walking around Karen. "These are the real deal sweet heart. I hear congratulations are in order." She moved to keep him in her sights at all times. So he knew about the baby too. Well, he was just full of surprises. She spared a glance at the naked man on the floor and wondered for a moment if the two of them hadn't been in this together, after all Richard hadn't threatened to tell Tobin about the affair back in L.A.? But one look at the cowering, broken man lying on the floor told her that he truly believed that Tobin was some sort of avenging spirit come back to get him.

Sighing she turned back to her brother and found that he had crossed half the distance between them while she had been distracted. Quickly she reached into her jacket and drew out a small snub nosed pistol. "Not another step Tobin or I will kill you." Tobin spread his arms wide and smiled pleasantly at her.

"Why Karen, you seem a bit upset, was it something I said?" He laughed. "You do know that if you shoot me, you will lose any chance of getting my money, right?" His money? Rage filled Karen. The money was hers and hers alone. What had Tobin ever done except be born? What gave him the right to claim anything that should have been given to her? Without a word she fired three shots into her little brother's chest.

The gun shots were deafening in the apartment, and the smell of cordite filled the frosty air. Beside her on the floor Richard wailed, and in front of her Tobin slowly lowered his arms and began walking toward her. Her own fear beginning to build Karen fired again, and then again as Tobin stopped directly in front of her. Lazily he reached up and wrenched the gun from her numb hands.

"Now look at what you have done." He sounded almost petulant as he looked at the hole in his chest. "I am going to have to get a new robe when we get home." He sighed and tossed the gun across the room.

"A vest?" Karen couldn't believe it, did he plan for everything? "You have a bullet proof vest on."

Tobin shook his head. "Sorry to disappoint." He laughed but the sound carried no humor in it. Karen watched as he pulled the robe open to expose his pale chest, and she could see three perfect holes in his body.

You see, a lot has changed since I fell from the balcony." Karen flinched as smoke began to rise out of the holes in her brother's skin, followed by thick greyish red liquid. It took several moments for her to figure out what was happening. Tobin was melting the bullets inside of his body and purging them through his wounds. This time it was her turn to scream as she tried to bolt past her brother toward the front door.

Tobin's hand darted out and caught her by the wrist, spinning her back into his arms. Karen stood rigid in terror her back against Tobin's chest. She could feel heat rising off him and moaned. Slowly her brother's hands slid down her body, caressing her breasts tenderly as he made his way down to her stomach.

"Ohhhhh." His breath whispered right next to her ear like a lovers' kiss. "Good news Richard, the baby really is yours." Karen began to cry.

"Shhhh." Tobin turned her gently to face him and

stroked her hair. "No. Don't cry Karen, it's going to be okay. I would like you to meet a friend of mine." Karen became aware of a shape rising up behind Tobin. The creature towered over the two humans, and seemed to be made of bone and fire.

"Karen, this is Ted." Tobin turned to look at the winged monstrosity. "Ted was the first thing I met when I got to Hell, isn't that right Ted." The thing that Tobin called 'Ted' stared in silence at Karen with its glowing eye sockets. "Well, Ted's not much into conversation, but he will see that you get settled in." Tobin stepped away, and Ted moved forward. Karen screamed in terror as the thing reached for her, its flaming claws wrapping around her shoulders.

"Karen." Ted gurgled and her screams rose in pitch and intensity.

"See?" Tobin smiled crazily. "I knew the two of you would hit it off." Karen was lifted off her feet and she struggled uselessly against the creature as they both began to sink into the solid floor. Within moments Karen's screams became muffled and then ceased all together.

After a moment Tobin turned to regard Richard lying on the ground. "Well, it looks like it's just you and me now lover."

"Please please don't kill me Tobin." He crawled, naked across the floor and kissed the tip of Tobin's black boot.

"Kill you?" Tobin asked as if the very thought was ridiculous. "Richard, I would never kill you." Slowly the man raised his head, his blood shot eyes hopeful.

"Come on." Tobin gently helped him up on trembling

legs. Slowly Tobin pulled him into an embrace. Richard sighed as he slid his arms around Tobin, his body conforming to his.

"I won't kill you." Tobin whispered in his ear. "But, I am sure someone in Hell will do that for me." With those words Tobin pushed Richard away from him and watched as he fell through the gate that had opened behind him. Richard was gone from Earth. Randomly flung into the world of Hell. Tobin hoped that he suffered forever.

Slowly he turned to regard the penthouse, taking one last look. Now that he was alone he could let his real feelings show. A child. Karen was pregnant with Richards's baby. The one thing that he could never give to the man he loved. What was he going to do with Karen now? But then, what was the rush? After all he had an eternity to decide, didn't he?

Slowly he raised his hand and made a small, almost dismissive gesture and a line of fire struck the Baby Grand Piano, causing it to burst into flames. He watched as the fire spread through the room, burning away his past. Sighing one last time Tobin Masters, Observer to the Throne of Darkness, turned away from the world of his birth and returned to the one that had become his home.

Detectives Strickland and Alexander stood in the burned out ruin that had been the Masters Penthouse, surveying the damage. It was unrecognizable as the place where they had questioned Richard Murry earlier in the day. Nothing had escaped the blaze, no room was spared. Strickland figured that Masters, if he were still alive, had lost millions.

This had been the second fire that the Detectives had

been to tonight that was connected to the Masters case. The first one had been a small house fire in the City proper. This fire had been localized to a bed, and the man who had been sleeping in it at the time. Nathaniel Stone, Attorney at Law had burned down to his bones, the words 'I am the Observer, everything you do I see, to all those who betray me I am judge, jury, executioner. The sentence is fire." No one could explain what the cryptic message meant. While they had been pondering the words the call had come in that the Masters penthouse was also on fire.

They arrived just after the fire had been put out and stayed as arson investigators searched through the ruins. No bodies had been found, though a small hand gun had been recovered under the remains of the couch. The gun was on its' way to forensics.

"So what do you think?" Alexander moved up next to him.

"Don't know." Strickland shook his head in frustration. Nothing in this case seemed to make any sense. Why would Murry go and kill off the Lawyer right after the Detectives got through talking to him. He had to know they would suspect him immediately. Then you added the fact that Karen Masters seemed to have gone missing as well. Did they go together, or had Murry decided to cut his losses, kill the Lawyer and the girl, before running?

Strickland shrugged before walking off toward the balcony where this case began.

Alexander watched his partner walk away and felt sorry for him. Under his gruff exterior Lance Strickland was a good cop, and an even better man. He wished that he could tell him more about what was happening here, but he knew that he could not. Slowly he pulled his cell phone out of inner jacket pocket. He looked around to make sure no one was close by before dialing a number from memory.

"Articulate Dry Cleaning Service, how may I help you?" A cheerful male voice answered. "Watchtower." Alexander answered.

"Please hold." There were several clicks before a strong female voice picked up.

"Report."

"It's just as we feared, Tobin Masters has been chosen as The Observer." Alexander ran his free hand over his bald head. "He returned to Earth and seems to have taken his ex-lover and sister. He also killed a Lawyer named Nathaniel Stone." There was short pause as the woman on the other end copied the names down for further research.

"The Council has been convened and you are to come before them to confirm your report." Alexander could feel his heart racing in his chest. He couldn't believe that it was finally happening.

"I understand." He said. "Is there anything further?"

"You are to have no contact with any of the six families."

"But I am on this case."

"The case will be transferred as soon as you return to your Precinct." The women's clipped voice held no room for argument. "You will await the call from the Council."

"I understand." Alexander hated being pulled off the case, but he understood the concern. The council couldn't risk alerting the Families that they were aware of what was happening. The Shadow War they had been fighting for centuries may finally be coming out into the light, and the fate of the entire world hung in the balance. "God be with you Guardian." The woman said.

"And He with you Keeper." With that the connection was severed. Alexander took a deep breath and put his phone away. He had known that this case was something important from the moment he heard the name Masters, but he never guessed that it would lead to all of this. But he was a soldier in God's Army and he would face whatever came with His light at his side.

No matter what the Throne of Darkness threw at them, they would be ready.

CHAPTER 10

Taken from the personal journal of Tobin Masters, Observer to the Throne of Darkness.

It began today.

Malice.

There was no sun that rose or set in Hell. Instead the sky was always covered with a roiling red storm that flashed black lightning, like a strobe light. It was the same over every continent, over every city. The only way to tell the difference between night and day was by internal clocks and by the way the storm either lightened (day) are darkened (night).

Kretia, a simple demonic peasant had been getting up at the first sign of 'dawn' her whole life. Her family had never been prominent in any way and their standing in Demonic Society, was just above humans. She owned no slaves and therefore had to do the unthinkable (at least to those with high standing) and work her small farm outside the city of Malign, herself.

Yes, she was poor, but she knew that one day everything would change for her. One day she would be in a position to have revenge on all the stuck up Demon Lords and Ladies who crossed to the other side of the street when they saw her coming their way. Oh, how she would make them all suffer.

Kretia thought about these things as she pulled herself out of her small bed as the storm above just showed hints of lightening. Her arms and back ached from harvesting Blood Pods the day before. Blood Pods were a type of fruit that grew within the rotting corpses of humanoids or animals. Kretia had gathered a reputation as a body collector over the years, as she was known to frequent the worst parts of the city early in the mornings. Here she could find victims of murder from the night before and collect them for her farm. As a result of the bodies Kretia's entire farm smelled of rotting meat, as she did herself.

Maybe today was the day. Something in the air told of great things to come. Perhaps today the Great Lord of the City, a Demon Lord named Vercrine, would come to her again. He had passed by her farm several years ago while she stood out in her fields planting Blood Pod seeds in half buried corpses. She had looked up to find the Lord and several of his Honor Guard, the Bone Riders, sitting on his huge skeletal mount looking at her. Vercrine was the perfect specimen of demon masculinity, with light green skin and long pink face tentacles. His muscular body covered in razor sharpened bone spurs.

As they looked at each other across the fields of the dead, Kretia felt their souls connect and knew that her Lord felt it to. If it hadn't been for his Guard she knew he would have come to her right then, perhaps taking her right there on the ground of her farm. He sat there for almost five minutes, sharing her elation at finding one another, before turning his mount around and riding off towards the city.

Many nights after that day Kretia lay alone in her bed, her hand slid down between her legs imagining the feel of his bone spurs slashing into her as he thrust inside of her. She knew that on these special nights he was up in Castle in the city, pleasuring himself, sending his thoughts out to her. She dreamed of the day when he would stop dreaming and come and get her. He would take her back to that great Castle, and make her his wife. Of course his old wife would have to die, but that was okay.

She would bathe in dark perfumes, washing the smell of rot and dirt from her body. Then those who had snubbed her would kneel and beg for her attention. And would she give it to them? Maybe. After they crawled on the floor and cried out for her forgiveness. Perhaps she would make them work on her old farm, and then they would know what it felt like to be shunned.

Yes, there was just something in the air today, Kretia decided as she ran a clawed hand across her mottled black face tentacles (they were rotting away from a disease she contracted from the corpses she harvested). Slowly, her back screaming in agony she limped across the room and pushed open the rickety wooden shutter that covered the only window in the small cottage. She looked out across the fetid, stinking, insect fields toward the main road, hoping to see her Lord waiting for her.

Lord Vercrine was nowhere to be seen though and her heart fell just a little. Maybe he would come later, the day had just started after all. She started to turn away from the window when she noticed something strange. The sky had suddenly become darker again, as instead of it being dawn, it was evening all of the sudden. How was that possible?

She raised her eyes to look at the ever present storm. At that moment, a boulder the size of an Earth elephant slammed into her window, shattering wood and stone. In an instant Kretia was smashed against the rock, and she felt bones in her face, arms and chest splinter as she was carried across the room and out through the back wall. Outside, the boulder bounced once before depositing her shattered body onto a pile of corpses that had been prepared for today's planting. Her lifeless eyes stared up at Set's dread Ships as they glided over her farm, hurling boulders at the city of Malign.

Lord Black, true vampiric son of the Necromantic Lord Set stood at the bow of the largest of his father's Dread Ships, watching death rain down on the city of Malign. He stood eight feet tall, with a well-muscled fur covered body, under a suit of black lacquered armor that looked like old Samurai armor from Earth. His head was shaped like a demonic jackal, with black fur and glowing red eyes.

Lord Black could feel the thrill of war coursing through his veins, as he watched several large buildings crumble under his assault. His father was down below-deck sequestered away with his prized stone. The Vampire Lord was more than content, for now at least, to allow his son to guide his armies. Of course the Lord Set also knew that there was bad blood between Black and the Lord of the city, Vercrine. As a matter of fact, there was only one person he hated more than Vercrine, and that was his half-brother Raven.

Black's hatred of Vercrine had started about thirty years ago, when the vampire had traveled to Malign to meet with the Lord on his father's behalf. Set had heard of an artifact that Vercrine had is his possession, sent his son to negotiate for it. This artifact was something called a Conipic Jar, used by ancient humans in a kingdom called Egypt to store the organs of their revered dead. Black had not seen the importance of the jar, but his father insisted that it had necromantic value. However, his son suspected that it had more to do with his father's trying to re-live the days when he had been on Earth, worshiped as a God.

No matter what he thought, Set was his Lord and Master, so Black had traveled to this vile little city to make an offer for the jar. It was during this time that he had met Vercrine's daughter. She was a stunning demoness, with long thick black hair and soft green skin. Her eyes were pure color of lavender that matched the tips of her facial tentacles. Her body was slender with the swell of her firm breasts rising from her chest in perfect symmetrical mounds. Black had heard stories of this girl's beauty, but they did not do her justice as she sat across from him, looking at him coyly through thick black lashes. He had also heard of the things she did in her bed for her own father, and he knew if they were true, he had to have her for himself.

It had taken a week, but Black finally seduced the young woman and found that every story ever told could not do her justice. Unfortunately as they lay in his bed, her bone spurs slashing his body to ribbons, he lost control of himself and he had bitten her. Upon seeing his daughter (and lover) marked, Vercrine had flown into a rage, demanding that Black explain himself, decreeing the event an attack on his house.

The Lord refused to believe that his daughter had

gone to Blacks' bed willingly, even after she herself readily admitted that she herself had sought him out, and would do so again that very night. Enraged beyond thought, Vercrine slit his daughter's throat, saying that Black had corrupted her through necromantic magic. He smashed the Conipic jar, and banished the vampire from his city.

Black left, but not before paying a huge amount of soul stones to a castle guardsman, who delivered the girl's body to him. Later, after Set's anger at losing the Jar faded, Black re-animated her and kept the zombie in his own private quarters as his own personal sex toy. Even after all these years, he enjoyed the caress of her mummified hands in the dark of night. Her father had sought to take her away from him, and he would pay for that hubris today.

"Lord Black." A vampire servant stepped up to him and bowed low. "The final assault on the city has begun." Black watched as fires bloomed across Malign and his lips drew back in a snarling grin.

"Drop the ground forces."

At his command, crew members began dropping rough sacks sewn together from mortal flesh. These sacks rained down over the city, doing absolutely no damage.

On the ground two demonic children, their blue facial tentacles twitching with fear, stopped to look at a strange burlap sack that had fallen from the sky with curiosity. Slowly, they approached the bag, wondering what it could possibly mean. At that moment the bones that had been placed within the bag burst free forming an animated skeleton under the control of the necromancers floating on the Dread Ships above. In an instant, before the two doomed boys could react, the skeleton swung on them with the long sword that it carried. Without a sound, two heads dropped to the street at the skeleton's feet. All over the city the demons fled through the streets only to be cut down by undead warriors. If this was not bad enough, Necromancers would then come in right behind their warriors and raise the recently killed as zombies. They would supplement the armies of the Lord of the Dead.

Within twelve hours the once proud city of Malign had been reduced to rubble and the Dread Ships moved on toward their next target. Still standing on the lead Dread Ship. Lord Black turned away from the burning city to look at Vercrine who had, on his order, been taken alive. The once High Overlord of the city lay cowering on the deck, a golden chain around his bleeding neck. Black had already fed off the man once and looked forward to centuries of doing so. Beside him Vercrine began to sob and rock back and forth.

"Ahhhh." Black licked the blood that dripped from his muzzle. "Music to my ears."

Wrath.

While day was just beginning on Malice, night had fallen on the kingdom of Skrell on the continent of Wrath. Skrell was a medium sized kingdom ruled by large furred humanoids called Skrellions. These creatures had lived on this corner of Wrath since the first recorded War of Ascension. They were a war like race that craved conflict at all times. The citizens of Krellos, a medium sized city on the border of Deceiver's jungle kingdom were no exception. For generations the warriors of Krellos had struck into the jungle kingdom, trying to push into the heart of their enemies' kingdom and kill the Lord of Deceit. Each time they had been beaten back and their Battle City attacked, though to their credit Krellos had never fallen into the hands of the hated serpents.

Krellos was a shining jewel of combat mastery. First the city was surrounded by a large fifty-foot wall, with a burning moat circling five feet away. The fire served two purposes. The first being the obvious deterrent of anyone foolish enough in trying to climb the walls. The second, was that the fire illuminated the fifty yard circle that had been stripped of all vegetation around the city. No one could possibly hope to sneak up to the walls of Krellos.

In this way the guards, could use their bone bows to rain death on anyone trying to attack the city. However, even if an invading force were able to get through the gates an event that had not happened since the city had been founded, they would quickly discover that their fight had only just begun. Like all cities in the Skrellions empire, every person, man, woman, and child, were ready to fight to the death. It was not uncommon to find toddlers with small bone daggers in their tiny hands, fighting during a siege.

As was befitting a great Battle City, Krellos was prepared for war, and yet today the streets were filled with more tension than usual. Skrole, the War Master of the city had recently captured a runaway slave from Lord Deceiver's kingdom. Usually these slaves were put to death immediately, but this young woman carried with her valuable information. Lord Deceiver had been named a Stone Bearer by the Throne of Darkness. Even now the Reptile Lord had one of the Stones of power in his possession. Upon hearing this he declared that the human would be left alive, chained to his personal Throne.

He then immediately ordered the entire city to prepare for battle. For generations, the Battle City and the reptiles to the west had fought small battles for small prizes. But all of that had now changed, indeed the stakes were immeasurable. Skrole would not send a simple raiding party against his hated enemy this time, tonight he would literally spill the entire city out into the jungle kingdom.

Deceiver would fall before the terrible might of Krellos and more importantly Skrole would become a Stone Bearer. Sitting upon his Throne, the War Master dreamed of his rise to the Throne of Darkness. In his mind, the contest had already been won. Who better to rule Hell after all? This was the reason that the Throne had chosen Deceiver as a Stone Bearer. So that Skrole could slaughter the Serpent King and show all those who would defy the greatest War Master in the entire world.

While Skrole sat upon his Throne and dreamed of war and glory the slave woman that had given him the glorious information sat on the floor, watching him. She was pale and thin, with long stringy brown hair. She wore rags and a large metal collar that kept her chained to Krellos's Throne. Slowly this woman stood and looked around the room. They were alone, which was not surprising since Skrole considered himself the greatest warrior alive. What would someone like that need with guards to protect him?

"Dreaming of the entire world bowing to you, Skrole?" The human spoke her voice holding a hint of humor to it. Upon the Throne Skrole blinked and looked down at the woman. Something he saw in her eyes disturbed the War Master. When she had been first brought to him she had been terrified, begging for her life. She had been weak and pitiful, groveling on the floor as a good human should. However, what he saw now was a defiance that bordered on contempt in her manner.

"How dare you speak my name, Bitch!" Skrole roared at her. Perhaps he was going to kill this insolent soft fleshed creature after all. "Remember that you live by my sufferance alone." At this the woman laughed, actually laughed as she walked toward the Throne and her death. For surely he would kill her, breaking her spine with bare hands.

"Oh Skrole," The slave almost sounded sad "You were always so full of yourself." The woman stopped at the foot of the Throne and raised her eyes up to him. "I warned you that your pride would one day be the end of you didn't I?"

Skrole had actually raised out of his seat and taken three steps toward the human, when she began to change. Her body began to elongate and fill out, growing muscles where before there had been none. Her skin rippled, as if it were made of water and began to change color and texture. The stringy hair writhed around her head like the living serpents that made up a medusa's hair, solidifying into thick tendrils, before melding into her skull, leaving her bald. Bones popped and snapped as she grew larger before his very eyes. Her face began to elongate as metal bands and a gauntlet tore through the skin of her right arm. Within seconds what had been a simple, weak human female, was now Lord Deceiver. Skrole stood staring at his nemesis in shock and confusion. This was not possible, he could not have brought his most hated enemy to the very heart of the great Battle City of Krellos. All without a single fight.

"You look surprised Skrole." Deceiver laughed and glared at the War Master through his orange reptilian eyes. "Of course, the dead usually do just before they fall at my feet." These words galvanized the other demon into action.

Skrole began to turn, his right hand reaching for the huge Battle Sword that he left sitting next to the Throne. In a blinding flash, Deceiver's gauntlet covered hand slammed through his chest and ripped his still beating heart free. For just a moment the War Master looked at the huge hole in his chest and then slipped down to his knees before finally falling on his face. Deceiver crushed the heart, enjoying the feeling of warm fluids flowing through the plates of his armored fingers.

Slowly he turned, lowered his large snout towards the stone floor, and vomited a large steaming pile of snakes onto the ground. He repeated this twice more before stopping. By the time the third string of writhing vomit had left his mouth, the first group of snakes had grown into forty serpent warriors. Feeling a great peace fall over himself, Deceiver walked across the body of the city's one time great ruler and found the seat that Skrole had once occupied and sat down to watch his warriors grow. Soon his second in command, a large humanoid snake named Sssithak bowed before him.

"We are ready, my Lord." He hissed.

"Then let the destruction begin," Deceiver commanded, his metal hand absently squeezing cooling blood from the heart he still clutched.

The city of Krellos soon fell burning from the attack that came from within its very heart, instead of from without. Before the storm above began to light with the coming of another dawn, the city was alight with fires that burned out of control with no one to stop them. Not a single citizen-man-woman, or child had been spared the slaughter. Deceiver, who had lost only a handful of men turned to the west and the next city that lay within the kingdom of Skrell. He would not be satisfied until the kingdom had been scoured clean of non-reptilian life.

Sheol.

Sentinel was a walled city built on the ridge of a great crater that had once held the capital city of a great kingdom which had ruled over half of the continent of Sheol. It was said that this kingdom could match the Dark City itself, in grandeur and decadence. But some terrible madness began inflicting the ruling Demon Lord's bloodline, driving them to slaughter each other. Ordinarily, such whole sale slaughter would have been considered normal, after all this was Hell. However, there was nothing to gain by the family turning on itself and in the end the kingdom fell apart and was separated into nine different kingdoms. The last ruling family member used dark and terrible magic to claim the area where the capital city had once stood.

The city sank into darkness, as if the ground itself was swallowing it into the depths of a great crater. Afterwards a black fog, like a hideous veil, slid across the top of the crater cutting off the city from the rest of the world forever. The crater was said to be a place of madness and horror, that could chill even the greatest Demon Lord's blood. Indeed, any who were brave enough could go to the lip of the great crater and listen to the wails and screams of torment that drifted out of the ever roiling black fog. Then if this was not enough perhaps they would watch the faces that raised up out of the darkness. Formed of nothing more than black mist these faces twitched between hatred and agony as they glared out knowingly at the watchers.

This was the home and prison of the creature called the Nameless One. It was said that she was forever trapped within the twisted mockery of the city, from which her family had once ruled. Of course this theory had never been tested fully, since no one had ever seen the Nameless One. Those brave or foolish enough to enter the black fog had never returned. But then, if you knew who you were looking for, you might just catch a glimpse of a familiar face writhing in the black fog.

Sentinel had originally been built by the first Demon Lords to break the Old Kingdom apart. Its purpose had been to keep an eye on the crater as a first warning to an impending attack. Back then several war parties or bands had gone into the consuming blackness in the hopes that they would kill the final ruler of the Old Kingdom, and therefore eliminate the fear of any reprisal. Of course, these war bands were never heard from again. After a thousand years of silence, the scholars and Throne Bound sorcerers put forth the theory that the madness had somehow locked the Nameless One in the crater and that the newly formed kingdoms had nothing more to fear from her.

"Then what to do with the city of sentinel" the Lords wondered. The Master of the city, a female with bony spikes protruding from her face and arms came up with the most novel of ideas. Sentinel would be turned into a prison city. But not just any prison, Sentinel would be the most feared prison in the entire world. For it would be a way station for its inmates, before they traveled on to their ultimate destination. The black crater and the madness beyond. It was a novel concept amongst creatures that simply murdered their enemies. Here was a chance to not only ensure death, but also a way to torture them before they died. There was nothing like the anticipation of unknown torture. A way for the Demon Lords to savor the defeat of their enemies. Soon, prisoners came flowing into the city gates from all over Hell, and with them soul stones to pay for their confinement.

These soul stones were divided up amongst the nine kingdoms and each kingdom in turn paid for the upkeep of Sentinel. Many a Demon Lord praised that first Warden and her brilliant ideas. Of course during her tenure as Warden at Sentinel she managed to anger a powerful Demon Lord, who paid well to see her dropped from the large wooden platform that had been built over the crater, like some giant version of a walking plank from a pirate ship.

The current Warden, a toad-like demon, with gray flesh hanging from his face thought about these things as he moved through the metal prison city. Like all the guards, he wore a thick chainmail suit which protected him from the inevitable Groach infestation that ran rampant through the prison population. This, of course, was actually promoted since it only added to the degradation of the prisoners. Often when a new prisoner would arrive, he or she would be placed in a specific cell with a known groach nest. Indeed some prisoners had found out that if they had a sufficiently large groach nest that they could be kept from the black mists of the Crater by becoming groach breeders.

"Greetings Warden." One of the armed guards employed by the city of Sentinel greeted him as he walked along the street. Smiling behind his chain-mail mask the Warden nodded in the general direction of the guard. Life was good. Here he was one of the most feared creatures in all the world, and getting paid for it. Of course he was also skimming soul stones off every payment made to house and torture the enemies of various demon lords. Sure, he never took more than ten percent, but at the rate that the prisoners had been pouring into the Warden was already richer than he ever dreamed possible.

Then to hear the glorious news that the Ruling Satan had finally died and that they were now entering the Great War of Ascension. At the news, the Warden had gone to the heads of the nine kingdoms and suggested that they triple their normal fee for accepting new inmates. Soon, the war would more than quadruple the amount of prisoners to come through the city gates, since it was the Warden himself that counted each new arrival for the books, no one would ever notice a dozen or so that didn't get written down.

These payments would go directly into his personal vaults, hidden within his personal rooms within the city. He dreamed of a time, very near, when he would retire to the splendor of the Dark City itself. Perhaps he would even get a home next to the famed Lake of Fire. He was so caught up in his dreams of the future that he had overlooked the sounds of screaming that echoed along the city streets. Of course the streets always seemed to echo with screams, but these were somehow different.

Suddenly, out of the night three guards came running past him. "You there," he called. "What's happening?" For a moment he thought that they were going to simply ignore him and continue in their flight, but then one stopped and turned. The Warden frowned and made a mental note to collect the other two and drop them into the Crater in the next day or two.

"It's the Black Fog, Warden. It comes out of the Crater." The guard who had stopped gasped, his eyes wild with terror. "The Nameless One comes for the city."

"Impossible!" The Warden snapped." That creature has been trapped for over a thousand years."

"Look for yourself!" The guardsman pointed and the Warden turned to look at the walkway that went around the wall protecting the city. Sure enough thick, black fog, poured over the top of the wall like smoke from some great hidden fire. As the Warden stood gaping at the sight a wall guard wheeled out of the mists writhing and screaming as shadows made of fog clung to him. Then, to his utter horror he watched as the guard began to change. No, this was not the right word for it. The guard's body began to ripple as if it were made of water. As the ripples ran down his body it changed shape, only to change again as if some madman were shaping clay. Indeed, even the wall, which was ten foot thick iron, danced and melted as the fog engulfed it.

Knowing his first real taste of terror the Warden turned

to where the guard had been standing to find himself alone. He croaked once, the sound being beaten down by the multitude of screams as the fog began entering the city, before fleeing blindly away from the madness of the Nameless One.

Gasping for air with lungs that burned like fire, the Warden ran down random alleyways between the prison buildings hoping to reach the other side of the city where he would do his best to climb the outer wall and escape into the wilderness beyond the city. He regretted the fact that he would have to abandoned his hidden vault and all the soul stones that it held, but at least he would be alive. At that moment a wall of black fog rolled through the street cutting him off.

Sobbing in horror he turned and found that he was trapped in the alley As he watched he saw familiar faces moving around in the roiling blackness as it drew nearer to him and at last he understood. Over the centuries the city of Sentinel had thrown unfortunates into the fog, thinking it a grand torture, but never thinking of what their actions could really mean. The fog was a powerful manifestation of the Nameless One's madness and they had fed that madness, adding more and more psyches to the Darkness, essentially giving the Nameless One an army of psychotic ghosts.

"You are the one they call The Warden." The voice that came out of the dark fog was like shards of glass being dragged through his mind. Screaming, the Warden dropped to his knees, blood spilling from his eyes and nose.

"You are just one of many who have claimed what is mine." The voice continued as the fog enveloped the twitching demon. Within seconds the Warden was completely surrounded by the fog and he began to scream. He screamed so loud that his voice box ruptured and he would have surely drowned in his own blood had the fog not absorbed his body into itself. Within less than an hour the city of Sentinel was gone, replaced by a landscape drawn by powerful madness and the fog that was the Nameless One crawled toward the next city.

❦

Somewhere on the Blight Sea between the Continents of Armageddon and Malice.

"Please, Mistress." The human begged as he was led toward the front of the large wooden ship, where a large altar had been erected. Legacy watched him impassively. The man had served her well for over one hundred years, but her Shamans had told her that the signs called for a sacrifice on her part. A blood sacrifice to the Throne and all the dark spirits surrounding the War of Ascension.

It was these spirits that the Shamans really cared about. Bonedancer, the First amongst her Shamans had come to her and explained how these spirits danced around her trying to get her attention. They spoke to her, but the Stone of Power had blinded her to their voice and they were growing angry. Now was not the time to let go of the old ways.

If Legacy truly intended to lead her people to victory in the War of Ascension, then she needed the wisdom of those who had gone before her. If these spirits were not appeased, then they could turn against her people and support her enemies. For a few moments Legacy had sat silently on the floor of her cabin, listening to the sounds of the waves pushing up against the wooden hull of the ship. She strained to hear the voices of the spirits that Bone Dancer saw. Was it possible. Had she already began losing touch with the spirits that had guided her for so long?

"What is required of me." She asked, locking eyes with the dark furred Shaman sitting across from her.

"The Spirits call for a duel sacrifice, you must give them blood of your line." Legacy nodded in understanding. This was a kind of sacrifice that she had performed many times in the past.

"You said dual." She pointed out.

"They require the life of your favored servant, to be sacrificed on an altar before them and your people."

And so it came that Krane, her human servant. was taken to the altar for sacrifice to the Ancient Spirits of the War of Ascension. Legacy stood exactly six feet from the altar watching impassively. Behind her and on every deck of the thirty ships that sailed with her, the demon wolves gathered to watch her make amends with the spirits. Bone Dancer, his dark fur painted with crimson paint chanted in a guttural growl as Krane, still begging for his life was tied to the wooden altar. Finally, the First Shaman turned to where Legacy stood.

"Let the one who has wronged our Dark Spirits come forward" Keeping her head held high Legacy stepped up to him.

"I am the one you seek. "Looking at her sternly, Bone Dancer raised a bleached white demon wolfs skull before her. It was the skull of Legacy's own mother, whom she had killed to take over the demon wolf tribes.

"Speak your name so that the Spirits may recognize you."

"I am Legacy, Alpha of the United Demon Wolf tribes." Legacy snarled. All around her the Demon Wolves howled and yipped in response. This continued until Bone Dancer raised the skull above his head.

"The spirits know you Alpha and they are disappointed. They say that you have lost your way and ignore their voice." At this several of her people let out mournful howls.

"What is it that you seek?" The Shaman asked.

"I have come to seek forgiveness and hear once again the council of the Dark Spirits." Legacy spoke without hesitation.

Slowly the skull was lowered, its jaw bones opening so that the contents, hidden until that very moment could be poured into Legacy's waiting mouth. The Alpha swallowed the bitter liquid, feeling it burn as it went down her throat. Without a word Bone Dancer turned and set the skull upon the altar where the human had fallen into silent sobs. Still silent he turned back to his leader and placed a large bone knife in her clawed hand.

"The spirits call for sacrifice, willingly given." Bone Dancer called out as he stepped away from the altar. Knowing what she must do Legacy stepped up to the altar and raised her gray furred arm up over the still crying slave.

"I offer first my own blood, may it open the gates between the living and the dead." With these ritual words Legacy drew the blade against her arm, cutting deeply. Krane began to writhe and scream with renewed vigor as crimson blood began spilling across his naked body. All around her the world seemed to slow as the special herbs she had swallowed began taking effect.

"My favored servant I offer up to the spirits so that the bridge between us may be repaired." Without warning Legacy drove the bone knife into Krane's chest, piercing his heart. On the altar the human arched his back, as if forcing the blade deeper into his chest, his mouth open wide in a silent scream. Slowly Legacy turned away from the dead man, her arms open wide in supplication.

All around her the world shivered and then she could see them. Dark shadows dancing amongst her followers. The spirits flew around her and she barked a laugh. Once again the Demon Wolves lifted their muzzles to the cold sea air and howled. Legacy turned and looked out over the crimson sea and watched in fascination as a large wave rose up, the water taking the shape of a great wolf's head. She watched as the things great eyes looked across the deck of the ship, finally coming to rest on the Alpha.

"Great things are to come for you Alpha of the tribes." The giant head spoke, its voice made up of the voices of all of the dark spirits.

"Your time has come and you will spread our glory throughout the world." With that the great beast opened its jaws wide and amongst those jagged teeth Legacy saw her destiny rise. Set, the so called Lord of the Dead would fall before her unimaginable might and she would rule as the next Satan.

The spirits said so.

Blasphemy.

Despite Tobin's concerns that the Lady Darkstar would remain sitting in the corner of her war room staring at her Stone, she was ready to begin her participation in the War of Ascension. As a matter of fact as soon as the Observer had left, she snapped the box closed and turned to her Gargoyle General.

"Did he see the maps"

"As you ordered my Lady," Chantric turned his reptilian eyes toward her.

"Good, let him think that we seek our deaths at the hands of Set." Darkstar walked back over to the table and ran her red hand over the map that sat there. The map rippled as if it were a puddle of water that her hand had disturbed. Within moments the features of the continent of Malice had changed to Wrath.

Darkstar laughed at her own brilliance. She had successfully tricked the Observer into believing that she would seek out a war with Set, when it was the Serpent King Deceiver whom she sought. Of course none of this truly mattered to Tobin. He knew of her plans the minute her time come up to be recorded within the Great Book. In the end it didn't matter if she sought her death at the hand of the Lord of the Dead or the Serpent Lord's. If she died Tobin would simply record her death and move on.

All of this had taken place weeks ago and now Darkstar was ready to make her first move. She called Chantric to the War Room one last time to go over their preparations. It was one of Darkstar's greatest achievements that she ruled not one kingdom, but two.

Everyone thought her the pathetic ruler of simple frog-like creatures that would never amount to anything. However, the daughter of the last Ruling Satan had not chosen this Kingdom at random. Indeed it was the Gargoyle kingdom located within the cliffs to the west that had brought her here. Within fifteen years of taking over the kingdom of Blight, by killing off its pathetic Royal Family, she had infiltrated and subverted the hierarchy of the Gargoyle Aries.

She watched their King and his family preparing for her eventual take over. She seduced the King's youngest son, a brute named Chantric and whispered in his ear that he was the only one fit to rule the Aries. That his father and brothers, thirty-two in all, were weak. She would help him gain his rightful place, if only he would allow her. Within a year she had made him her slave through a mixture of subtle magic and sex.

Chantric rose up with followers that he had gathered in secret and slaughtered all those in his family. claimed the Stone Throne of the Gargoyles, but it was the Lady Darkstar who ran things from the shadows. Now the time had come to put her warriors to the test. They would fight and sacrifice themselves for her war. They would help her ascend and then she would destroy them all.

But, there was one thing that needed to be taken care of first. For to long she had been stuck in a prison of her own making and tonight she would be free of it. "Is all ready?" She asked Chantric, trying unsuccessfully to keep the excitement out of her voice. It was time for her to take her rightful spot on the Throne of Darkness.

"All is as you have commanded it, My Lady." Chantric bowed low before her.

"Then do it." Without another word, the great Gargoyle turned and dove through the large window. His wings taking him out over the city to where a large force of his people waited for his orders. They thought that their king had been planning on betraying his concubine for some time and tonight they would finally attack.

Within moments, the sky was filled with reptilian warriors with skin as strong as stone. Darkstar closed her eyes and listened as the first sounds of battle reached her throne room. Screams and shattering glass were like the sweetest of wine to her. Soon all living things within the capital city were dead and Chantric had taken the Lady Darkstar "prisoner."

Leaving the blood stained city behind, Darkstar was taken to her new palace in the Aerie of the king. From here they would, under the command of Chantric, begin a march towards the kingdom of Deceiver and her second stone. However, that night she rewarded her slave with sex.

After all one had to keep their pets happy.

———◆———

The Island of Scab in the Boiling Ocean.

Severikhan, Lord of Lust stood at the highest point on the island of Scab, where a lookout had been built centuries before to watch for storms and pirates. However today neither of these things concerned the small city of Trench. The docks were filled with War Ships and the streets teemed with Mercenaries as they prepared to move out to fight in the great War of Ascension. Severikhan stood nude in the hissing rain and looked down upon the city with very little interest. Soon he would be away from this wretched island where he grew up learning the ways of the monk from a small monastery attached to the Church of Sin.

Movement, out on the tumbling ocean caught his eye, and he lifted a spy glass, an ingénues human invention up to his left eye. Yes, there definitely was a ship out there. And what an odd ship it was. Built entirely of wood instead of bone, and like nothing Severikhan had ever seen before. At the top the main mast a black flag snapped back and forth in the fierce wind and he could just make out what appeared to be a human skull with two bones crossed underneath it. How odd. Slowly he lowered his eye, searching for the ships name......there it was Black Rose. Something about the ship drew him, he wanted to know more. Perhaps even send one of his Warships out to intercept it........

"........even listening to me?" An irritated voice snapped from behind him. Severikhan sighed heavily and turned to face the owner of that voice. A large priest, his purple scales immaculate as he stood up under a tent not to far away, scared to get his robes wet. Beside the priest stood a small rodent of a demon, with a hairless wrinkled body and large square teeth. This Acolyte sneered up at Severikhan as he approached his Master. Behind the pair stood four towering Minotaurs, representing company commanders of Severikhans' army.

"Did you hear me?" The Priest demanded as Severikhan brushed past him to get a goblet of wine. "I said you should have turned those mercenary contracts over to the Church of Lust." He continued when Severikhan didn't answer him. "You had no right to use them." At this Severikhan finally lost his patience.

"No right?" He turned and glared at the priest. Did he honestly think that he still held sway over him? He. Severikhan who was now a God amongst insects.

"That's right, I said…." Severikhan lashed out with a flurry of hand strikes, moving faster than the eye could see. The priests snout shattered, followed by his right and left shoulder bones. His rib cage cracked in five different placed and finally his larynx was crushed. All in a matter of seconds. Gurgling, drowning in his own blood and agony, the priest fell and began the slow agonizing process of dying.

The Acolyte yelped in terror, the glare wiped free from his face as he turned to flee, only to be cut into two perfect halves by a minotaur war axe. Not looking at the two bodies Severikhan went back to the look out and searched for the intriguing ship, but it was gone, lost in the storm. Sighing he turned to look at the four commanders awaiting his orders.

"You may begin." Was all he said as he turned back to the storm and the city below. Within moments screams could be heard over the wind, and fires began breaking out here and there despite the rain. Soon the only living people on the island would be Severikhan and his mercenaries. And that was alright by him.

The ruins under the Dark City.

"Get down." Forgotten Child screamed at the young woman who had broken from cover. He could see the terror in her eyes and knew that she had run in a blind panic. All around the crouched group the air seemed to fill with a sound like knives being sharpened against a whet stone.

Forgotten watched as dark crystalline shapes swooped from the ruined ceiling to swarm around the running human.

The woman, Forgotten tried to remember her name, screamed in horror and pain as she was engulfed in a flurry of blade like wings. As he watched, several of the creatures began to glow crimson. They looked exactly like large bats from Earth, except for the fact that they were made of black crystal. They were called crysbats and were amongst the deadliest of all the creatures found in Hell. They attacked anything that bled, flying around them, cutting with their razor sharp wings. These cuts were always deep and bloodless, as the foul beasts fed at the moment that they cut into flesh.

As they fed, they would begin to glow with a deep crimson light which would slowly fade over the next few days, until they were ready to feed again. It had been six months since the fall of The Pit and Forgotten had already lost five members of his original twenty. Two had fallen in raids from Baal's demons who seemed to hound their every step, knowing exactly which tunnels to follow no matter what they did to cover their tracks. One had fallen through a weakened point in an old street to the level below.

The unfortunate soul had shattered his ankle and while Forgotten had prepared to rescue him, the man was discovered by a small pack of devourers. Forgotten could do nothing but listen in frustration to the man's screams as he was eaten alive before their very eyes. Shortly after that a woman woke up to find that she had contracted groaches. She died, as Raven tried to remove the single queen through primitive surgery.

And now another body lay on the ground, her eyes staring at him in accusation. Their deaths were his responsibility. He felt their weight, even though in his heart he knew that he had done all he could for these people who had chosen to follow him out into the ruins under the Dark City. What had he been thinking when he had taken the Stone from Father Michael? He should be with his daughter right now, traveling to the safety of Haven.

Thinking of Cassandra was the worst thing that he could do at this time. Was she out there right now facing her own horrors. Had she been killed by some random creature looking for its next meal or perhaps she had fallen to Baal's men. But he knew that he was just thinking the worst. If Cassandra had died he would have felt it, he was sure of that. Best to concentrate on getting out of this chamber alive.

"Well Blade Master?" a voice whispered into his right ear causing him to jump. It was all he could do to keep himself from going for his sword which would have surely drawn the attention of the crysbats. Turning Forgotten looked into Shard's bright hazel eyes. Once again he was drawn to their familiarity. He had seen those eyes somewhere before, but where?

"Are you going to come up with a plan, or stare into her eyes all night?" Another voice, this time at his left startled him again. Raven, the Throne Bound half-vampire. Forgotten shuddered at his nearness but did not pull away from him.

"What do you suggest?" He snapped at them.

"My wife may have a spell that could help." Raven smiled showing his fangs. Magic. Spells granted by the Throne of Darkness itself. The very thought made the Blade Master sick. He hated all Throne Bound. The fact that two of them had chosen to accompany him had not made him change his mind. He had forbidden Raven, and his wife Kara from using their magic unless he gave them the okay. So in honor of his order they had watched five people die when they could have easily saved them. Now, here they were pinned down by creatures that could easily kill the remaining fifteen and their only hope could lie within magic. There seemed to be no other choice.

"Okay, fine." He spoke, his voice a hoarse whisper. Raven smiled again and Forgotten swore he could smell old blood on the man's breath. He felt bile rise in his throat as he waited for the Throne Bound Cleric to slip away to talk to his wife. Instead of leaving Raven simply closed his eyes and appeared to drift off into sleep with his face cupped by his hands.

"I know you didn't just go to sleep after I've finally given you permission to use your vile magic!" Forgotten's voice quivered with suppressed rage. This could not be happening. If they got out of this alive, he would kill the Throne Bound himself, he swore it.

"Have patience Blade Master." Raven spoke without opening his eyes. "I am speaking with my wife." Forgotten looked at the man as if he had lost his mind. This was too much. He opened his mouth to say something, but at that moment the half vampire opened his eyes.

"I would cover my ears if I were you." He said and did as he suggested. Forgotten had just enough time to put his hands up to his ears before the air was filled with a screech that caused his teeth to rattle in mouth. So loud was the sound that his ear drums reverberated even though they were blocked off. He was certain that had he not covered them, they would have burst.

Above them the crysbats began to vibrate in agony as the sound penetrated their crystal bodies and caused them to crack. One by one they shattered, showering the humans with sharp dagger-like crystal shards and a syrupy slime that was the creatures own blood. Within moments the sound ceased, leaving everyone's ears ringing. Hesitantly, Forgotten pushed himself to his feet, his hands still clamped over his ears. Only when he was certain that the sound would not return, or the crysbats would not attack again, did he finally lower his hands.

"Wow." He whispered as one by one the others began standing. Forgotten looked over at the human Throne Bound woman named Kara. For the first time he understood what powerful weapons they could be.

"Thank-you." She smiled at him.

"For what?"

"For letting me touch my magic again." There was a light in her eyes that said that doing so was pleasurable beyond anything that the Blade Master could understand. He wanted to be sickened by this, but at the moment he was just happy to be alive. Slowly, he forced himself to turn away from the Throne-Bound and the look in her eyes, and began giving orders to the stunned survivors.

They stripped the fallen woman (her name had been Kali) of all her useful items before burning the body. Fifteen minutes later they were on the move again, heading for the coast and a secret human cavern that awaited their arrival. As he led, Forgotten thought about Kali's eyes staring up at him. Silently, he added her to the list of those he had failed. That night not even the closeness of Rachel could fill the emptiness inside of him.

He was going to fail and all of the rebellion would pay for his failure.

CHAPTER 11

Taken from the personal journal of Tobin Masters, the Observer to the Throne of Darkness.

All my Life, I have dreamed of what it would be like to be a father. It was this dream, amongst all the others that my sister and Richard took from me, that hurt the most. How it galled me to know that Karen, with her hate and lies, now carried Richard's child. To know that she had not been satisfied in taking my very heart away from me, she also had to take this most sacred dream as well. But, I know something that Karen doesn't. A secret that is in the very fabric of life. It is a truth that many simply do not see. For every dream that dies, a new one is born.

Tobin sat at the table in the great library writing in his personal journal. For now the Great Book that contained the beginnings of the War of Ascension sat closed and awaiting the next passage to be inked onto its pages. The Stone Bearers had finally begun their movements, which signaled to the other kingdoms that the time for war had come. Indeed, several kingdoms on all the continents had started attacking one another.

Even rival neighborhoods within the Dark City, itself had had a few skirmishes. But, none that mattered right now. Not to Tobin. He was waiting for his final revenge on his sister. It had been seven months since he had traveled back to Earth to get his revenge on the two people who had hurt him the most. Seven months and still he waited for his ultimate revenge. Richard had been thrown randomly into the world of Hell. Where he was at this exact moment, Tobin did not know. He had not bothered to look through the Throne to see. All he knew was that Richard was still alive, somewhere out there.

As for Karen, Tobin had her brought directly back to the Great Palace. He had her placed in an opulent apartment where she screamed, ranted and threw pieces of furniture against the walls. She made such a ruckus that several visiting demons had approached her door wanting to know if a new breed of demon had been discovered. Several of them, upon being told that the sounds came from a human, had even offered to pay Tobin several thousand Souls Stones for her.

Apparently, her ferocity actually turned them on. Tobin had been tempted to tell them that she was a deceitful back stabbing bitch, but then he didn't want to encourage them. Instead he politely turned each of them down. He hadn't turned down the money out of any sense of loyalty, or fleeting sibling love. No, she had destroyed those feelings as surely as she had destroyed his dreams. There had been a demon whom he had actually considered accepting payment from. A hulking creature with black and red spikes protruding from its armored skin. His Lord (a Demon named Blotar) was said to be a sadist and this servant promised the Observer that the woman would know pain like never before.

But no. Tobin had other plans for his sister.

Perhaps in the future. So, he had gone into the room and faced his sister. She lay on a large bed, which had been carved from the bone of some demonic beast. The room was a mess, with bone shards from broken furniture strewn about. Karen did not acknowledge him, as she lay face down, sobbing.

"Karen?" Tobin walked up beside her. "Are you done tearing things up?" At that moment she turned and with a shriek plunged a piece of sharpened bone into his chest. Tobin felt the shard scrape against his ribs, before sliding between them and into his lung. On Earth, the injury would have surely killed him as he drowned in his own blood. However, they were no longer on Earth, and Tobin was no longer just a mortal man. He was the Observer to the Throne of Darkness and his Master would not allow him to die so easily.

Sighing, Tobin reached up and pulled the bloody bone shard from his chest. "I see we didn't learn from the gun back on Earth." He smiled, as he held the make-shift weapon out to her.

"Try again?" And try she did. Several times in the weeks following her arrival. Karen tried everything she could to kill him, from keeping silverware from her meals to stab him, to trying to push him from the balcony outside her window.

But after some time she began to see that her efforts were futile. "Am I dead?" She asked one night in a soft, trembling voice, her eyes on the floor.

"No" Tobin had answered pulling a shard of glass out of his neck. "Not yet."

"Then, what's happening?" There was a tremble of panic to her voice that Tobin cherished. So Tobin had explained to her, in a soft gentle voice where they were. He explained about the Throne and the War of Ascension.

"No more!" Karen sobbed as she covered her ears.

"But, don't you see Karen?" Tobin reached over and pulled her hands down. "It was you and Richard who brought me here. It was your treachery that made all of this possible." He looked deep into her hazel eyes, so much like his own before his enslavement by the Throne.

"Are you going to kill me?" She whispered, fear flooding her eyes.

Sighing heavily, Tobin leaned back and looked at her. "When I first came after you, that is what I intended to do, but then I found out that you were pregnant." Tobin paused and wiped a black gloved hand across his face. "I can't kill you. You are my sister, no matter what you've done."

And so, they had come to an agreement. Tobin told her that he could not open a gate back to Earth so soon after bringing her and Richard here. If Karen would take care of herself and quit trying to kill him (not that it did much good) within a year he would send her back. As an extra added bonus he would send with her papers that would ensure the transfer Tobin's estate to her and the baby. Never once during these negotiations did she mention Richard's name.

For the first couple of months, Tobin would visit her and the human slave, a mid-wife named Stella, that he had assigned to her. As her belly grew his visits came less frequently. The pain of knowing that Richard's child lived within her was too much for him to bear. Stella reported to him on a daily basis, letting him know that the child was strong. She, also spoke often of Karen's attitude toward her pregnancy. Tobin had expected indifference, after all the child had been conceived as a way of ensuring that Richard would do what she had wanted. However, Stella said that Karen showed a surprising amount of tenderness toward her unborn child.

Whispering words of love to her swelling stomach and singing to it. It had now been four months since Tobin had visited his sister. He knew that the time was approaching quickly. When he would have to see her one last time before sending her on her way. Strangely, he looked forward to this. His last deed, as her brother.

"Master!" Tobin looked up from his journal to find Steven standing in front of the table. The sight shocked him, since he had never seen the red headed slave outside his rooms.

"What is it Steven?"

"The mid-wife bids you to come to your sister's room." The slave looked around the Great Library nervously. Slaves were never allowed here. "She says that it is time." Tobin tried not to run through the hallways of the Great Palace, but just couldn't seem to help himself. It was time. After all this time, his final plans were coming together. If all went well, after tonight he would be rid of Karen for good.

Several demons and slaves bowed to him as he moved passed them, but he hardly even glanced at them. Nothing mattered at this moment, except getting to where he had held his sister prisoner for the last seven months. Oh, if she only knew what he had planned for her. If she had gleaned even a sliver of his thoughts, then surely she would have thrown herself from the balcony into the streets below. So, he stayed away, sending her messages of love and compassion. What he had really wanted to do was spit in her face.

How weak she must have thought him to be, believing that he would simply forgive her, after what she had done. Bringing her to Hell had only been the beginning of the things that he had planned for her. Originally he thought to torture her unendingly, rip the unborn fetus from her, and make her eat it. But the child was innocent in all of this. Why should this small life pay for what its parents had done to him. And then he knew what he must do. And he had set into motion his own great deceit, weaving a web of lies in which to trap his tormentor. Tonight all would come to an end and Karen Masters would know what it was like to suffer.

Finally, after what seemed an eternity, he arrived at the doors to his sister's room. From behind the thick door, he could hear Karen's unmistakable screams. Without knocking, he walked in. The room was dark, with shadows cast by the fire burning in the fire place. Karen lay on the four poster bed, her legs spread wide before her. Blood stained the rough wool-like sheets, as the mid-wife urged the girl to push for her baby's life.

Karen's face was covered in sweat and twisted in pain as she screamed and tried to do as Stella ordered her. Hours passed, with nothing happening beyond Karen screeching and cussing the old mid-wife out. During this time slaves had brought Tobin a large Throne like chair for him to sit in and await his nephew arrival into this world. "I can see the head, child!"

The mid-wife exclaimed. "Push!" Karen looked at the older woman as if she would get up and strangle her.

"I am pushing you old bitch!" She snapped in-between gasps of pain. It looked, as if she was going to say some more but then she bared down suddenly and let loose a shriek of pain. At that moment the old woman leapt forward and caught the blood covered child. With a deft flick of a bone dagger the child's umbilical card was severed, followed by a swift slap, which caused the baby to gasp out in fear and pain.

Instantly, the room was filled with the high pitch wails of a healthy child. Tobin let out a sigh of relief. He had been afraid that the stress Karen had been under would have affected the child, a child that she had conceived out of deceit and had grown to love over the last seven months.

"It is a boy, My Lord." Stella passed him the tiny form wrapped in a blanket, made from the fur of a demonic rat. Tobin looked down into the boys' pink face, all scrunched up from his efforts at crying. His little fists flailing at the world. Tears filled the Observer's eyes, as he looked at the child.

"This boy will be strong, My Lord" Stella whispered and smiled. Tobin could not trust himself to speak, so he only nodded that he understood her.

"Tobin," Karen called weakly from the bed where she had been left to lay in her cooling sweat and afterbirth. "Let me see my baby" Leaving the mid-wife cooing at the boy Tobin walked over and looked down at his sister. Her face was still red from her exertions and her hair was soaked with sweat. For a moment he stood there and tried to remember what it had been like to love her. To be proud that she had been his BIG SISTER. When he was a boy he always thought of her like that, in capital letters. As if she were something truly special.

"Did you always hate me?" He finally asked.

"What?" Karen tried to push herself up, but fell feebly back on the bed. "What are you talking about?" Tears welled up in her eyes. "Please Tobin, I can hear him crying."

"You have no baby Karen, he died the day that you conceived him with Richard."

"No!" Karen's cry was cut short, as her hoarse voice gave out. "You can't have him Tobin, I won't let you take him." She gasped as she slid her hand slowly under the pillow next to her head.

"I already have." Tobin whispered as his hand darted out and pulled the bone dagger from under the pillow, before she could get to it. In an instant Karen's features hardened with hate.

"Damn you Tobin, God damn you!" She screamed spitting into his face.

"God doesn't have to damn me, Karen, you and Richard did it for Him." Tobin stood up, slipping the dagger into his black robe. "You will not be going back to Earth, Karen." He smiled with cruelty down at her as she began to sob. "This is as much your home as it is mine."

"What are you going to do to me?" She asked, her voice catching as she struggled to gather control of herself. "Please Tobin, I never meant to hurt you." Her eyes softened as she plead with him.

"You can't lie to me Karen, you forget that I can look into your memories." Tobin shook his head in sadness. "I have tasted your hate for me, and if anybody deserves to spend eternity in Hell, it's you."

Tobin turned away from her and walked back over to where Stella stood holding the boy, watching the scene with troubled eyes.

"Give the boy to one of the other slaves Stella, I would have a word with you in private." A few moments later they stood out on the balcony overlooking the Dark City. Somewhere in the distance Tobin could see the flickering light of a building burning.

"I hope that I haven't done anything to offend My Lord." Stella's voice trembled. "I did everything that I could to ensure that the child was born healthy."

"Are you a spy for the Free Humans?" The Observer asked, without taking his eyes from the city.

"What?" Stella exclaimed. Her voice now bordered on panic.

"No, you came to feel sorry for her, that's it, isn't it." Tobin kept his voice soft.

"My Lord please, I don't understand." Without speaking, Tobin turned and laid the bone dagger on the black marble of the rail. He watched as all the blood drained from the slave's face and her eyes grew wide. If Tobin hadn't already knew that she was guilty of giving his sister the weapon, she had just given him all the proof that he needed.

"Please My Lord, I just told her that you were planning to betray her" The slave began to cry.

"I never intended for her to hurt you." Tobin barked a laugh at that, as if anything could have killed him. That would have been a mercy to him. However, the Throne denied him this and there was nothing to be gained from dwelling at that which he couldn't change. He was on the path that had been chosen for him and he meant to see it to the end.

"How did you know?" He asked. It was a foolish question, they were in Hell, of course he was planning to betray her it was what one did.

"It was the crib My Lord." There was shame in the slave's voice now and Tobin wondered if it was real or feigned. No matter, he had his answer. She must have seen Stephen buying the crib in the market. Of course she had been told that after she gave birth, the Observer planned on returning Mother and child back to Earth. But then she had seen the crib and understood that Tobin had every intention of keeping the child. She had come back here and warned Karen of the deceit.

Sighing, Tobin shook his head. Part of this was his fault. He had spent so much time with the demons that he had forgotten that some people could still feel compassion for others. Taking his silence for condemnation Stella fell at his feet and began begging for her life. For a few moments Tobin remained silent listening to her promises of loyalty and faithful service in raising the boy. Finally, he had had enough.

"Stand up." He snapped. Trembling she rose up in front of him, keeping her eyes cast down at the black marble of the balcony. "You are a product of Hell and betrayal is a way of life." He whispered. Stella heard hope in his words and tentatively raised her eyes. "If it was just me you had betrayed then I could have easily overlooked the incident."

"What?" The midwife blinked in confusion, the fear returned to her eyes.

"The dagger was never meant for me." Tobin's voice became cold and hard as he reached out and grabbed her by her arms. "She meant to kill my son and you gave her the means to do so." It was in that moment that Stella knew that she was going to die and yet she tried one last time to bargain for her worthless life.

"Please Master, I didn't know!" Tobin looked at her

and saw that she was speaking the truth. She had honestly believed Karen, when she had said that she wanted the dagger to kill Tobin. But, none of that mattered now. Tobin had already made up his mind. Before his resolve could fade and he gave into the older woman pleas, Tobin thrust her away from him, using all his newfound strength. Stella screamed as she flew out and away from the balcony. Within seconds gravity snatched hold of her and she plummeted from sight. Tobin followed her screams, until her body smashed into the street far below.

"What did you do?" Karen screamed at him as he stepped back into the room. "Where's Stella?"

The remaining six slaves in the room kept their heads down, barley daring to breathe. None of them knew what the mid-wife had done and they were afraid that Tobin would punish them since they had served her.

"Stella is dead." Tobin said not even bothering to look at his sister. "The rest of you need not worry that the mid-wife's transgressions will fall to you." He addressed the other slaves. Several of them visibly relaxed and Tobin smiled. "Each of you will be given a position in my House." He decreed. Never mind that the Palace was technically not his house. Gasping the slaves each dropped to one knee before him. To his surprise, he saw that several of them traded smiles. They saw his taking them as personal slaves as an honor.

"You will each be charged with the constant care of my son." Tobin spoke to each of them. Behind him Karen began screaming at him again. He simply ignored her, as he stepped up to the woman that held the still crying child. "Are you capable of nursing my son." Tobin asked.

"I can Master," the woman spoke without looking up

from the floor. "It is why the mid-wife chose me to be here this night, in case the mother was unable to feed her child." At the mention of Stella, the other slaves flinched but Tobin did not react to their fears.

"Stand child." Tobin commanded and the woman obeyed. Slowly Tobin took the boy from her and cradled him against his chest. "You will be the First amongst my new slaves, their failures are now yours." Tobin told the woman in front of him, without taking his eyes off the baby.

"Now, call for a Throne Bound Healer and get her cleaned up and ready for travel." The Observer indicated the still railing woman on the blood and sweat stained bed. With that, he turned and began walking toward the door, his sister's screams, and curses following him until he could no longer hear her. Tobin took the boy back to his own rooms where Steven waited, with eight chests that had been delivered within the last hour.

"The servant of Lord Blotar delivered these for you, My Lord." Tobin thought of the demon visitor with the spikes on his face and smiled. He remembered well the promise of pain that had been given for Karen's future, should he decide to sell her. "Five-hundred-thousand Soul Stones, My Lord." Steven explained, as if he had counted each stone himself. Tobin had no doubt that he probably had.

"Very good Steven." The Observer spoke softly. "Tell Lord Blotar's retainer where he can pick up his Master's new slave." Bowing low, the red headed slave left Tobin with the boy. Who was now his son. Slowly, still without taking his eyes off the baby, Tobin sat down in a large chair.

"Thorn." He whispered. "Your name will be Thorn, and the nations off Hell will tremble at your feet.

CHAPTER 12

Taken from the personal journal of Tobin Masters, Observer to the Throne of Darkness.

I understand that I have covered the tenants of betrayal and deceit many times through my journal, but I have only been here in this world for a year and have learned some heart wrenching lessons myself, concerning these things. But how does somebody live their life day to day not being able to trust anything people tell us? How do you get beyond the fact that you can never let your guard down for one second? And when we slip up and forget this, how do we reconcile within our own hearts that we should have known better and because we didn't others have paid the price? I believe that Nicholas actually fell into this trap as he set out to fight his war for the Throne of Darkness. He forgot that sometimes humans could be just as evil as the demons, it was a lesson that he needed to be re-taught, with heartache and loss.

"Aye, does my heart good to see yer mug again." The woman sitting across from Forgotten smiled. Her name was Nala Darkwynd (at least that is the name she gave) and she was definitely one of the most colorful people that Forgotten Child had ever met.

She wore a black and white striped waistcoat, which had been altered to be a brazier that managed to accent her ample breasts while covering them at the same time. Around her waist she wore a short Sari that was reminiscent of Ancient Egyptians, her flat stomach exposed and flaunting the Black Widow spider that she had Tattooed on her skin in that area.

At her waist was a large cutlass that had spilled the blood of many a man, both human and demon. Her lovely shoulders would have been left bare if it were not for the leather and bone shoulder pads that held the medium length spider silk cape that she wore. Leather straps crisscrossed down her right arm, ending at her right fore-finger. On her feet, she wore leather knee high boots, adorned with golden skulls whose eyes glowed with blood red gems.

Her long dark hair was tied in a tight braid that snaked out from underneath an old pirate captain's hat. On her shoulder a demonic looking miniature dragon sat, eyeing Forgotten balefully. She was a beautiful, exotic woman with dark eyes and mahogany skin. The perfect combination of African and Asian. Anyone seeing her on Earth in modern times would have thought that she was either a stripper, or on her way to some costume party. But, they would have been dead wrong. She was exactly what she looked like, a pirate.

Nala had come to Hell from the year seventeen-fifty six, where she was a scourge of the known seas, terrorizing any vessel that had the unfortunate luck of crossing her path. A tradition that she carried on in Hell. Beyond those things Forgotten knew nothing of the woman's past. They had met almost fifty years ago when the Resistance first hired her ship, The Black Rose, to help move them from continent to continent.

That had been when Nala's husband, a seaman named Barnabus, had still been alive. Back in those days the female Captain had been more mercenary, allowing her ship and her crew to be hired out to anyone, human or demon alike though it was said that she would have nothing to do with the transportation of slaves. Then about twenty-five years ago tragedy struck. Barnabus had been killed by a group of demons that had hired the Black Rose to transport some goods from Wrath to the Dark City.

Once the ship reached one of the hidden ports that the Rose made use of, the demons had turned on the crew, trying to add them to their profits by selling them as slaves. The human crew fought back valiantly and when the smoke cleared all the betrayers were dead. The crew had suffered many losses themselves, Barnabus was among those that had been lost. Nala's attitude changed on that day. Gone was her mercenary attitude. She and her children, a son named Stephan, and a daughter named Shauntra, had joined the Resistance, turning all their hatred against the demons and any who would support them.

"Aye." The pirate woman spoke again, bringing Forgotten back to the present. "Thought fer sure yer bloody head would have been cut from yer fool shoulders by now Blade Master." She hid the harshness of her words with a smile.

"Well, it hasn't been like they haven't tried." Forgotten mumbled, as he reached across the small table and grabbed a hunk of the dry coarse bread that he and the Captain were sharing. The little dragon thing on Nala's shoulder hissed at him and bared its sharp teeth in his direction.

"Spaz," Nala turned to eye the creature. "Be nice, the Blade Master is our guest." With that she pulled a severed finger from a demon, which she kept in a small leather pouch on her sword belt, and lifted it up in front of the things face. Without hesitation Spaz took the offered treat, forgetting all about the unfamiliar human that sat across from his mistress. Forgotten watched as the thing crunched through bone and flesh before setting aside the bread he had taken. He was no longer hungry.

"I hear yer people whisper of some great mission Blade Master." The Pirate Captain turned away from her pet and looked directly into Forgotten's eyes. "Tell me" Sighing inwardly, Forgotten leaned forward and told her what he had been charged with doing. He watched as the woman's eyes grew wider the further he got. Finally, he told of the destruction of The Pit and his taking the gem and becoming a Stone Bearer in the War of Ascension.

"I had heard talk of great tragedy within The Pit, but nothin' such as ye have told me." The Pirate looked at him skeptically. "Do ye speak truth?" She asked her eyes sliding to the satchel where the Stone rested like dead weight against his side.

"I do speak the truth." Forgotten whispered, the memory of The Pit's destruction haunting him. "Do you want to see it?" For a moment, The Blade Master saw a calculating look cross the woman's face and knew that she was weighing her options.

After all, the Stone could gather her and the crew of the Black Rose untold riches. Blade Master or not, Forgotten was only one man and she had an entire crew backing her, should she wish to make such a move. But after that moment he saw that she rejected the thought.

No one in their right mind would want to take on

the responsibility of carrying such a tainted prize. Besides, whomever she tried to deal with would surly try and betray them once again. Forgotten smiled to himself not in the least bit upset by the woman's thoughts. After all she was a Pirate and while vengeance was very important to her, greed was still very near and dear to her heart.

"Will you still help us'" Forgotten asked. Knowing if she said no, that they would have another four to six month trek through the under city to find another ship to take them to Wrath. He was still unsure about why they had to go to that particular continent.

Raven had saved a few of the volumes from the secret library and he was convinced that he could find some ruins left behind by the original inhabitants of Elysium. For the life of him, the Blade Master didn't know why a bunch of ruins left behind by those who had lost the war meant anything. Of course he had no other plans in mind, so he chose to indulge the Throne Bound half-breed.

"All me and mine have to do is to take ye and that infernal Stone, and then we be on our own again?" Nala asked while feeding Spaz a second finger.

"Yes." Forgotten answered without a thought.

"And the price?" Without a word, Forgotten lifted a large sack containing five thousand Soul Stones off the floor and laid it on the table in-between them. For a moment the Pirate waited to see if he would offer more and when he didn't she shrugged and simply took the bag setting it on floor on her side of the table.

"And will there be fighting." Nala looked eager at this prospect and Forgotten wondered if Nala perhaps got high from the danger inherent to her chosen profession.

"You can count on it." The Blade Master told her truthfully. He didn't need the ability to see the future to know that there would be more blood spilled. He just didn't know whose it would be.

An hour after his meeting with Nala, Forgotten Child stood on a wooden catwalk overlooking a large craggy cavern. For just a moment, his mind flashed back to The Pit and the terrible struggle that destroyed it. The Pit had been the closest thing that he had been able to call home since coming to Hell. But, all that had ended. Now he was set adrift again, perhaps even lost. With a frustrated sigh, he shook his head and looked down at the scene below him.

This place may have had bridges and ladders crisscrossing it, but that was where the resemblance to the Pit ended. For one, there were only three levels to this cavern with the main level actually resting on the stone floor. From where he stood, Forgotten could see several wooden huts where the Pirates lived with their families while they were ashore. These huts looked small and sometimes resembled little more than a shack, but the Blade Master envied the occupants never the less. After all, he had lived in a ruined building with fifty other people around at all times. At least in one of those rough shacks down there, there would be a modicum of privacy. This was not the only difference between this place and the one that Forgotten had called home. Floating in a natural cove not twenty feet away from where the huts sat on their ledge, was Nala's ship, the Black Rose.

The ship, a British man'o'war if Forgotten remembered correctly, had three masts, from which at least twenty skulls of demons were hung like grotesque wind chimes. The main mast was so thick, that a grown man would have had trouble wrapping his arms around its full girth. Forgotten let his eye trail up this mast until he come to a man sized basket, called a Crow's Nest and then above this to the flag pole which almost scraped the caverns ceiling.

Connected to this flag pole was a black cloth, limp in the still air of the cavern, though Forgotten could easily imagine the thing snapped taught in the harsh wind of the open sea, bearing its skull and cross bone motif. The deck of the massive ship was black as was the hull, which sported two gun deck, from which the Black Rose could fire her forty two cannons, in what must be an awesome display of fire power for its time. Forgotten had heard that the crew actually slept on the gun decks with the cannons, or on the main deck out under the perpetual storm of Hell's night. It was also said that the crew ate out on the main deck, with the cook preparing the meal right in front of them.

The Captain's living arrangements were drastically different though. Nala had her own private room, located at the rear of the ship, this was where the Blade Master had met with the Pirate and he knew that the room was large and opulently decorated with fine spider silks and the skin of more than one hapless demon. There was also a large desk in the captain's quarters where a map of the eight Blood Seas of Hell were depicted, as well as all major demonic trading routes.

Finally, the back of the room was dominated by a large four poster bed, that Forgotten believed Nala had placed after she acquired the ship. Certainly the pirate caught him looking at the bed one time during their meeting and had suggested, in her up front manner, that perhaps he would better negotiate from a position between those silk sheets. Forgotten had blushed a deep red and the Pirate laughed uproariously. All in all, it was an intimidating ship, but even Forgotten knew that a ship was only as good as her crew. However, there was nothing lost when it came to the crew of the Black Rose.

The First Mate, Nala's daughter, was as ruthless as any man Forgotten had ever come across. She was beautiful, taking most of her physical make up from her Asian heritage and wearing long spider silk kimonos as she went about her business upon the decks of the Black Rose like a slave master. Whenever she moved the eyes of the crew moved with her, not out of lust, but out of anticipation as to what tasks she may need completed. There were times that Forgotten thought that the crew was more frightened of her, than they were of the Captain.

However, if little five foot Shauntra was domineering, then her brother, Stephen was downright terrifying. Stephan stood at least seven and a half feet tall and was as black as midnight, with muscles bulging from places Forgotten hadn't even realized existed. On his back the huge man wore three spears, which he used with deadly efficiency against the enemies of his ship. He was a warrior to his heart, waiting on the decks for the cry to battle. It was said that when it came to boarding an enemy ship, Stephan was always the first across the ropes and the first to draw blood. Beyond those two the rest of the crew, while not as strong, had never faltered in their mission to drive the demons from the seas of Hell. To a man (and Woman) they were loyal to Nala. There was no doubt in Forgotten's mind that they would be traveling with some of the most dangerous humans in all of Hell.

For the first time since he and his band of survivors had been smuggled into these hidden caverns three days ago, Forgotten felt himself relax. Perhaps everything would be okay after all. It was at that exact moment that he felt the stirrings of danger nearby. With a flash the Blade Master drew his sword, his eyes darting around.

Suddenly off to his left, the shadows of the cavern began to deepen. Preparing for battle Forgotten held his blade out before him as small tentacles made from the shadows reached out from the darkness, groping like blind things. Suddenly a man, dressed in black studded leather stepped out of the Darkness and grinned at the Blade Master.

"Hello, Forgotten." The new comer said, with a heavy Spanish accent. Forgotten could only stare while the Spanish man laughed at him. Finally he was able to find his voice. "Hello Triv."

Triv looked from the Blade Master to the sword that the man still pointed at him, this smile widening. "Um, Forgotten?" His smile widened even more. "Is that any way to greet an old friend." For a moment Forgotten stared at the man in front of him before sheathing his blade.

"How did you do that?" The Blade Master asked, his voice quivering with pent up emotion. He had been certain that they were under attack from one of the many demonic factions that were surely searching for them by now. Triv seemed pleased by Forgotten's reaction and that only served to aggregate him all the more. My powers have grown since the last time that we saw each other." The man bragged.

Triv called himself a Shadow Master, with the power to move through the smallest shadow as if it were a doorway, going anywhere he wanted to, as long as there was another shadow at his destination. Distance was not a factor, so the man could quite literally go anywhere in the world of Hell that he wanted. As if this power was not enough, the man could also take shadows and turn them into physical things. Forgotten had once watched him scoop up shadow stuff and begin shaping it like clay. In just a few moments, the man had formed a dagger made entirely of shadow, which he used to slay a nearby demon.

But even with all his experience with the Shadow Master, Forgotten had never seen anything like what had just happened. He shuddered again as he remembered the shadow tentacles as they groped outside the shadow gate that Triv had made, as if they were living things, independent of their Master. He did not want to think about such things, so he concentrated on the man himself.

Very little was known about the man and his life back on Earth. What was known was that the tan man looked like he had been born in India although he was actually from the South American country of Belize where he trained himself to be a Master Thief. What was commonly known as a Cat Burglar. It was rumored that no security system was safe from the thief and that he took on many jobs for the sheer joy of the challenge. Certainly he had done such things here in Hell, even sneaking into a part of the Great Palace itself to steal a small bauble from one of the Noble's rooms. It was said that Triv was truly without fear.

The Resistance used the Shadow Master as a thief and a spy gathering information and collecting items such as souls stones that the fighters used to free humans from Demonic Over Lords. And even though he exacted a huge amount for his services. Forgotten had always thought that the only reason Triv worked for them at all was due to the nature of their enemy.

After all, whatever thrill there had been stealing from humans had been lost since there was very little challenge in robbing slaves. The demon lords however had their castles, armies, and even magical protection. To defeat these things meant to have a power that even the demon lords themselves did not.

"Did you find what you were looking for?" Triv asked and Forgotten realized that he had been staring at the man.

"Sorry." He looked away from the Shadow Master and back down at the huts below.

"I am just surprised to see you here."

"Nala hired me to kill a Demon Lord in the Dark City." Triv said in the way of explanation.

"Assassination?" Forgotten turned to look at the dark haired man again. For his part Triv simply shrugged and offered another smile.

"What can I say, soul stones are soul stones." Both men fell silent as they turned their attention to the crew of the Black Rose, as they went about loading supplies onto their ship. Preparing to set sail in three days' time. The two friends remained silent until Triv let out a low whistle of appreciation.

"Wow, I heard that you were traveling with an assassin, but didn't really believe it until now." Forgotten followed the mans' eyes and found himself looking at Shard. The assassin knelt beside the edge of the cove, splashing water across her face and hair. For a moment the Blade Master watched her his mind trying desperately to understand the familiarity that constantly plagued him whenever she was close by. What was it about the woman that drew him to her?

"She's more beautiful than I thought she would be." Triv spoke up suddenly, causing Forgotten to jump. "Easy there, nothing to get excited about." Triv smiled at him and for an instant Forgotten saw into the little man's mind. Triv thought that the Blade Master was attracted to the assassin.

"No way, she's the enemy!" Forgotten snapped, letting the little thief know that he had read his mind. Triv smiled again (a knowing smile, damn him) and held his hands up in mock surrender.

Forgotten would have said more, but something down below drew his attention. Shard had suddenly stood up and he could see her hazel eyes moving around the cavern, never resting in one place for more than a few moments, almost as if she were searching for something. And then her hands were suddenly clutching red crystal swords.

"Something's wrong." The Blade Master whispered to the man next to him. At that moment, shouts of alarm rang out from all around the cavern as demonic creatures charged out of the caves that lead into the ruins under the Dark City Forgotten watched as the half demon army that had once belonged to Thonatutus and which surely now belonged to his son, Belial, fell on the unsuspecting pirates. Several of them fell before the deformed monstrosities but others reacted drawing blades to meet the oncoming onslaught.

Nala, drawn by the call to battle, rushed out from her quarters on the Black Rose took in the scene and began barking orders. Instantly the pirates began moving as one, some of them fighting off the half breeds, while others gathered everything they could and tossed them to those still on the deck of the ship.

Forgotten knew without having to look, that most of

the chests being delivered aboard ship would not contain supplies for the weeks' worth of travel they would undergo on the blood seas. No these chests would contain soul stones. The pirates would not part with their wealth so easily.

Meanwhile, down on the cavern floor, Stephan moved through the pitched battle skewing half demon after half demon on his spears. Forgotten watched in amazement as the huge man lifted one screaming monstrosity by his spear and tossed it over his head as if it had weighed nothing at all.

The creatures' screams of protest stopped abruptly as Shard's crystal sword cut the thing in half in midair. A flash of light then drew the Blade Master's attention and he watched as Kara and Raven rained magical death on the attackers from the deck of the Black Rose.

Suddenly the roof of the cavern grew darker and the air was filled with a low moaning that reverberated in Forgotten's bones. Slowly, tentacles made of darkness, each as thick as a human man's leg, slithered down from the ceiling and began attacking the half demons.

In awe, Forgotten turned to look at the man standing next to him just the screams of attackers reached a new crescendo. Forgotten turned to run to the ladder that would take him down into the battle but was stopped by Triv's hand catching his shoulder.

"Let go of me!" Forgotten yelled at the thief. "I have to help them."

"No." Triv shook his head one time. "Don't you understand? They are here for you."

"All the more reason for me to get down there."

Again the other man shook his head. "If you die, then we have already lost." He pointed down into the cavern.

"Listen to me, you know that there is no way we can win this battle!" Turning, Forgotten knew it was true. Most of the Pirates had already fallen back to the ship, while the others were engaged in a fighting retreat.

Meanwhile half breeds still poured from the cavern entrances. Forgotten felt his shoulders slump in defeat. Another home destroyed because of the Stone he carried. Because of him. Within moments, every surviving human was aboard the Pirate ship, except Forgotten and Triv.

"How do we get down to the ship without fighting?" Forgotten asked and then instantly regretted it. Without warning shadows leapt up covering him and the Shadow Master. He had just a moment to feel panic before a pain ripped through his body threatening to pull him apart. And then in the next instant he was stumbling across the deck of the Black Rose, having come out of the shadow cast by the main mast.

"Now ye Throne Bound dogs!" Nala yelled as soon as she saw Forgotten and Triv appear. At her command both Kara and Raven began a spell. Instantly a gust of wind leapt forth snapping the sails tight and pulling the ship away from its once safe harbor. Forgotten stumbled to the railing, his legs barely responding. He had just enough time to grip the rail, before he was shoved with enough force that he literally slid five feet across the deck.

Thinking that somehow one of the enemy had made it on board without anyone noticing, Forgotten drew his blade and prepared to defend himself, but when he looked to where he had been, the only person he saw was Stephan.

Slowly the huge man turned to look at the fallen Blade Master and he heard the high piercing wail of the man's sister ring out. Stephan had not been attacking him. The man had pushed him aside to keep him from being hit by the crossbow bolt which now stuck out of his throat.

As Forgotten watched blood began spraying out of the man's neck, and, his eyes rolled up into his head. Within moments he fell, dead before striking the wooden deck. Almost instantly Nala was there, cradling her son's head in her lap, whispering to him.

Behind her, her daughter stood, eyes glistening with tears that she would not shed in front of the rest of the crew. After a few moments Nala raised her eyes to where Forgotten still sat, his sword drawn. There was a fire in the woman's eyes that caused him to want to back away.

"There be no way the Half Breeds could have found us on their own." The Pirate Captain's voice was cold and hard. Forgotten knew that the Pirates had hidden the entrances to their caves well. Even going so far as to cover any tracks that Forgotten and his people had left behind and using Throne Bound servants to make the cavern itself invisible to anyone who might be searching. She was right, there was no way they could have been followed.

"I know." Was all the Blade Master could manage to say.

"Ye know what that means, then?" Forgotten could only nod. Yes, he knew. It meant that somebody that he was traveling with had betrayed them. Had most likely betrayed The Pit as well. Someone he trusted was working with Baal.

CHAPTER 13

Taken from the personal journal of Tobin Masters, Observer to the Throne of Darkness.

As the Observer to the Throne of Darkness I have seen many things in this world of Hell. I have witnessed events from far away, while never leaving my seat at my desk. This power to see, to sometimes even foretell events is potent and one can become drunk on power. Believing that, as the Observer my own plans must end the way that I believe they should. But, this is Hell and in Hell Murphy's law, the law that says anything that can go wrong, will go wrong, rules. I will know better next time.

The sky lightened slowly over the City of Black Forge, in the kingdom of Ash, located on the continent of Wrath. The kingdom was called Ash due to the large number of volcanoes that constantly filled the air with black and gray ash. Nothing in the way of vegetation could find the strength to take root in the ash covered ground, though the dead blackened skeletons of trees gave testimony that at one time life did actually grow here.

Likewise there were very few indigenous animal life to

be found here. Though the fool who believed themselves safe, walking through the perpetual ash-fall soon found themselves feeding some hideous mutant beast that lurked in this hateful land.

All across the ash choked realm were small mining towns, where human slaves were used to dig deep into the mountains, in search of ore to send to the City of Black Forge, the capital city of Ash. These mining camps (one really couldn't call them towns) were miserable places filled with dirty humans who were destined to die slow deaths at the hands of ash lung, starvation, or if they were very lucky a cave in would crush them beneath several tons of stone.

It says a lot about a place when the inhabitants actually cheer when they feel the ground shake with an Earth quake while they are underneath it. The city, of Black Forge was located in the center of a volcano called Satan's Cyst.

The Cyst was easily the highest point in all the world of Hell, being almost twice the size and height of Earth's Mount Everest. The City floated only two hundred feet above the magma boiling in the center of the Cyst, suspended by some age forgotten magic. Anyone trying get into the City, had to pay for a ride on the back of one of the great fire worms which swam through the lava flow like a fish swims though water. These travelers would be protected by thick magical stone carriages which had been fitted to the backs of these beasts.

Each traveler was responsible for their own carriage and there had been a few deaths when the hasty travelers had failed to ensure that their Carriage was properly sealed. After being submerged twice, these carriages simply vanished from the backs of their worms, the magic destroyed as the stone melted from the inside.

One may wonder why anyone would want to travel to a city such as this and the answer is fairly simple, the city of Black Forge was the location of the greatest black smiths in all of Hell. It was known that the city produced the best quality weapons and armor anywhere. As such, there was a constant line of demons moving in and out of the city, looking to purchase arms for their various armies. Now during the time of the War of Ascension the fire worms (of which there were at least two hundred) had trouble moving fast enough to transport the great crowds of Demon Lords who now filled the entry ports waiting to get into the City. Fights between these Demon Lords were not unheard of and even encouraged by the Worm Riders who drove the creatures from port to port.

After all, if a few Lords died, it meant less trips across the Cyst. The largest structure in the City of Black Forge, was the Royal Palace, which shot from the center of the city like a huge erection. It was from this Palace that the rest of the city spiraled out forming the spokes of the city proper. Indeed anyone standing at the top of the Palace would surely notice how the city resembled a giant spider-web made of stone and metal, with the Palace as its central focal point.

This was actually more truth than anyone could know. The original founders of the Kingdom of Ash had been large spiders. These spiders, simply known as Crawlers, had exoskeletons that were made of black and red obsidian, and they had ruled Ash for several thousand years before being tricked by a demon Lord named Baltizar. This Demon Lord had come to them with what he called a business proposition, which turned into an invasion. The crawlers were decimated, leaving only a few thousand enslaved to the new Master of the Kingdom.

Standing at one of the top balconies of the Palace a human slave looked out across the city and thought of these things. Ancient history and yet he could see it all in his mind as if he had lived every second. Maybe he actually had, after all hadn't pieces of his soul been replaced by the fractured souls of Crawlers who had lived and died within this city? What did this make him, more, or less than human? Did any of it even matter anymore? So much had changed in the year that he had lived in Hell.

He still remembered his arrival like it had been yesterday. The portal had dropped him, naked and terrified into the ash covered wilderness. He wandered for days without food or water, his skin covered in burns from the hot ash that fell from the sky. Just when he was ready to lay down and give up he had been discovered by a group of outriders from the City of Black Forge. He thought at first that he was being rescued, only to find out that his nightmare was only just now beginning.

He was taken to the bowels of the city and put to work in the foundries, where ore from the many mines was processed using the unbearable heat from the volcano. The work was hard and human's rarely lived very long. This is where the majority of the Crawlers had been exiled to, forced to work where they once ruled supreme. The man had found himself tormented from all sides, his mind recoiling in horror at the eight legged creatures that he was forced to work with, and his body slowly breaking down from the work and physical abuse he suffered from guards.

However, the human refused to be broken and still he struggled every day to pull himself out of his cell and back to work. The guards had begun taking bets on how much longer he would last. He had already out lived most of the other humans who had been there before his arrival, and even half of the ones that came after him. He was pretty sure that it would be one of the guards that finally killed him, he could see it in their eyes as the weeks and months passed and they continued to lose their bets. Eventually, one of them would take fate into their own hands, bet on a day, and then kill him.

Then one day, four months into his suffering everything changed. The day started like any other, with the human forcing himself to his feet, second and third degree burns screaming in agony as he moved. He stumbled out into the hallway to find the shift guard, an ugly brute named Fragnar glaring at him, and he knew that today was the day that Fragnar had bet the human would die. And if the look in his hate filled eyes said anything, he would.

The man tried to be extra carful and by mid day he had only burned himself five times, and while this was a great way to start the day, he was falling behind in his work.

"Faster!" Fragnar lashed his razor sharp whip across the man's back and he cried out in shock and pain. He stumbled forward and barley caught himself on the edge of the trough of molten ore, burning both of his hands. The man knew better to seek any kind of medical attention and tried to push himself harder, but the blisters on his hands made it even more difficult. He knew that he wasn't going to make it. The next time Fragnar came past him, he would get more than just a single lash, the demon would use his inability to work as excuse to beat him to death.

Suddenly, a screech of pain echoed throughout the foundry. The man looked around until he found the source of the sound. A young Crawler writhed on the floor as Fragnar poured a stream of molten ore across it's back. This did not concern the man, he should have simply done what every other human was doing and simply turn back to his work, but the Crawler's mewling agony resonated deep within his core. Before he knew what he was doing, the man was moving across the room.

"Hey!" He screamed as he swung his fist at Fragnar's head. The man felt several blisters pop as he connected. Fragnar turned a surprised look at the human who had the audacity to strike him. All around them humans and crawlers had stopped their work to watch.

"Well, well." Fragnar smiled when he recognized the man. "You just made it easy to collect my money human." The guard's hand lashed out and caught the man by the throat. The Crawler, now forgotten limped away and was quickly surrounded by its fellow spiders. The man struggled uselessly as he was lifted up into the air and slammed hard onto his back.

Gasping for air he was dragged over to the nearest trough and his face lowered into the pool of hot ore. Blazing agony filled the human as he screamed and the molten metal melted his flesh. It didn't take long for darkness to claim him.

Sometime later the man drifted back into consciousness. He was being carried through dark hallways, seeming to float above the floor. Slowly he rolled his eyes to see that he was being held by a large Crawler. He wanted to lift his hands to push the creature away from him, but his arms refused to obey him, and the effort made the world swirl. Slowly he drifted off into darkness again.

When he opened his eyes again, he was laying on his back in a large metal chamber. Slowly he turned his head and found himself on a raised dais and down below him, a group of Crawlers watched him intently. No. Not watching him, something behind him.

Slowly, his body in agony he turned to look the other way, and instantly wished he hadn't. Standing there was the largest Crawler he had ever seen. Easily as big a S.U.V., this Crawler moved toward him slowly, as if each step caused it pain.

As it came closer the human realized that this creature was truly ancient, he could feel it in his soul, as if he were being approached by God Himself. He could see that it was missing three of its legs and horrible scars marred its' obsidian carapace. Slowly the creature lowered itself toward the man on the alter in front of it.

"Okay." The man whispered in pain. He was ready. "Go ahead, finish it." The ancient Crawler clacked its' fangs together and the man could see a thick green liquid dripping from them. Poison.

"Well, what are you waiting for?" The man gasped. "Come on! Finish it!" He yelled. At that moment the creature struck, driving its' sharp fangs into the human's chest, piercing his heart. A new kind of fire filled the mans' body as he arched his back and closed his eyes and waited for the poison to kill him. Death did not come. He felt the Crawler continue to pump poison into his heart, and his still beating heart pumped that poison through his veins. It spread through him like a raging fire.

Finally the fangs were withdrawn and the man was left to wraith in pure agony as he screamed his throat raw. He lay like this for three days, begging for death to claim him as his mind and soul were shattered and put back together. And as the days passed he began to realize that he was no longer alone in his body. He could feel hundreds of other minds within him. Could access a thousand memories from a past that was not his, and yet felt as familiar as his own.

On the fourth day he woke up to find that the pain was gone. Slowly he sat up and looked around. He found the dry dead husk of the ancient Crawler lying next to the alter and felt a profound sadness. He ran his hand gently across her scared body. She had been the last of the living Queens that had ruled the city before Baltizar came. He had thought to kill all the queens, but this one had survived, remaining hidden all this time in unexplored sections of the city. She had given the last of her life to ensure the survival of her people.

It had not been poison that she had injected into the human, but Royal Jelly, her very essence. In giving it to the man, she had changed him into a new being, a powerful hybrid that she hoped would one day liberate her people. The man also knew something else, there were other Queens waiting to be hatched, their egg sacks hidden until the time was right. With wonder the human closed his eyes and felt their life pulse through him. He could feel their desperate need to be born. They called to him, asking if the time had finally come.

"Not yet." He thought to them. "Soon." Disappointment filled him as they withdrew back into their slumber. A gentle nudge against his mind told him he was no longer alone in the room and he turned to find a Crawler by the entrance. The Crawler came toward him, stopping at the bottom of the dais. Slowly, the creature dipped its (no, his) front legs to bow before the man.

"Tyrant." The man spoke the Crawler's name and was surprised by the sound of affection that filled his voice. Slowly the man walked down and placed a hand on the creatures' hard carapace. Underneath his touch Tyrant shivered and the man understood.

He was their King. The first of his kind. He closed his eye and found that he could see through the eyes of the creature in front of him. He gasped as he saw his face. The left side was still strong with its sharp handsome features. However, the right side of his face was a mound of metal and scar tissue, from being pushed into the molten ore. He opened his eye and shuddered at the horror of it.

"You are magnificent Majesty." Tyrant's voice filled his mind and the man knew, that the Crawlers were now truly his people. He could feel every single one of them throughout the city as they suffered under the heel of the Usurper Baltizar and he vowed that one day soon, he would free them all.

That had been six months ago and in that time he had learned much. Tyrant had become his constant companion as he grew in power and understanding. He studied the ways of magic and became a Throne Bound Sorcerer.

He protected his people from the shadows when he could, because the minions of Baltizar must not find out about his existence, lest they destroy him. The last six months had been an agony of impatience. Every time the man felt the pain of a Crawler under the whip, or beaten he wanted to rise and attack, but Tyrant had kept him from doing anything rash.

But now as he stood on the balcony overlooking the city, his city, he knew that the time had come. He felt Crawlers preparing themselves for the uprising that would come this day. Slowly he turned to look at Tyrant standing off to his right.

"The time is upon us my son." He whispered and could feel excitement ripple through the large spider. "Let us reclaim our home."

As the man moved through the Palace hallways, working his way toward the Throne room, Crawlers began joining him. At first it was only three or four and then a dozen. Soon more and more followed him, turning on those demons who had subjugated them for three thousand years. Soon the halls were filled with an army of black spiders crawling on the floors, walls, and even on the ceiling itself. All following their Messiah, leaving in their wake the twitching paralyzed bodies of future meals.

Word had not reached Baltizar in his Throne Room, so he was quite surprised when a black robed human smashed through the ornate doors to the Throne Room, followed by hundreds of Crawler slaves. The self-proclaimed leader of the kingdom of Ash watched from his Throne, as the spider slaves spread out across the room taking up position near his guardsmen and he shifted uneasily. This could turn very ugly; however he had always known someone would one day attempt to take his Throne from him. Though he must admit that a human with a bunch of slaves was the last one that he would have suspected. After all, what could a human possible do to him?

Baltizar could barely suppress his laughter, obviously this human didn't expect that he would fight. Perhaps he thought Baltizar would be afraid of his scared face and spider slaves and would drop to his knees and beg for forgiveness. If that was the case, then the human was in for a nasty surprise. Baltizar had no intention of losing his seat today. Or any other day for that matter and certainly not to a human mongrel and a bunch of slaves.

"What is the meaning of this!" Baltizar demanded glaring down at the man. "How dare you defile my Throne Room with your filth." He fully expected the human quake in terror at the sound of his wrath, but instead the man stepped forward and looked the usurper in the eye.

"It is you who have defiled this entire kingdom by your very presence and it ends now." The man's voice was low and menacing. For the first time in his very long life Baltizar felt a tickling of fear run through him. What was happening here? What was he missing?

"You cannot hope to win here, today." He spat, trying and almost succeeding in keeping his voice from trembling. Without another word the man slowly bowed his head closing his eyes. That was more like it. Baltizar settled back into his seat fighting off the urge to sigh in relief.

"Kill them." The human whispered into the silence. Baltizar started to stand as Crawlers suddenly swarmed over all the guards in the room. They shrieked in pain and terror as they were ripped limb from limb.

"Damn you!" Baltizar screamed, his hand thrusting toward the magical staff that he kept hidden in the arm of his chair. "Die!" He thrust the staff forward and watched in triumph as the human was engulfed in the jet of flame, but his look quickly changed to horror, as the man seemed to absorb the magic.

"My turn." The human raised his one eye to look at the usurper. Slowly his hands began to move and he spoke ancient words of power. Baltizar tried to stand, but suddenly his body refused to obey him. Deep within himself he felt a tearing sensation and he wailed in terror and agony. Within seconds, the demon's soul was trapped in a spiritual web cocoon where he would be forever trapped awaiting man's call so that he could serve the human for as long as he lived. Baltizar would know no rest.

Later that night after every loyal demon to Baltizar had been found and killed, or fled the city the man sat on his new throne and waited. Tyrant reported that the Crawlers were meeting little resistance in the outlying mining camps, as they rose up against their slavers. The Kingdom was once again the province of the Crawlers but this was not enough for the man.

He had his eyes set upon another prize. It was the time of the War of Ascension. Out there in the world wars were being fought in the name of winning the Throne of Darkness. He was now in control of a city full of master crafted weapons and armor. He would begin his own hunt for the stones and would himself rise to the Throne of Darkness.

"My Lord." Tyrant interrupted his thoughts. The man looked up to find that another demon had joined them in Throne Room. The new comer was a small thing, with ragged clothes, blue skin and a long horse-like face. "This demon is a messenger from a Lord Blotar who in the city to buy arms."

"If it would please the new Lord of the City, my Master would like to offer you a gift." The horse face demon slobbered. The man waved his hand in bored fashion. He had more important things to consider and wanted this intrusion over with. Taking his wave as permission to continue, the horse faced demon turned and pulled a human female into view.

The woman trembled on long pale legs and her hair was long and ragged. She kept her face down, looking at the floor, like a good proper slave. Intrigued despite himself, the man leaned forward. There was something about the slave that seemed familiar. He looked at her pale naked flesh, covered in small bruises. At the swell of her firm breasts, the purple nub of nipple.

"Show me her face." The man commanded. Slowly the woman raised her face, her hazel eyes filled with fear.

"Oh...no." The woman sobbed. "Please God no!" She wailed as she tried to pull away from her horse faced keeper. The man on the Throne began to laugh, deep chuckles that held a dark delight.

Hell was such an unpredictable place. What were the chances?

"Hello Karen." The man who was once called Richard Murray said from his Throne. "It's so good to see you again. You may call me Nemesis." Falling to her knees Karen Masters began to wail as Nemesis laughed even harder.

CHAPTER 14

Taken from the personal journal of Tobin Masters, Observer to the Throne of Darkness.

Realizing that you have an enemy is always the first step in defeating that enemy. However, what can you do when you do not know the identity of your enemy, but you suspect that he or she is somebody close to you? Someone that you have always trusted? It is easy to slip into paranoia suspecting every smile and every look. What happens when you have a small group of people that you already don't trust? They become easy targets and we watch their every move for the traitorous acts, that must surley be there. We slowly slip into the Salem Witch trial mentality and before it is over we have burned all the innocents out of our village. Only as the smoke from the charred bodies clears do we finally realize that we are now truly alone with the very evil that we sought to destroy.

Shard stood at the rail and looked out across the endlessly rising and falling crimson waves of the Sea of Despair. She now understood why it was the Sea of Despair, after five months of seeing only water she was ready to throw herself over the rail just to end the boredom. And then there was the fact that Forgotten was becoming more and more obsessed with the idea that someone in his little band of so called heroes was actually in league with Belial.

Shard had shrugged upon hearing this, so what? This was Hell, of course there was a traitor. Honestly, she would have been more surprised to hear that there wasn't one. But for some reason, Forgotten took this fact as something very personal. None of this had really mattered to Shard, until she began to realize that the others were beginning to avoid her more so than usual. And then there were the times that she caught Forgotten Child watching her from the other end of the ship.

Ordinarily this out of place with its lace curtains and canopy. Nala would have not bothered her, but the combination of being bored out of her skull and always being watched had her ready to snap. Several times she had been tempted to approach the one they called Triv, and ask him to take her wherever he jumped to get supplies for the crew and passengers. But every time she came close to doing so, some excuse for not doing it always came up.

Sighing, the assassin turned around to find Forgotten Child watching her from the wheelhouse. Triv was standing next to the Blade Master, his dark head leaning forward as if he were whispering. For just a moment Shard's eyes locked with the Blade Master's and then he turned away from her. Anger flared deep within her chest.

Why would the stupid man think that she had anything to do with Beliel? She was the one on the run from the demon lord, wasn't she? She wanted nothing more than to go up to Forgotten, snatch him by that oh so blond ponytail and rip it off his fool head. And maybe she would have, but at that moment someone stepped up in front of her cutting off her thoughts.

"And just what do you think you are looking at?" Shard rolled her eyes and sighed again as Rachael glared at her. She definitely didn't need this right now.

Shortly after they had left the remains of The Pit, Shard began to sense a silent hostility building within the Blade Master's wife. For the most part this hostility was limited to dirty looks from a distance and a whispered word to one of their travel companions. But every once in a while it bubbled out into a confrontation. It was almost as if Rachael wanted to start a fight with Shard. If that were the case then the female Blade Master was going to get much more than she bargained for. Shard had fought Forgotten Child twice, neither of them being able to gain the upper hand in either fight. His wife lacked the capability to face her and live.

"I don't want to deal with this." Shard mumbled to herself and tried to walk around the other woman only to have Rachael grab her by her elbow.

"Oh you are going to hear me, loud and clear." Rachael hissed through clenched teeth, her eyes flashing in a bolt of lightning that suddenly lanced across the red and black sky.

"I see you looking at him." She hissed.

"What are you talking about?" Shard looked around confused and was dismayed to find several of the survivors from The Pit watching them, some of them fingering their weapons.

"You will never have him." Rachael continued as if Shard hadn't spoken.

And then understanding finally dawned on the assassin. This stupid woman actually thought that Shard had designs to sleep with her husband. "Have you gone mad?" She laughed in the other woman's face. "Your so called man and I hate each other."

"Oh I know he hates you, but I have seen the way you look at him." The Blades Woman insisted causing Shard to laugh even harder.

"You can't be serious," Shard gasped. "The only reason we aren't trying to cut each other's heads off is because of the deal that I made with your Father Michael." Then just as suddenly as it came, the laughter left the assassin and she looked defiantly into Rachael's eyes. "Now get out of my way." Shard tried once again to push past. Shard's head snapped to the side as Rachael slapped her. Without looking Shard reacted slapping the woman back. In the next moment Rachael reached for the blade at her waist, as Shard reached out to her Blood Kindred magic to call her weapons to her.

All around the two women blades were drawn and Shard was pretty sure that she was going to have to kill every survivor from The Pit and probably half the crew too. But at that moment a strong hand clamped down over Rachael's hand as she tried to draw her sword and Shard felt a bone dagger slide around to rest uncomfortably against her throat.

"Tis enough of this stupidity on me ship." Nala snarled at Rachael. "Ye draw weapons on me ship and I will drop ye both off into the waves this very second."

"Don't" Shauntra whispered into Shard's ear when she tensed. The dagger was pressed harder against her flesh.

In front of them Rachael seethed with anger. "Don't you see?" She screamed at the pirate Captain. "She's the traitor, she killed your son." Now Nala turned her piercing gaze back toward the assassin behind her.

"Aye, tis a possibility." She acknowledged before turning back to the other woman. "But I have been here long enough to know that it's the last person ye'd expect that will stab ye in the back." Slowly the pirate stepped back away from them and Shard felt the dagger leave her throat.

"Ye will stay away from each other until I figure out which one of you filthy landlubbers killed me boy." At this point she raised her voice until all of those on board could hear her. "And if I find ye before I put yer filthy carcasses ashore I will personally gut ye."

With that she was gone leaving the two women to glare at one another before retreating to opposite ends of the ship. Everyone knew that it was far from over between the two of them.

Forgotten Child stood on the wheel house and looked down at Shard as she stood at the rail on the starboard side of the ship. Her back was turned to him, her shoulders hunched. The assassin had been edgy since they had begun their journey, tired of being cooped up on the ship, no matter how large it appeared. In this, Forgotten could almost sympathize with the woman. There had been only one more attack since they had been forced to flee the pirate's hidden cove.

This attack had involved a small ship filled with half breed monstrosities, which the Black Rose had easily sank before it even became a true threat to the ship. It wasn't that Forgotten actually wanted to fight, but anything would have been better than sitting around day and night trying to figure out who was the traitor. Which of course brought his mind back around to the woman standing at the rail.

Was it possible that she was the one? Of course it was. But did he believe it? He wasn't sure. And the fact that he was unsure bothered him even more. If anyone on this ship could be capable of selling them out it was Shard. It was her name that he first thought of when Nala had spoken out loud what he had already come to suspect and yet there were two others that he didn't trust either. The Throne Bound husband and wife. But, for reasons that he could not even begin to explain he wanted it to be Shard. Needed it to be her.

Down below him Shard turned her head slightly, looking out over the endless swells of crimson colored waves. Forgotten looked at her profile intently, willing her to tell him that she was the traitor. As he watched the wind stirred her hair and for the first time he realized that Triv was right, she was a very beautiful woman.

"For someone who only thinks of that woman an enemy, you spend an awful long time staring at her, mi amigo." Triv whispered in his ear, his Spanish accent thick. Forgotten felt his face heat as he blushed.

"I thought so." Triv nodded his head as if he finally got the answer he had been looking for.

"It's not like that." Forgotten tried to recover himself. "She could be the traitor." He spoke to the small man next to him but could not drag his eyes away from Shard.

"Uh-huh, and you don't watch the other two half as much." The Shadow Master patted him on the shoulder. "Face it mijo, you like her" Forgotten opened his mouth to protest, but at that moment Shard turned around and looked directly at him. Well, more like glared, but their eyes met and the Blade Master felt like he had been jolted by electricity.

In that moment he understood that she was mad at him and for some reason her anger troubled him. He wanted to go down there and talk to her. Find some way to prove once and for all her guilt, or innocence. Instead he forced himself to turn away from her and look out across the sea.

"Si, this one troubles you, very much." Triv sounded almost happy about this and Forgotten scowled. It didn't help any that the small Belizean was right. Things had been so much more simpler when Shard had fit nicely into the role of enemy. Now he was unsure what the woman was and he hated it.

"Looks like your problems are getting worse, mijo." Triv's voice was suddenly very serious. Forgotten turned and watched as his wife walked up to where Shard stood. The Blade Master felt his heart sink. While he might be unsure of who the traitor was, Rachael let it be known every chance that she got that it had to be Shard.

He watched as the women exchanged words and then the last thing that Forgotten had expected happened. Shard burst out into laughter. Watching this the Blade Master felt the tension leave his body. If they were laughing, then they were not going to cut each other's hearts out. And then suddenly the two women slapped each other the sound like two whips cracking in the sudden silence left behind by Shard's laughter.

"No." Triv grabbed Forgotten's shoulder as he moved toward the two women as they went for their weapons. "They must find their middle ground."

Nala and her daughter had stopped the fight, declaring that any who would draw weapons against each other on the Black Rose, would be left to the mercies of the sea. Almost as soon as it begun the fight was over, the two combatants retreating to opposite ends of the main deck glaring at one another under the stormy sky.

Later that night Forgotten lay with his wife on the main deck and they whispered about what had happened. He kissed her bruised cheek and together they formulated a plan that would remove all three of the possible threats. The plan would work, even against the Throne Bound magic users.

After all had been said and the plan decided, Forgotten lay awake. He knew in his mind something had to be done. They could not allow the traitor, no matter who it was, to continue to give information to their enemies. And yet in his heart he felt like a traitor himself.

CHAPTER 15

Taken from the personal journal of Tobin Masters, Observer to the Throne of Darkness.

Just as it is the nature of demons to betray one another, so is it in their nature to scheme. They are constantly looking for ways to out-do all those around them. They form alliances believing that in the end they may betray those foolish enough to support them, without a second thought. I find it strange, that the thought that their allies may themselves scheme the very same thing against them never seems to occur to the various demon lords'. The histories are rife with such instances. And yet when they are betrayed and brought low by another, every Demon Lord appears to be shocked. There is a lesson to be learned in all of this. One that my son will need to learn ifI he is to survive the ravages of this twisted and decadent world. As you scheme against others, so shall others scheme against you.

The six large war ships sailed into the harbor, to the sounds of cheering and roaring. It seemed that the entire port city, of Carrion had turned out to see the arrival of the Stone Bearer, named Legacy. The city, if it could really be called that was small with squat, ugly buildings, much like the inhabitants, which were drwarven carp looking things that constantly reeked. The only reason the city had even survived for as long as it had was simply because nobody cared about it enough to attack, destroy, or enslave it. This was the very reason Legacy had chosen this place as her entry point onto Malice. Nobody would suspect somebody as powerful as she to ally herself with such pathetic creatures.

"Welcome, Great One." The city leader, a large, actually standing as tall as Legacy's breasts flabby creature with dull green scales, greeted her as Legacy walked down the short plank to the docks of the city. She tried very hard not to turn her sensitive snout away from the offensive little beast but simply could not do it.

"Is all ready?" She asked, turning her head back to the sea. In front of her the Carp thing smiled, its lips stretching in a big flabby line.

"Oh, yes great one. All is prepared." He bowed low again. "We have also prepared a great feast in your honor." Legacy shuddered to think of what these things thought a "great feast" consisted of but she nodded in agreement. Anything to get things moving so that she could get out of this filthy city.

With agonizing slowness Legacy, her Honor Guard, and the city leader traveled through the Carp choked streets of Carrion. If the Stone Bearer had thought the docks area had smelled, now she really understood the meaning of the word. The collective stench of the crowd had already driven two of her four guards to vomiting and then ultimately back to the relative solace of the ship. She would have liked to retreat as well, but to do so would have shown weakness and the Great Spirits would have been offended by such a display. Finally, after what seemed like hours they arrived at the ugly, square box that the inhabitants called a palace. The only good thing about the building was the fact that it was actualy large enough for Legacy and her Wolves to stand upright within.

"Only the Stone Bearer may enter the Great Palace." The leader spoke with a gurgling authority. Legacy rolled her eyes. Oh, how she just wanted to turn and order all her warriors to kill these wretched creatures but to do so could draw unwanted attention right now. Set was one of the most dangerous Demon Lords in all of Hell if she had any chance of winning his stone, it had to be through surprise.

"So be it." She turned to her two remaining guards. "You two stand out here and see to it that I remain undisturbed for one hour." With that, she turned and entered the Great Palace.

The first thing that Legacy noticed upon entering the room beyond the door was that the stench from the city seemed to be absent here. Instead, the air was filled with the sweet smelling smoke of burning incense. The second thing she noticed was how dim the light was in here. Slowly, she moved deeper into the room, searching for any sign of the banquet that the little Carp had promised her. As a matter of fact she wondered why the little son-of-a-bitch hadn't followed her in. "Hello?" She growled into the dimness. "Is there anyone here?"

Suddenly, in front of her a shadow arose and she stopped. "Who's there?" Legacy demanded. "Reveal yourself or die!" The threat came across cold and hard, and she was confident that whoever was in the room would now come forward and present himself to her, at which point she would probably kill them anyway. That is what they got for skulking about in the shadows instead of greeting her properly. On the first part of her thought, Legacy was not going to be disappointed. Almost immediately, the large shadow (larger than any Carp, she was sure) moved forward and in that instant, as she went for the sword at her waist Legacy knew true fear for the first time in her long life.

"Welcome to my victory banquet." Lord Set whispered.

Above the city of Carrion six Dread Ships suddenly appeared as the magic that had made them invisible faded. This was of course no big surprise to the Carp like demons who lived there, for they had known about them the whole time. It was however, a great surprise to the demon wolf ships that were resting in the harbor. One by one the wolf warriors let out cries of surprise, followed by calls to arm. This was an absolutely useless act, since the flying ships of Set hovered well out of their reach, and used their catapults to fling boulders at them.

One by one Legacy's ships were smashed to bits and those wolves who were not fortunate enough to be killed by a flying rock found themselves drug down to the bottom of the harbor by Black's zombies. Soon, the ships had turned back to the still cheering Carp city. They were still cheering, when the first boulder slammed into a crowded street killing at least a dozen of the Carps. On that one street, the survivors stopped in mid cheer to stare dumfounded at the approaching Dread Ships. Slow realization filled their fishy eyes and they began to panic.

Elsewhere in the city the cheering continued. All too soon, it turned to screams.

"I will not die at your hands, you filthy blood sucking bastard!" Legacy howled as she drew her spear from her back. Slowly, Set pushed himself from his throne and pulled his lips back from his teeth in a silent snarl.

"You cannot win," he whispered in a voice that carne straight from the grave.

"Give me the Stone and I will let you live on as one of my personal concubines." Roaring in anger Legacy charged the Vampire, her spear held out before her. Set stood his ground until the last minute, before spinning to his left, his hand snatching the wooden haft of the spear just below the spear head that his enemy had intended to pierce his heart.

Without a sound he spun the stunned Stone Bearer around and let go of the spear. Legacy found herself flying through the air, unable to stop until she smashed into the back wall. Pain flared up through the demon lords' back. She yelped as she felt the stone of the wall crack and the entire building shook. Gasping Legacy leaned back against the wall and fought to keep from sliding to the floor.

Not wanting to lose his advantage Lord Set leapt forward with the speed of the dead, lifting his leg and kicked out, smashing his ebony boot into Legacy's chest. Legacy howled in pain as three ribs snapped in her chest and she smashed through the wall out into the streets of the city. Set waited a moment smiling to himself.

This was going to be easier than he thought. He was going to defeat the wolf, collect her Stone. And then he would feed on her, slowly draining the life from her body as she struggled against him, against the inevitable death that had come for her.

Still taking his time Set walked up to the hole in the wall and stepped out into the street beyond. In that instant Legacy, the pain in her chest burning like the fires on the Burning Lake itself, came at the vampire from his right, driving the head of her spear deep into his flank. It was the Lord of the Undead's turn to howl in agony as the wound sizzled and steamed. Silver. The spear head had been made of silver, a very rare metal in Hell. One that could do serious damage to vampires.

"Die!" Legacy snarled as she pressed forward, trying to drive the silver tip through him. Set found himself on the retreat, stumbling to his left down the street. He tried to move faster than the hated wolf using his blood tricks, but found that he could not access his powers with the silver still stuck in his side.

Legacy smelled her victory at hand and howled to the Ancient Spirits that had guided her to this moment. In her mind she saw her rise to the Throne of Darkness. Her rule would be the darkest Hell had ever seen. So deep into her fantasy was she that she failed to see the shadow hurtling towards her from a side street.

"Master!" The vampire screamed as she brought a short blade down on the haft of the spear, severing the wood of the weapon a few inches from the head. Legacy stumbled slightly forward and her prey was free of her. Snarling the humanoid wolf righted herself, prepared to regain her advantage but instead found herself facing the half human vampire that had freed her Master. This vampire stood between Set and Legacy her red eyes blazing, fangs bared in a hiss.

Without a word Legacy dropped the now useless spear shaft and quickly drew two tomahawks (also made of silver) and moved to fight the pathetic creature that stood between her and her destiny. Behind them Set grabbed at the wood still connected to the spear head that remained in his side and pulled.

Hissing in pain, he freed the offending piece of metal from his still steaming flesh, just as Legacy dispatched the vampire that had intervened in their fight. Mentally, Set shrugged at the loss of the vampire, after all who had she thought she was getting involved in a fight between two Gods? Her death at the hands of his enemy only saved him the trouble of killing her later. Slowly the two Stone Bearers eyed each other more wearily, and began circling.

Suddenly, with a roar and a hiss, the combatants came at each other; the wolf swinging her deadly silver tomahawks, and the vampire attacking with his teeth and claws. Within seconds both were a bloody mess of scratches and steaming wounds. Their fight moved through the streets, passing by soldiers of both of their armies, as they tore each other apart.

Buildings fell as the two demon lords passed by and people died before their fury; neither creature gaining the upper hand in their epic combat. Anytime that an unfortunate fighter from either army, or even natives from the besieged city came into their proximity they were slaughtered by one or the other combatants. Any who had a death wish and wanted to find them, would only have to follow the swath of destruction and the streets that ran crimson with blood.

Finally they separated in what once had passed as a park, now it was a graveyard. What once was a huge fountain lay smashed amongst bodies of Wolfen warriors, hacked apart zombies, and dead fish people. Here and there one could spot piles of ashes that represented fallen vampires. Set was satisfied that this was as good as any place to collect his second stone.

"The time has come for you to die." The Vampire Lord whispered through the pain of a thousand burning wounds. Legacy, her eyes never leaving her quarry barked out a laugh and raised her weapons to her muzzle and inhaled the haughty scent of Set's blood. Blood that she had drawn. Blood that she had spilled all through the city.

"Oh there will be a death; vampire," she could not quite keep her own voice steady. "But it will not be mine." Slowly Set began to chuckle, the sound like fingernails being drug across a chalk board, and Legacy could feel her fur standing on end. What was he doing? And then he knew, he was calling on his black Throne Bound Sorcery.

Enraged, the Wolfen leader leapt forward, her tomahawks swinging for the neck of her enemy. But rage turned into shock, as her blades passed through the Demon Lord without hurting him. Again Set laughed and the sound rang out around her as if she were surrounded. Bewildered she turned and once again her fur stood on end. The park was filled with Sets, ten, twenty, maybe even one hundred of them. All pointing, all laughing.

"Come out and fight me you coward! Legacy roared as she moved her way through the illusions of her enemy swinging wildly. "The Throne take you, you bastard!"

Suddenly one of the illusions moved behind her, the others remaining still. Set, swiftly stepped up behind the Wolf brought his clawed hand back and drove it into his enemies back. Legacy howled in pain and terror as Set dug his way to her spine. The once proud warrior could do nothing but hang in the air, her back arched, blood running from her nose and mouth.

With a sickening sound, like that of wet cloth ripping, Set pulled, tearing Legacies spine from her body. Blood soaked and defeated Legacy stood on her feet for a moment, her eyes blank and uncomprehending, before she fell to the blood soaked black grass. There she twitched for a few moments and then died.

Set looked down at his enemy for a few long moments before raising his arms out to his side (one still holding Legacy's spine) and bellowed his victory for all to hear. All across the world of Hell, five Stone Bearers stopped whatever they were doing as a lancing pain shot through their backs. After the pain was gone each one knew, without knowing how, that a Stone Bearer had fallen. Each one turned and looked out from where they were in the direction of that shared death, each wondering which had died and whether they would be next.

CHAPTER 16

Taken from the personal journal of Tobin Masters, Observer to the Throne of Darkness.

To find anything good in Hell is next to impossible. This is not a place that nurtures dreams, or the dreamer. But there are a few people who do not give into the hate and ugliness that breed, like cockroaches in the souls of many who live here. These rare few have found a light to help illuminate their darkness. However, they must fight on a daily basis to keep that light safe, for at the end of each day one never knows what might change within them. So, those unlucky few who have anything good, find themselves locked in an endless war to keep that which they have found, whether it be friendship, or even true love, only to find a terrible truth about Hell. All good things must come to an end.

Forgotten Child cursed as the pain shot through his spine. His knees buckled underneath him and he dropped to the crimson sand of the beach where Nala's people had put them ashore. Instantly there were people on either side of him asking at first if he was alright and then simply glaring hatefully at each other over his head. Shard was the first of the two women to back off, leaving Rachael with her husband, though for some reason Forgotten missed the other woman as soon as she moved away.

It was silly, especially with what he, Rachael and Triv had planned but with the pain coursing through his head and the knowledge that somewhere out there a Stone Bearer had died he felt somehow safer with Shard standing next to him. He could still feel the place on his arm where her warm hand had touched with such gentle concern. And then he was looking out over the ocean, past the spot where the Black Rose was still anchored wondering, am I the next to fall?

"What is it?" Rachael asked her voice soft with concern. For a moment he longed to have her arms around him, protecting him from the pain that the world had in store for him, but he knew that she could not protect him. He could not even protect himself. He had changed everything the day he stepped up and took on the title of Stone Bearer.

"One of the Stone Bearers has fallen." He said, his voice barely above a whisper

"What?" Rachael looked around as trying find the body. "How do you know?" It was hard to put into words, but he tried. He explained the pain and the sure knowledge that one who carried a stone had died. He left out the feeling of dread that had accompanied this knowledge not wanting to upset her any more than she already was.

"Hey Chica!" Triv, who had decided to join Forgotten Child, called from his spot near the edge of what appeared to be a jungle full of trees with large black and red trunks. "You and your Chico gonna lay there all day, or are you going to help set up this camp?" Forgotten couldn't help but smile. There were times that he was sure that Triv was actually Cheech Maron in disguise.

"We're coming, we're coming." Forgotten pushed up to his feet slowly making sure that he wasn't going to fall back to the ground. Out on the water a horn sounded on the Black Rose, signaling their departure. Nala had been disappointed that the traitor had not revealed themselves while they had still been on board the Black Rose. The night before they reached land, she had taken Forgotten back into her private cabin where she had extracted an oath from him.

"When ye find the piece of dung, be sure to gut them fer me boy." She had said and Forgotten had sworn to it. The next day they had taken small boats to the shore of Malice, though he was having second thoughts about the place where they had decided to stay. They should have come ashore in one of the many hidden coves around the continent and went straight on from there to the Free City of Haven.

Instead Forgotten had allowed Raven, the half vampire to talk him into coming here. But even he had to admit that the Throne Bound had a point. One night after the fight had broken out between Rachael and Shard, Raven had come to him and asked if they might speak in private. Not knowing what to think Forgotten had agreed and the two of them had walked to a spot next to one of the rails.

"I have been studying one of the books that we were able to get out of The Pit." Raven spoke after a few moments of silence. "I think that I may be able to locate some ruins left behind when Elysium fell." The Throne Bound paused here as if he had just announced the answer to all their worries. If that was the case then Forgotten failed to see the connection. What good were a bunch of ruins?

"We have to go there." Raven suddenly blurted as if Forgotten had denied his request already.

"Why?" The Blade Master wanted to know. "What is so important that we should go there instead of trying to get to Haven.? That's where our army is." Not to mention my daughter, he added to himself. He missed Cassandra dearly and wanted to see her again, and know that she was safe. Sighing, Raven pulled out the book that he had been studying and opened it up to a page that he had marked.

With mild interest the Blade Master looked at what he was being shown. On the page was a beautiful drawing of the most spectacular city that Forgotten had ever seen. The city seemed to glow on the page, with crystal towers, golden peaks, and silver streets. Humans walked through those streets, while angels flew overhead. All in all, it was surely breathtaking, but Forgotten still didn't see what the man was so upset about.

"It's a beautiful drawing, so?"

Sighing is exasperation Raven pointed to the clouds above the city. "What do you see here?"

"Clouds, a few angels, what looks like a ray of sun light shining down on all the happy shoppers." Forgotten was getting tired of this game. For a moment Raven looked at the other man in confusion and Forgotten realized that he had confused him with the shoppers comment. Of course the Hell born half vampire wouldn't understand the reference. He opened his mouth to explain, but Raven cut him off

"Look closer at the ray of light." And so Forgotten did. After a few moments he began to see what he thought were letters hidden within the shaft, like those old picture puzzles that he used to do in school and then the letters solidified for him. For a moment he could do nothing but stand there and stare. Could this be a Throne Bound trick?

He hadn't heard Raven speak any words that could have cast a spell, but what did that matter? He wanted this to be trick, but deep down in his heart he knew that what he was seeing had been in the book a long time before Raven ever stumbled upon it There in the little shaft of light were the words' FORGOTTEN CHILD'.

Forgotten Child sat in the tent that had been set up for him and thought of the future. The whole tent thing had seemed very silly to him. Nobody else in his group had the luxury of having even the meager shelter that the demon hide tent provided Rachel and himself, but Raven had insisted.

After all, Forgotten Child was as Stone Bearer in the Great War of Ascension. He was a Demon Lord in the eyes of the world of Hell. The thought of this had sent shivers down the Blade Masters' spine. To be labeled as one's own enemy was almost too much to take. However, in the end he had given up the argument and moved into the tent.

Now, as he lay on his cot, staring at nothing, he was beginning to have misgivings about the plan that he, Rachel and Triv had come up with concerning the possible traitors. What if they were wrong? What if they took out the wrong ones and left the traitor to continue the destruction of their group? Without warning an image of Shard standing at the rail of the Black Rose, her hair lifted by the wind filled his minds' eye. Her face highlighted by the flashes of red lighting that danced across the sky. Here in the darkness of his tent he could admit to himself that she was the reason that he was second guessing the plan.

"It's the right thing to do." Rachel whispered in the dark, her breath hot and soft against his ear. For a moment he tensed, afraid that he had not masked his thoughts well enough and that his wife had read them. But no, what Rachel had sensed was his unease.

"Are we sure?" He asked turning as he slid his arms around her warm body, pulling her close to him. Deep inside of him he felt guilty over his thoughts of Shard. This was his one true love, his rock, his everything.

"They are all Demon Spawn no matter how they look." Rachel whispered, her lips brushing his lightly, sending an electric charge through his body. "They are the enemy." Rachel leaned forward and pressed her lip firmly against her husbands, her tongue sliding into his mouth to explore across his teeth. Moaning, Forgotten rolled over on top of her and in the back of his mind silently thanked Raven for forcing the tent upon him.

Night had come by the time that Forgotten and Rachel emerged from their tent to see that the others had settled down upon the beach. A fire burned and what appeared to be several six legged fish were affixed to a spit above it. Despite the creatures hideous appearance the smell of its roasting flesh caused Forgottens' mouth to water in anticipation of dinner.

Triv, who had been adding strange herbs to the demonic fish turned a knowing smile to the pair and Forgotten felt himself blush. The moment passed and Triv's look became serious. Forgotten watched as the Spanish Shadow Master slid a small bottle from one of his many pouches and slowly began pouring its contents over one of the fish.

It was the poison that Triv had prepared for the three

that Forgotten had labeled as possible traitors. It wasn't deadly Triv had insisted, instead the poison would attack the nervous system of anyone ingesting it, paralyzing them for several days. It also had the extra added benefit of cutting them off from their source of magic for at least forty-eight hours.

Without a word Rachel and Forgotten sat down close to the fire and watched as Triv began carving cooked meat onto metal traveling plates and passing them out. One by one the travelers were fed and only Raven, his wife, and Shard were given meat from the poisoned fish.

Unable to stop himself Forgotten Child watched the three of them waiting for the poison to set in. Just when he thought that there had been some sort of mistake Kara began to tremble her plate falling from her hands.

"Kara?" Raven was at her side instantly and Forgotten could actually hear fear in his voice. Fear for the one that he loved. Was it possible for demon spawn to love? Again Forgotten felt misgiving for what they had done.

Suddenly, Kara began to scream her body thrashing about in what appeared to be a seizure. Raven held tightly to his wife horrified panic in his eyes. All around people had jumped to their feet eyes locked on the spectacle. And then just as suddenly as the seizures began they ended, with Kara's body locked rigid her eyes wide open as if in death.

"What have you done!!?!" Raven's eyes flashed red with fury as he held his wife's rigid body and he began to shake. He glared hate at Forgotten. "What have you....?" The half vampire started again before the seizures overtook him.

In seconds it was over and Raven lay on his back in the sand, his face locked in fury and hatred. Horrified at what he had done Forgotten turned to find Shard also lying rigid in the sand having succumbed to the poison without a sound.

"What the fuck was that!?!" Forgotten turned on Triv. "You never said it would be like this."

"Actually, I told Rachel that there would be pain." Triv whispered his eyes on the fire. Silently feeling his own anger rising, Forgotten turned to his wife. Rachel sat on the sand looking up at him serenely.

"We did what we had to do." She smiled. "You did the right thing."

"No," Forgotten felt tears rising in his eyes. "I didn't want them to suffer like that." He turned and looked at Raven and his wife and then to Shard. He was no better than the demons that they fought he saw that now. Without another word he turned his back on the people that had chosen to follow him and walked into his tent.

Several hours passed, before Rachel finally joined her husband in the tent. She found him sitting on the bunk where they had made love earlier, the black lacquered box containing the Stone resting next to him. Silently she went to him and slid her arms around him.

"It's okay, they are bound and safe." She whispered gently to him. "I'm sorry, I should have told you about the side effects."

Slowly Forgotten turned to look at her. "Why?" He whispered his voice hoarse. "There had to be other ways, ways that would not have done that to them."

"Yes, there probably were other ways, but we didn't have

the time and they had to be taken care of." Forgotten looked at his wife and for the first time felt that he really didn't know her at all. He had never before seen such hate in her eyes. He wanted to ask her who she was and what she had done with the woman that he had married, but restrained himself somehow. Instead he simply turned away from the hate filled creature that was wearing his wife's face and looked down at the box that carried his curse.

"I guess I'll go and see about setting up guards then." She kissed the side of his head as she rose. Rachel stood there for a few moments looking at her husband before sighing and turning away. Forgotten closed his eyes and again heard the horrible screams coming from Kara as her body rocked in agony and then suddenly it wasn't Kara, but Shard that he saw.

"No." He whispered to himself trying force the terrible images out of his head, but they refused to go. Suddenly, without warning, he felt a chill run through him, a warning of danger. He snapped his eyes open, his hand darting towards the hilt of his sword, knowing even as he reached that he was too late.

The hilt of a sword smashed into his temple causing the world to explode in bright white stars. Again he was struck, and the stars were replaced an all-consuming darkness. Rachel caught her husbands' unconscious body and lowered it down gently to the cot.

"It will be okay." She smiled down at him her eyes showing the gleam of madness "You will understand, Baal has promised us a kingdom of our own." She nodded as if he had spoken to her.

"That's right, our very own kingdom, where we can be

together forever." Slowly, she stood up and lifted the box containing the Stone. "I'll be back soon." She whispered. "I love you, Nicholas."

She spoke his true name. A name that he had never told her, a name she should have not known. With that the traitor turned and slid out of the tent and out into the night where she planned to deliver the Stone to her demonic master.

EPILOGUE

Taken from the personal journal of Tobin Masters, Observer to the Throne of Darkness.

The world of Hell trembles at the sound of war. Kingdoms fall and new ones shall arise. The world is lit with a thousand burning fires. A traitor is revealed and lives will never be the same again. What does the future hold for all of us caught in the Throne's shadow? Will there be anything left of who we were, or are we doomed to become the very monsters that we struggle against? Or have we always been that which we fear and hate the most? There are no easy answers. We are each like a shattered pane of glass which has allowed darkness to seep in between the cracks and into our very souls.

The War of Ascension continues and in its cold hall of black bone and marble the Throne waits.

TO BE CONTINUED.

APPENDIX 1

THE HUMANS

Tobin Leon Masters: First human taken by the Throne of Darkness to be an Observer.

Karen Masters: Older sister to Tobin. Karen has been sold into slavery by her little brother and is currently owned by the half demon Nemesis.

Richard Murry: See Nemesis

Thorn: Baby boy born to Karen Masters and Richard Murry. The baby has been taken by his Uncle Tobin.

Forgotten Child/Nicholas Miller: First Blade Master, leads the warrior branch of the human resistance in Hell. Father to Cassandra. First Human to become a Stone Bearer.

Rachel: Blade Master. Married to Forgotten Child. Spy for the Demon Lord Belial. (see appendix 3 Demons & half Demons)

Cassandra: Daughter to Rachel and Forgotten Child. She has the potential to be a great Blade Master and has begun developing powers beyond anything seen in Hell before.

Father Michael: Priest. Formal leader of the Human Resistance.

Shard: Assassin raised by the Demonic Seekers. **Nola:** Pirate Captain. Ship named the Black Rose. **Triv:** Human with the power to control shadows.

Kara: Throne Bound Magic User and wife to Raven (see appendix 3 Demons & half Demons)

APPENDIX 2

THE STONE BEARERS

Lord Deceiver: Reptilian Shapeshifter. Ruler of a Kingdom on the continent of Wrath. Currently in possession of one Stone.

Lord Set: Vampiric Lord of Necromancers. Rules a desert Kingdom on the continent of Malic. Currently in possession of two Stones.

The Nameless One: Last surviving member of a Royal family on the continent of Sheol. Currently in possession of one Stone.

Lady Legacy: (Deceased) Died at the hands of Lord Set. One time ruler of a Kingdom on the continent of Armageddon. Currently in possession of one Stone.

Lady Darkstar: Daughter of a former Ruling Satan, ruler of a Kingdom on the continent of Blasphemy. Currently in possession of one Stone.

Lord Thanatutus: (Deceased) Killed by Shard (see appendix 1 Humans). Ruled a neighborhood in the Dark City.

Forgotten Child: See Appendix 1 Humans. Currently in possession of one Stone.

APPENDIX 3

DEMONS & HALF DEMONS

Raven: Half Vampire son to Lord Set. Throne Bound Healer. Husband to Kara.

Lord Black: Pure Blood Vampire son to Lord Set. Necromancer. Hates his brother Raven.

Belial: Son to Thanatutus, he is hunting the Stone of Power that was taken by the assassin known as Shard.

Chantric: King of the Gargoyles, and lover of the Lady Darkstar.

Ssithak: Serpent General to Lord Deceivers' armies.

Nemesis: Born a human named Richard Murphy, Nemesis bonded with the spirit of an ancient demonic spider. He is no longer fully human. He currently rules in the city of Black Forge.

Tyrant: From a race of demonic spiders called crawlers, Tyrant is Nemesis's second in command.

APPENDIX 4

MAPS

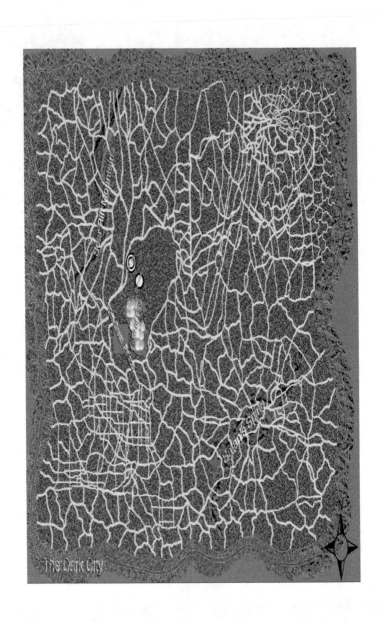

Legacy

Armageddon

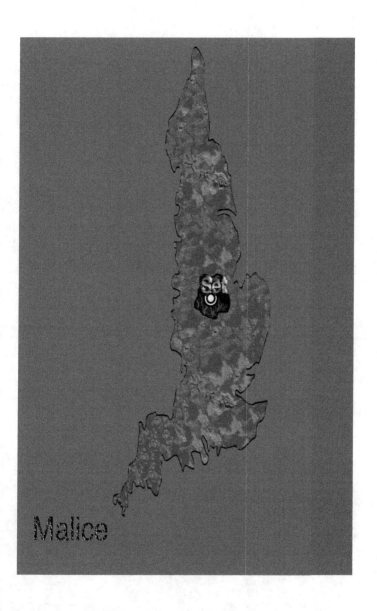

Sheol

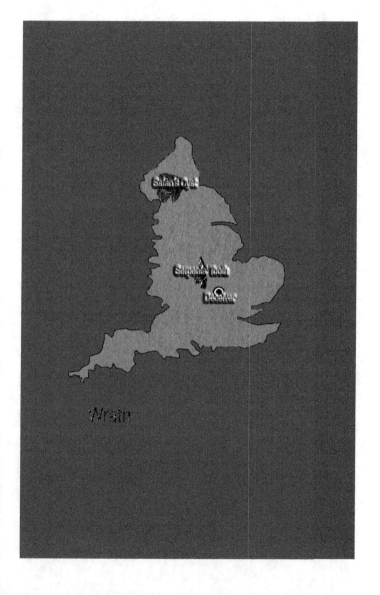

Satan's oyst

Serpents tooth

Deceiver

Wrath

Printed in the United States
By Bookmasters